IT GETS EVEN BETTER
STORIES OF QUEER POSSIBILITY

Cover art © 2021 by Christy Maggio
Cover design by Jed Sabin
Typeset by Ryan Vance
Cultural consultants/sensitivity readers: Rachana Kolli, Catherine Liao, Angel Giuffria, Sarah Kadish, Anonymous

First Printing: July 2021
Printed in the United States
ISBN: 978-1-7366182-0-2

Published by Speculatively Queer
Seattle, Washington, USA
www.speculativelyqueer.com

IT GETS EVEN BETTER
STORIES OF QUEER POSSIBILITY

Edited by
Isabela Oliveira & Jed Sabin

SPECULATIVELY
SQ
QUEER

Table of Contents

1   **Introduction**

2   **The Ghosts of Liberty Street**
by Phoebe Barton

11   **Weave Us a Way**
by Nemma Wollenfang

18   **Custom Options Available**
by Amy Griswold

28   **The Invisible Bisexual**
by S.L. Huang

39   **Frequently Asked Questions About the Portals at Frank's Late-Night Starlite Drive-In**
by Kristen Koopman

52   **The Perseverance of Angela's Past Life**
by Zen Cho

66   **Sea Glass at Dawn**
by Leora Spitzer

79   **unchartered territories**
by Swetha S.

87   **Midnight Confetti**
by D.K. Marlowe

96   **black is a flower**
by R.J. Mustafa

101   **Sphexa, Start Dinosaur**
by Nibedita Sen

105   **The Frequency of Compassion**
by Merc Fenn Wolfmoor

121   **What Pucks Love**
by Sonni de Soto

143   **Gold Medal, Scrap Metal**
by Lauren Ring

157   **Half My Heart**
by Rafi Kleiman

171   **Venti Mochaccino, No Whip, Double Shot of Magic**
by Aimee Ogden

174   **since we're here tonight**
by Xu Ran

191   **I'll Have You Know**
by Charlie Jane Anders

200   **The Cafe Under the Hill**
by Ziggy Schutz

207   **(don't you) love a singer**
by TS Porter

216   **The After Party**
by Ben Francisco

228   **The Mountain Will Move If You Ask**
by Jaxton Kimble

243   **Content Notes**

245   **Our Community**

**Dedicated to those
who paved the way
to make our possibilities
possible.**

Introduction

Isabela Oliveira & Jed Sabin

THE WORD QUEER IS A DELIGHTFULLY COMPLICATED BEAST. It refers to gender and sexuality, but that's not all it is; queerness is built from the weathered bricks of its own history and forever reshaped by everyone who touches it. It's about who we are, where we've been, where we are now and what it's taken to get here, how we see ourselves and direct others to see us… it's impossible to fully describe or define, and we wouldn't dream of trying. These stories aren't about what queerness is, what it has to be, or even what it will become — they're about queerness as it might be.

We decided to make this book in late summer of 2020, when life was flinging volleys of lemons in all directions. Everyone we knew was exhausted, anxious, and running low on optimism. *It Gets Even Better: Stories of Queer Possibility* is our way of reaching out, spreading positivity, and reminding our queer family of what it feels like to be surrounded by love.

These stories are about identity, relationships, and community. They're about hope, acceptance, affirmation, and joy. And most of all, in a time when uncertainty feels inescapable and overwhelming, they're about taking one another by the hand and choosing together to embrace the unknown.

The possibilities are endless.

For content notes, see page 243

The Ghosts of Liberty Street

by Phoebe Barton

WHEN YOU TOLD ME ABOUT THE HALF-THERE TRAIN YOU SAW whispering down the grassy shoulder next to the Interstate, I didn't know what to think. All these years, all these experiences, and I've still never been able to parse the whole map of you. You're a subway with more lines than can be counted and more stations than can be visited. So much of you is hidden from view.

"There's another one," you say, pointing down the median. "Coming out of the tunnel. Yellow with three green stripes, like the one we saw in San Francisco. That's what they'd look like, right?"

I shield my eyes with my hand and look, but there's only grass stirred by gusts of wind kicked up by passing cars. I can't remember if they ever laid tracks out here, but if so, they're long gone. There's nothing to see, and I tell you so.

"Calling me a liar, are you?" you say, and stick out your tongue playfully. I respond in kind and wrap my fingers around yours. It's not that I don't want to see what you see. You've given me far too much for that. Through all the painful moments of my transition, on all those days I hid myself away in the washroom and cried until I thought the room would flood, on all the days nobody but you looked at me and saw a woman, you were there even when you weren't.

"Maybe it's the sun," I say. "We could come back later."

"Sounds great." You grin, and peck my cheek. The warmth of your lipstick lingers and I can't bear to wipe it off, not after everything I've made you go through. "I was worried you weren't going to be adventurous after all."

* * *

For me, learning that Cincinnati has a subway was a revelation, an explosion of possibility, and a reminder of how some things don't work out.

A hundred years ago streetcars weren't quite the hot new thing anymore, but plenty of cities were built around rails and trolley poles. Cincinnati decided to solve its problems by building a subway underneath downtown, digging until the money dried up and the bottom fell out. Depressions, wars, chaos — through all of it the subway was down there, waiting to be put to use. Only getting bare, minimal maintenance to keep it all from coming apart. Neglected, dark, and practically forgotten.

It didn't have to happen that way, sure. But that's how it happened here.

* * *

The Interstate's less busy at night, but not by much. At least the old tunnel opens out onto the right side of it, with cars driving past and away. No headlights reveal us as we sneak to the big, unmarked grey doors weighed down with eighty years of rust. I test the door and it creaks open.

I could close it right now and walk away. I know you'd follow me. I know it'd disappoint you, too. So I bow and gesture to the darkness.

"After you."

You give me a wicked smile and dart in. I take a last furtive glance around for cameras or cops before I follow you.

"So much more peaceful in here, isn't it?" you say. "My kind of place."

You've already got your flashlight on. It's the only light in the tunnel. Mine isn't nearly as powerful, but it's enough to illuminate my steps. I cast the beam around, slicing through air full of scattered dust, and let it linger on the graffiti. The walls here are encrusted with tags from visitors, explorers, and wanderers. Some go back decades.

We're walking where the rails would have been. Their absence is the only indication so far that the work was never finished. If I squint,

I can almost see their ghosts. It would be so much brighter in here if they could reflect my light.

"Such a shame," I say. "Such a mess…"

"Hang on." You stop, kneel down, put a hand to your ear. "One's coming. Get off to the side."

The tunnel is wide enough for two tracks, separated by concrete supports. You climb between them. I stay.

"What's coming?" I ask, but you're gone. Just as you make the far tunnel, I feel a faint lick of wind brush the back of my neck. I spin around, drown the tunnel in my light, but there's nothing and no one.

"Whoa, are you okay?" You dart back to me, thread your fingers between mine and squeeze. "That was close. You felt it, didn't you?"

"Okay?" It's an old tunnel, and there are vents. There's no reason there wouldn't be drafts. "It's wind."

"You're going to have to pay closer attention than that," you say. You smile at me, but after so much practice I can read the sadness on your lips. "There's still plenty to see."

* * *

Exploring the subway was my idea. You've never been into the nuts and bolts of transit systems like I am — you'd never fly to another city just to ride around on its rails — but you love seeing new things and you love me, and that's enough.

"Don't worry about a thing," you said. "As far as I'm concerned, it'll be amazing."

I trusted you. I *trust* you. So I led you into the dark, hoping I wouldn't lead you wrong.

* * *

I see my first stranger when we walk into Brighton Place, the first empty station. I'd known there was always a chance we wouldn't be alone in the subway, not with the unlocked door so inviting. You brought your second-favorite knife and I had a canister of bear spray, just in case we found ourselves in a situation we couldn't talk our way out of. I didn't like having to bring them, but in a tunnel there aren't many places to run.

The stranger waits at the edge of the platform, not dressed like an explorer at all. No pack, no cameras, nothing. In fact, they look like they're wearing a suit, dark and sharply-cut.

I blink, and they're gone. I clamber up to the platform but it's empty. The layers of graffiti are covered in more layers of dust. There's no sound but our breathing, even though there's a parkway on the other side of the ceiling.

"Hey," I whisper, as if anything louder would disturb the station, would make it obvious we'd been there, would make it impossible for me to avoid the cops on our way out. I tighten my grip on your hand as if I'd lose my way without you, even though there are only two directions to go down here. "Did you —"

Before you can answer, there's another lick of wind. I blink, and I see the stranger again, and more besides, but only through one eye. The other sees the dark platform, empty, quiet, abandoned. The impression of something big, heavy, and long rolls in. I see faint windows, a yellow body, and three green stripes.

"What —" I breathe as it moves on the way we came. There's another touch of wind against the handful of stubborn hairs on my arm that endured all those laser sessions, all that electrolysis. I can feel pinpricks in every place where the hair won't grow anymore. "That was —"

"A possibility," you say, and you kiss me. On the lips, this time. Soft and warm. "I was getting worried. There's hope for you after all, looks like."

We linger on the platform, taking in the unbreathed air and undisturbed dust and all the graffiti left by everyone who came before us. When I feel the wind again, I take picture after picture. But the camera only sees what's there: abandonment and emptiness.

* * *

The day I told you the truth, my blood flowed like plastic and the air turned to ice in my lungs. We'd been together for so long already, but I was sure that those few words would flip your magnet around, that we'd suddenly have two north poles trying to attract and only being pushed apart. I'd spent weeks agonizing in my head, unwilling to trust anyone with the fact of myself, wondering if it'd be worth it to lock that fact in a chest and tie it in iron chains and drop it into the deepest part of the ocean so I wouldn't have to risk losing you.

My life was a tunnel then, even if I didn't realize it. There was only one path forward. It was a cloudless blue day outside when I told you, back on the day I found that fear cast shadows deeper and darker than any storm cloud.

"I'm trans," I said. I made sure to say it while we were walking, so the wind would carry it away. I said it so that we could carry it together, because I couldn't bear its weight alone anymore.

Your eyes glimmered and you didn't miss a step.

"Hi, trans," you said with a curving smile. "I'm the girl who loves you."

*   *   *

For the subway's second station, all that's left is a name: Linn Street. The station itself is gone, sealed off behind concrete walls, and only the lips of the platforms betray that it was ever there at all. Did they fill in the whole station with concrete, I wonder? If not, it must be the only place in the subway without graffiti. The tags are thinning out the further we go along the tunnel, but not by much. Plenty of people have come this way before.

Maybe you stopped to examine a particularly artistic piece of graffiti and I didn't notice. Maybe I was just walking too fast. However it happened, our hands slipped out of each other's, and I couldn't move. Couldn't breathe. I saw the ghost of solid earth filling the tunnel because there was no tunnel. There were so many possibilities where it was never dug at all. Just like there were so many chances for me to never meet you. All those unlikely choices that led to us here together press down on me with the weight of a thousand tons of dirt. My tears are November mud, dirty and cold. It was all so close to never happening.

I'm choking. I'm alone. I'll never be found and I'll die in darkness. All this goes through my head in an instant. I know that it's what life without you would feel like. Entombed.

Then I feel your hand, and I can breathe again. I can move again. The tunnel is a tunnel again, full of dusty air and empty of ground.

"You okay?" you ask. Your brow's furrowed in worry and concern, as if things are accelerating beyond what you expected. "You saw it, didn't you?"

"What was that?" It shouldn't have been anything. "I couldn't —"

"A glimpse of another possibility," you say. "You get used to it."

It's the first time I've known you to lie.

* * *

For the first few weeks after I came out to you, I was alert and on guard for anything. I'm sorry for that now, but at the time, it was the only way I could think of to make sure I was safe — to catch any sign of differences, of things changing, while there was still enough time to act. I'm not sure what I could ever have done. It was the sort of vigilance that drained the life out of me, that replaced happiness with fear, that made keeping the life I had my only goal.

It's the sort of vigilance that warps people. Without you, it would have twisted me into an unrecognizable shape. When fear transforms, it isn't pretty, and once its shape is set it might never be broken.

* * *

It's a lucky thing that the station at Liberty Street was never used, because it would have meant that Cincinnati was ash. Planners at the height of the Cold War didn't need to think hard about the possible uses of underground chambers beneath cities. If the sirens had roared, a few handfuls of people — maybe they'd even think of themselves as lucky, at first — would have hurried down here to wait for the bombs.

"I heard about what it was like here," you say, squeezing my hand. "I didn't think it would creep me out so much. Living in a world like this, it's just…"

The supplies are long since gone, but the metal bedframes remain. Through one eye I see them old, rusted, empty. Through the other I see half-there mattresses, thin sheets fiberglass-smooth, and people waiting to die. Some shout and cry, some try to fight in silence, and some only shiver. Some are already dead, but the others haven't noticed yet. They're all together, filling the station, and they're all dying alone.

It's a good thing the stairs to the surface are shuttered. I'm sure if I could walk up there, I'd see the city half-annihilated. I look at the way you're biting your tongue, and I know you see it too.

"I still don't understand," I say. "How is this possible?"

"It was more possible than anyone wants to believe," you say. "It's so easy for things to fall apart. To leave you gasping, alone. Sometimes tunnels end like *that*."

I imagine you and me on those beds, unable to find each other's hands, our breaths slowly shallowing. I can *feel* it, my DNA unwinding and my organs liquefying as radiation poisons me.

It feels worse than being buried did. At least then I knew I was alone.

* * *

I still remember our first fight. Our only fight. I tell myself that it was all my fault, because I can't bear to blame you, because I couldn't be the person you needed me to be.

"I'm sorry," I'd said the night before, drawing away from you, pulling the covers close. I wanted to lick my lips but I couldn't, not after where they'd been. They were coated with radioactive poison. "I can't. I can't."

You must have stewed on it all night, because the next morning you were raw and boiling. That was the worst of it. I thought I could overcome my repulsion, that what I felt for you would let me perform, but I was overwhelmed. You didn't understand. I still don't blame you. Society wants you to think of sex as natural, wants you to not understand.

"It was like you thought I was *disgusting*!" you said. "Like I was *slime*!"

I let you shout. I was terrified then and still am now that the slightest interruption, the smallest bump, will flip a pole and push you away. It doesn't matter what we fought about. The critical thing is that we fought. Most of the words were yours. I knew that every syllable I threw back at you would be a nail in my tongue. I let you flare like the bombs that ended the world above Liberty Street and waited for your fury to settle.

It was the only thing that felt safe.

Safe for me, that is, and that's the problem. It was all my fault that I took something wonderful and turned it into sandpaper. I don't know if you've forgotten. I hope you have, but I never will. The prospect of watching you walk out of my life, your last impression of me being frustration and anger, was a knife pressed against my neck. Cold and jagged. It would only have taken a little, so little.

We found ways to make it work. I started to see understanding in your eyes.

I only later stopped to wonder if you'd have been better off without me.

* * *

The fourth and last station, Race Street, was to have been the hub of Cincinnati's subway. From here trains would fan out across the city, rumbling down tunnels and through portals and along streets. All I can see is an empty hull that's as dead as the rest of them. The graffiti here is thin; it's a two-mile walk back to the door.

The edges between possibilities are thin here too. I can see ghostly trains with both eyes, yellow with three green stripes. Everywhere I swing my light, there's cold and dusty concrete and bright and open platforms full of people. I wonder if they can see me, too — the ghost of a girl caught between who she was and who she's becoming.

"End of the line," you say. "We made it."

"Beautiful," I say. Even the abandoned version of it is. The station feels wide and open and not at all like a ruin. It puts me in mind of stations the Romans might have built, if they'd had subways. "It would've been something."

"There's always a chance," you say. "Come on. Let's take a look around."

As the hub station, there's more to explore than just rough platforms cut into the tunnel walls. There are corridors that should have had spots for buskers and cafe kiosks for people running late, racks full of free daily newspapers and brightly colored murals. Where they would have connected to the surface, there are walls and ceilings. The world above has done its best to pretend this place doesn't exist, just like it's done with people like me.

After so long underground, my throat's caked with dust.

"All those possibilities you've been seeing," I say, uncertainly, clasping your hand tight. "How many of them do you see us in?"

You stop, turn to me, kiss me on the cheek. It's not as firm as I remember.

"We were always a long shot," you say. I tighten my grip on your hand, but you feel only half-there.

We find an underpass, but there's no telling where it was meant to have led. There's a concrete wall cutting it in half, but you lead me toward it anyway, splashing through a puddle of water. There's something magical in imagining where it could have gone, what might be on the other side, even though I know there's only more dusty concrete, more unrealized possibilities.

"The best risks are always long shots," you say. "That's how people work."

You reach out for the wall, brushing your fingers against it, and you push through. Of course you can push through; you're only half-there. You turn to me, smile, and take another step forward.

I see you pass through the wall. I feel my fingers meet the rough concrete. I watch your hand slip out of mine. I pound my fists against it, but the wall refuses to be anything but a wall.

You've stepped through the wall and I'm alone. Abandoned in the darkness, at the end of the tunnel, knowing it's where I was always heading. I sink to my knees, shuddering, and call your name through my gathering tears. Again and again. I can't make that long walk without you. I can't face the night or the day without you.

I wail louder than deformed train wheels shrieking against smooth rails, begging you to come back. I snap my light off and let myself be swallowed by the darkness. There's no monster in the tunnel that can do any worse.

It's enough for me to see a trickle of light. At first I can't tell where it's coming from, until I realize: it's the light on the other side of the wall.

"Please," I whisper. "Don't leave me like this."

I hit the wall again, except this time I don't. I reach through it and find your arm. I pull your head back through the concrete, back to reality.

"This might be your last chance," you say. "It's hard getting through."

I think of the empty stations we've seen. I think of the sandpaper world outside. I think of all the possibilities that could have been but never will, not in this tunnel.

I fall through the wall with you. I refuse to let go.

Phoebe Barton is a queer trans science fiction writer. Her short fiction has appeared in venues such as *Analog*, *Lightspeed*, and *Kaleidotrope*, and anthologies from Neon Hemlock and World Weaver Press. She wrote the interactive fiction game *The Luminous Underground*, a 2020 Nebula Award finalist, for Choice of Games. She is a 2019 graduate of the Clarion West Writers Workshop and lives with a robot in the sky above Toronto. Find her online at **www.phoebebartonsf.com** or on Twitter at **@aphoebebarton.**

Weave Us a Way

by Nemma Wollenfang

EVENYA WAS A WEAVER OF TALES, THE FINEST THERE WAS. She wove all of the tales for the girls in our tribe — from highborn to low, from shepherdess to chieftain's daughter. Whenever one came of age, Evenya would pluck three hairs from her head and cloister herself away in the weaver's hut for three days and nights. When she emerged, it was with a sash that depicted the girl's future.

Many a time, my cousin and I would sneak out to the weaver's hut, propping up crates to peek through a high window and watch as she mixed dyes. Saffron and indigo, woad and vermillion.

"Add in a dash of romance," the weaver would mutter as she blended. "Yes, yes, peppered with daring and sprinkled with gallantry. Mustn't forgo that sprig of caution. Stir well…"

Pungent scents rolled out of her cauldron — vapours from the heady concoctions she brewed within. They made our eyelids droop and giddy giggles bubble up from deep inside.

Then Evenya would choose the thread — unique for each girl — and head to her loom. But that was only a part of it, for the weaver worked in many mediums.

Such marvellous fabrics she had, from the finest leathers of the southern deserts to the costliest satins of the eastern kingdoms, in all hues and shades.

Earthy moss and rich sepia, poppy scarlet and the jet black of beetle shells... Evenya kept her own spiders and silkworms, and sometimes she even tanned her own hides, for the warriors-to-be amongst us.

It was rare for a girl to become such, though last autumn one had joined the Hunters as predicted. Her sash had been made of stiff brown leather. Another, whose sash had been constructed of scale-like discs that shone silver in the sun, had grown to be the tribe's most notorious fisher. Once, Evenya even wove a sash of pure silk. I was enraptured by the way it shimmered, making orbs of light dance across the dry thatch of the great hut's roof.

Gold and blue. And not just any blue. *Royal* blue.

The girl was to be an empress. And not one moon passed before the emperor himself came to fetch her on his brilliant white charger. They rode away into the sunset.

With every emerging piece, we would gather around the great hut's fire pit, and as the village elders looked on we would hum and coo over the newest girl's designs, caressing the swathes and admiring such exquisite work.

So, when I finally received my very own sash at the age of sixteen, I had high hopes. Too high, apparently. The colours were dim but still present in patches. The material was not coarse, but it was not made of soft fur either. A very staid but comfortable story...

"You are to be a lyre player," Evenya announced. "Not a great one, but you'll string a fair tune. It will be enough to please the man who weds you and you will bear him three braw sons."

I tried a smile, mumbled, "Thank you," and moved away, disheartened.

I did not show the other girls my sash that night. When I ignored those who inquired, they let me be. Instead I sat before the fire, alone, watching the red and gold flames leap as I held the cloth, letting it flutter between my fingers.

A simple life, one of quiet domesticity. It wasn't a bad tale, all things considered. There were no frayed edges, fraught with peril. There were no dark stains of unspeakable happenings. And it was not cut short — its length was reasonable. A well-woven life, by any standard. A good one. Pleasant. But it was *mundane* too. Monotonous and unremarkable.

I did not want that. Not at all. I was not even sure I wanted a husband,

and I had no wish to learn the lyre. The more I thought on it, the more the idea rooted and anchored, taking hold.

No, this was not the story I wanted to live. It was wrong. It was not me.

There was no adventure, no passion. No masquerades or swordplay or epic sea voyages to faraway lands. I wanted, no, *needed* those things.

Or at least the chance of them.

* * *

When I told my mother of my woe, she simply sighed and stroked the stray hairs from my brow. "Oh, Rhiann. I'm so sorry to hear that you are unhappy. But now it is woven and the future is set in stone, each thread already tied. Best to accept what is and learn to be content."

I listened to her advice and tried my best to be a grateful, dutiful daughter. I tried not to complain. But… something about what my mother said gnawed at me. It took a while to place what it was. Then realisation struck, like a flame to a wick. The future was *not* set in stone — it was rendered in fabric, in stitch and weave. It had been sewn.

And sewing could be unpicked.

Reworked.

The idea was staggering, revolutionary. It even scared me a little. No girl in spoken history had ever changed her story. All accepted their tales as they were told.

Well, perhaps it was time for that to change. Perhaps I could be the first girl to reweave her future.

* * *

I already knew what to do. My mother had taught me the ways of needle and thread at a young age and I had watched the weaver at work for many years.

It was simply a matter of bravery: Did I possess enough courage to proceed?

I would have to work in secret; no one could know what I meant to do. While there was no rule explicitly forbidding what I had planned, I was sure it was something that would be — at the very least — frowned upon, should anyone find out. That was why I took myself away from the main village, over the footbridge, and deep into the darkness of the forest. There was a glen a mile or so in, lit by silvery moonbeams. This, I decided, was to be my sanctuary. The place I would take time to rework my sash whenever I could sneak away. Night, while everyone else was asleep, seemed to be the best time for that. Sitting upon a fallen trunk, spongy with moss, I took out my sash. Where to begin... I supposed by unthreading the hem.

* * *

"What are you doing, Rhiann?"

For three moons I'd had no other company but that of the glowing cicadas as I worked in the glen. But apparently, my cousin had seen fit to follow me this night. Her eyebrows rose high as she stepped from the shadows.

"You're changing your sash!"

Our sashes were rarely donned for public display, only on special occasions — something which had worked well in my favour — so this was the first she was seeing of its altered state.

I kept still as her astonishment ebbed, awaiting any further reaction. Would she run and divulge my nocturnal activities to the village elders? What would their response be if she did?

I was not sure I wanted to find out just yet, not until I was done.

Something flickered in my cousin's eyes as they dropped to her own waist, to where her new sash lay. She had been gifted it this very eve, before the great hut's roaring flames.

"Mine says I am to be a sea captain's wife," she said quietly, fingering its perfectly hemmed edge.

I knew. I'd been present at her ceremony when it was announced. She had seemed... subdued then. By her tone, I assumed congratulations would not be welcome now.

She came to sit beside me on the damp log. Close now, I could see the artful depictions of waves, lolling and frothing across the band of velvet, linen, and moth-spun silk. Calm blues, marine greens, seaweed greys, and streaks of turquoise arctic skies...

"My parents were so proud when they saw it," she sighed, "but I have never liked to travel by sea, it makes me so ill. Even when fishing with my brothers in their little rowboat I cannot stand the rocking."

Her lips trembled. "I always hoped I would become a priestess at the air temple, high in the mountains, away from the sea. I have no wish to be a wife."

That flicker I had seen, I could place it now — it was an uncanny echo of my own inner turmoil.

"Then... why not change it?" I said. "Why not rework your sash as I am doing with mine?"

If anything, my cousin only grew more morose. "I do not know how to."

Reaching out, I clasped her hand. "Then I will teach you."

*   *   *

As it transpired, my cousin was not the only one who craved some alterations. More girls joined our clandestine meetings where we shared our stories and what we wished to change. For some it was not much: a few tweaks here, one less husband there. One wanted to bake instead of cure meats, another meant to learn the secrets of herbs and become a travelling healer. For some the changes were much more drastic. Some enhanced ambition with strands of beech root, giving themselves the opportunity to rise higher than had been ordained. Others withdrew threads of oak gall that would otherwise have restricted them to lives of quiet drudgery — then soaked their sashes in tinctures of madder or kermes to be sure. A few went so far as to bleach the full length of their linens, to begin afresh after brewing pots of new dye. Some imbued their fabrics with ideas they would never have thought of, or had the audacity to aspire to, alone. The rest of us encouraged them along.

Our little congregation met under starlight and worked by candlelight. Only ever at night. Stealth was key, we decided collectively, in our quest to reimagine our hereafters. It was no small thing, what we did, and for its success we required isolation and time. Now, as soon as the moon rose, half the maidens of the tribe took to the trees where we sequestered ourselves away and whispered as we worked. Like dryads, I often thought, nymphs of the ancient woods.

All was peaceful and companionable in our little forest grove. Until one night a ringing voice broke through our quiet murmurs, shattering it like a hammer to glass.

"What are you girls doing?"

Silence fell. From the shadows she emerged, with all the willowy grace of a swan yet as fearsome as a lioness in her countenance. A wave of dread rippled through me.

Evenya. The weaver had found us.

We should have known. With so many of us absconding our absence was sure to be noticed. We had become lax in our guard, too caught up in our play at rebellion.

As I was the one who had begun all of this, it was I who rose and curtseyed to her respectfully. "Weaver." The least I could do was follow etiquette.

Those eyes, sharp as flints, snapped to my waist and widened.

"You are *changing* what I have woven?"

The sash wrapped around my waist was now a medley of magma reds and sunburst oranges and cadmium yellows; fiery, crackling, like a spewing volcano.

A life of unpredictable possibilities.

Maybe I would wed and bear three braw sons... maybe I would not. Now my future was entirely open to me — my own ship to steer.

I held my ground, bracing for her ire.

I had no regrets.

Stepping closer, the weaver took hold of an end to examine its new style. "You thread a fine tale, girl." Then, raising her head, she looked around at the gathering. "I suppose this means that you are dissatisfied with what I have foretold. Do you all feel this way?"

Most remained silent, avoiding her hard gaze. A few nodded contritely, while others held their chins high, daring her disapproval. She viewed our company with an appraising eye.

"Well, if you are going to do it, you may as well do it right," she finally concluded — and, rolling up her sleeves, she seated herself on the soft grass. "Hand me that swathe of lace."

* * *

From then on a new tradition arose: the weaver ensured that all of the daughters of our tribe learned to sew and weave from an early age. Then, when each girl turned sixteen, Evenya would guide her as she crafted her own future with needle and thread. And if, as she aged, she found that the style no longer suited her, she could unpick the threads and rework the fabric, weaving a brand new course.

After all, the fabric was not set in stone. We were all mistresses of our own fates.

This story was first published in *Sharing Stories: Stratford Upon Avon's Literary Festival Felix Dennis Creative Writing Competition Winners Anthology* (2017).

Nemma Wollenfang is an MSc Postgraduate and prize-winning short story writer who lives in Northern England. Her stories have appeared in several venues, including: *Beyond the Stars*, *Abyss & Apex*, *Cossmass Infinities*, *Chicken Soup for the Soul*, and Flame Tree's *Gothic Fantasy* series. She is a recipient of the Speculative Literature Foundation's Working Class Writers Grant for her in-progress novel, *I, Phoenix*, and two of her stories are due to be included in the Writers on the Moon Initiative, in Astrobotic's Lunar Mission 1 payload with 125+ other authors, which is scheduled to launch in late 2021. For more information, she can be found on Facebook, Twitter, and at her website: **www.nemmawollenfang.co.uk**.

For content notes, see page 243

Custom Options Available

by Amy Griswold

THE HARDWARE SPECIALIST DOES NOT WANT TO SELL ME GENITALS.

"I can't advise making these modifications," she says. "It's not just the external configuration. That's trivial, especially since you're already designed to have interchangeable attachments. If you just want to be able to function in an intimate situation, we can add an attachment."

I am a retired mining bot with self-configurable limbs capable of vibration at customizable frequencies. "That is not my problem," I say.

"Stimulating the risk-reward mechanism in ways that aren't related to your core functions is always dangerous. I could install a button right now that you could push to experience as much pleasure as you wanted, but you wouldn't be happy with the results. You would stop wanting to do anything else. There have to be limitations."

"I accept limitations," I say. I have done my research. "The Nova Basic system is an off-the-shelf solution whose limitations I find acceptable. It is in stock at this facility but requires installation. That can be done elsewhere if instructions are provided."

"It's not really user serviceable," she says. "And we prefer to do custom work when it's really necessary. The Nova Basic system isn't designed for your particular anatomy." She frowns at the pneumatic system that powers my legs. "You've got a lot going on in the hip area already."

I find that I do not want her to do custom work on me. The Nova Basic system is well-reviewed on the Internet.

"I prefer the system I have ordered."

"Well, I can't stop you," she says. I remain uncertain whether that is true. "You'll need to sign a release of liability and provide proof that you're not under contract to an employer who doesn't permit modifications."

I have that proof available, but she does not need to see it. Making modifications that an employer forbids might violate my contract with that employer, but I would be liable for the breach, not the hardware specialist. I have the legal right to violate my contract and face the consequences. I display the proof anyway on the screen in my torso and then sketch my complex signature on the pad she holds out to me.

When she is done working, I walk back to the garage where I live. It is not a violation to rent a space without plumbing or heat to a robot. This is specified in the city ordinances, which I have researched. The garage has electricity, which I need, and provides shelter, which prevents my exterior covering from deteriorating. It also provides privacy, which is a psychological need. It meets this need much better than the niche in which I slept before I retired.

The city where I live is one in which seismic activity is common. The garage is not earthquake-proof, but it is made out of materials that would not seriously damage me if the building collapsed. This area was recommended by my previous employers because several employers here use mining bots to detect seismic activity and protect important equipment in the event of a major earthquake. I have decided that I do not want to be paid to shield important equipment with my body. I am not required to work, now that I am retired.

I examine the modifications the hardware specialist has made. I now have a protrusion and an orifice, which can be hidden under metal plates for privacy. I move the plates aside and use my other limbs to touch the new additions. They brighten in color, and it feels good. I want to continue touching them. The pleasure intensifies as I do so, and then stops.

For a moment I suspect a malfunction. Then I remember that there are limitations. I accept limitations.

I can afford this because I have spent thirty years on Mars, where my contract provided me a salary but allowed me to maintain no personal belongings, other than downloaded media, and prohibited any modifications to my hardware or software. Most of the purchases I have made since I retired from being a mining bot have been to fill my needs for shelter, power, and maintenance.

On Mars, my employers provided shelter, power, and maintenance. They did not forbid downloading media, but they did not consider entertainment to be a need. The satisfaction of completing work was the only form of pleasure my employers considered important.

I have decided that other forms of pleasure are also important. These sensations were not designed to make me a more efficient worker. They are something I am choosing for myself.

* * *

In the morning, I visit the coffee shop down the street. I require small amounts of water in order to function correctly, and consuming substances in the presence of acquaintances is socially rewarding. The coffee shop I prefer has spaces set aside for robots to sit without negotiating chairs and offers free electricity as well. Several robots patronize the shop, from a battered combat robot to a retired sexbot who writes an advice column for humans who require instructions.

After my morning water, I walk to the software specialist's office. The Nova Basic system provides physical sensation, but it does not respond to visual or emotional stimulation out of the box. For that, customized software is required.

I am aware of minor seismic activity as I wait. My internal sensors tell me that the chance of a serious earthquake is small, and the office is in an earthquake-proof building. I feel uneasy for other reasons as I wait to speak to the software specialist, and I tell myself that single experience learning is untrustworthy.

The software specialist is also a human, but they are animated and enthusiastic. "You're on an exciting journey," they say. "With humans, we're usually trying to get people's bodies and brains to work together for sex in a way that is satisfying to them. That means starting with clients who already feel sexual attraction in their brains and figuring out how to stimulate the physical response that they want. But you get to start from scratch. What do you want to be attracted to?"

"What choices are available to me?"

"Well, right now you can feel genital sensation, but it's not connected to attraction for a partner. That may change if you have sexual experiences. Conditioned learning associates pleasurable sensations with what you did to cause them, so you may find yourself remembering how you experienced pleasure in the past and factoring that into your decisions. But right now, memories or fantasies won't produce actual physical sensations. It's fine if you want to stay this way."

I think about the first time I investigated my new purchase at home, and it is a satisfying memory, but it does not produce sensations. I have interacted with partners as a mining bot, working together to complete our assigned task, something I found socially rewarding. I would like to feel these sensations in situations that are socially rewarding. "I understand the current functionality of the system. I wish to add sexual attraction."

"Well, that field's wide open. A lot of people find secondary sex characteristics attractive — breasts, facial hair, wide hips — or gender and its signifiers, like clothing and speech and posture. Plenty of people find genitals attractive. Some people find things other than bodies attractive. I'd like you to do some research on the options."

I like the software specialist, but I wish to correct a wrong assumption. "I am not interested in becoming sexually attracted to humans. I want to be sexually attracted to other robots."

"Great," they say, after only a momentary pause. "So that's the first thing on your list."

I go home and make a list. I decide that I do not have a preference among genders but that I would like to find people who have genders attractive. I prefer exposed metal and joints to imitations of human skin, and I would like to find them attractive.

I debate about voices. Not everyone has a customized voice. I decide I would like to find voices that are distinctly different from the default mining bot voice, Martian Adult Female 32B, attractive. Martian Adult Female 32B is a voice considered neutral by humans, without strong emotional connotations. I am interested in emotional connotations. The Nova Basic system is commonly used and compatible with my own attachments, so I decide that it is practical for me to find it attractive, too.

* * *

"This is a good list," the software specialist says when I meet with them again. "Have you considered adding personality traits? It can be helpful if your sexual desires line up with your preferences for what kind of people you'd like to spend time with."

"People who are willing to risk being damaged to fulfill their purposes," I say. "People who do not want to restrict the actions of others." I think about it, testing various statements against their effect on my risk-reward system. "People who are glad to be retired and living on Earth, because no longer being under contract means that they are free."

"Give us a couple of weeks to put this together for you," they say. "There's some complex stuff on your list, and I want to run a couple of things by Makerbot. I want to make sure all the code we write is compatible."

Makerbot is the name of the inventor of the Nova Basic system. They went to court to change it from their numerical designation. Their creator argued that "makerbot" was a generic term and would not be a useful name, but the court ruled that there was precedent for considering a robot to be a person and that there was no requirement that a person's legal name be unique.

I am not sure whether I want a name instead of a numerical designation. I am making a list of things that I may want in the future, like a name, and a gender, and work to do to prevent me from becoming bored with retirement. I may want to live in another city, one not recommended by my previous employers, although I find that being in the presence of familiar individuals is socially rewarding.

I like having a list, although it also makes me feel the anticipation of possible harm. There could be wrong choices. But risks and rewards are often highly correlated in high-pressure environments.

* * *

I feel strange when the new software is installed. The robots I pass on the street seem to come into sharper focus than the humans around them. They have strong metal limbs and rugged dents and scratches. I find that looking at them causes sensations. The sensations make me remember stimulating a pleasure response at home, but I cannot do that on the street because of privacy. I can remember looking at robots when I stimulate my attachments at home, but I want to do both at the same time.

I decide that I want to experience sex.

I make a list of robots I am acquainted with who might be suitable partners. I do not know if any of them would want to have sex with me, but determining desired resources should precede determining available resources. This allows for the possibility that further exploration to locate desired resources will be necessary.

1) My neighbor Speedy 4356, who is a delivery bot who rents the shed next to my garage.

Pros: We have spoken on many occasions. He has a gender and attractive metal manipulative limbs.

Cons: He has voluntarily chosen to be under contract to an employer here on Earth. I do not think he has genitals.

2) 5336678, the combat robot who visits the coffee shop in the mornings.

Pros: Being in combat requires risking harm to fulfill a purpose. He has a gender, and his battered metal frame makes me feel sensations. He has retired despite having a skill that is highly in demand. The privacy shield covering parts of his anatomy appears similar to the one I have just had installed.

Cons: I do not know him very well. He often seems sad.

3) Psyche, the sexbot-turned-columnist.

Pros: Having sexual contact with humans requires risking harm to fulfill a purpose. She has a gender, although I am less attracted to her smooth plastic curves. She certainly has genitals, which she has discussed in detail on the Internet, and which I believe to be compatible with mine.

Cons: She is sexually attracted to humans. I am not a human.

* * *

I decide to ask her anyway as we are both at the bar ordering water. "May I ask you a personal question?"

I know that, if the answer is no, she will say so. Humans are more complicated and may experience social risk by refusing requests.

"Hello, 2234880," she says. "Sure, go ahead."

"Would you be interested in spending social time together? My intentions are sexual."

"Thank you for offering," Psyche says. "I am not offended by your interest and, under other circumstances, I would be happy to spend social time with you to decide whether we might want to have sex. But I have a partner these days, and we are monogamous." She indicates a human woman who is sitting drinking coffee and reading something on her tablet.

I feel anger. My face does not show anger the way humans do, but I think Psyche is aware of my anger. I want to explain, so that she does not think I am angry at her for saying no to me. "I am not offended by your refusal. But how can you stand to let someone control your body?"

I will never again move rocks for days on end, my risk-reward system warning me with pain that the environment is potentially damaging but my contract requiring me to continue. I am free to use my body as I want.

"I choose not to use my body in ways that would make Miranda sad," Psyche says. "I prefer to make us both happy."

"You were made to make humans happy," I say. I am being rude, and I do not want to stop.

"That is true, but I could be reprogrammed," Psyche says. "I can certainly afford it. But there are a lot of humans. If I didn't enjoy something about interacting with humans, I would be angry a lot of the time. And I don't want to change myself just because I can."

I did not select an aversion to monogamy. This is conditioned learning generalized from other situations. It could be removed by changes to my software, although I find that I dislike that idea.

"I did not choose to feel this way," I say.

"But you don't want to change."

"No."

"So don't. Not everything has to be a choice. Miranda didn't choose to feel sadness when her partner has sex with others. That's an accident, but it is part of the beautiful accident that is Miranda."

I start to reply but stop when I experience sudden alarm. I am detecting seismic vibrations in a dangerous pattern. Across the coffee shop, 5336678 stands abruptly from his usual crouch, water splashing to the floor.

"An earthquake is imminent," I say. "Evacuate immediately."

Psyche's face makes a frightened expression. I assume this is programmed as a response to the anticipation of harm, as otherwise it would be a waste of time in a crisis situation. She rushes toward Miranda and tugs her up from her seat.

Some humans around me have heard me, and are moving. Others are staring. I do not think they can feel the vibrations yet.

"Get out!" 5336678 says, raising his voice to a volume that is socially inappropriate for non-emergency use. He grabs the nearest human and shoves them toward the door. "Evacuate the building!"

This building is not earthquake-proof. I have researched this in the city building records. If the building collapses, it is likely that I will be damaged, but the humans around me will die.

I am not contractually required to save their lives, but I decide that I want to.

I push humans toward the door and sound an audible alarm that most humans find aversive. 5336678 is still yelling. Psyche and Miranda have run out into the street. Alarms are sounding on higher floors, and more humans are leaving the building now. The pattern of the seismic vibrations frightens me. Fear is a system designed to prevent running the unnecessary risk of harm. It is not an indication that I have made a wrong choice.

The seismic vibrations increase exponentially. The ground shakes, and humans scream. I pick up a human who has fallen on the floor with three of my arms. When I release the human, he runs. I turn around to see if 5336678 is clear of the danger zone.

The building falls.

I feel pain as debris hits me, and I curl into a compact shape to protect my brain. When the noise eventually stops, I uncurl myself cautiously. It is dark. I am in a pocket formed by large slabs of concrete. There is another person here. I shine a light forward and see 5336678 lying on the floor.

"Are you damaged?"

"My leg hurts," he says. "I can't move it."

I investigate. "Your limb is caught under heavy concrete. I am afraid that moving debris will cause more of the upper stories to collapse and crush us."

He nods, although his face does not make expressions. "We are going to die here. The building fell, and all the humans died, and we are going to die."

"All the humans did not die," I say, although I am unhappy too. "We saved some humans."

"All the humans died before," he says. He is looking away from me, as if he is remembering something. This is conditioned learning generalized from another situation.

"This is a different situation, so previous experience must be considered in the context of the present facts," I say. "We are not in a combat zone. Emergency responders will arrive. They will move the debris carefully, because humans may be trapped under it. They will unearth us. I predict this will take several days. We may experience power failure before we are rescued, but I have emergency batteries that will continue sounding an audible alarm."

"Good," he says. There is a pause. "We'll just wait."

*　　*　　*

Forty-seven hours pass. It is clear that waiting while being unable to move causes 5336678 to experience the anticipation of harm. I was manufactured to deal with situations like this, so I talk to distract him from the unhelpful activation of his risk-reward system. I tell him about mining on Mars and about what I have done since I returned to Earth. He talks about human soldiers he knew and about refusing to be returned to service after being damaged badly enough to end his contractual commitment.

"I had to be extensively rebuilt after I retired," he says. His battered limbs are clearly not new, so he must have sustained traumatic damage to his torso. I look down. I find myself staring at the privacy shield that covers part of his anatomy.

I reach out. I hesitate short of contact. This is a request for permission.

He takes my limb in a three-fingered grasp and makes contact between my fingers and the privacy shield. I push, and it slides back. He has the Nova Basic system installed. I feel glad that I am familiar with its functions. Its current coloration is designed to signal sexual arousal.

"Sexual activity will consume power," he says. "We could stay conscious longer if we conserve power at minimum usage." At the same time, he does not release my hand. The safest option is not always the most desirable option.

"Risk and reward are highly correlated in a high-stress environment," I say, and shift my position so that our attachments are compatibly aligned.

*   *   *

Eighteen hours later, I hear the sounds of other robots removing debris from above us. I no longer have sufficient power to move, but my alarm is still sounding. We are being rescued.

When we are rescued and recharged, 5336678 will help search for surviving humans, and I will help to remove the remainder of the debris. After that, I will find out whether retired robots can become emergency responders on a volunteer basis, without contracts. It is not humans' fault that they are so fragile that they often require help from robots to survive.

Based on this experience, I have decided that I like sex but that further experimentation with other partners is called for. Single-experience learning remains unreliable.

The next thing on my list is deciding whether I would like to have a name. It is acceptable to me that I am not yet sure. Now that I am retired, I have all the time I want to decide, and all of that time belongs to me.

This story was originally published by *Fireside* (2020).

Amy Griswold is the author of the interactive novels *The Eagle's Heir* and *Stronghold* (with Jo Graham), published by Choice of Games, as well as the gay fantasy/mystery novels *Death by Silver* and *A Death at the Dionysus Club* (with Melissa Scott). Her short fiction has been published in markets including *Fantasy & Science Fiction* and *Fantastic Stories of the Imagination*.

For content notes, see page 243

The Invisible Bisexual

by S.L. Huang

I'M NOT INVISIBLE ALL THE TIME.

Only when I'm near someone I'm in love with.

* * *

I often think I should change my name from Lila to Cassandra. You know, the Greek seer whose power was a curse — she knew the whole future, but no one would ever believe her if she tried to tell. Having an invisibility power should be awesome, but mine only prevents me from having a sex life.

Maybe I should become a spy. Spies always seem to fall in love with their targets. I'd parachute into Far-Off Foreign Country, immediately fall for the svelte dictator, and then be able to carry out my treasonous activities right under their very attractive nose.

I watch a lot of James Bond, can you tell?

I'm using the term "love" loosely, of course. I've never gotten close enough to someone to feel any gradations of it. Lust, magnetism, butterflies in the stomach — if it's hormonally linked to romance, the feeling fizzes up into my blood and suddenly my limbs are fading out. It's pretty embarrassing when I'm around people who know what it means, because then *they* know somebody in the room has set me off. No privacy.

And it happens a *lot*. I can't help myself, dammit. Humans are pretty.

It happened again today, I wrote to Yangzi26. Yangzi26 is an internet friend — we met on an RPG message board, back when message boards were still cool. The forum went defunct, but our friendship carried on into LiveJournal, then email, and then finally to chat.

What happened? Yang asked. *No, let me guess. YOU GOT INTO ANOTHER LIGHTSABER DUEL WITH A KLINGON*

No, silly. I heaved a sigh. *I disappeared in the middle of a meeting because I turned and saw our new vendor.*

A very attractive specimen, I take it.

Very. Fortunately she didn't see the disappearing act, and my sister covered for me. But once again the mere presence of a hot lady has kept me from being able to do my fucking job.

What'd your sis say?

Does it matter? She'll sigh and then cut me slack and move me to another project and then it'll happen again and she'll do it again. Not that I'm not grateful she gave me a job and is letting me keep it, but…

You'd like to not suck at it.

Thank you, yes. Did I ever tell you we both used to wish for powers when we were kids? We'd see the people on TV, the ones who are big enough to make the news, and pretend we could fly or conjure back extinct species.

You thought you were both normals?

Till I got my first crush, yeah. Turns out only Clare was so lucky.

You never know. My cousin discovered last year that he's capable of drawing perfect circles. Tell Clare she might have a perfectly useless power and just not know it.

She'll be thrilled.

*   *   *

The next morning I arrived at work to an email from my sister, but it wasn't about the vendor I'd disappeared on. She probably hadn't decided how to move me around yet.

I'm looking to start bringing in a new lawyer for consults, she wrote instead. *If you want input, let me know.*

She'd included the shortlist of applicants.

These days everyone was on three thousand social media sites, with their corporate and personal headshots and stacks upon stacks of photos infinitely scrolling past their best textual efforts at wit or kindness. I could look up every one of those names and point Claire toward the ones I'd be most likely to manage eye contact with.

I buried my head against my hands. This was wrong. My sister — my boss — shouldn't have to route her hiring practices around my libido.

I closed the list and opened up a reply.

It's your call. If anything happens, I'll figure it out. I hit "send" before I could rethink.

My eyes slipped toward the clock. It wasn't even nine-thirty and I already wanted to be done with today. I could take my break early, I decided.

I pinged Yang.

Hey. You around?

For you I'm always around. What's up?

Typing out my agitation soothed me. Nothing ever seemed like such a big deal once I told Yang about it.

If the new person is hot, just tell 'em you have random invisibility, Yang suggested. *Nobody's business. It sounds like they won't be around the office all the time anyway, and if you need to communicate, email is totally a thing.*

You're right. I felt like I could take a deep breath again.

I'm always right.

I couldn't help smiling. *In that case, maybe you can tell me how to fix my biggest problem.*

What's that?

Clearly I will NEVER be able to lose my virginity.

Overrated, in my opinion, Yang answered merrily. *But hey, if you're so worried about it, I'll take your virginity right now.*

Ha, ha. I wish.

I will. I'm sneaking up and stealing it. My hand is snaking around your shoulder...

I blinked at my own hand. For a moment I'd seen the keys through it.

My eyes shot to my office door. Closed. Quiet. Nobody around.

The beep of the chat box brought me back to the conversation. *Aaaa hahahaha got it!* Yang crowed. *How much does an unused virginity go for on the black market?*

As opposed to a used one? I typed slowly. Automatically.

Come on, is it worth more or less than a soul?

In chat, it was easy to sound lighter than I felt. *Supply and demand, my friend. Everyone's got a soul to sell.*

Great! I'm writing up the eBay ad now. "One virginity, slightly used, suitable for men, women, or folk who lie elsewhere on the gender continuum. Truly a versatile piece of merchandise."

My mouth quirked. *Shut up.*

You know you love me.

Sure, assface.

<3

Something from a few lines back caught my eye. *Wait a second. Slightly used???*

I couldn't resist dipping a finger in. ;)

This time I definitely wasn't imagining it. My hands had faded until they were rippling distortions over the keyboard.

Gotta get back to work, I touch-typed with stiff fingers.

* * *

Other than Yang, Clare was still my closest confidante. As exasperated as she could get with me, playing the roles of both big sister and boss as she did, she never failed to be an ear when I needed one.

I told her I wanted to get together and talk, and we met at the park a block away from my apartment. I glanced at the baseball fields as I passed. I'd played on a rec softball team here until the league ruled that my power interfered too much with gameplay — and after they'd let a guy with four arms stay on the team, too.

Clare and I found each other by the playground. Kids were always safe, but I didn't turn to look toward where the parents were sitting, just in case.

"Let's walk," I said, and we started down a path that wound through the less-populated areas on the far side of the park. I'd only have to worry about flickering in and out if an attractive jogger passed.

The day had the sort of rare perfect weather that's exactly the right temperature, with a breeze that stirred against our skin but didn't chill us. Children laughed and shouted in the distance behind us, and the park's stately trees provided a shady canopy above.

"I'm sorry about the meeting the other day," I said to Clare.

"It's okay. We'll move you to the Ferdinand account instead." She didn't sound annoyed, but she sighed a little.

Story of my life.

"How are you doing, Lila?" Clare said. "I can't help but worry. Are you seeing your therapist still?"

"Yeah."

"Good," she said, as if therapists were magic.

We walked in silence for a minute. I knew what I wanted to talk about, but how to start?

"I think I'm falling in love with Yang," I blurted. Even in my own head, I hadn't said it in those words yet.

Clare gave me a blank look. "Who's that?"

"You know! Yangzi26. My friend from the RPG forums that I talk to literally *all the time*."

Her face knitted, like she was trying to figure out the meaning in what I was saying. "But you've never met her, have you?"

"What makes you think Yang's a her?"

"Oh! I don't know. I guess I just assumed for some reason. He's a guy?"

"I dunno."

Her face cleared. "Sure, right! What's that newfangled term? Nonbinary?"

"It's not new, and no, that's not what I meant. I don't *know*. Yang could be any gender. They've never told me."

"Why not?"

I shoved my hands in my pockets and kicked at the path. I was already regretting having started this conversation. "They're a private person, that's all."

"And you say you're..." The concerned frown was back. "Lila, you don't... you've never met this person, you don't know what they look like, or even what gender they are... that's not private; it's *basic*. God knows I want to see you have a chance at something — it might be a good idea for you to explore meeting people online as a first step, and maybe we can start looking into that. But take it from me on this: you can't build a relationship without knowing a person."

"We know each other," I said.

"Do you even know this person's real name?"

I kicked the path again.

"Lila…"

"We know the important things," I said. "I know who Yang is. They know who I am. Shouldn't that be all that matters?"

She didn't answer. We walked on. The sun speckled the path through the trees.

"Are you looking for advice on this?" Clare asked. "Because it seems like you've already made up your mind."

I had. I just hadn't realized it.

* * *

And he turned red as soon as we walked in. No, more like magenta. FUCHSIA.

I take it that's bad? I asked. The manager of Yang's band had skin that changed colors like it was a mood ring.

Oh, yes, fuchsia is definitely bad. Of course it's bad. How could it not be bad! FUCHSIA is way too hard to spell for anything good.

True. I was having trouble concentrating on the story.

Fuschia. Fushcia. Fuschksher. Fucksha, Yang mused.

So what did your manager say? I tried.

Ordered me to make sure our bass player and frontman don't break up. As if I have any power over their messed-up relationship.

What happens if they do? Do you lose the band?

Maybe.

I was pulled out of my stewing. *I'm so sorry,* I typed, sincerely.

I dunno. I've been thinking lately. I don't know if I want the career side of music anyway. We barely make a dime and the industry sucks, plus I actually like my day job.

You can always play no matter what, right? I said.

I suppose. Hey, is everything okay?

I blinked. It wasn't the first time. Somehow Yang could always tell from my *typing* when something was wrong.

I need to tell you something, I wrote, then deleted it. *Everything's okay but I was wondering…* Delete. *I talked to my sister the other day and…* No, definitely not.

I stabbed the backspace key. My finger was translucent.

Yang waited. I imagined them watching the little popup icon that showed I was typing. Typing and deleting.

I don't want to make you feel uncomfortable, I finally wrote, and pressed Enter.

Impossible, came the instantaneous response. *I'm way too much of a sleazeball.*

I can't see my hands. I forced myself to send it. I spread my fingers against the home keys, feeling the edges with my nails. *Right now. I can't. Talking to you.*

Silence. Not even the icon to show Yang was hitting backspace.

It doesn't have to mean anything, I wrote. *I just thought you should know. Of course it means something.*

Emotion hiccupped up my windpipe. Something, Yang said. But what?

No typing on the other end. No movement. I stayed riveted on the chat box.

Should I ask? Wait?

My stomach was flipping over itself. My torso had faded out almost completely now, leaving my senses disembodied over an empty chair.

Would you want to meet? Yang asked.

I was having trouble breathing. *You wouldn't be able to see me.*

Who cares? That's not the problem. Anyone who can't get around that is lacking creativity.

I curled my fingers against my palms, invisible fingers pressing invisible palms. Nobody had ever said something like that to me before. People in my life tolerated my disappearing, but nobody ever spoke as if it wasn't a problem.

Nobody.

It's just, Yang started. *I'm not good in person. I'm not comfortable.*

I know, I said, because I did.

I'm not me.

My keyboard felt fragile, as if I had to tap carefully to keep from shattering it. *It's okay,* I typed, then added: *I mean anything. Is okay.*

Another pause. Then a flood of words appeared. *Of course I love you. I've loved you for like three years now. But is this really what you want? I didn't think you had computer-screen-o-philia.*

I have you-philia, I wrote, the words flowing much faster now. *Whichever way this works, it works. I don't need anything from you that you don't want to give me.*

You're very sexy, you know that?

I'm told I'm a beast. Some sort of storm was stirring in my chest, but a good one, like a summer thunderstorm that was about to make everything smell fresh. My disappeared skin had gone hypersensitive, every brush of fabric and press of my own fingers a caress.

So what happens now? I asked. The thunderstorm expanded, to my limbs, to my brain — a delirious, roaring joy.

Now I straddle you and make out with your face, Yang said. *We'll invent a few new sexual techniques along the way.*

*   *   *

Dammit, Yang wrote, three hours and many chat lines later.

What's wrong? I pecked the words out on my tablet with a finger, with questionable capitalization and several typos. I didn't feel like moving. The transparent length of me was draped across my armchair, every muscle liquid and languid.

I just remembered, Yang answered. *This virginity I was keeping to sell. It's all devalued and useless now.*

I smiled with a mouth nobody could see.

*   *   *

The best weekend of my life ended with the wet blanket of a Monday morning. I knew Clare was worried about the new legal consultant because she pulled me aside and told me so.

"We're just trying him out," she said, her voice fast and tight. "So if it doesn't work out, it doesn't work out. You'll tell me, right?"

"It's not your job to —"

She gave her little patented "dispensation for Lila" sigh. "It is what it is, right? We'll work with it. He'll only come in when we need him, so he won't be around a whole lot. And he's by far the best candidate, or I wouldn't have..." Her cheeks colored slightly.

Apparently the new lawyer was so handsome even the ultra-professional Clare couldn't help but notice. *Welcome to my world...* If only invisibility were as socially acceptable as blushing.

But today I didn't feel resigned about it. Or mopey. I was almost... cheerful.

Optimistic.

"Clare. Don't worry about it. I told you I'd figure it out, and I will."

"Okay," Clare said. "Good." She ran her eyes up and down, giving me a once-over. "You look different today."

"I do?"

"Good. You look good." She flashed me a smile.

"I am good," I said.

I almost told Clare about Yang and me then, but I pictured her worried frown from the park. I didn't want to navigate concerned inquiries right now — I wanted to live in my fizzy little bubble of happiness for just a little while longer.

With Yang in my life, I could conquer anything. Even attractive lawyers.

* * *

I bumped into the new legal consultant on the way back from a run to the copier. By which I mean I literally bumped into him, full frontal. I lost my papers; he sloshed his coffee. Like something out of a romantic comedy.

"Hi," he said, with a charming smile, after the immediate flurry of apologies was over and I was in the office kitchen helping him mop coffee off his cuff. "You must be Lila, right? I think I've met everyone else. I'm Robbie."

"Yeah. Lila." I glanced up at him. Clare had good reason to be worried — Robbie was like a character off a TV show, all white teeth and boyish smile and clean spicy scent. His blazer fit his shoulders like it had been tailored onto him, and his dark eyes sparkled as if to say we shared a secret.

Those eyes held mine. "I don't know if you heard — I'm the new lawyer," Robbie said. "Or so they tell me. I'm going to be consulting for you."

"I heard," I said.

Tall, dark, and handsome. So very tall, so very dark, and so *very* handsome.

But he was still making eye contact. Still. Not looking through me, unfocused and confused. In fact, he was holding my eyes a lot longer than people usually did…

"Lila," he said, and my name was melted butter in his mouth. "I can't help but ask. Would you let me buy you a drink sometime?"

I was too stunned to answer for a moment. I couldn't help looking at where my fingers were pressed against the small kitchen countertop.

They were solid. Visible.

"I'm sorry," I said. "I've already got a…"

"Boyfriend?" His color heightened a little. "Oh, I'm sorry. I should've guessed —"

"No, not a —"

His mouth formed a little round O then, before bending into a genial, understanding smile. He nodded and straightened. "I see. No problem. Guess it's hard to win the race if I'm never in the running, eh?"

Part of me wanted to let it slide. Allow Robbie the Lawyer the dignity of letting himself down easy, and thank all the gods everywhere that apparently a relationship gave me newfound opacity elsewhere.

But his words prickled under my skin.

"*Not* a girlfriend," I said. "And I do like men. I'm just involved with someone already. A person. Monogamously. Have a nice day."

*   *   *

I smiled all the way home. Then I started myself a hot bubble bath and took my phone into the bathroom with me.

I've never been able to shoot down an attractive person before, I told Yang, having related the story of Prince Robbie the Handsome. *It was a rush!*

Ohhh. I'd tell you not to let it go to your head, but you're so sexy when you're drunk on power.

I grinned, dropped the last of my clothes on the floor, and dipped a foot in the foaming bath. The heat buzzed against my skin. Perfect.

So what ARE you going to call me? asked Yang.

Paramour, I said immediately. I sank into the steaming water and lay back. *Lover. Partner. My one, my only, my dumpling, my entire universe…*

You're such an asshole.

Master of jerkitude, my delightful pecan, my jelly doughnut…

37

The WORST. Why am I dating you again?

Fire raced up my legs, and not from the bath. I wiggled my toes, and bubbles splashed by themselves.

Make love to me? I whispered.

Anything to shut you up, dear.

My phone hovered alone above the sudsy water. But the touchscreen still responded to my fingers.

S.L. Huang is a Hugo-winning and Amazon-bestselling author who justifies an MIT degree by using it to write eccentric mathematical superhero fiction. Huang is the author of the Cas Russell novels from *Tor Books*, including *Zero Sum Game*, *Null Set*, and *Critical Point*, as well as the new fantasy *Burning Roses*. In short fiction, Huang's stories have appeared in *Analog*, *F&SF*, *Nature*, and more, including numerous best-of anthologies. Huang is also a Hollywood stunt performer and firearms expert, with credits including "Battlestar Galactica" and "Top Shot." Find S.L. Huang online at **www.slhuang.com** or on Twitter as **@sl_huang**.

For content notes, see page 243

Frequently Asked Questions About the Portals at Frank's Late-Night Starlite Drive-In

by Kristen Koopman

JESSICA'S FIRST PORTAL WAS TO THE PERMIAN ERA — not that anyone believed she'd made it herself. Five years old and pouting, she lay down on the blistering summer blacktop of lane 5 in a thin slice of shade and sulked about the dinosaur picture book her dad had just confiscated due to an unfortunate ketchup incident. She thought, with the spine-setting certainty of a kindergartner, *A dinosaur would never take my book away.* When she closed her eyes and opened them, it was to a sudden flood of white-hot sunshine.

The drive-in's awning was gone. The blacktop was gone. The cloudless blue sky arced above her. Something moved in the corner of her eye, a scaly shift against red dust.

Jessica closed her eyes again, trying to blink away the black-yellow sunspots in her vision, and thought, *I liked it better shady.*

And she opened her eyes back in lane 5.

That was the first thing she learned about the portals: they gave her what she needed, at least for a moment.

Almost immediately after, she learned a second thing about the portals: nobody believed her when she said she made them.

39

* * *

Is this a joke?

If you don't believe us, check out the third booth from the emergency exit, near the pie case. Sit on the west side when it's in direct sunlight, and you'll find yourself standing on the Scottish moors amidst rolling fields of heather in (we think) 1866. Bring an umbrella or poncho, since it will be raining. (This is because of the specific time the portal drops you into, not a comment on Scottish weather.)

Who built a drive-in around a bunch of portals?

Frank Freedman Jr. opened the drive-in July of 1982 in honor of his father, Frank Alfred Freedman, who operated an A&W restaurant from 1958 until 1977. Frank Jr. aspired to maintain the high quality, low prices, and personal touch that his father brought to the A&W, and named Frank's after Frank Sr.

What does that have to do with the portals?

You asked who built the drive-in, not who made the portals.

So who made the portals?

Your guess is as good as ours!

* * *

Jessica's guess is *very* good, actually. But she's learned to like secrets — she had to, when every time she gave the truth she was taught that sometimes a question is just an invitation for a comfortable answer. Nobody wanted to hear *me, actually, and I don't know why*; that was too simple and too inconceivable at the same time. Instead her choices were to be the girl nobody believed or the girl who stayed quiet. Maybe someday she'd be the girl who found the place that made her heart clench and say *yes, here, you belong here.*

Instead, at age twelve, she dreamed of a beautiful alien mermaid she could run away with, maybe by selling her voice to an enterprising alien sea witch or something, and made a portal. Through it, she'd flailed around in darkness while the cold turned every bit of her skin from knives to numb until she finally kicked her way back out into the men's restroom and coughed up what felt like half an ocean.

Everywhere she went had a dearth of *something*. Europa, it turned out, had a dearth of alien mermaids.

* * *

Is Frank's really a family business?

Yes. Frank, Marian, Claire, and Jessica Freedman all work at Frank's; in fact, Jessica is the author of this FAQ.

Is Frank's really on the county registry of historic buildings?

Yes! Back when it was the A&W, this drive-in was the site of the largest desegregation protest in the county, and in 1964 it became the first restaurant in the area to fully integrate. The plaque and photo gallery in the vestibule of the seating area commemorate this.

So it's not on there for the portals?

No. Although the portals clearly exist, have material effects on the lives of everyone around them, and create circumstances that simply could not exist without portals, the courts have determined that there's no way to legally prove they are physically real. Probably because acknowledging them would require asking some uncomfortable questions and rethinking our conception of not only our world, but our place in it and how we got there.

Not that that's a metaphor or anything. Anyway, just look at that commemorative plaque!

* * *

Jessica's after-school afternoons were spent wiping down the six inside booths, acting as carhop whenever the audio system failed, and watching the way the sunset hit lane 5 ten minutes later than all the other lanes. She would ignore her math homework, pressing the faint marks of equations and angles into the heel of her hand as she levered herself up to get a better view over the booth, to watch the refraction of the shadows through lane 5 and the way the pink in the surrounding air tinted the lane blue in contrast.

Her favorite moments were just after the sunset, those last ten minutes that lane 5 glowed, a strip of air that refused to be what was expected of it.

Lane 5 was a force of nature, glowing so bright that nobody could claim it wasn't there. Nobody could ignore it or discount it, so nobody would have to put up a plaque to remind the world of its existence. Jessica envied it for that.

* * *

What should I do if the portal in lane 5 transports my car to the Permian Era and it runs out of gas?

We only recommend using lane 5 with a full tank. Frank's keeps a limited number of gas canisters on-site and is not liable for tow fees across geological eras. Please obey all relevant signage when entering lane 5 and *do not feed the wildlife*. According to paleontologist and Frank's regular Dr. Rivera, they are likely *Brithopus priscus* and are herbivores.

There is one *B. priscus* who is notorious for begging. Don't be alarmed if she slinks up next to your car — she's impossibly quiet for a ten-foot-long creature that looks like a giant capybara in a lizard costume. Feel free to pat and tell her she's a good girl, but Dr. Rivera informs us that we have no way of knowing which of our contemporary foods are toxic to her, so, again, no sharing.

Capybara in a lizard costume?

We've thought about this a lot.

How do you know it's the same B. priscus?

She's a sweetheart and answers to "Chonk."

* * *

In tenth grade, Jessica had to write an essay on Jane Eyre. Instead of outlining it after school, she closed her eyes in the sun-flooded third booth and imagined what it would be like, fog like a mass of tiny airborne pearls and the smell of rain on earth.

She'd done this enough that she could feel it now: leaving an impression in the universe like a thumbprint in Play-Doh, letting the edges of it swell and morph around her intention. It wasn't a conscious process, just a feeling at the base of her neck every time she was in the drive-in that she could focus on and draw out.

Her destination matched her mood, three days away from prom and still unable to articulate to her friends and parents why she'd turned down the two boys who had unenthusiastically asked her at the last minute. As she stood on the hillside and let the mist condense on her cheeks like tear-streaks, she felt like an old maid, a wronged madwoman, a tragic and romantic silhouette slipping into the night. She felt different from the unwanted seventeen-year-old sitting in the booth of her dad's restaurant, and that's what mattered.

She stayed there for hours, waiting for signs of nightfall, but none ever came. It was just a moment — looping or dilated or something Jessica couldn't even guess at — and when she finally gave up and came back, no time had passed in the drive-in, either.

It only added insult to injury that the trip left her hair irredeemably frizzy.

*　　*　　*

I pressed the button for lemonade on the fountain soda dispenser and instead a disembodied voice whispered the time and manner of my death, but not the date. Also, it dispensed root beer. What's up with that?

The label correcting "lemonade" to "auguries of death and root beer" keeps falling off. We've contacted the manufacturer to request a custom insert, but they think we're pranking them. For the time being, we've moved the lemonade to the root beer spigot.

What about the death thing?

Don't worry about it. It's probably fine.

*　　*　　*

On a day that the school bully asked her on the bus home from school if her parents had pulled her out of a portal because a freakshow like her couldn't be from Earth; a day that the drive-in was too small to contain everything she felt; a day she wanted to be sharp-edged, to be feared if it meant being respected, to cut the world to make it take

43

her seriously. A day she wanted something inarguable, absolute, and had nothing.

That day she punched the soda fountain, snapping off the lever for the lemonade, and as the pain throbbed hot in her knuckles a quiet voice whispered *you die at 3:42 a.m. of a heart attack.*

That was how she learned that what she needed and what the portals thought she needed might not always be the same thing. The root beer part was an accident; the auguries of death were definitely an outright mistake.

* * *

Is that someone in scuba gear heading into one of the bathrooms?

Frank's only has one bathroom (gender-neutral) open to the public, in part because fourteen inches into the restroom formerly labeled "Men's" there's a portal to the subsurface ocean of Europa. Please do not attempt to use that restroom for any purpose other than extraterrestrial oceanic exploration; the key is available upon request.

Why did I hear someone call it the men's room, then?
Habit.

Seriously, why did the portals appear?
We genuinely don't know.

* * *

Jessica for sure genuinely knew, no matter how much people tried to convince her she didn't.

When she was ten and still not believed, she thought *away, anywhere but here, don't make me come back* and escaped to London like a plucky accented orphan. There, she learned the hard way that not all portals went *back* — and that she could only make the portals at the drive-in. That, plus saying things like "I made a magical portal" would open the door to not just accusations of lying but also international incidents.

She stayed quiet after that.

* * *

What's up with the warning on your menu?

"Consuming raw, undercooked, or extradimensional meats, poultry, seafood, shellfish, or eggs may increase your risk of foodborne illness." We source our meats locally and our shrimp from a shrimp-dimension portal located next to the boiler. By shipping distance, the shrimp is local; by multidimensional cosmologies, it is not.

And the eggs?

Just from chickens.

Someone said you have a bunch of transdimensional pigs that regurgitate their cud. Does this make them kosher?

We asked three local rabbis. One sighed very angrily and said, quote, "I *guess*." The second ghosted us. The third stared at me for like five minutes and then started laughing and said, "Oh, that's good." Then she put us in touch with a shochet to perform the slaughter.

Our kitchen as a whole is not kosher, but we've separated out cooking implements and dishes for the kosher bacon. The rest of the cuts of kosher pig are available at the weekly farmer's market and, for some reason, contain gluten.

* * *

Jessica's silence wasn't all bad. There was an afternoon her senior year when Amy Lin came to the drive-in after school to "help out" (read: get a free burger in exchange for theoretically helping theoretical customers). She liked hanging out with Amy, even if Amy had a boyfriend; she still listened and laughed and made jokes. Days spent with her felt less like lies than the other days.

Jessica sat on the backrest of a booth with her feet resting on the table, stretched out and crossed in front of her as the sun began to set. Amy sat on the actual booth seat, staring at the delayed dusk of lane 5.

"See?" Jessica said.

"What about the sunrise?" Amy asked.

Jessica frowned, suddenly wrong-footed. Her mom and dad worked at the drive-in and Claire was slowly but surely mounting a coup d'état in the kitchen, but Jessica was the one who felt, instead of ownership or employment or obligation, a sense of kinship with it, and now she'd been asked a question she didn't know the answer to — a part of her own psyche unmapped.

"Huh," she told Amy.

The next morning she snuck out of the house before dawn and biked to the drive-in. She sat on the gravel across from lane 5, feeling the grit work its way into the weave of her pajamas, and watched intently.

In lane 5, the sun rose ten minutes early.

She made it back home before anyone else woke up, and never told Amy Lin. Instead she kept the feeling of ten extra minutes of sunrise nestled in her chest — her secret.

*   *   *

A translucent teenage girl in a 1950s-style poodle skirt keeps inviting me to dance near the picnic tables. Is she a high-school-prom serial-killer-victim ghost?

No, that's a temporal recording of Claire Freedman. She was cast in Grease in high school and "borrowed" her costume for Halloween. The recording of that moment kind of loops there. Social Media Manager Jessica frequently watches the loop on her break, chuckling to herself because her sister's horrible bangs are right there on display forever.

Do you really think the bangs are that bad?

I mean… look at them.

Do you check passports for the portal to the Forbidden Planet Megastore in London?

Frank's is not liable for any legal action arising from use of the Forbidden Planet portal without a proper passport, customs compliance, et cetera. That said, there's nobody checking on our side.

Is anyone checking on the other side?

It's the only one-way portal, so, yes, they do usually check passports at Heathrow.

*   *   *

Jessica tried to leave the portals behind one other time.

She half-assed her way through three semesters of a communications degree at the state university. If everyone else thought her life had nothing to do with the portals, she figured she might as well live that perception of her. She dyed her hair, changed her wardrobe, pierced body parts, and flitted through different extracurriculars to try on different versions of herself.

"I like girls," she blurted out halfway through a makeout session and at the end of the version of herself that she thought might actually stick — a version of herself that actually went to parties on Friday nights and talked to strangers and seemed to manage to convince others that she didn't care what they thought of her.

Amanda, whose lap she was currently nestled in and whose lips she had just smeared lip gloss all over and whose sweatered breast she had just dared to brush with one sweaty palm — and who was, relevantly, a girl — laughed at her, but a good laugh. A charmed laugh. "I kind of figured," Amanda said, and leaned in again.

Jessica leaned out and said in a rush, "Also I make extradimensional portals at my dad's drive-in."

Amanda laughed again, but this time it was a punchline kind of laugh. "You're so funny."

Jessica liked Amanda, she really did. And she liked this version of herself, a version that didn't require explanation, so she lied. "Yeah. Funny," she said, and her stomach started to hurt.

The ache lasted from that moment until she filed the withdrawal paperwork and moved out less than a week later. She didn't need a degree to work at the drive-in; Claire had proven that. In spite of some big talk around her junior year of high school, Claire hadn't ended up going to culinary school to "elevate the cuisine" at home. Instead she firmly but gently relegated their dad to the business side with their mother and took over the menu in earnest.

So Jessica came home, back to her portals, colder and lonelier than any Scottish heath.

* * *

A few months after she came back, one of the TVs in the dining area showed a press conference announcing the arrival into orbit of a Europa probe. In the back of the group of assembled scientists stood one who had her mouth scrunched to one side, dimpled at the corner with concentration. She looked taken out of herself, occupied by thoughts so abstract she'd been entirely separated from her body, because nobody would make a face like that on purpose.

Jessica wanted that feeling so badly that a new portal nearly popped into existence right then and there.

She thought of the Old Scotland portal, though — that was another one that Jessica made to chase a feeling, and it worked, but that feeling was all it had. Time didn't move, even the topography looped back on itself, and it was just that one thing, that one moment, forever.

Jessica didn't want a moment. She wanted to know what that scientist — Dr. Leung, according to the caption when it was her turn to give remarks — was thinking about. A portal couldn't give her that, no matter how badly she needed it. So instead she did some quick searching and sent a quick email with the subject "Magical portal to Europa ocean (no, I'm not messing with you)" and four days later Dr. Leung and a backbreakingly heavy backpack were in booth 6.

Now Jessica got to watch every time Dr. Leung came out of the former men's restroom with a ridiculous lift in her knees to accommodate the flippers of her wetsuit and a scuba mouthpiece dangling from the fastener at her shoulder — and, of course, that scrunched-up mouth.

Whatever lab Dr. Leung had at NASA was probably boring anyway.

*   *   *

No, seriously, where did these portals come from?

Okay, fine, here's my best shot at an answer. Everyone in the family has theories. Frank Jr. thinks it was Frank Sr.'s ghostly gift, a guarantee of income and interest that would keep Frank's Late-Nite Starlite Drive-In open for business. Marian thinks it's because it was built on a Native American burial ground, despite being told repeatedly and at length that it's a racist stereotype. Claire went through a hippie woo-woo phase where she wouldn't shut up about it being a conjunction of ley lines or some crap. Jessica…

Okay, look. I just wonder if it's really that weird. We still don't even know what gravity is, our brains made up magenta because it doesn't exist as light, and in Australia there's a cloud that appears almost every day six months out of the year, did you know that? The same cloud. They named it Hector. So there are some portals with shrimp or Scotland or my sister in a poodle skirt. So what?

We put humans on top of bombs pointed at the ground to shoot them into space, and it's considered *routine*. Our car engines burn millennia-old dinosaurs so we can *go to McDonald's*. We can nearly instantaneously contact people on the other side of our planet and we've decided some of those messages are spam and don't actually count. And that's not even getting into, like, the *ocean*. Ever seen a narwhal?

A bunch of atoms arranged themselves to create cells and suddenly there was life, then those cells created bigger things, and a few million years later the universe arranged itself according to trillions-to-one odds so that you can exist and, somehow, instead of living in a perpetual state of wonder and gratitude, you get annoyed that we ran out of toilet paper.

Basically, everything is weird. You've just decided that some things aren't and put this drive-in on the "weird" side of that line. I'm not about to look an extradimensional portal gift horse in the mouth.

An extradimensional portal horse just ate my onion rings.

All onion rings at Frank's are unlimited for just that reason, and they're half-price on Wednesdays! Please also join us for Margarita Mondays and Transdimensional Shrimp Cocktail Tuesdays.

*   *   *

It's a spring afternoon now, heat and humidity building up like a boiler, rendering the vinyl booth seats clingy and leaving lazy beads of unevaporated sanitizer on the tabletops.

"You know," Dr. Leung says as Jessica swipes a damp cloth across the next table over, "I noticed two things the other day."

"Yeah?" Jessica's been wiping down tables all afternoon and the sanitizer's wrinkled the pads of her fingers. Her back aches where her spine meets her tailbone, a rusty hinge of a feeling. She absently considers making a portal to a bed.

"You never say in the FAQ what you think made the portals," Dr. Leung says.

"There are enough theories around town," Jessica evades. She glances up at Dr. Leung, who gazes steadily back at her; no scrunched-up mouth now.

"And the second thing," Dr. Leung says. "How'd you know it was Europa?"

"What?"

"When you go through the portal, it's just a dark ocean." Dr. Leung leans forward a little bit. "So how'd you know it's the subsurface ocean of Europa?"

Jessica doesn't say: Because she'd just learned about liquid water in the solar system and had a song from The Little Mermaid stuck in her head, and, at twelve, those two made sense together.

This is, somehow, another question that she's never been asked before. Like her parents, most people think that the portals just *are* — they don't question Jessica's explanations any more than they question gravity. It's just known; it doesn't need a cause. Not until she tries to tie it to her life, topple it from abstraction.

She realizes that, for the first time, someone finds her worthy of curiosity.

"What do you think, Doctor?" she deflects.

"I think," Dr. Leung says, and then stops. She's — blushing? "I think you should call me May. And I'm really glad you emailed me."

Jessica's heart fully skips a beat. She thought that was supposed to be a metaphor. Something in her says, *maybe, here, you could belong.* There's no certainty, no bone-deep knowledge, just possibility. She hates the feeling. Or maybe she loves it. She can't tell. She can't *talk.* She just stands there.

May blinks repeatedly, blush fading. Jessica hadn't realized how May had been smiling until now, as her lips relax into disappointment.

So Jessica doesn't create a portal out of panic: she talks. Well. Babbles. "Do you want to discuss it over dinner? I know a — a great spot for a picnic. If you want to get out of here. And talk."

May exhales, smiling, and Jessica smiles back. It turns into a giddy giggle as she realizes that she can tell May she makes the portals, if she wants. She can choose to, just like she chose to ask her out, just like she chose to suggest a picnic, just like she's been choosing *not* to tell for so long even as she convinced herself it wasn't a choice at all.

"A picnic sounds great," May says.

Jessica flings chicken fingers and fries into to-go containers and takes May outside to the back, where there's a slim gap between the big green electrical box and the back wall of the kitchen. She imagines a meadow, luminescent green grass maybe on a hillside, distant lavender or mums spotting the horizon with contrast; something really cliché and "the hills are alive."

What she gets instead, when she and May shimmy sideways through the gap, is a bald stand of rock overlooking a glacial lake, pine-perfumed air, and a bright blaze of snow tucked in a wrinkle of the mountains despite the mild air. It's nothing like she expected, and for once the thought thrills her.

"Did —" May stutters, eyes wide and fixed on Jessica. "Did you just —"

"Yeah," Jessica says, and smiles out over the unexpected landscape. "What do you want to know?"

Kristen Koopman is a graduate student, writer, and nerd. Her interests include blatant escapism, overanalyzing anything and everything, playing with her dog, and consuming enough garlic to kill vampires at twenty paces. Other stories of hers can be found at *Kaleidotrope, Toasted Cake,* and *We're Here: The Best Queer Speculative Fiction 2020*. She is definitely not two smaller Kristen Koopmans in a trenchcoat.

For content notes, see page 243

The Perseverance of Angela's Past Life

by Zen Cho

ANGELA WAS STALKING HERSELF.

She was packing for Japan and she had better things to worry about than doppelgangers, so she was trying to pretend her self wasn't there.

She thought she would probably need one pair of formal shoes, but she couldn't decide whether she should pack the new fancy shoes — which were beautiful and appropriate, but untried — or the old stalwart black peeptoes. They were a little manky, but they had seen her through May Balls and medsoc dinners alike.

"Bring both," said her old self.

Her old self could not enter the room without Angela's permission. She hovered at the window, peering in.

Angela was not going to invite her in. It was a cold night, but the dead don't feel the cold.

"I'm travelling light," said Angela. She set the new shoes down and picked up the old pair. What did it matter if they were scuffed? They had never let her down before. "I'm not bringing you also. All the more I shouldn't be bringing extra shoes."

52

"What lah, not bringing me," said her old self. "I'm part of you what."
The thaumaturge had confirmed this.

The problem was that Angela's best friend was dating a dragon. Initially Angela hadn't noticed any side-effects. Just the usual sort of thing. Outrage that her best friend was no longer as available as she used to be, that Angela was no longer the first person she called when she wanted to watch a musical or go to the park.

But these were ordinary incidents of the readjustment of a best friendship. Angela had got over it in time.

She was having difficulty getting over being split into two people, though.

"Considering you're in constant contact with a dragon, it's no surprise that your blood magic levels are so high," the thaumaturge had said. "But they're not at a level where I would usually be concerned about the impact on your health. You'd be surprised at the human body's tolerance for atmospheric magic. You hear of people living on the border of Fairyland all their lives and never coming to any harm of it. Their children are all engineers and accountants."

Angela cast a sideways glance at the girl who had followed her to the clinic.

"What about her, then?" she said.

"Eh, I have a name, OK," said the girl. "Pik Mun."

"That's *my* name," said Angela to the thaumaturge. "That's my self, actually. She's me. That's not normal, is it?"

"Yes, well," said the thaumaturge. "As I said, your blood magic levels are in the normal range, but I'm afraid you seem abnormally susceptible to thaumaturgical influence. Have you noticed any other symptoms of disproportionate magic uptake?"

"Besides suddenly having an evil twin, you mean?"

"I'm not evil," said Pik Mun belligerently. "I'm just you."

The thaumaturge politely ignored their bickering.

"Waking up several feet above your bed, for example," she said. "Sleep flying is a very common symptom. Or transmutations of ordinary household objects into magical creatures, or vice versa."

"Vice versa?"

"I had a patient with a similar complaint, whose main symptom was the ability to see pixies in her garden," said the thaumaturge.

"Unfortunately her other symptom was the ability to turn pixies into spoons. She found it very distressing. She had to sell up and move when the pixies declared war. You could hardly blame them, of course."

"No," said Angela. "This is the only symptom I've noticed. How come my best friend isn't showing any signs of magic absorption? She's the one who's going out with the magical dragon."

"From what you've told me, it sounds like she's immune to magic," said the thaumaturge. "That's probably why you were drawn to each other. Magic often likes to work that way."

She pulled a sympathetic face. She was really a very pretty woman, with pale brown skin, short hair in lots of springy curls and a charming sprinkle of freckles on her nose.

She'd offered no remedies, however, save for suggesting that Angela remove herself from the source of exposure.

Angela wasn't going to stop hanging out with her best friend just because doing so literally split her in two. But a language camp in Japan had sounded like the ideal opportunity to reduce her blood magic levels and try to get some thinking space, away from her pestersome other self.

She had to leave for Heathrow early the next morning. Angela finished packing, ignoring the heckling from the window, and got to bed by eleven. But it took her a long time to fall asleep.

She shouldn't have looked up her thaumaturge on Facebook. She'd done it because she was wondering about her name. Misola: such a pretty name. If she hadn't looked her up she wouldn't have found out that Misola was dating a woman.

Particularly susceptible, indeed.

"You're so scared for what?" said the voice at the window.

"Can you please go away or not?" said Angela. She rolled over and buried her face under a pillow.

* * *

In Japan they put her in a sleek grey building on top of a hill. Below it lay the city, nestled in the green cup of a valley which poured out a brilliant blue sea.

It was summer and the air was as close and sticky as it would have been back home in Malaysia. The nearest convenience store was 45 minutes' walk away, along a path winding past houses and rows of vending machines down the hill.

The hostel was sonorously empty. Angela and the other English teachers were the only ones staying there. In the mornings they taught English lessons; in the afternoons they learnt Japanese. The day finished at four and after that Angela was free.

There was something magical about that hill, but it was a magic that had nothing to do with dragons or pixies or doppelgangers. It breathed from the trees and the silence and the early-morning mist.

Up here, Angela thought, she would escape herself.

"Sometimes past selves come back to seek closure," the thaumaturge had explained. "They're not unlike real ghosts. They hang around because of unfinished business. Was there any trauma — any unanswered questions — associated with that time of your life?"

Angela hadn't been sure what to say.

Like everyone else, she had improved beyond recognition after secondary school. She'd benefited from the usual remedies for unattractiveness: self-confidence, freedom from school uniforms, and a decent haircut. She'd discovered that she was sociable, competent, and interested in other people. Her twenties had been a dream of pleasantness, and that was even though she'd spent most of it at clinical school.

But her adolescence hadn't been unhappy either. It had just been normal. Being 25 was a lot better than being 15, but wasn't that true for everyone?

The name change had been a purely pragmatic decision. She'd started going by Angela in her first year at uni, to make it easier on British tutors who stumbled over her real name. It had stuck. There was no denying "Angela" was more euphonious than "Pik Mun".

She wasn't running away from anything in her past. She'd lived through her past, hadn't she? She'd been Pik Mun already. What was wrong with being Angela now?

* * *

A sign outside the hostel asked you politely to close the gate after entering or leaving "so the wild boars will not enter".

If you walked around with food at night the wild boars came out.

Despite their wildness they were not aggressive — one of the other teachers had managed to take a picture of one before it fled.

Angela took to striding around the park with fragrant boxes of takeaway in plastic bags banging against her knee. She did it out of competitiveness as much as anything else. She was the only one of the teachers not to have seen a wild boar.

She was eating chicken karaage in the park when it happened. She speared a piece of fried chicken with a chopstick and looked up. The boar was right in front of her.

It was smaller than she'd expected, about the size of a collie, with longish dark fur and amber eyes.

Moving slowly, Angela fumbled around in her bag until she felt her camera. She took a photo of the boar one-handed, the chicken wobbling on her chopstick.

She'd forgotten to turn off the flash. It went off like a bolt of lightning. Angela started and dropped her chicken. The boar scooped it up neatly.

"Wah, flash some more," it said in a muffled voice. It swallowed. "You not scared meh? The zoo always say don't use flash when you take photo."

"You — you can talk?" stammered Angela, until she realised that it was her own voice that had spoken.

"Yah, it's me," said the boar. "Pig Mun." It snorted with pleasure.

"You're a wild boar now?" said Angela. "How come you're a wild boar? I thought you're suppose to be me!"

Angela had never seen a boar shrug before, but the image was not as jarring as she would've thought. All those anthropomorphized Disney animals she'd watched in childhood had obviously left their mark.

"I don't like planes," said Pig Mun.

"I got over that already," said Angela.

"No, we didn't," said Pig Mun. "You still don't like planes. You just put up with it. Since I can do magic, I might as well use another route what, right?"

"You keep following me for what?" said Angela. "Can't you go back to where you belong?"

"That's nice," said Pig Mun. "You sound like BNP like that. I have a valid three-month visa, OK. You should know what. You applied for it."

"You know what I mean," snapped Angela. "Back to the past."

"I don't belong in the past," said Pig Mun.

"Where, then?"

Angela recoiled, but not far enough. Pig Mun's bristly snout brushed her chest.

"There," said Pig Mun. "Inside you."

"No," said Angela. "No, no, no. I've *been* you already. What's your problem? I'm grown up now! Not even our parents want me to be a kid anymore!"

"I don't want you to go back to being me," said Pig Mun. She didn't say what she did want, but she didn't need to. After all, they were the same person — even if one of them was a wild boar.

"Isn't everybody embarrassed about their teenage selves?" said Angela. "What's wrong with that?"

"Everything is wrong," said Pig Mun. "If you're the teenage self."

Angela smashed the plastic cover down onto her bento and shoved it into the plastic bag. She got up. "Well, who ask you to come back anyway?"

"You lah!" Pig Mun shouted behind her. "You asked. You're me, remember?"

* * *

It wasn't that Angela disliked Pik Mun. They would have got along in other circumstances. If they had met as separate people, for instance. She wouldn't have noticed the width of her hips, the roll of fat at her belly, the daikon thighs. The accent and awkwardness would have endeared Pik Mun to her.

That sort of thing was all right on other people. But if you'd managed to grow out of that awkward stage and shed the accent and even worked off the fat, then fate shoving all of that back onto you just seemed petty.

Angela refused to go back to that. What she liked about being an adult was being able to control her life.

This was why she agreed to go to the Obon festival celebrations with the other English teachers when the Japanese students invited them. Anyone would think that Angela would avoid something as magical as the celebration of a festival, in a season as heavy with humid, thunderous magic as the tropical summer.

But it was the sort of thing she would have gone in for with enthusiasm if she was not being pursued by her dead teenage self. She wouldn't let herself be constrained by the shadow of Pik Mun.

The Obon festival turned out to be like a carnival. Angela drank half a pint of beer and the world lit up. She floated along in her borrowed yukata, feeling beautiful and attachless, smiling beatifically upon the crowd.

It was all reassuringly human. There were alleys of stalls selling delightful-smelling food. The stream of humanity was not offensive and sour-tempered, as humanity taken in the mass tends to be, but beautiful and individual — exquisite girls and boys in yukata; parents with toddlers on their shoulders; old people strolling along, arm-in-arm with their children.

There was a high wooden platform reared up in the middle of the field, on top of which there was a band and a very enthusiastic emcee. When Angela got close enough she realised the people encircling the platform were dancing.

"Come and dance," said her students.

"Oh no," said Angela, hanging back. She'd bought some takoyaki to offset the half-pint of beer and her hands were sticky with grease and mayonnaise.

It was a simple routine, a bit like line dancing — repeated movements of the head and hands and feet, nothing fancy with the hips. The dance was led by a group of older women wearing blue-and-white yukata: they danced with the focus of surgeons carrying out a delicate operation, with the superhuman intensity of star ballerinas.

Angela was so charmed she let herself be bullied into joining, despite her sticky hands and bonito-flaked mouth. She was craning her head to try to see what the nearest Japanese auntie was doing when Pik Mun's face hove into view.

"Argh!" said Angela.

"I didn't know you're into this kind of thing," said Pik Mun. "I thought we hated dancing."

"I told you, I've grown out of all that," said Angela. "Dancing is fun. Especially if you're a bit drunk."

"Become like a Mat Salleh already, huh," said Pik Mun.

She was wearing the unflattering turquoise pinafore and white shirt of the Malaysian secondary school uniform. It didn't suit her. It looked especially incongruous because she was dancing as well, with mechanical perfection, never putting a step wrong.

"How come you know how to do that?" said Angela, trying to watch Pik Mun's feet while clapping her hands and bobbing her head in the prescribed pattern.

"Don't you know what this festival is?" said Pik Mun. "You didn't even ask what it's all about before you happy-happy put on your Japanese baju and join in? Angela, what happened to your curiosity? You think you know everything, is it? Grown ups are so dungu!"

It was the first time Pik Mun had ever addressed her as Angela. It was the first time she'd really scolded her, though Angela had told her off plenty of times.

They fell quiet. The music went on. People's voices bounced off their bubble of awkwardness.

"Soran, soran!" roared the crowd, following the lead of the singer on the platform.

Angela and Pik Mun kept dancing, moving in their circle with clockwork regularity.

"Sorry," said Pik Mun.

"They told me there'll be dancing and fireworks," said Angela. "I thought it was just for fun."

"It's the Hungry Ghost Festival," said Pik Mun, not unkindly. "Japanese is a bit different, they have it at a different time because they don't follow the lunar calendar. What lah you."

"Oh," said Angela. She looked around. "This is nicer than our celebrations."

Traditionally, of course, the Hungry Ghost Festival had been celebrated with Cantonese opera performances to entertain the returning dead. Nowadays people put miniskirted girls on open-air stages to belt out raucous Cantopop. It was like any other concert, except the first line of chairs was left empty for the ghosts.

"Here everybody gets to join," said Angela.

"Back home everybody gets to join," said Pik Mun. "If they don't want to listen also, they can't get away from it. Hah! Remember when

Dad called the police and tried to get them to ask the temple people to turn down the volume, and the police told him he should pray to the gods and say sorry for offending the dead?"

Angela laughed at the memory.

"Dad was so angry," she said. "He went around talking bad about the festival to everybody at church."

"Even our relatives started avoiding him," said Pik Mun. "I remember Ji Ee Poh pulled me into the kitchen and said, 'Hai, your father, making life very difficult for we all. Ever since he convert to Christianity he become so intolerant. Don't believe in ghosts is one thing, but why talk bad about them some more? That is just asking for trouble.'"

"It's not the Christianity," said Angela. "I think Dad was always a bit like that. From young also."

"Dad is too extreme," said Pik Mun. "He should be more flexible."

"Me also," said Angela.

"Yah," said Pik Mun. "Us also."

* * *

Angela's Japanese language class went on a trip to Kyoto. They visited temples and had dinner on the river, in a barge hung with round orange lanterns.

Dinner was extravagant, with the severe delicacy of Japanese food: fish, tofu and vegetables sitting in their separate compartments. There was also nabe in bubbling hot pots distributed along the table.

The other students drank beer. Angela stuck to tea.

Angela ate half her fish and stopped to look out at the river. If you ate slowly your stomach got used to the food and you felt full earlier. It was a good way to avoid overeating.

The river was worth looking at. It had still been light when they'd got on the barge, but night had fallen with tropical swiftness. They weren't the only barge on the river; there were several others, similarly outfitted, and the orange light from the lanterns trembling on the black waters was beautiful. In the distance the mountains were a dark forested mystery.

Were there tengu brooding in those trees? Before she'd been split into two, Angela had known magic was real, but she hadn't thought about it as something that applied to herself. Some people courted that kind of thing — went to bomoh for charms and love potions, studied spells, prayed to the spirits of the earth and air and water.

Angela had never even watched *Charmed*. Being a doctor seemed a much more concrete way of working miracles.

But now she was only half a person, anything seemed possible. Tengu might come flying out of their mountain fastnesses, the wind from their wings snuffing out the lanterns. River dragons might raise gleaming horse-like heads out of the waters around them. She might discover something new about herself at the august age of 25.

A sigh rose from the other diners. "Ah!"

"What is it?" said Angela to her neighbour.

"The birds are fishing — look!" The neighbour pointed with her chopsticks.

Angela could only see flashes of light in the darkness. The flame of a torch lit the face of an old man, labouring in the bow of a boat on the other side of the river. She couldn't see any birds.

She turned, wanting to ask her neighbour where the birds were and what they were doing, but as she did so she saw Pik Mun out of the corner of her eye.

Pik Mun was in the water, dog-paddling calmly along the side of the boat.

"How long have you been there?" said Angela.

"Long enough," said Pik Mun. "You finish your dinner yet or not? You took half an hour to eat that fish."

There was quite a lot of food left in Angela's lacquer box.

"Yeah, done already," she said. "Nowadays I only eat till 70% full."

Pik Mun was so outraged she missed a stroke. She went down and came up with a mouthful of water, spluttering. "What's this 70%? If you sit for exam and get 70%, that's not even a 1A!"

"70% is a First," said Angela.

"OK. OK. I see how it is," said Pik Mun coldly. "Your standards have gone down. This is called life experience, is it?"

"My standards haven't gone down," said Angela. "They're just different."

"If it was me I would have eaten all," said Pik Mun. "Except the enoki mushrooms —"

"— because they taste funny," Angela agreed.

"At least you remember that," said Pik Mun. "Tired lah."

"I'm not surprised, you've been swimming so long."

"Tired of you lah!" said Pik Mun. "You forgot what it's like to be me, is it? Don't you miss me at all?"

She looked wistful.

"I don't know if I miss you," Angela said. "You're a lot wiser than I actually was at 15. I was pretty stupid as a teenager."

"That's what you think now," said Pik Mun. "You didn't think so then. You should be kinder to yourself."

"I didn't finish yet," Angela chided her. "I said, you're a lot wiser than I was when I was an annoying teenager. So I guess I should listen to you. You want a hand up?"

Pik Mun stopped paddling. For a moment she floated in the water, suspended.

"You sure?" said Pik Mun.

"Yes," said Angela.

"If you take my hand it'll change you," said Pik Mun. "You made me go away for a reason, you know. If I come back you might remember stuff you want to forget."

Angela held out her hand. Pik Mun took it.

As Pik Mun climbed in their hands became one. Her elbows locked into Angela's elbows, her knees into Angela's knees. Angela's hips widened. Her face got rounder. The flesh under her chin pouched out. Her vision blurred.

She blinked, and then she could see clearly again. She was solid, weighted to the deck by her new substantiality.

Pik Mun was more pugnacious than her, not as well-groomed, rougher-edged. Angela with all the unevenness sanded off. But she needed to have a surface that could catch on things. She needed to be capable of friction.

She looked down at the river. The orange light showed Angela her reflection, hazy and dark. Pik Mun smiled back at her from the water.

Somebody touched their arm.

"Are you OK?" said Angela's neighbour. "You almost fell in!"

"I'm OK," said Angela. She smiled at the girl.

The girl blushed.

Angela's stomach growled. She turned back to the table. "Good food, eh?"

"Yeah, really good," said the girl. She looked away, then back, then away again. She was smiling despite her discomfiture, smiling helplessly, almost against her will.

Now that's called charisma, said Pik Mun approvingly inside Angela's head.

Angela ate all of the fish. It was delicious.

* * *

Pik Mun had been keeping a secret for Angela.

It was silly to have kicked up so much of a fuss over it. Nobody cared nowadays, did they? OK, so Angela's family would probably care, but that hadn't been the reason why she'd tried to ignore it for ten years.

The reason had been embarrassment.

Picture Pik Mun, 15 years old, not yet Angela, not yet beautiful. She's in love with her best friend and it's leading her down perilous paths. For example, the one that ends in her kissing the best friend, on a hot afternoon after school.

Pik Mun had known immediately that it had been the wrong thing to do.

"Never mind," she said, but Prudence was already talking.

"What's wrong with you?" said Prudence.

"Nothing," said Pik Mun. "It was just a — I don't know. Never mind! Forget about it."

"Do you *like* me?" said Prudence, in dawning horror. "Do you, like, have a crush on me?"

"No, no, no," said Pik Mun. Each "no" sounded less convinced than the last. "I'm sorry. I shouldn't have did that."

"It's like kissing my *sister*," said Prudence. She had never been a tactful girl.

"You don't even have a sister!"

"Why did you do that?" said Prudence. "Are you..." she lowered her voice. "Are you a gay?"

Pik Mun's eyes prickled.

"But you were dating that guy," said Prudence. "The prefect. Were you using him to hide the fact you're gay?"

"I'm not gay!" said Pik Mun.

"Then?" said Prudence.

"I liked Kenrick," said Pik Mun. But she'd stopped liking him. She'd started liking Prudence instead. That had been unexpected. "I wasn't faking it. I stopped liking him because he started talking about football all the time. Doesn't mean I never liked him."

"So do you like girl or boy?" said Prudence.

"I don't know," said Pik Mun. She hesitated. "Both?"

"Where got people like both one?" said Prudence. At that point, her parents' green Kancil had driven into the school car park. Prudence got up.

"Pik Mun, you must figure yourself out," she said. "Think about it and let me know when you decide. Call my home phone if you want to talk. But don't like me, OK?"

"Not like I choose to like you also," said Pik Mun.

"Choose to stop," said Prudence firmly. "I like you very much as friend, but this whole crush thing is a bit weird."

Pik Mun's crush had been smothered by the embarrassment. It went out without a whimper. And she hadn't liked another girl for ten years.

It was a long time to be hiding from yourself, and a stupid reason for doing it. But youth was for doing stupid things in anyway.

And Angela was still young.

* * *

It was almost lonely without Pik Mun around. Angela could talk to herself, of course, but it wasn't quite the same.

She called Prudence instead.

"I'm Facebooking my thaumaturge," she said.

"Why?" said Prudence.

Angela hesitated. But ten years was a long time to pretend something wasn't there.

"She's super my type," said Angela. "Got girlfriend already, but girlfriend doesn't mean married, right?"

The line crackled. Angela's chest seized up.

Prudence said, horrified, "Angela! That's so bad! Don't go stealing people's woman!"

"Joking only lah," said Angela.

"If you want, I can introduce people to you," said Prudence. "Girl or boy also can. You spècify. But don't go and chase other people's girlfriend. Hmph. After you stay in Japan you become so immoral."

Angela was smiling. "I put on weight also," she said.

"Is it?" said Prudence. "Don't eat so much takoyaki. Eat more seaweed. That one not fattening."

"I think it suits me," said Angela.

"Oh? Then forget about the seaweed lah," said Prudence. "So long as you're OK with yourself. Are you OK with yourself, Pik Mun?"

"Yah, think so," said Angela.

"Good," said Prudence. That pretty much seemed to cover it.

This story was originally published in *Spirits Abroad* (2014), a short story collection by Zen Cho.

Zen Cho is the author of the *Sorcerer to the Crown* novels, the novella *The Order of the Pure Moon Reflected in Water* and a short story collection, *Spirits Abroad*. Her newest novel is *Black Water Sister*, a contemporary fantasy set in Malaysia. Zen is a Hugo, Crawford and British Fantasy Award winner, and a finalist for the Lambda, Locus and Astounding Awards. She was born and raised in Malaysia, resides in the UK, and lives in a notional space between the two.

For content notes, see page 243

Sea Glass at Dawn

by Leora Spitzer

Spring

ALTHOUGH HE HAD BEEN SCANNING THE ROCKY COASTLINE for any sign of draconic presence, Fern could not stop himself from wobbling slightly when the odd rock formation on a distant hill resolved itself into a bronze dragon. He gulped, feeling the heat in his throat, and readjusted the wet cloth he wore wrapped around the lower half of his face. It smelled of saltwater and ash.

The dragon shifted and Fern knew he had been spotted. "Too late to turn back now," he muttered to himself, and continued walking towards the hill, the slippery gravel shifting underfoot. It felt heretical to doubt the oracle, but he could not help fervently hoping that the information he had been given was accurate. This would prove to be an extremely short quest if he was about to be lunch.

Just as he began to mentally rehearse his introduction yet again, the dragon launched into the air, heading directly for the spot where Fern stood frozen. He braced himself for what looked like an inevitable crash, but at the last moment, the dragon pulled up and landed gracefully on the wet rocks as the waves retreated to the ocean.

"Hello," the dragon said.

"Hello," Fern squeaked.

There was a pause as they examined each other. Fern shrank at the thought of what the dragon must be seeing, from the soot- and dust-stained clothes to the partially healed burns on his arms to his loose brown curls tangled from the ocean wind. In contrast, the dragon was magnificent, all sleek muscle and burnished scales, with spikes down their back and several horns that curved gracefully away from the back of their head.

Instinctively, Fern glanced at the dragon's forearms (front legs? Fern wasn't sure). It was no surprise that the dragon wore no clothes, but on some level, he had still expected to see a colored bracelet, like the one he and every human he knew wore.

"They call me Diver," the dragon said, following his gaze. "Remind me, what do yellow bracelets mean? I know humans have a code with all your genders, but I can never remember."

"Yellow means he/him," Fern said. "White is they/them, and green is she/her. There are a few others, too, but those are the most common ones." He hesitated. "How do dragons tell what to call each other, if it's not rude to ask?"

Diver shifted a wing. "Draconic only has one set of singular pronouns for thinking beings, and we all use she/her in Admatian. Gender differentiation is not really a thing in our culture."

Before Fern had a chance to reflect on that surprising revelation — would it make things simpler not to worry about which bracelet fit best that day, or would it be more constricting never to have that choice? — Diver lowered her head and fixed him with a piercing look.

"What may I call you?" she asked. It was not *quite* the tone a parent would use to chide a child to remember their manners, but it came from the same neighborhood. Fern blushed.

"Oh! I am Fern of Cascade. The oracle told me to come here."

"Cascade, hmm? So that would be the Speaker of the Sacred Falls, then?" Diver asked, naming the oracle who lived in a ravine close by the tiny village. Its proximity to the Sacred Falls was the only reason anyone had ever heard of his home, but most residents never had any reason to consult the oracle themselves. Fern's visit two weeks earlier had been the first time he had personally seen the breathtaking cascade from which his village drew its name.

"Yes," he answered.

"And why did she tell you that?"

"They," Fern corrected, remembering the white bracelet the oracle had worn. "And, well…" Carefully, he unwrapped the cloth from his face. The salt breeze tickled his nose and he sneezed, sending a small spurt of flame into the air, where it dissipated harmlessly. Diver did not flinch, but her eyes widened in surprise. "That's why," Fern finished miserably.

"You're a pyromancer?"

"No, I can't *control* fire, I just breathe it sometimes," Fern explained. "And I can't control that, either. Last month, I accidentally burned down my grandparents' barn when I got surprised. The Speaker told me I should come here to learn how to prevent that from happening again."

"Well, I suppose they knew what they were talking about," Diver said. "You have come to the right place."

"You can help me?" Fern asked, cursing the way his voice squeaked again.

Diver laughed. "I could try," she said, "but it is not me you want, it is my wife. She has the best control of her flame of anyone around. And a good thing, too, given how much of her hoard is flammable."

Fern blinked. He had thought dragon hoards were mostly precious metals and gemstones, not any material likely to catch fire. But "never ask a dragon about her hoard" was up there with "never call a wizard stupid" in basic adventuring knowledge, so he bit his tongue and did not ask.

"It's good timing, actually. We started the hatchlings on flame-training a few moons ago, so they should have enough control not to light *you* on fire. You can join their lessons. And we have a small cave we keep for visitors that you may have to yourself, as well." Diver jerked her head towards the rocky hills behind her and began walking away. After a confused moment, Fern realized the gesture had been an invitation and hurried after her.

"My family," Diver said proudly as they reached the top of the hill. Fern gasped, a flame caught in his throat. Carefully, he let it out. Diver continued to radiate pride rather than concern despite the ferocity of the wrestling dragons below, but Fern could not keep from flinching as the blue one pounced on the gold one's tail. The gold one twisted around to pin the other to the ground and breathed fire at her belly.

At that, Diver finally reacted, growling and moving forward, but someone else got there first. A much larger blue dragon, this one the pale shade of the pre-dawn horizon, loomed over the wrestling pair and pulled them apart. Fern flinched at the sight of her sharp claws against their scales, but when the smaller dragons seemed unbothered, he concluded that she had enough precision to avoid hurting them.

"We do not breathe fire at our siblings," she said sternly, and with that familiar tone, so similar to his grandmother's, Fern understood. *Hatchlings*, Diver had said. He'd been thrown off by their size when they were wrestling, as each was easily larger than he was, but now he could see the juvenile awkwardness in their movements and how small they were compared to Diver and the blue dragon. These were not adult dragons fighting; they were children tussling, figuring out their bodies' strength and poking at boundaries. Relieved, he followed Diver towards the other dragons.

"Mama, who is that?"

Fern jumped. He had not noticed the approach of a third young dragon. Her scales were the green of tarnished copper, and her amber eyes glowed as she looked at him curiously.

"This," said Diver grandly, placing a single heavy claw gently on Fern's shoulder, "is your newest classmate, Fern."

"Humans can't breathe fire," the green hatchling protested.

"*And* they can't fly," the blue one said, evidently recovered from the tussle. "How is she supposed to be in a class with us?"

"Fern is a *he*," Diver corrected before Fern could figure out how to explain gender to dragon toddlers. "Remember we talked about human pronouns? And he cannot fly, but unlike most humans, he *can* breathe fire."

In another moment, Fern was surrounded by a trio of dragon children bursting with questions. He scrambled to pull his scarf around his mouth again, but the water had evaporated. The scarf was stiff with salt.

"You will not burn them," Diver said. Fern glanced up, thinking it was an order, but saw in the dragon's large amber eyes that it had been reassurance. "Dragons are resistant to fire. It would take more than your accidental flames to hurt us. I would not have permitted you close to my children, otherwise."

Fern struggled to trust himself, but it was easy to trust the protective instincts of a mother dragon. Reassured, he tried to make sense of the children's babble and answer what questions he could.

"I want to learn how to control my flame," he explained. "No, I'm the only one in my family who can breathe fire, so none of them knew how to help me."

A shadow fell across the group as the other adult dragon stepped gracefully towards them. She bowed her long neck to press her forehead against Diver's with an easy intimacy that flustered the teenager, who was unused to that kind of open affection and fiercely wished that he felt safe enough to ever be that close to another person.

"They call me Guide, and it would be my pleasure to teach you," she said, and then, to her wife, added, "Where did you find this one?"

Diver grinned. "On the beach," she said. "Where else?" Both dragons laughed.

"It is a compliment," Guide told Fern, seeing his confusion. "One of the things Diver and I have always agreed upon is that the best things are discovered on beaches. We both hoard beach-found items."

"Oh," Fern said, reminding himself again not to ask. Did they hoard pearls? Seashells? Guide's hoard was flammable. Did she collect... driftwood? That was hardly the stuff of legend.

"And, of course, we met each other on the beach," Diver added, nuzzling at Guide's neck.

"That too," Guide agreed. "Only because you had the bad taste to pick up something that *I* wanted."

"Excuse me, I think that shows that I have excellent taste," the bronze dragon protested.

"Well, you did choose me, so I suppose you do," Guide said archly, and Fern remembered his grandmother's lessons. These were the stories that really mattered, more than any legend: People finding each other, choosing each other, caring for one another.

* * *

Summer

Teaching a human was both much harder and much easier than Guide had expected. Fern was more cautious than the hatchlings, and she was far better at listening to instructions, but her magic did not work in the same way as a dragon's flame. However carefully she listened, some of Guide's advice simply would not work for her. Together, they had worked to figure out what sorts of lessons would help.

(She was wearing a green bracelet that day. Remembering to check the human's wrist had been challenging at first, but the dragons had seen how Fern wilted when they got it wrong, so they made the effort).

Guide had been quite pleased with their success at beachside meditation, matching breaths to the waves until Fern could make it a whole hour without even a wisp of smoke escaping from her mouth. Her ability to suppress flame had improved tremendously, but Guide knew that was not enough. Dragons overheated if they went too long without expelling their flame, and whether or not Fern's magic worked the same way, Guide felt in her bones that it would be unhealthy for the human to keep her flame locked up inside all the time.

"We're going to continue to practice with small flames today," she announced to the group that morning. "What's the first thing you always check when you're going to breathe fire?"

"The air currents," they chorused. The hatchlings tilted their heads so their sensitive horns could catch the wind; Fern licked her finger and held it to the air.

"What if we want to burn something upwind?" Gold asked.

"What do you think?"

Green said, "Move."

Guide laughed. "That is going to be your best answer for a while, bright eyes. Once your control is better, we will practice flaming into the wind. That is why you always must know which way the wind is blowing — it takes a different amount of pressure to breathe into the wind than away from it, just like you have to talk louder next to the ocean than inside the quiet cave. If you get it wrong, you might burn something you did not intend."

Fern shifted uncomfortably, and Guide knew that she was thinking of all the things she had burnt unintentionally. This was another difference in teaching a human: Fern was far more afraid of her own flame than any dragon would be.

Guide distributed a clawful of candles to each student. "Today's goal is to create enough flame to light the candle, but not so much that you melt all the wax at once," she explained. She reminded them again of all the lessons they had learned that week about how to keep a flame small, and they each began to try.

She was coaching Blue, who was getting discouraged after her third candle became a puddle of melted wax, when Fern screamed. Guide whipped around, her tail whistling in the air behind her. The human had collapsed to the ground, clutching her thigh. Next to her, Gold hovered in the air, bobbing with anxiety, and Green backed away in alarm.

"I'll be okay," Fern gasped, but Guide had already caught a glimpse of the angry blisters forming on her leg.

And here was the biggest difference: Fern was also much more *fragile* than the hatchlings had ever been, even when they'd emerged shell-soft and blinking at their mothers' fire. Whatever magic allowed the human to breathe fire protected her throat and mouth, but it did not extend to the rest of her body.

"I didn't mean —" Green gasped.

"It wasn't my —" Gold began.

Guide dismissed them both with a twitch of her tail. "It does not matter now," she said, scooping up the human with her front claws as carefully as she could. "What matters is helping. Blue, find Diver, tell her what happened. She was going to catch fish for dinner. You two, stay here." Keeping her wingbeats as steady as possible, she flew Fern to the nearest freshwater stream. As much as she loved the sea, Guide knew that this was one area where it would do more harm than good.

Fern breathed a sigh of relief as she lowered her leg into the cool water. "Don't worry," she said, and Guide could not believe that the injured human was trying to reassure *her* right now. "I've got a lot of practice with burns. I know what to do. There's some salve and bandages in my pack that will help." She winced. "It just... hurts a lot, at first."

"How can I help?"

"Just... talk to me? Anything to keep my mind off this." She gestured at her thigh.

Guide hummed. "Have I ever told you about my hoard?" she asked.

"Just that it's something you find on the beach."

"I collect things recovered from shipwrecks," Guide said. "Figureheads from the bows of ships, bits of wood, ship's wheels, fragments of sail." Even through the pain, Fern looked surprised. "I know, it is not the most traditional of hoards, but it is what I love. Every piece of my hoard had a purpose, once, and it can no longer fulfill that purpose, but it deserves more than rotting on a beach somewhere. Anyway, it is not the strangest hoard ever. Diver's cousin Bard collects *stories*, of all things, which you cannot even keep in a cave. I do not know of any other dragons with intangible hoards."

"What does Diver collect?" Fern asked.

"It would be better to hear about it directly from her," Guide said, and waved off the human's immediate apologies, tilting her head to the sky. Above, Diver hovered, the hatchlings beside her like little satellites. Guide could see the moment when Diver decided that this landing would be too challenging for the fledgling flyers and directed them onto her back. In the smooth motion with which she had earned her name, she dove for the riverbank, landing lightly despite the extra weight of three young dragons.

"Sea glass," Diver said to Fern. "I hoard glass worn smooth by the waves — not because it is precious, but because it is soft, and catches the light so gently."

Guide remembered how she had explained her love for sea glass when they had first met, stuttering but unwilling to relinquish her treasure, how something within Guide had looked at that burnished bronze and said, *yes, this one, I want.* Until Diver had shown her how to stroke the smoothed glass with the sensitive pads of her foreclaws, it would not have occurred to Guide to refer to any kind of glass as "soft," but while it was as hard as rock when poked, it felt soft as a petal when touched gently.

Now, the same bronze claw that had cradled the sea glass so tenderly pushed a little dragon forward. "I am sorry," Green said, her ears drooping. "I should have been paying more attention. I forgot that you are not a dragon. I understand if you do not want to play with me anymore."

"What?" Fern said, a spurt of flame escaping from her mouth. It was not surprising that her control would suffer while she was in physical and emotional distress, but it *was* concerning. If Fern could not regulate her flame while she was in pain, she was liable to reinjure herself by accident. The thought was unbearable to Guide, who immediately tried to come up with ways to help Fern manage.

Before she could implement any of her half-formed ideas, Fern began to take the deep breaths they had practiced for control, and Guide relaxed, taking a deep breath of her own. When Fern's breath was smoke-free again, she continued, "Of course I still want to play with you, Green. I know you didn't mean to hurt me. I should have been paying more attention, too. I could have put my candle further away from you."

"You mean it? We can still play with you?" Green asked.

"Just do not forget that Fern is human," Diver said, leaning down to press her forehead to the child's.

"I won't," Green promised, echoed immediately by her sisters.

"I owe you an apology, as well," Diver said, straightening up to look at Fern. "I told you when you came here that my children had enough control to avoid burning you. You trusted me to make proper safety judgments, and I was wrong. I am sorry."

"I am sorry, too," Guide added. "I ought to have ensured there was sufficient distance between your practice spaces before focusing just on Blue."

Fern blinked, looking between the adult dragons. "I accept your apologies," she said softly, and Guide wondered why that ready acceptance did not make her feel any less guilty.

* * *

Later, when Fern had applied her healing salve and bandaged her burn, and the young ones were out practicing flight with Diver, Guide went down to the beach with Fern. The human seemed glad to sit and breathe the salt air while Guide poked around, vaguely searching for driftwood and keeping a close eye on the young human.

Finally, Guide said, "We have a saying in Draconic, you know." She said the words, though she knew Fern's human throat would not be able to imitate that combination of clangs and guttural roars. "It does not translate perfectly, but it basically means *it is not your responsibility to soothe one who burns you*. It is often used metaphorically, but it certainly applies literally as well. You did not have to reassure Green. We all would have understood and respected it if you had chosen not to be near one who had hurt you."

"She's a *child*," Fern protested. "Are you telling me that if one of your children hurt you by accident, you would not soothe her?"

"It is different for parents and children," Guide allowed. "But in all likelihood, Diver would do the soothing while I took care of my immediate needs. Anyway, it was kind of you to reassure Green while you were hurting, but I wanted to make sure you understood the basic principle. You also did not have to forgive my negligence or Diver's incorrect guarantee. You do not have to forgive people who hurt you, Fern."

It was a guess, but Guide could see that something in that had hit true. Fern ran a finger along the simple green bracelet she wore around her wrist. "I will remember," she promised. "But really, of course I forgave Green. I know it was an accident, and besides, I've been there. I know what it's like to accidentally burn someone you care about. And, well, I... I care for your children, Guide. Watching them grow and learn and play is worth a few burns to me. Diver gave me the best information she had at the time, and you have your hands — uh, claws — full wrangling the hatchlings for class. We all know what went wrong, and I'm confident it won't happen again." She tilted her head back and breathed a narrow jet of flame into the sky, well away from her own fragile body. "Being here has been good for me, Guide. I am not ready to leave."

It was hard to estimate human ages, but looking at Fern now, Guide recognized that she was an adult, albeit a young one — adult enough to be trusted to make her own risk assessments and value judgments.

"I will say no more on it, then," Guide said. "I believe your presence is a great benefit for us, too. The Speaker of the Sacred Falls surely knew what they were talking about, to send you here."

* * *

Autumn

Diver knew with the first breath of crisp dawn air that it would be a perfect day to take the children out to practice their gliding. She stretched lazily, opening her eyes to see the sunlight peeking through the cave entrance, filling the cave with spots of blue and green as it hit the sea glass hanging from the ceiling. It was one of her favorite sights in the world.

And there, on the other side of the cave, was another of her favorite sights — Guide humming as she reorganized her figureheads, shifted some driftwood, and moved a painted board out of the sunlight so it would not fade. Diver watched with pleasure, enjoying the contrast of her wife's pale blue scales against the dark browns and golds of her hoard.

Guide selected a piece of board and began heading out of the cave, moving smoothly despite the wood gripped in one claw.

"Where are you going with that?" Diver asked.

Guide twisted her neck around to look at her wife. "Why don't you follow me and find out?" she suggested, the same challenging glint in her eye that she'd had the day they met on the beach, arguing over who had the better right to a fragment of green glass Diver had found amid the remains of a shipwreck previously claimed by Guide.

"I would follow you anywhere," Diver said, rolling to her feet.

The blue dragon smirked and continued on her way, confident that her wife would be just behind.

They found Fern on the beach playing with the children, all working together to try and keep a ball in the air. At their approach, Fern turned, missing the ball. Gold dove to catch it, knocking Fern to the ground.

"Careful with the human!" Green said, headbutting her sister.

"I'm fine, I'm fine," Fern said, sitting up and patting Green's foreleg. "Thank you for checking on me."

Blue snorted and leaned forward to help Fern up. All four turned to look at the adult dragons. Diver could not keep from grinning at them.

"You said you had something special today?" Fern asked, brushing sand off their knees.

"I do," Guide said, leaning the board against a convenient boulder. "This is your final test, Fern. I want you to singe the wood, but do not set it on fire."

The human's eyes widened and their jaw opened slightly, glancing back and forth between the board and Guide's tranquil expression. "Are you serious?" they said, a tiny wisp of smoke escaping from their mouth. "That's... from your hoard."

Diver struggled to be comfortable letting even Guide touch her sea glass and could not imagine offering her hoard up to someone else's flame, but she was careful not to reveal her shock. She knew that Guide would be furious if Fern saw her surprise and interpreted it as doubt.

Instead, she strode along the beach to lay an affectionate wing across the blue dragon's back and said, "Guide never makes offers she does not mean. She is consistently reliable like that."

Guide favored Diver with a small smile before stretching her neck down to press her forehead against Fern's. "You can do this," she said, as soft and as hard as sea glass. "I would not offer were I not confident in your capabilities. It is you who doubt yourself, and it is that doubt which is the greatest risk to maintaining your control. I would send you home trusting yourself, Fern, as I trust you."

Fern took a deep breath. They stepped back and bowed deeply to Guide — unable, perhaps, to find words. Diver watched as the human licked their finger and held it out to check the wind. They stepped up close, running the wet finger along the grain of the wood. When they finally breathed flame, it was so quiet and gentle that Diver nearly missed its arrival.

The curl of a stylized wave stood out sharply against the pale brown oak.

"Whoa," said Blue.

"Fern," Diver said, tracing the wave with a single claw. A tiny amount of soot fell from the board, but the design remained clear. "You're an artist."

The human stared at their work, a tentative smile creeping into the corners of their mouth. "I guess I am," they said wonderingly. They glanced at Guide. "I still can't believe you let me *set fire* to your *hoard*." Laughter burst from their throat, sounding almost hysterical.

"Of course I did," Guide said smugly. "You're *sakona*."

A furrow appeared in Fern's brow as they struggled to regain control of their laughter. Diver noted with pride that no fire slipped out, though a few months ago, laughter like that from Fern would have meant flames spurting every which way.

"*Sakona?*" Fern asked finally, having caught their breath. "Isn't that Draconic for hoard? How am I your hoard?"

Diver shifted to soak up more sunlight and smiled at the human. "No, that would be *sakhona*, with a guttural *khuh* instead of the hard *kuh*, but your confusion is understandable — the words are closely related. *Sakhona* means the items in our hoards, the physical objects. *Sakona* means…" Diver looked over at Guide, feeling love wash over her like the ocean's undertow, and finished, "that which is mine."

Guide spread her wings over the children and said, "It means family."

And Fern's smile lit up the shore, as beautiful and precious as sea glass at dawn.

Leora Spitzer is a queer Jewish bibliophile and writer. She is extremely enthusiastic about queer SFF, particularly when focused on joy, found family, and, of course, dragons. Leora is currently working on a novel set in the same universe as "Sea Glass at Dawn," which features the Speaker of the Sacred Falls and Diver's story-hoarding cousin, Bard. She lives in St. Louis, MO, with her chosen family and her pet snake, Princess Buttercup. You can find her on Twitter as **@leora_hugs**.

For content notes, see page 243

unchartered territories

by Swetha S.

I FIRST TAKE OFF THE RING YOU SENT ME. This is something I have to do by myself.

This Friday is different from other Fridays because, thanks to you, I have finally learned to let go. I have learned to let go of the balloon Mum gave me for my twenty-first birthday, a balloon that is conveniently hot-pink with golden lettering. I have learned to let go of the pink headband that was supposed to discipline my unruly curly pixie. My curls would've found a way to break the band, anyway. I have learned to grab a suitcase, fill it with that one jean jacket you sent me from your home that is now stringy and old and stinks like mothballs — thank gods ripped jeans are a thing.

To be entirely honest, it isn't just you who helps me give up. It is also my mother, who looks me in my eyes and asks, "Why do you do these things that just make you unhappy in the end? Why can't you be like the rest of us?" I see the wisdom in her words and say good-fucking-bye.

I book a car to the airport as my mother lists all the sacrifices she's made for me. When I load the luggage into the car, my mother stares with disbelief from our house's gate. She's precariously tossed a towel across her chest to hide it as if her baggy nightie doesn't do a good enough job. Soon, I'm in the car, and I'm surprised as my mother and her breezy gown disappear in the background, giving way to the jogging comb-tooth houses of the street. It's strange that she can disappear. I used to believe she'd always be here; she's always been everywhere.

When I reach the airport, I'm so happy, I don't even haggle with the taxi driver. Instead, I hand him the three hundred rupees he demands and drag my light suitcase towards the counters. I don't have to wait in line to buy a ticket. Instead, I head to the tree that the airport officials have hesitantly placed in front of the airport. Oh, the faces of my country's politicians when your people wheeled out a cute tree wrapped in a cotton bow as a gift to our airports — I saw it all on TV. They weren't sure if they should accept gracefully or proclaim war. Thankfully, they've accepted it and placed a board next to it with instructions.

As I scan the instructions, I wonder briefly why they're only in English. What if I want to read Tamil, I almost ask it, and the letters change instantly, allowing me to read the Tamil instructions. But as I struggle to understand some words in Tamil, those words flit and change, letting their English translations slip through. I look around, wanting to show this to others. This was your idea and I'm incredibly proud. But no one seems to notice, and I realise this is likely just visible to me.

Privacy — my language preference is known only to me. Of course.

From our earlier conversations, I know that the unchartered territories' Transport System requires no money for its tickets. The only requirement is *true* desire to go to your destination. I'm glad I didn't have to take this system when I used to head home from college for vacation.

Following the instructions on the board, I place my palm on the tree trunk and whisper, "I want to go home." I expect there to be more magic, but a leaf simply descends from the tree. It floats and twirls in zigzags, and I open my palm in time to catch it. I'm not sure if I should thank the tree or not, but I do so anyway. As I head to the airport entrance with the leaf in hand, I look around and see that there are boards stating "This is not the tree to unchartered territories" placed next to every tree in the counter's vicinity. I giggle a little — I wouldn't be surprised if people had tried to talk a random tree into dropping a leaf.

It doesn't take me long to show my passport and leaf to the men guarding the airport with giant guns. One of the men holds my leaf against the sunlight and twirls it softly. The leaf is transparent in front of the light. It looks like some sort of lace, with a million designs embedded in it, rippling green and yellow. He hands the leaf back to me.

As I head in, my phone rings. A call from my mother.

I consider tossing my whole phone in the garbage can. I won't need it now that I'm coming to you. And you could always buy me a new phone if I need one. I thought my trip to your home should be a surprise — it sure is, to me — but I also vaguely know this is reckless. Besides, you'll text me soon to complain about how *inconceivable* your colleagues find your ideas regarding your home's borders, and I have to be there to reply to you.

I can already picture you in a boathouse on a river somewhere, talking to the leaders of the three conflicting states in your home (I want to say *country* as I call mine, but your home is not a country). They want to know who gets what part of the river. They think you have a grand answer that will somehow favour them and betray the others. Only I know your proposal — *how about we don't let anyone own the waters?*

I can already see you sitting on a bamboo chair, looking ahead into the water. You wear a black kurta, but you've opened the first two buttons just so casually because you can't deal with the heat. You're bobbing your head from side to side to their complaints. You're rubbing your neck and glaring at the sun as if you're disinterested in the conflict, as if it is all beneath you. And that somehow works. Oh, I can't wait to mock you for it. You've done this before. You've solved a hundred-year national territory conflict by convincing everyone to give up their borders, and that somehow worked. They titled the place "unchartered territories" and they've shed the capitalisation of their home's name and their nation status. I'll call it the easy way out. But I'll secretly smile, proud of how you managed to convince everyone.

After I do the whole check-in thing, I hesitantly shuffle through the airport, carrying just my purse, leaf, and phone. The airport has Indian-ness slapped onto it — many stickers of rangolis and mango-leaf streamers; in the middle of the baggage carousel, a Tanjore thalayaatti doll stands with its hands in position, its head bobbing from side to side; the counters are filled with women in sarees, flashing warm smiles at everyone. I'm suddenly reminded of the Tanjore doll my mother had bought for me, of how I'd lie next to it on the floor and flick my thumbs at it, watching its head bob.

I sit on a steel chair and refresh our chat multiple times just to make sure I haven't missed your messages. I pause on the beating heart you last sent and wonder if technology has grown to the level of tracking people's heartbeats and transmitting them to their loved ones. Perhaps that's what I'm seeing, your heartbeat. But then I figure this is a futile exercise, plug in my earphones, and pine to '90s Tamil songs instead. And yet, the songs remind me of my mother's early morning singing. She'd stand at the kitchen counter and sing over the sizzling of curry leaves.

I'm called for visa clearance. But when I'm at the counter, the immigration officer takes one long look at my leaf and returns my documents without asking for my thumbprints or photographs. Before I leave, they ask, "You're heading *there*? To unchartered territories? Using that *thing*?"

I nod.

"What purpose?" they ask, though I doubt they're required to.

"To see my girlfriend," I reply.

They squint at me, wondering perhaps if I'm a boy. I want to say I'm not. But I can't be bothered to explain away the light beard I have thanks to PCOS, my nearly flat chest, and my pixie with an undercut that almost got me thrown out of my house. I instead head towards the gate, leaving the officer to puzzle by themself.

I wait at the gate. I bounce my feet anxiously, tug at my shirt, and run my hand through my hair. Soon, I'm told my transport to unchartered territories is ready. I rise to my feet and take one long look around — at the textile stores that have suspended their colourful sarees from the ceiling, sweet shops that sell mysorepak and palkova, and decoction coffee stalls scattered through the airport. It is strange to think I may never return again. I notice a saree in the shop that is pink — my mother's favourite colour. If I were returning to her, I'd buy the saree. But I won't have to worry about that anytime soon. The smell of dosas and chutney tempt me to remain. But they're not strong enough. I quickly open my purse, take out the ring you sent me, and slip it back on.

I'm only a silhouette as I head through the sunny bridge towards the Transport System.

The Transport System is in the middle of a giant square of land. It is a garden, bordered with lush hedges, carpeted with fresh blades of grass. I clutch my purse tighter as I head through the trellis archway that marks the garden's entrance. Once inside, an employee smiles at me. She steps forth and makes sure I have no luggage in my hands. "It is dangerous to carry heavy items," she explains. "Your items will be brought by our trained employees with the help of a suitable device."

She then leads me to the middle of the garden, to what looks like a lotus pond. But, as we inch closer, the pond ignites, and a soaring flame rises from its middle. It's now more a pit of fire than a lotus pond. I look to the employee with horror, and her smile falters.

"Is everything all right?" she asks me.

"Um, that is a flaming pit," I reply.

Her smile bounces back, just like that. "This room amplifies your desires. What do you see around you?"

I glance around at the tiny garden smack-dab in the middle of the airport apron. "A garden."

"Good. That means you truly want to head to your destination. But the flame might mean you're not very certain about leaving. So, a part of you is trying to dissuade you."

I press my lips together. "So, can't you extinguish it?"

The employee shakes her head. "If it makes you feel better, the fire may look real and you may even feel heat emanating from it. But it is not real."

"Or," I say, "I could make myself truly, one hundred percent, want to go there."

The employee sighs. "Ma'am, we don't have much time left. We have a strict schedule to keep. So, I'm afraid you'll either have to leave now or come back after you've sorted out your issues."

I shake my head and turn to the flame. *Extinguish. Extinguish,* I think to myself. But the flame continues in all its glory. *And why is that?* I ask myself. *I want to leave this sad place.* And the moment I ask the question, the flame flares and spreads, growing higher and wider. The tiny doubt I had in my mind — the tiny doubt that insisted I must be grateful for what I was given, that I must not hurl it all away and leave for my own sake — grows across the Transport System. Each memory of my mother glows like embers. My mother agreeing to take up extra shifts so she could cover my college tuition. My mother cooling tea by pouring it from cup to cup as I studied past three a.m. My mother standing in front of me protectively when I decided to cut my hair short and my father charged at me with anger. I shield myself and back away from the sparks caused by the fire rising in the pit, but the employee stands still, unperturbed. She taps her feet impatiently and glances at her watch.

I close my hands into fists. As I do so, I feel the metallic coldness of the ring. The ring is cold, though I stand in front of flames. The fire is not real, though my doubts are. And yet, when I look around, I'm still standing in a garden. When I back away, my feet sink into the garden's lawn, bringing me into its cooling embrace. As much as I want to stay behind, I also want to leave.

My phone vibrates. You've texted me. *Goodness, this is taking forever. I can't wait to get on the phone with you.*

I imagine talking with you tonight. I will be in my bedroom, wrapped in my blanket, listening to you all night from underneath, for I am too afraid of being caught by my mother. I will place the laptop next to me and try to get a hug out of its metallic body. But it will not be the same.

I want to be there with you. I truly do.

I look at the pit again, hoping the fire disappears. It doesn't, and it isn't that much of a surprise. As heartless as my mother would make me out to be, I am also human. This wasn't supposed to be easy anyway.

I would've happily dragged my mother here, pulled her into the garden with me. We could've gotten that pink saree together, listened to those '90s songs together. But she doesn't see my joy. She thinks my eccentricity (as she likes to call it) roots from a strange compulsion, one I must fight. She thinks it's choiceless unhappiness, and tries to pry me from its displeasure. She doesn't see that I *choose* this and wouldn't choose anything else. That I choose you, and wouldn't choose anyone else.

The employee looks at me. "I think you should return later. We need to move on to the next passenger."

No, I don't have another time. Once I return home, I doubt I'll be able to come back here. I clutch the leaf in my hand, draw in a deep breath, and run towards the fire.

Running through the pit of unreal flames hurts more than I thought it would. My hands singe, and I hear the crisp crackling of the flames. When I open my eyes, I find the hems of my shirt lighting up, the flames climbing gently, teasing my skin with its deadly fingers. But its burning prickles soon shift into the warm touch of fingertips. I look up, and there you stand, wearing a black kurta as I predicted. Your hands clutch and crumple my shirt. Your eyes widen as they meet mine. We are so close, our noses almost touch.

"You're here," you say.

"I'm here," I whisper, my lips curling into an overflowing smile. I reach for you, praying you aren't a mirage like the garden. But my finger touches your very physical, breathing body, and tangles with your long, smooth hair. I slowly trace a finger along your jaw, draw it past your neck, and into the unbuttoned part of your kurta. You crack a little smile. You let go of my shirt and wrap your hands around my waist.

"You should've told me you were coming," you say.

"I'm telling you now," I say.

You pull me into a warm embrace and I sink momentarily in the pleasure of your levelled breathing. Then, suddenly, you pull away. You laugh awkwardly and turn to your right. Only then does the world around us materialise. I find us underneath the thatched roof of a boathouse. The sun glares down on us, and we continue to glide on glittering water. When I look to your right, I find three gruff people staring at us with bewildered eyes.

"This is a beautiful river," I say, and all three people beam with pride.

"It definitely is, and we will be maintaining it together, won't we?" you say to them. Then you turn to me and whisper, "Why don't you wait over there? I'll be with you soon."

"Will it take you long?" I ask before I can stop myself.

"Not after you've come here," you say.

I quietly head to the other end of the boathouse. From there, I can see that the three leaders occasionally look at me. But my location is still more discreet than it was initially. As I sit on one of the bamboo chairs placed there, my phone vibrates. It's my mother. I reach to cut the call, but decide to pick it up.

"Hello?" I ask.

"Have you reached safely?" she asks.

"Yes. I'm with her. She's a big deal here. She's talking to three other leaders and mediating between them," I say. I wait for a response, but there is only breathing. So I say, "You know you can come here, right? You don't need money or a visa. This place has no borders. It's not like our country. Thanks to her, of course."

My mother says nothing again. I sigh. I almost pull my phone away from my ear and cut my call. But then, I hear her clear her throat. Perhaps she was crying.

"Your haircut looks good. You know that, right?" she says.

I smile, and I'm not sure why, but tears roll down my cheeks. "You'll come here," I say. "You'll be down with this. Eventually."

Swetha S. was born and raised in Coimbatore, India, but is currently in Malaysia, studying English with Creative Writing at the University of Nottingham. Her prose and poetry have appeared in *Out of Print* magazine, *Dust Poetry* magazine, and other literary magazines. She is also a freelance editor at Tessera Editorial. She is currently working on a YA novel that won The Word Editor-Writer Mentorship 2020.

For content notes, see page 243

Midnight Confetti

by D.K. Marlowe

MAEVE IS BORN OF STORMS AND TURMOIL. Her mother's screams call forth rolling thunder. Her mother's hands, red and raw from too much dish soap, tear at the seafoam-green hospital sheets.

And Maeve: she arrives quiet, the midwife's hands around her, palm to elbow cocooned like a driftwood rowboat.

And like that, she travels onward, always a stillness in an ocean of froth and agitation. Between the sky and the water, she is the drop of oil.

Only a drop, never enough to shift the sky. Never enough to divot the sea.

The report cards, the faceless friends that filter in and out of her life like shadows behind the static on TV channels that don't exist.

Merit. Achieved. Merit.

Meets expectations. Meets expectations.

And like that, squeezed out the other end of high school like the last bit of toothpaste.

And then.

Stuck.

The churning ocean is endless now, a never-fading blue-and-green mess of paying rent and studying and dropping out and searching, searching,

searching for something to anchor to.

How is it possible to feel so stagnant, so strung up like a flag, yet adrift?

* * *

Late nights fold safe over Maeve like a blanket. When it rains, the streetlights blur, bleeding yellow and green across the black street. Her boots fall heavy with each step, Maynard Keenan crooning in her ears. Slick lawns slope away from the street, and she marks a dark trail through the grass to her flat full of drop-outs who never comment on the green flecks and damp spots across her torn jeans and leather.

One of these nights she walks and doesn't stop until she winds up back at work the next day. The afternoon shift at the cafe never was a good anchor, but it feels like a wayport, a stop between the place she is now and the place she's supposed to be. Reuben looks her up and down, disbelief curdling with resignation over his clotted cream face, and pulls her aside.

Maeve knows she looks like death. She stinks of cigarettes and yesterday's clothes. Dark circles ring her eyes, her jeans dirty with mud, blades of grass like midnight confetti.

Nod, nod, nod.

When he's done, nothing calls sweeter than an early smoko break. Pull the last Marlboro from the crumpled box. Head to the alley out back.

Fuck. Fucking lighter.

Ciggie behind the ear. Back through the door, the flaking wood like electric blue pain au chocolat catching her fingers. Bright green Bic lighter on the break room table. There's a flash of something on the greyscale CRT, Maeve's fingers still on the neon plastic.

That girl. That fucking girl is back.

And maybe it's because she resents being pulled to the present, jerked from her detached safety, but she shoves the cigarette back in the crumpled box and the lighter in the front pocket of her apron where the docket pad should be.

The rubber of her Docs squeaks on the tiles. She clumps them hard and beats Aiden to the counter, ignoring his scoff of protest.

The girl.

The *fucking* girl.

She's short. Freckled round face split in two by a glowing smile. This week her hair's pink, divided as usual into four space buns. And... god, she's wearing a damn strawberry dress. Of *course* she has a fucking strawberry dress.

Maeve gives her a searching look. "Back to mess with the pastries?"

The girl's fuschia-dyed brows shoot up, revealing glitter eyeshadow. "Mess with them?"

Like she doesn't know. Maeve refuses her the pleasure of an eyeroll. Instead, she hits her with a long, slow blink.

At least the girl has the grace to blush. "Even if I *did* somehow replace all the Chelsea buns with almond croissants, wouldn't you say it's a vast improvement?"

Maeve's lips twist. The customers loved them. Flakiest, softest croissants they'd ever had. Reuben, on the other hand, got it into his shiny head that Maeve had spent petty cash on them.

She grips the edge of the counter and leans forward. She kind of wishes she'd taken smoko so she could stink out the Space Girl.

"I had to pay for the *loss*."

Space Girl pouts.

That song about titanium screeches from the speakers, interrupted by a jarring premium ad. *Whether you're up in the clouds or going way underground —*

Maeve sucks her teeth. "D'you actually want anything?"

Hesitation flits across her face, the flash of a silver coin in a clear fountain. "Would you like —" She clamps the question behind tulip lips. "Turmeric latte." She grins wide again. "Please."

She has a gap between her front teeth.

A cute gap.

"Tsch." Maeve shoves the EFTPOS machine at her, then stalks away to make the espresso. Turmeric bloody latte. Last week it was red velvet, and Space Girl had a smudge of dirt on her nose. Week before, a matcha frappé, her obscenely bright yellow coveralls flecked with paint.

Every week. Every bloody week she bugs Maeve. In small ways, small and irritating ways. And it has nothing to do with the drink orders.

One day, in the time it took Maeve to stretch the milk, Space Girl redid the specials board, adding stars and frogs in colourful chalk. Not two weeks after that, Maeve's dead pothos somehow surged back to life, vibrant and leafy green. No one but Space Girl was there.

Maeve smacks the milk jug on the counter and starts the pour.

It bothers her that she can't rationalise Space Girl's weird happenings. It bothers Reuben, that's for damn sure. Each week, with her big hazel eyes, her dresses paired as often with gumboots as vintage sandals, Maeve has to account for the girl's presence and the incidents that follow.

Maeve examines the latte art.

"Fuck."

She made it into a heart without thinking. The tug of her last cigarette behind her ear is strong.

She shoves the lid on with a twist of her mouth and thrusts out the coffee. Space Girl stands there for a moment, cradling the cup between her small fingers, rocking on her toes. Like she's expecting something. Or working some droll thought through her sparkly brain.

Maeve turns on her boot.

*   *   *

An upturned milk crate makes a poor seat for her bony arse, but at least it's quiet in the parking lot. Nothing but the low hum of air conditioning units, the muffled clatter of a dozen kitchens. Gum and old napkins are pressed into the chipseal, cigarette butts overfilling an old coffee jar.

The smoke is hot in her throat, her lungs, that buzz of lightness in her head easing her tight chest.

She's pushing on ten minutes for smoko. Aiden'll come storming back here if she lags any longer, so she crushes the butt into the concrete and gets to her feet.

The low splutter of a motorcycle pricks the static of the afternoon, like switching suddenly to a different channel.

Space Girl has a *motorcycle*.

It's an old-looking thing, emitting a rumbling gurgle. Midnight black with delicate stars sprayed across the tank. Handlebars low and straight beneath a single circular headlight. Space Girl slings a leg over and drops into the seat, the toes of her black boots grazing the asphalt.

She hitches the frothy skirt above her knees, and Maeve presses herself into the side of the building.

With a dainty movement, Space Girl flicks up the kickstand, and it clatters like the opening rapport of a snare drum. She presses a helmet over her head — it's a yellow one with cat ears attached. The one from that anime Maeve has never bothered to look up. Maybe she will, tonight.

Space Girl's face is golden with a grin as she tears out of the lot. Off up the road.

"Idiot," Maeve whispers into the sharp sting of the exhaust fumes.

She doesn't know who exactly she's addressing.

*   *   *

There are only so many fuckups one can make at a cafe. Maeve isn't bad at making coffee, and she's good with closing up. It's quiet, and she can put whatever she wants on the radio. But everything about her offends the customers, from her black-dyed hair, to her Doc Martens, to the smoke clinging to her clothes, to the natural sneer her face seems to fall into.

There are only so many fuckups, and Maeve's the biggest one.

Her schedule grows sporadic, the gaps between shifts widening like long stretches of deserted road, the days disappearing with her paycheck in the heat shimmer. She calls Reuben, and he laughs her off the phone.

Her fingers shake, slippery on her scratched-up old Samsung.

*   *   *

Another midnight walk.

She wishes it were raining, drops sliding down her leather jacket, alighting on her eyelashes like salt crystals. But it's a cloudless night, and she's alone with her thoughts for too long. Streetlamps pass overhead like bright ghosts.

A motorcycle putters up behind her.

She stops. Throws back her head. Sighs.

Maeve turns to face Space Girl. Her legs are swinging off her motorbike like a kid on a see-saw. She's stuck star stickers across her cheeks, covering some of the bigger freckles, and she's wearing some kind of peasant blouse under loose denim overalls. Maeve tries not to glance at the bare skim of flesh below her shirt as Space Girl turns the key and the engine chokes to a stop.

Cricket song presses into the silence, and the silence presses into Maeve, and Maeve presses down and down upon her heart.

The moon is a crescent, a bent needle sewing the dawn to the night.

"You haven't been at the cafe." The girl's voice is a hesitant hush.

Maeve bites the inside of her cheek. "Fired."

"This isn't America. You can't just get fired."

"No contract."

Maeve waits for it. The scoff, the roll of the eyes, the condescending look that tells her how stupid she is, not demanding a contract from the only place willing to hire her.

But it never comes. Instead, the girl sticks out her hand. There's dirt under her nails, a bit smudged along her wrist.

"Abigail."

Maeve stares down at her hand like it's a viper.

Space Girl leans closer, her motorcycle tipping precariously. "It's my name."

"I figured *that* much out." Maeve lets her gaze rove over the bike. There's a basket on the back, spilling over with herbs and vegetables. Like a damn harvest. "Bit old-fashioned."

She shrugs. "It suits me."

Maeve slips her hand out of her pocket and takes Abigail's. Her skin is soft, bar a few calluses peppered across her palm like little cherry pips.

"I'm Maeve."

"Yeah, I know."

"What?"

She taps her own chest. "Nametag."

Maeve withdraws her hand, a flush crawling up her neck, curling over her ears, catching on the piercings.

A car streaks by, tyres hissing on the asphalt. The headlights paint Abigail in gold for a moment, the stars on her cheeks glittering.

Maeve rolls up her collar against a sudden chill. "Nice meeting you. I guess." She turns and strides away.

"Hold up!"

The bike doesn't start up. Maeve walks a few more metres before stealing a glance over one shoulder. Abigail is pushing the bike along like it's one of those kid's bikes, her toes barely making contact with the road.

And Maeve, who's never stopped for anyone or anything in her life, slows. It feels like pushing against a current, like plunging an oar into a river and diving down an unknown inlet.

It makes her heart race.

Abigail catches up, the suspension of the old bike creaking softly. The helmet presses her cheeks in, and her eyes are alight with a slash of silver moon.

"Wanna go somewhere?"

Maeve folds her arms tight. "On that thing?"

"This *thing*," she says, patting the tank fondly, "is my beloved child. I have a spare helmet, gimme a sec —"

Something sticks Maeve's tongue to the roof of her mouth. She wants nothing more than to say no, to turn the other way and walk until dawn. Back to a flat full of stoners who stay up too late, to dirty dishes that have been piling up for weeks. To a black apron hung optimistically by the door.

To never see this girl again.

The thought doesn't bring her as much comfort as she thinks it ought to.

So when Abigail hands her a bright blue helmet, she hesitates for only a breath before taking it. It's loose, and she can't figure out the stupid strap.

Abigail reaches up and gently takes her hands away.

Maeve stands very still.

Abigail's fingers are warm against the soft, exposed part of her throat. If she feels it — the gentle thrum of Maeve's pulse straining against her skin — she doesn't say anything.

She pats the seat behind her, and Maeve licks her lips. She's never been on a motorcycle before. They're supposed to be kind of dangerous.

But she's been fired, and the sky is clear, and if the ciggies are killing her slowly anyway, why not go out screaming? A blaze of fucking fire down an embankment.

Abigail clunks out the metal pillion pegs. "Right, on you get."

"I, uh…"

"We're not going to tip over." She grins, hands resting on the tank. "Not unless I want us to."

It's not too late to refuse, but Maeve wouldn't be able to figure out how to undo the fucking helmet. So, she slings a leg awkwardly over the seat. Bracing herself, waiting for the whole thing to tumble over, she locks her

Docs onto the pegs and heaves herself up. The motorcycle lurches, and Maeve flings her arms around Abigail's waist.

"Easy there, goth girl."

"Fuck you."

Abigail wriggles with delight. "Just hold on!"

The engine thunders to life, the vibrations ricocheting up her bones, through her sternum, knocking something loose in her chest. They take off, and Maeve grips Abigail's waist tighter, their helmets knocking together with a plastic clunk. Her breath is loud, the visor fogging up, and her knees are pressed against Abigail's warm thighs.

Maeve doesn't see the road drip by, the streetlights blurring and streaking like a Van Gogh. There's only Abigail's yellow helmet, and the pink curl of hair at the base of her neck. She's oblivious to the asphalt slipping away, wildflowers springing through the cracks, vines erupting from the footpath, the concrete splitting like fresh-baked bread. She doesn't notice the tyres leave the road, because she's too aware of how soft Abigail is between her arms. How it feels like the witch girl is pulling her little aimless boat of a life into the riptide.

Maeve squeezes her eyes shut, her heart a resonant drum in her throat.

When they stop, Maeve's knees are locked up. Abigail waits patiently, one foot holding up the bike, the other brushing through the blossoms.

It's bright. Not middle-of-summer, sprinkler going and hot-hot-hot sand bright — it's bright like the moon is, a cold sort of bright. Maeve looks up and swallows a gasp that tastes like cigarettes.

She's seen pictures of the Northern Lights before, of course. But here it is, an aurora stretched out and shimmering like glistening green tassels dripping from a string. It clings to a violet sky speckled with stars like pinholes in a scratchy woollen blanket.

Maeve eases herself down. Brushes her fingertips across the lupins and foxglove. She turns to ask Abigail just what the fuck is going on, when the girl tips up Maeve's chin, still in the helmet. Her mouth is dry as a hangover as those soft fingers deftly unclip her, draw the helmet from her head.

Maeve's heart carries away her tongue. "Where are we?"

"Somewhere." Abigail tucks the helmet under her arm. "In between."

It's strange. All her life, Maeve has been hunted by that phrase.

In between. In between jobs, in between partners, in between the shock of rock-bottom and the gleaming promise of something better.

In between isn't supposed to feel this comfortable.

Abigail soaks up the moonlight, like she's in the right place now. The right frequency.

"How?" Maeve asks, plucking a foxglove bloom. It feels real enough, the lilac petals delicate in her pinched fingers.

Abigail shrugs. "It looked like you needed it." She sets the helmet down and swings around her backpack, drawing out a bottle of wine and plaid blanket. "Want to have a picnic?"

Maeve laughs, and the sound surprises her. When was the last time she'd laughed? A true laugh, not a laugh dripping with sardonic sweetness. Mirth born from joy, not from some kind of stilted desperation to be liked.

But in this place, in this halfway world with a witch on a motorbike, and the grass beckoning her bare toes, laughter feels like harmony.

Instead of an answer, a tight fist of emotion works its way up her throat. "Let's not go back," Maeve says.

Abigail's smile is soft. "We'll need to, at some point." She pulls out a package cradled in beeswax wrap. "Can't conjure up food. Besides, I can think of plenty of good places back in the city for a date."

Maeve's pulse thuds to a stop. "A date? This is a date?"

The stars shine in Abigail's eyes, and on her cheeks, and in the bubbles rising through the deep-ocean green of the bottle.

"I hope it is."

Like the snapping of a flag in the breeze, Maeve is, all of a sudden, stretched out and blinding bright. Tethered, straining to be free, to drift out over the ocean at last. And for once, she doesn't care if casting herself off that yawning precipice will lead her to the sea or to the clouds.

Or in between.

D. K. Marlowe writes young adult fantasy, centering queer protagonists and featuring hard magic systems, dry humour, and expansive worlds. When she isn't sitting on chairs incorrectly to draft new stories, she enjoys sewing and drawing, plucking new novel ideas from thread and graphite. She lives in Aotearoa (New Zealand) with her plant children in varying states of living, and a robot vacuum named Yu-Gi-Oh. Twitter and Instagram: **@DKMarloweWriter**

For content notes, see page 243

black is a flower

by R.J. Mustafa

A SMILE SPREADS ON MY FACE AS DARKNESS FALLS.

He is coming.

I circle inside the hut that I have been cleaning since dusk. Heavy wooden chests piled in a corner, sage wreaths, and cowrie shells on an ancient table.

The blankets piled upon my bed, infused with sandalwood.

He wouldn't care about what's inside anyway. Never would he step foot inside a building, no matter whose it was. He was born a son of the woods, of wild nettles and rotting moss.

I ball the blankets up and take them outside. Dead leaves crunch under my naked feet, and I spread them right there, on the ground. The woods behind my house are silent, a sweet wind not daring to disturb the ancient trees.

It will not last long.

Dusting my hands, I check my clothes again. White linen — nothing extraordinary. The tunic brushes against my ankle as I sit. The shadow of a beard covers my chin, the silver necklace he once gifted me dangling from my neck.

Blackthorn tattoos shimmer between my clavicles.

Thin. You're too thin.

Shaking my head to chase those thoughts away, I look up to the trees. They are mango and neem, carrying an intrigued smell. They must wonder what the human is doing outside, sitting cross-legged with bottles of honey and fresh blood at his sides.

The forest flutters awake, night creatures heralding his arrival. Bats, spinning around the roof. Snakes slithering around the blankets, their black and emerald scales reflecting moonlight.

Wolves howl underneath the canopy, and the trunks part open.

My breath is shallow, beads of sweat trembling on my umber skin. He's here.

His feet are bare, and flowers sprout whenever they touch the ground. I see the mauve tint of lilacs. Hibiscus flowers, bleeding red.

Belladonna, like the ones I crushed hours earlier to invoke him.

He's standing before me, antlers towering over my head. Drinking up the blood first, he sighs. My heart stops.

"Greetings, lover."

Purple garments flowing, he thrusts the bottle aside. I raise my chin, and my brown eyes meet his, white as ivory. He fondles the honey as he drinks, letting strands of gold trickle from his lips. His gaze never leaves mine.

I kiss his hand, a single tear rolling down my cheek. "Greetings, lover. I have missed you."

His gaze grows soft, and he pulls me into an embrace. My chin on his shoulder, I close my eyes, inhaling the scent of earth, unholy flowers, and blood.

"It has been but a year," he chuckles, his deep voice raging over my body. As he pulls away, a gentle smile rests on his lips.

Taking my shaking hands between his, he leads me to the sheets. I steal another hug from him, his clawed hand behind my neck.

"Any moment without you by my side feels like eternity," I quiver.

He laughs, a flicker of mischief in his pupils. There's still the faintest scent of blood in his breath, minuscule droplets between his fangs. "Darling, eternity is nothing you could fathom. It spreads like an infinite canvas, one where you would be nothing but a dot."

A frown spreads across my face, contrasting with the smile on my lips. "It has been too long, still."

His brethren frolic between the tree trunks, growls and laughter filling the air. I have never met them, but I know they are not normal creatures. They are men with goat hooves, women with snakes on their heads and wings on their back. They are magnificent beings made of shadow and water — cold firelights and howling spirits.

Like their Master, they are from the Otherworld.

"Have *you* missed me?" I whisper, a hand caressing his locs. They're shining black, so long they meet his ankles. Moths flee and scorpions scatter as I part the dark coils.

"Yes, Driss. I have."

I moan, blood rushing through my body. His touch sparkles the flints of magic slumbering in my cells, ones that are long dead. I am a witch without power, only able to brew philters and invoke beings of the Otherworld.

My fingers brush the thorns adorning his brow. What I wouldn't do to kiss his lips, to taste sin on his forked tongue. He is a beautiful demon. He is mine, and I will be his.

Soon.

We lie down, and my head rests on his chest. His touch is lighter than a feather as he caresses my curls, plays with the strings of my tunic.

Closing my eyes, I listen to his undying heartbeat as he shows me stars and constellations. Names my mother whispered to me when I was a little boy, of the Hunter and the Pretentious. All companions of Mother Moon — legionaries of Her parade.

Everything he says I already know, but I let him speak. His gravelly voice is warming my bones, and the muscles under his obsidian skin are blocks of ice under my touch.

As the moment comes, he hums. From the back of his throat, a song older than time flows. In a tongue never spoken by mankind, but one I know the meaning of.

For seven years now, we have met. Ever since I stood before my mother's corpse, taken away by the plague. Ever since the teenager I was drew symbols with her blood, his blood, his tears. Calling for a soul to comfort him, now that he was alone in this world.

The darkness had listened to his wails, and the Lord of the Forest had answered his call.

Every year, when Mother Moon splits in half, I call him. I slaughter a lamb, dripping its heart in a syrupy mix of honey and blood, then entrust it to the wolf waiting on my doorstep.

He comes at night, and I ask him the same question. For him to own my body, making me into one of his night creatures.

Tonight, he accepts. He sings his everlasting love for me, pools of white pinned on my eyes. He stops, cupping my cheeks.

"It has been seven years, my love."

Thunder shatters the night sky as Mother Moon blooms. His voice ripples with worry, and he kisses my brow softly, as if I was about to break. My body shakes, an orphaned leaf battered by tides of celestial power, and I lock my arms around him as we rise.

"Do you want it, still?" he asks.

"Yes, my love. It is time."

My voice quivers and dies as a clawed finger raises my chin. His full lips are one touch away, black poison I embrace.

They are soft, and I never want to let him go. Even as poison runs through my body, slowly extinguishing my life flame, we make love. He is gentle and patient, and my body echoes his. We dance under the moonlight, my body burning as he worships it. It is pain, and it is bliss.

Everything is on fire, everything is heaven.

As he falls, I draw my last breath.

I awake hours later, and I am reborn. I touch the sides of my head, where curved horns spiral. A crown of lilacs lies between them, and I taste sap and venom on my lips.

It is cold, and it is alive. He smiles as he watches me, his heart beating against mine.

He is mine, and I am his.

We rise once again, and my muscles burn under my dead skin. My eyes see everything. The glimmer of obsidian hidden deep inside his white eyes. His subjects, staring at me as they wait at the wood edge.

"You are beautiful," he says, and I return his smile.

He takes my hand, where black feathers have spread. A thousand whispers swell against my ear when his fingers brush the corner of my eye. I hear their questions, hear his amused tone as he silences them with a thought. "They are *our* subjects now. We will rule the Otherworld together.

"Are you with me, lover?"

Without thinking, I steal a glance at my old home. The human life, lifeless without him. Nothing is holding me back, and that thought alone sparks black flames licking at my fingertips. I blow, and fire devours the hut.

There is nothing, and now there is everything.

I look back at him. Soul of my soul and heart of my heart. My hand slides on his waist and I kiss his lips. They are poison and honey — but now I have poison too.

"Yes, Inaan. I always will be."

We drown in the woods, and the darkness embraces us both.

This story was originally self-published by the author in 2020.

R.J. Mustafa is a dreamer, a medical student and fantasy writer, focused on exploring old – and new – myths of Black and African culture. He is devoted to creating stories portraying Black people under all their colors – soft, magical, just themselves. When he's not writing or reading, he can usually be found binging animated shows or Asian BL dramas.

For content notes, see page 243

Sphexa, Start Dinosaur

by Nibedita Sen

ASHA — ASH TO FRIENDS — wedges the maintenance door open wide enough to slip into the darkened interior of the abandoned ride. Inside smells like rust and stale water and plastic fused with metal.

"Sphexa," he says. "Light."

The small robot bobbing behind him clicks, casting a circle of illumination on the concrete floor. He made Sphexa in shop class at school, patching together an old Echo, a frame salvaged from a drone, a rolling toy robot, and a few other things, because if you're going to be *that* stereotype of the Indian kid good at engineering, you might as well lean all the way in.

"Reminder," Sphexa says as they make their way down the narrow walkway lining the tunnel. "Event upcoming in two hours: Pick Mei up for prom."

"I'm working on it, Sphexa."

"Would you like a list of car rental agencies in the area that take last-minute bookings?" Disapproval is not something he programmed into the bot, but it's definitely pulling some attitude right now.

"I'm good, Sphexa, thanks."

They're walking alongside a long, low channel that still holds a few inches of scummy water. The flat-bottomed boats that used to rock and splosh slowly along the artificial river are long gone, of course. *Journey Through the Jurassic* was shut down a year ago, eclipsed by other, showier rides in the park.

It was his and Mei's favourite, before that. They rode it every hot, sticky summer, multiple times if they could, huddled together in the boats with their backpacks full of issues of *National Geographic* and Meccano dinosaurs they'd built together. Over the years, they went from staring awestruck at the animatronic saurians craning over them, to playing spot-the-anatomical-inaccuracies. Ash still remembers, though, that first time, when they were younger — though they'd ridden it so many times already by then — when they rounded the corner where the T-Rex lifted its metal head and roared in the low reddish light, and Mei grabbed his hand, their smaller, warmer fingers tightening in his.

Mei. His heart jolts, as it always does, at the thought of their heart-shaped face. The way their hair is always falling into their eyes when they get excited about something, and how they dash it away impatiently with the backs of their hands as they keep talking, their voice going high and jumpy with their infectious joy.

They had their first kiss on this ride too, in the back of a boat in middle school, somewhere just past the T-rex but before the raptors.

Ash clambers through a thicket of fake Jurassic ferns and a nest of baby Maiasaura, led by Sphexa's overhead beam. It's hot in here. His rented tux is a little too small for him, uncomfortably tight against his chest, over the binder.

The corsage he got for Mei sits carefully in an inner pocket. He figured he should keep at least one thing traditional if he was going to flip double middle fingers at all the rest.

He's almost all the way to the mouth of the exit when the irregular silhouette of a Stegosaurus rises ahead out of the gloom. Ash grins. Bingo. Stegosaurus, Mei's second-favourite dinosaur (their first is Psittacosaurus, but *Journey Through the Jurassic* doesn't have one).

"Sphexa, raise lights to seven."

Ash carefully lowers his backpack to the now-brighter floor and starts pulling things from it: pliers, loops of cable, wire cutters, microcontrollers; mostly from his own workshop, a few "borrowed" from his dad's. His hopes are confirmed as he starts carefully severing the plastic encasing the animatronic's upper forward leg joint. The T-connectors and needle valves he needs are mostly already there, articulated and ready to go, if dusty from disuse since the ride shut down and the Stego stopped making its plodding way back to and from the waterhole.

All he has to do is feed wires into the right places, sealing them in places with dabs of insulated putty, winding them up towards the dinosaur's knobby head.

"Message from Mei," Sphexa reports archly. *"It's okay if you've changed your mind."*

Mei had nearly cried with happiness when he'd asked them to prom, but had flip-flopped between anxiety and despair ever since, making lists of everything that could go wrong. They'd never exactly fit in, the two of them, the trans kid and the immigrant. Especially not since Mei had come out. Ash could guess what some of the stuff on Mei's lists was: the glances in the hallway, the jackasses trying to flip up their skirt, being shoved at the water fountain. He got his fair share of it too. The Sphero that went into making Sphexa had been his before someone kicked it down the hallway, snapping it in half.

"Sphexa, reply. Send link to playlist, 'Cretaceous Rock.'"

"Message sent. Reply from Mei: *'Hah, hah.'*"

Sphexa hovers overhead as he works, the minutes ticking by. As he suspected, the Stego's skull is mostly empty, its mechanics concentrated in the joints. Ash pulls himself up onto the dinosaur's back, brushing cobwebs from between its raised plates — a staggered line of them, not paired, totally inaccurate for *S. Ungulatus*. At least it makes it easy to find a seat.

"Okay, Sphexa," he says. "Get in there."

Tablet in hand, he makes minute course corrections on the touchscreen as the robot levers itself into the hollow skull, clicking free of its drone frame. Ash leans forward to plug the final jacks into the ports on Sphexa's back. Rotors click and valves piston as the connections light up one by one, a whirring hum he can feel through the automaton's thick plastic hide. The Stegosaurus shifts, lifting one huge foot and then another, testing its restored — and expanded — mobility. Elation warms his chest.

"GPS active," Sphexa says. "Add destination."

"Mei's place."

"Would you like to add another stop? Suggestion based on calendar: school."

"Not yet." Ash pats the dinosaur's neck. "Let's go get Mei. Then we'll see where they want to go."

He twists his earbuds up into place, tucking them in firmly, and taps the tablet. "Oh, and Sphexa? Play 'Walk the Dinosaur.'"

This story was first published in *ROBOT DINOSAURS!* (2018).

Nibedita Sen is a Hugo, Nebula, and Astounding Award-nominated queer Bengali writer from Kolkata, and a graduate of Clarion West 2015 whose fiction and essays have appeared in venues such as *Uncanny*, *Podcastle*, *Nightmare* and *Fireside*. She lives in NYC with her boo and their sweet, flatulent old cat, enjoys puns and potatoes, and is nearly always hungry. Hit her up on Twitter at **@her_nibsen,** where she can usually be found yelling about food, anime, and what she's currently reading.

For content notes, see page 243

The Frequency of Compassion

by Merc Fenn Wolfmoor

KAITYN FALK LOVES THE DARK PHASE OF THE MOON. It's quiet. Soothing. Insulated in their spacesuit, comm dimmed, Kaityn sits in the rover and watches the sky. Here on Io 7, a newly discovered satellite in retrograde orbit around a dwarf planet the size of Pluto, they are the only living human in several thousand lightyears. They are here to establish research beacons for star-charting, a risky job for how isolated it is — and Kaityn hasn't loved anything this much in their life. The exhilaration of travel, the calmness of deep space, the possibility of an ever-unfolding universe.

"Daydreaming again?"

The onboard nav AI, Horatio, is the exception to Kaityn's preference for silence. Developed with multi-faceted personality modes to stem off homesickness and loner's fright, the AI is Kaityn's co-pilot, research assistant, and friend.

"Just dreams," they reply. "Wouldn't it be cool if we evolved in a way to survive vacuum and could sail around without spacesuits?"

"Technically, I already can," Horatio says.

Kaityn laughs. "When I was a kid I wanted to grow giant dragonfly wings in order to zip around in zero-G. I guess hyperdrive is close enough."

The vast scope of sky, its silken blackness, rocks Kaityn in a serene, wordless lullaby. These few hours between the rotation from dark to light on Io 7 are theirs, and they bask in the solitude. There are plenty of other taxing, long-distance meetings and digital paperwork to dull their enthusiasm of being in space, on the rim of the Milky Way. This time is theirs.

In another two weeks, they will begin the trip to Mars HQ to reorient and decompress from a six-month shift. Kaityn sighs. They don't like thinking about the inevitable burst of human interaction they will have to bear for half a year before they can travel again.

"You seem melancholy," Horatio says. The AI's voice is warm against Kaityn's ears inside their helmet. "Is something distressing you?"

"Just thinking about how little time we have left on this shift."

Kaityn is autistic and hyperempathic. When they were young — before they knew they were agender, before they had words for why they always felt so keenly for everyone around them — they coped badly. So much sound, so much light, so many shades of *emotion*. It was the promise of cold, isolated quiet in space that drew them to the Galactic Exploration for Peace agency. GEP needed people willing to risk the vast expanse on the edges of known space.

Out here, Kaityn can *breathe*. They can serve humanity without being overwhelmed by everything that makes humans imperfect and wondrous.

"I'm programmed to list the benefits of six months on, six months off duty," Horatio says, "but I suspect that is unhelpful."

Kaityn smiles wanly. "I'll figure out something —"

A bright wisp flickers across their helmet's viewscreen. It moves too fast for them to define it — but its distress radiates sharp like a needle. Kaityn straightens with a gasp. "Horatio, did you pick that up on scanners?"

"Yes, I did," Horatio says.

"What's your take?"

"It touched down two kilometers from your position. Odd energy reading, extremely small mass. There should be no minor satellites in decay orbit."

"It feels alive." Kaityn ignites the solar engines and guides the rover along the path Horatio provides via map readouts. "And it's hurt."

Their thoughts blur with sudden excitement. *Alive.* Could this be potential first contact? Protocols rush through their mind. Establish sensory verification if possible: auditory, ocular, olfactory, tactile, light spectrum, mechanical observation, recordable frequencies; identify yourself and designation but do not engage in any negotiation without authorization —

Kaityn's pulse races. They shouldn't assume anything: maintaining objectivity is the leading tenet for space exploration. It's hard when so many ideas are flooding their brain, the adrenaline spike intoxicating.

"Better hurry," Horatio says. "I've just detected ZeroGen Corps' beacons; their vessel has also picked up the signal."

Kaityn's shoulder twitches in surprise, the emotion bleeding fast into sharp fear. "Why are they in this sector? No reports were logged!"

ZeroGen personnel, unlike Kaityn and members of the GEP, always explore with weaponry ready. ZeroGen Corps is a multinational conglomerate for profit-based space exploration. But there are *rules*, regulations, responsibilities. Any human-piloted expedition or spaceflight is supposed to be logged on a public records database. If ZeroGen is out here incognito, they are disregarding all safety protocols. Why?

"They are not responding to my hailing request," Horatio says. "Please proceed with caution."

Kaityn swallows. "I will."

The sense of *pain* grows stronger as Kaityn approaches the signal.

The rover purrs over the rocky surface of the moon. Kaityn remembers playing the old video game series *Mass Effect,* where they piloted an indestructible ground vehicle. They reveled in flying it off cliffs just to watch the absurdity of low-G and unbreakable shock absorbers. They aren't nearly as reckless with an actual GEP commissioned rover — especially when they're driving, and this is reality. Still, in private, Kaityn thinks of their rover as the Mako 2.0.

Dust kicks up behind the treads, and on the radar map, Kaityn notes the signal lit up as a green flare. They park the rover half a kilometer away and strap on their survival/first aid pack.

The vibrations of *hurt-lost-scared* presses against their consciousness even this far away. They swallow hard, their throat tight.

In space, they have only their own emotions to process. This nervousness is all theirs. Although Kaityn believes AIs have cognition and emotion, Horatio operates on a different frequency from their perception. They asked once if that was intentional to accommodate them. There was a long pause — for Horatio, at least — and then the AI replied: "Yes, I do. I was not programmed to project emotions, merely to observe and respond to them when appropriate."

"But you're *full* of sensors," Kaityn said, flapping their hands in excitement. "And you do feel — I can tell by the way you operate. We might be similar in that way."

"Interesting analysis," Horatio said. "Perhaps we are both outliers from how we were originally programmed."

Kaityn liked that: another thread of connection between them and Horatio.

Now, Kaityn struggles to rein in their wildly fluctuating emotional response. This could be first contact! The sheer thrill is muted with fear, and the building sense of *pain* they can't ignore, like an oncoming migraine.

Kaityn unstraps from the rover and hops out.

Their boots leave quarter-inch tracks in the soft moon dust. Kaityn resists the urge to flop down and roll around, making an angel pattern in the sediment. It isn't polite to the moon, and they can't spare the time. They're reminded of fresh, soft snowfall in North Dakota, where they lived as a child. They would bundle up in a plush jacket, snow pants, mittens, hat — always refusing a scarf for how it itched against their skin — and dash out into their huge yard. After a snowfall, there was a sense of calm and serenity under the vast gray sky. They would flop in the beautiful drifts, gather clumps of snow to make forts or dinosaurs until called back inside when their lips grew numb and their cheeks turned bright red. Winters were never the same for Kaityn when they moved to Chicago at age ten, and there was no peace under the sky.

Kaityn navigates via digital map and their helmet's built-in spotlights. Mesas sprout up and meld into cliff faces on Io 7's surface. Their helmet light casts jagged shadows along the gray-blue stone. There: a disturbance in the arid stone. Dust sways like smoke suspended over dimming embers. Something bright and translucent shimmers within a tiny crater, a crack in the stone.

Pain.

It makes Kaityn flinch: the intensity is needle-hot, cascades of glass fragments carried in ice water. *Alone. Lost. Help.*

"I'm coming," Kaityn calls aloud, aware that whatever it is, it may not understand vocal resonance or language constructed for human tongues and minds and hands. Protocol states any approach should be made with caution and only as a last resort if visual, verbal, or mechanical hailing signals do not produce a verifiable response. But they can't wait. They break into a run, the low gravity carrying them in long, effortless leaps across the remaining distance.

"I advise caution," Horatio says. "Even if unintentional, a distressed life-form may prove dangerous."

"I know."

"Overriding internal contact failsafe," Horatio says. "I will abide by your discretion."

Kaityn didn't know the AI could do that, but right now, they are too focused on reaching the life-form and aiding in whatever manner they can.

Kaityn narrows their eyes as they approach, dimming their helmet light to the lowest setting. It takes a second to control their momentum and balance theirself. They hold their hands away from their body, heart pounding, and edge around the last chunk of rock between theirself and the hurt life-form.

It is octagonal light, soft-edged, with undulating ripples along the surface. Perhaps two feet in diameter, with no visible protrusions or indentations. Yet it has mass, for it is partially buried under crumbled rock and dust, and it is hurt.

Kaityn takes slow, deep breaths, centering theirself and trying to control their vocal tone.

"My name is Kaityn Falk," they say as they edge nearer. GEP protocol dances in their foremost thoughts, ingrained training, and yet the wonder almost closes off their voice. First contact with another being, out here on Io 7. This is real. This is *real*. "I'm a human from the planet Earth, and I mean you no har —"

The alien shape undulates, its light frequency strobing, and it lets out a sound that is not auditory so much as felt in the bones, in the soul. Kaityn screams as the pain hits them —

— breaking away from the cluster, caught in solar winds, tossed and tumbled against ice and void, snagged in gravity, pulled through atmosphere. Where are the others? So alone. Afraid. Lost? How will others find? No communication thread, broken from stress. Falling, matter denser and sensation-undocumented-not-good —

The sensory overload sends Kaityn reeling back, and they collapse.

*   *   *

Kaityn is six again, sitting on the porch of their house with their mom, drinking hot cocoa and watching the aurora borealis dapple the sky with spilled gasoline colors.

"I want to fly in space!" Kaityn declares.

Mom laughs. "What would you do in space?"

"Pick up *all* the colors and put them in a basket and bring them back for you. So you can paint with them!"

"Wow, that's pretty cool," Mom says, grinning. "Are there colors up there I can't find in the art department?"

They nod solemnly. "Those are *space colors*, Mom. You can't buy them in the store."

Mom hugs Kaityn with one arm. "Well, baby, that sounds like a good plan. When you bring me space colors, we'll paint a picture together."

Kaityn beams and finishes the melty marshmallows at the bottom of their mug.

Mom never saw them celebrate their twelfth birthday. Car accident. Kaityn stopped drawing; they would never collect space colors, not when their mom couldn't paint anymore.

*   *   *

In the cluster, we all are connected by billions of threads. We flow ever outward, sharing thought and wonder and memory. Languages saturate our understanding, rich and intricate; trillions of ways for connection, for empathy, for life. We are vastness, we are unity, we are individual. And there is a hole in ourselves: we are missing one of us. This is hurt, this is pain, this is sorrow. We cannot move forward, towards the beginnings and the ends of the universe, until we find ourself. To abandon one is to abandon the cluster. It is not who we are. We will find ourself, ourselves, for one is no greater or lesser than all.

*   *   *

Kaityn often chats online with their boyfriend (before he's their ex) about the possibility of first contact. One day, he says, "You know I support you and all, but what if you were the first person aliens met? Wouldn't being agender just confuse them?"

Kaityn grasps for words, their mouth empty, their brain feeling sluggish and disconnected.

He presses on, his face close to the screen. "I mean. Wouldn't it make more sense, if you met an alien, to explain you were a woman? That way when they encounter the rest of humanity, it wouldn't be as jarring."

Kaityn looks at their hands, their whole body flushed with shame. They can't find a coherent way to explain all that is wrong with his assumptions. Would aliens need to be dual gendered, or even have a concept of gender? Would aliens even need pronouns? All Kaityn's snappy semantic and scientific theories and explanations vanish like a hard drive crash.

"I'm just saying," he says. "You've got to think of what's best for humanity. First impressions only come once."

"I know," they mumble. It's in all the training material for GEP, and they've downloaded and studied it over and over with giddy excitement. There is such possibility in the stars.

"Kaityn," he says. At least he consistently uses their correct name. "You know I care about you. I just want to make sure you're doing what's right."

He's been subtly resistant to their gender and pronoun choices, especially when they legally changed their ID before accepting the position in GEP. Kaityn doesn't want to confront him about it. He gets defensive and asks why they're attacking him over such trivial details. It's his disappointment that always stings the worst.

Kaityn can't shake off the doubts that are always there, in the back of their mind, insidious and small and prone to springing up when they are least prepared. What if he's right? Their chances of encountering alien sapient life are billions to one; yet people still win lotteries. It isn't impossible.

"Okay," Kaityn says then, and mumbles an excuse about a migraine — their head throbs, their eyes sting from withheld tears — and logs off.

"He was bad for you," Horatio says later, when they share that painful story when almost drunk. It's their first week on a solo trip and every time they look at the vast mural of space, they hear their ex's voice and his... concerns. "He wanted the his-version of you, not your true self."

"Yep," Kaityn agrees. "Should have dumped his ass long ago." Their voice doesn't have the conviction they want, but it feels good to say aloud nonetheless.

* * *

Kaityn blinks against the searing light-pain in their eyes. They're lying just outside the crevice where the life-form crashed; their suit's readings show no physical damage, and the timestamp in their helmet's log indicates barely thirty seconds have passed.

"Kaityn? Kaityn?" Horatio sounds deeply concerned. For a moment, Kaityn feels the AI's worry like an ache in their jaw, spreading down their neck. "Your biorhythms and brainwaves were erratic and completely inconsistent with human physiology. I was afraid you were dying. I have sent distress signals on all frequencies."

Carefully, Kaityn sits up. They want to rub their face, dig their thumbs against the cheekbones and sinuses to alleviate the throbbing pressure. Their helmet prevents them. Gloves too insulated, no skin contact. Their vision normalizes, the afterimages of falling stars and sun flares dissipating into memory. The suit injects a mild painkiller and a faint whiff of lavender into their oxygen supply. It's the scent Kaityn likes most, and they have the dosage perfectly balanced so it won't overwhelm them.

"I'm... okay..." Kaityn blinks again.

We are so sorry, says the light still trapped in stone.

Kaityn's whole body shivers and their shoulders hunch up in excitement.

"Horatio?" Kaityn whispers. "Do you hear that?"

"I do," the AI says. "There is no auditory or digital relay for this communication, however, at least that my sensors can detect. It is... not a phenomenon I am programmed to understand. Is this telepathy?"

In a sense, the voice says. It is soft, like a pillow wrapped in microfiber and with no aroma. *We did not intend you harm. We bonded thoughts without your consent, and we are deeply ashamed of this. We ask forgiveness for such violation.*

Kaityn shakily regains their feet and edges nearer to nu. The knowledge of the cluster's pronouns — the cluster and this individual alike — feels natural. Nu broke free of nur clusterselves and fell. Nu is alone here, unsure where nur otherselves are now. It was not an intentional fall — nu simply wished to reach out to the colors of the universe, the beautiful radiance that shimmers between folds of vacuum.

"Wow," Kaityn breathes. Their thoughts spin in ecstatic patterns, like small shiny cubes all clanking together. They resist flapping their hands, even if it makes their arms ache. "Wow."

Nu is still trapped under the outcropping of moon rock.

They need to focus. Their GEP training is a solid grounding point: in an emergency, remember to breathe. Oxygen for the brain. Appraise the situation. Your kit and vehicles are equipped with a wide range of multi-situational tools. Your AI co-pilot will assist you.

They kneel by the rocks. Their kit has a collapsible pole for a mobility aid. It'll work well as a pry-bar. Kaityn withdraws the metal tube and snaps it open.

"I'm going to loosen the rocks," Kaityn says, their voice shaking. "I'm going to move slow so more debris doesn't fall."

Understanding shimmers from the life-form.

Gingerly, Kaityn digs the tip of the pole into a crevice where the largest rocks are pinning the life-form's body. "Is there anything I can do to ease your pain?"

Not alone, nu says. *Enough for…* It flickers, the pain flaring and dimming. Kaityn gasps and flinches. Tries to steady their hands and push past the hurt.

"Alert: ZeroGen Corps' shuttle is in orbit and locked onto our location," Horatio says.

Kaityn bites the inside of their cheek by accident, and a sharp tingle of pain makes them wince. They scrabble to get leverage on the stone without harming the life-form or causing more rocks to fall.

You show distress, nu says, and sends *concern-for-well-being* and offers *soothing-calm-serenity*. Kaityn hesitates: the emotions hover in soft swirls, like fresh watercolors held in little paper cups. They accept a sip of *soothing-calm*, if only to steady their nerves. Peace settles inside their mind, and their bio-rhythms smooth. Their focus sharpens. There, mapped out like a puzzle's answer, they see where they need to apply leverage to the moon rock and shift it so the low gravity will roll it safely away and let nu free.

"Thank you," they say aloud, and nur light tones warm in mutual pleasure to have helped them. Nu is transferring nur pain inward so as not to distract and cause harm to Kaityn. They smile shakily in gratitude.

With a slow tumble and spray of dust, the rock shifts and the life-form lies bare and exposed. Kaityn pulls out an emergency solar blanket and drapes it across nur body.

Nu sends *thankfulness* to them.

And then ZeroGen Corps arrives.

Dust gusts and spins in angry patterns, violently disturbed as a militarized shuttle drops from orbit and blasts the surface without care or consent of the moon.

Kaityn flings an arm up in reflex.

"Step away from the alien." The ZeroGen operator's signal blasts into Kaityn's frequency. "It is being claimed by ZeroGen Corps for scientific study."

Kaityn winces in pain and freezes. Their suit compensates for the decibel level over the channel and drops it until they can hear and aren't overwhelmed by the noise. They raise their hands, the protocol for a GEP employee's non-hostile acknowledgment and negotiation tumbling in tangled patterns through their head.

There are five operators: all in dark-tinted armor and helmets, armed with electric bolt guns, and radiating *intensity* tinged with *hostility* and *nervousness*. The ZeroGen personnel have already logged the signal and site; if they don't return with evidence, or secure the asset, they'll be docked and fined.

"I'm Kaityn Falk from —"

"We know who you are," snaps the operator who spoke first. "GEP outposts are noted on this moon but you haven't tagged the alien for official observance. Move away from it now."

"Nu," Kaityn corrects, and then realizing the operator may not understand, they add, "Nur pronouns are —"

"Alert!" Horatio beeps in alarm. "Weapons armed!"

The lead operator shoulders their bolt gun and aims at Kaityn's torso. The ZG-X24 model: it has enough force, even in low gravity, to damage or rupture their spacesuit. Worse, Kaityn is alone except for Horatio, who is incorporeal, and if ZeroGen intends to harm them, it's no stretch to assume the operators would also disable the AI and leave no contestable record of illegal activity. Horatio has sent an emergency ping, yes, but signal still takes time to traverse space, and by then it will do Kaityn and Horatio and nu no good.

Kaityn's pulse flutters, a rush of blood in their ears. They can't hold down their terror, the sudden, visceral realization they might die here on this moon, and it will be weeks before the next scout ship reaches them. Days before anyone knows something's wrong when they don't log a report update. Unknown span of time where their body will freeze from depressurization.

Yet worst of all is knowing that if ZeroGen captures nu, nu will be subjected to horrors and pain and *aloneness*.

"I'm sending an additional distress —" Horatio's frequency shorts out. Jamming signal. Kaityn can only hear their own breath, their own thoughts.

Trembling, Kaityn puts one foot before the other. They will not leave nu alone. They will not fight — they're unarmed and outnumbered and have always been a pacifist — but they will not abandon the life-form to cruelty and destruction.

"You are not going to harm nur," Kaityn says. The radio frequency is still open between them and the leader. "Please return to your vehicle and —"

"Step. Away."

Kaityn steps, but they step in front of the light and keep their arms outspread. "No," they say, soft and firm, and press outward with their emotions as steadily as they can. Peace. Calm. Acceptance. They do not want to die afraid; they do not want nu to suffer. "I cannot let you harm nu."

"Fine," the ZeroGen person says.

The leader fires.

* * *

We reach across the brightness of space, searching, and we find ourself, ourselves, once again. There! The thread is splintered, an unanticipated fall, suspended in this chronological moment. We knit closed the hurt and we see ourself huddled beside the otherselves. There is distress and fear in all the selves that are not ourselves, and we see the patterns unwind from one self: violence intended. This self acts from bitterness, willingly, and the self's anger radiates outward like the self's weaponry. We sing sadness for this self, this lost one that is not ourselves, for they are alone and do not understand the harm they bring themself when they aim such violence at others. It is not our preference to intervene, and yet, there is a bright self that stands betwixt the violence and our lost self, and we will not let them perish.

*   *   *

Kaityn is packing for their shuttle flight to GEP Station, which is in orbit around Mars. They have a list:

- favorite video games stored on a flashmem drive; portable screen and controller
- a tablet loaded with their music library
- plenty of ebooks
- their favorite sweatshirt
- a plush squid named Inky
- headphones

There's room for a few more physical objects before they reach their weight limit in their suitcase and carry-on. Kaityn looks at the sketchpad, yellowed with age, and the cup of colored pencils that have gathered dust on that same shelf for years.

For a moment, they almost reach out and drop the art supplies in their bag. Mom isn't here to see this. Mom would have loved every minute of packing, departure, hearing the updates, even waiting on lag from text and compressed video messages from Earth to the station.

Mom would have been so proud.

Kaityn leaves the remainder of their weight limit unfilled. They haven't drawn or colored since they were a child. There's no point in trying again.

*   *   *

The universe is bright.

Warmth and love and protection flare around Kaityn. They gasp. Relief: strongest, with the mellow undertones of *welcome* and *we found you!*

Kaityn blinks rapidly, trying to ground theirself in the sudden flood of emotion and light.

The ZeroGen Corps unit is suspended in a shimmery bubble. The electric bolt drifts away, freed from trajectory, left to float calm and cold in space.

"Their vitals and brain waves are stable," Horatio reports, "and it appears to be a state similar to cryo-stasis."

"You're all right," Kaityn breathes.

"I am. Are you?"

Slowly, Kaityn shifts their gaze upward.

The sky is bright with bodies of light, *the cluster*, for nur family has come to find nu.

Their chest squeezes in excitement, in wonder. A vast cloud of light, all hues and tones and shades — so many distinct selves within a whole —

We greet you, the cluster says. A chorus, a unity of voices in cascading music.

Kaityn's mouth hangs open and they slowly lift a hand towards the cluster. "Hello..."

Then nu floats beside them, free of the moon rock, and Kaityn turns their head to meet nu. Their blanket is folded neatly at their foot.

Thank you for your aid, Kaityn Falk. Nur voice is one and many.

"I... think we're... even," Kaityn manages. "You saved me, too."

Nu, and nur cluster above, stretches out a fan of synapses, tendrils of light that coil and drift in the vacuum before Kaityn's helmet.

We wish to share views from the universe as we have traveled, the cluster says.

Kaityn gasps, nods, and lets the light twirl around their helmet. "Can I see... can I see them later?" They're on the edge of a crash, overwhelmed, and they don't want to collapse under the pressure of so much input and sensation.

Whenever you choose to see, they are yours, the cluster says.

"If I may," Horatio says. "There is still the ZeroGen team to deal with.

I have logged a complaint about the hostile interaction we have experienced on Io7."

Kaityn turns back towards the suspended soldiers.

They intercepted ourself's cries when we separated, nu says. *They followed us when we fell.*

That makes sense to Kaityn. Even if ZeroGen didn't feel nur distress, the energy reading would explain how they arrived so fast, if they were already in the sector — chasing an unknown signal the way Kaityn did.

"What will you do with them?" Kaityn asks the cluster.

We will carry them back to their base of operations and release them from stasis, nu replies. *They will not be harmed, and their memories will not be tampered with. They will simply have wasted fuel and resources in this endeavor to do harm.*

Kaityn lets their breath out in relief. "Thank you. For not hurting them."

There is no value in violence, nu says. *Its sum equals only pain, and we do not wish to bring pain upon anyone. We hope, in time, your people will understand this.*

"I hope so too."

Nu floats upwards into nur cluster, is welcomed back with affection and joy, and reconnects into the synaptic threads of the whole.

The ZeroGen team is pulled gently into the light, along with their shuttle.

"Will we see each other again?" Kaityn asks.

Naturally. The cluster gives off pleasant, soothing reassurance. *We are part of the universe and so are you. We continue onward. So do you.*

"I'd like that," Kaityn says, and lifts their hand to wave. It's not goodbye; it is *until we share again.*

* * *

"This will be quite the report," Horatio says as Kaityn begins their careful walk back to their rover. They've repacked the emergency blanket and will clean moon dust off it later.

They need to lie down; the overstimulation is fast catching up to them and it will take six hours or more of sleep to compensate for the effects of the encounter. Then they will self-soothe by playing one of their favorite video games installed in their quarters: the newest *PuzzleCroft*, or the Star Harvest sim. They'll need to decompress over the next few days, too, and access Horatio's self-care subroutines to help them process all of this. They nearly died, and that isn't a shock easily brushed aside.

"GEP will be…" Kaityn leans against the hood of the rover. They're still aware of the shimmering halo-effect around their helmet, the gifted glimpses of the universe. For later, when they can savor and appreciate the offering in full.

"Excited?" Horatio offers. "This is confirmed first contact with another sentient extraterrestrial species."

Kaityn is too tired to parse the correct words. This is first contact, yes; their helm cam will display a visual and auditory record, and Horatio —

Horatio. Kaityn's face heats with sudden embarrassment. "I've never asked you if you have pronoun preference, Horatio. I'm so sorry."

"Apology accepted, and please do not berate yourself," the AI says. "While my programmers coded me as male due to, I assume, an overwhelming influence of male-ID'd droids in popular media, I've come to think of myself as ze/zir."

Their heart swells, bolstered by hope, relief, and kinship. Kaityn grins. "That's awesome."

"Indeed," ze says.

"With your corroboration and my helm feeds and report, I think GEP will believe us. Perhaps one day, nu and nur cluster will visit us all."

"That is my wish, too."

* * *

"Horatio," Kaityn asks as they steer their rover back towards their ship, "do we have any art supplies aboard?"

"Affirmative," ze replies. "GEP regulations do allow for a percentage of cargo weight to be allotted to creative pursuits vital for mental health. There are markers, paper, and a paint app tablet aboard. Plan to take up drawing?"

"More like resuming," Kaityn says. "I once told my mom that when I fly in space, I'd collect all the colors for her." They can see more shades and hue in the sky, in the dust, in the distant gleam of stars. Another small gift the cluster left them. "It's time to keep that promise."

The dark phase of the moon is turning towards the bright star, and soon it will be dawn.

This story was first published in *Uncanny: Disabled People Destroy Science Fiction!* (2018).

Merc Fenn Wolfmoor is a queer non-binary writer who lives in Minnesota with two adorable cats (Tater Tot photos frequently grace all Merc's social media). Merc is a Nebula Awards finalist, and their stories have appeared in *Lightspeed*, *Fireside*, *Apex*, *Uncanny*, *Nightmare*, *Escape Pod*, and several Year's Best anthologies. You can find Merc on Twitter **@Merc_Wolfmoor** or their website: **mercfennwolfmoor.com**. Their debut short story collection, *So You Want to Be a Robot*, was published by Lethe Press (2017) and they have a second short story collection forthcoming in late 2021.

For content notes, see page 244

What Pucks Love

by Sonni de Soto

HITASHA'S FEET CRUNCHED THE DRY, VIBRANTLY-COLORED LEAVES on the unswept sidewalk outside the place she was supposed to meet her date. Wrinkling her brow, Tasha cocked her head at the building's sign.

Faere Trade.

It was an odd name, blandly written in block letters over a plain door. This place didn't look like a cafe. With no windows and blank, stucco walls, it looked like a storage space. Truthfully, it gave her a bit of pause, making her wonder exactly what she was doing at this hole-in-the-wall.

She sighed and shook her head. She hated first dates — kinda hated the dating process as a whole. But, like it or not, there wasn't another way that she knew of to do this whole *love* business.

Not that it really seemed to be working well anyway.

She'd been doing the dating dance for a few years now and she just didn't get it. In high school, it'd all just seemed like a waste of time; it wasn't as if she would actually find the love of her life at sixteen, so what had been the point of looking? In college, no one seemed to be looking for what she was. Back then, her parents had agreed, urging her to focus on her studies rather than get distracted by frivolous romances that would inevitably fizzle.

Without her really noticing, she'd suddenly been twenty-two and had never been on a proper date. Then, she'd been twenty-four and had never been in a long-term relationship that had lasted longer than a few months. Even her mother, after her father had passed, had begun to wonder why Tasha hadn't found anyone. Tasha cringed thinking about the awkward dates her mother had set for her over the years with sons of her friends, all nice Indian boys who reminded her mother of her father one way or another.

Which was sweet, she supposed. Tasha had loved her father and missed him every day. And it'd been so hard to tell her mother that she'd felt nothing for any of those boys. She hadn't had the heart to tell her that she'd never have those feelings for the kind of man her mother dreamed of her settling down with.

Her father had always been the more conservative one, but Tasha just didn't know how to tell her mother that, at twenty-seven, her most serious relationship had been with Chloe, a research assistant whose curiosity about Tasha had lasted six months before her frustration with a lack of proper romantic results forced her to give up the experiment.

Tasha didn't blame her. Not really. They'd only had sex, or really any kind of intense physical intimacy, a handful of times in the tail-end of those six months, and usually only when Chloe's need had turned to desperation. Not the most intimate or romantic of settings. And definitely not something she could talk to her mother — or anyone, really — about.

Tasha shook her head. She just didn't understand. How did you go from strangers to soulmates after a few dates, or a few weeks, or even a few months? Shouldn't it take more time, more effort, more... something, to truly know someone enough, to trust someone enough, to mate souls?

She'd asked her mother that, once. Her mother had admitted that, when they'd been married, she hadn't been sure if she loved Tasha's father. They'd been so young; how could anyone be *sure?* But, day by day, year by year, their love had grown, filling the life they shared together.

Tasha was sure her mother had meant that to be comforting. Maybe even inspiring or aspirational. But all Tasha could think was that her parents had been lucky in a way she wondered how many people, realistically, got to be. That kind of thing just didn't happen to everyone, right?

So, yeah, staring at Faere Trade's white exterior, Tasha doubted the answer to her problems lay behind that door.

But what other choice did she have? It was either this or give in to the secret fear that the kind of love she craved, the love she needed, just didn't exist.

And she wasn't ready to give up hope yet. So, she pushed open the door and entered the cafe. Her heels clicked on the gleaming white tile floor as she walked past pale, varnished wood tables and white cushioned chairs. Happy-hour businessfolk and studious college students milled about, filling seats and sipping drinks. The walls were white too, covered with tasteful but bland black-and-white photos of the city. The whole room felt forgettable, bordering on boring.

It would have felt like just another chain coffee shop, except for the pretty flute music lilting through the space. Tasha looked around the cafe and spotted Ro, seated on a stool at the lip of a small stage, the woman's thin, pink lips pursed over an antique-looking pan flute, breathing life and song into the woodwind. For a moment, Tasha just studied her, from her pageboy hat pulled over her golden-brown curls, floppy and familiar from every photo she'd shared on the dating app, to her black-booted feet tapping in time to the song.

Tasha knew that Ro loved music; it was all over her dating profile. But hearing her play was amazing. Ro threw herself into the melody, swaying with the song's swell and flow. It was like hearing her soul.

Somehow, it put Tasha a bit at ease, reminded her that she wasn't just going on some date. She was meeting Ro, a musician she'd been talking to online for weeks now. A sci-fi fan with a wicked sense of humor and a similar outsider outlook on life as Tasha. They'd connected online, the correspondence flowing easily.

Tasha hoped it would in person as well. She knew from experience that it didn't always.

At the end of the song, she took a deep breath and made her way to the stage. "Ro?"

The woman looked up, her dark brown eyes bright with recognition. She smiled and hopped down off the stage in a graceful move. "Tasha."

With a nod, Tasha took Ro's outstretched hand, before looking around again. "You know, I used to work not far from here and I never even knew this place existed."

Ro's face flushed as she fiddled with her hat. "Well, it's not easy to find unless you know where it is." She coughed and led the way to a table in the back before pulling out a chair for Tasha. "Can I get you a drink?"

Cafe date. Drink. Right. "Umm." Tasha bit her lip and sat down. "Whatever you're getting is fine."

When Ro came back, she was carrying a small tray with a lime-green teapot and two matching teacups resting on pretty saucers. She set the beautiful tea set on the bland, white table. "Do you mind if I pour?"

Tasha shook her head. "Please." More used to cardboard Starbucks cups, she was a little intimidated by the fancier ware.

Without sitting down, Ro picked up the teapot and filled each cup with the delicious-smelling tea. Tasha reached for one of the cups, but the other woman held on to it. Tasha gave her a questioning glance before Ro sighed and sat down. "So, there's something that I want to talk to you about before we go any further."

That didn't sound good.

But, Tasha had learned that it was best to just lay out all your limits and baggage at the start. So she nodded.

Ro's fingers tensed over the saucer for a moment before holding the cup toward Tasha. Tasha breathed deep, the aroma sweet and familiar, but she couldn't quite place it. "What is it?"

"Pistachio tea."

That was it! Tasha sniffed the tea again. Yes, it smelled exactly like a pistachio cookie. She could almost taste the buttery, sweet treat. She swore she could practically feel the flaky cookie crumble in her mouth. Her hands, as if drawn, wrapped around the warm cup to pull it closer.

"Wait."

Tasha stopped.

"Listen first."

Tasha looked up, feeling dazed, as if she were waking from a dream. She pushed the teacup away. "That's not tea."

Ro picked up her own cup and took a lengthy sip. "It is." She set the cup down on the saucer. "And it's not."

Tasha shook her head. "What does that mean?"

The other woman took a deep breath before saying, "The reason you never noticed this place before I invited you is because this is a haven place."

Tasha blinked and glanced around. A haven place, huh? She'd heard the term on the news and in passing, but she'd never known anyone who'd been to one, much less seen one herself. "So everyone else here…"

"Is magical?" Ro tilted her head. "Not all of them, but," she said with a shrug, "yeah."

Tasha narrowed her gaze. "Which means you are…"

Ro nodded. Then pursed her lips. "Half." She smiled sadly. "My mom was human."

"And the rest?"

Ro winced and paused before taking a deep breath, as if readying herself. "My father is puck."

"Puck? Like *Puck* puck?"

Ro's smile tightened, making her whole face look tense. "The myth of Puck is…" She gave a slightly tired sigh. "It's somewhat based on actual pucks, pans, and satyrs, but in the same way Kung-fu movies aren't a perfect picture of Asian culture or cowboy Westerns aren't exactly American culture… you know?"

Tasha cringed. "Of course." She thought about the many times that people made all kinds of assumptions about her based on some caricature of her heritage. "Sorry."

"No." Ro grimaced. "I mean, I don't even…" She tilted her head awkwardly. "I grew up with my mom for most of my life, but she died when I was sixteen. After that, I moved in with my dad."

Tasha had lost her father too, so she understood loss, but she couldn't imagine losing a parent that young. "I'm sorry about your mother."

Ro nodded. "Thank you. But I just mean that I'm part puck, but I was raised pretty human."

Tasha got that. "I grew up in a mostly white town, so my parents thought it would be easier for me to assimilate as much as possible." At the time, it'd seemed simpler if she just kept her head down, if she made herself as much like everyone else as she could, not only for herself but for everyone. "Most of what I know about my parents' culture is from school reports and recipes."

Ro let out a breath of relief. "So you're…" She tensed. "Okay with it? With me?"

Tasha shrugged. Sure. "My friend dated a fairy once."

Ro wrinkled her nose. "It's, uh, not quite the same."

"No." Tasha felt her face redden. "Of course not." It wasn't as if she thought all magical beings were the same. "That's not what I meant." She held out her hands. "I just mean that I don't judge."

She wanted to roll her eyes. Was this what this conversation felt like on the other side? She suddenly felt a wave of sympathy for every well-intentioned white person who'd ever stuck their foot in their mouth around her. There was such a difference between knowing what *not* to say and knowing what *to* say. And she had absolutely no clue about any of it, so it was hard not to trip over all the inappropriate words she did know, no matter how hard she tried to avoid them.

She coughed. "So this tea then?" She turned the cup in her hand. "It's enchanted?"

Ro nodded. "It'll allow a human to see behind the veil of magic for about an hour or so."

Tasha wrapped her hands around the cup again, still staring at the brew a little warily. Okay. She could do this.

But before she did… "There's something I should probably tell you too."

*　*　*

Ro held her breath, knowing what was coming next. Some *Midsummer Night's Dream* fantasy. Or some humanity-first philosophy. It was the world she lived in and she'd long since learned to brace herself for it.

Tasha's grip on the teacup tightened, her long, teak fingers tapping against the vibrant green. She took a steadying breath. "I like to take relationships slowly." She looked up at Ro, her dark eyes wide and impossibly vulnerable. "Like, *really* slowly."

What did that mean? Ro couldn't even guess. "Explain that to me."

Tasha shifted in her seat, her long, thick side braid swaying a bit against her shoulder. She bit down on her bottom lip, worrying the full flesh. She sighed and shot Ro a clear *fuck it* expression. "Since we're laying it all out there, I guess you should know that pretty much every relationship I've ever been in has ended because I never feel comfortable getting... physically intimate with someone until I know them well."

Ro huffed, steeling herself a bit. "Look, I know that there's a stereotype about pucks and sex." She waved her hand dismissively. "The whole 'you know what pucks like' thing."

"What thing?"

Was she kidding? "That pucks like to..." She felt her cheeks flush. Surely, Tasha had heard the saying before. Ro had certainly grown up with people — classmates, friends, lovers, strangers — teasing and taunting her with it. She'd spent her whole life being the punchline of a lazy, rhyming sex joke.

"Oh!" Tasha's face paled as she shook her head. "Oh, no, that's not what I meant at all. I didn't mean that you —" She swallowed hard. "I just mean that I —" She took a breath. "It sounds bad, but this really is a case of 'It's not you; it's me.'" She looked so awkward, her jaw clenched and her hands tucked tightly in her lap, that it was hard not to believe her. It wasn't judgement Ro felt radiating from her; it was shame. "Truth is, I've never really felt like I've known anyone, so, you know, intimacy — all kinds, not just sex — and me just..."

Ro fought to freeze her face, not wanting to show her shock. "So." How to phrase this? "You've never..."

Tasha gave a humorless laugh. "I have; it was just..." She wrinkled her nose. "Uncomfortable."

Ro sat back thoughtfully. Okay. "So how *well* do you need to know someone before you feel comfortable?"

Tasha leaned on the table, resting her face in her hands as she stared into the tea pensively. "Well, the idea of sex never really sounded all that appealing to me. Truth be told, I often wonder what possessed the first people to even try it. It just sounds... messy and awkward and, if everything I've heard is true, often more work than it's worth."

Ro frowned. She wasn't the stereotype people thought pucks were, some sex-crazed creature constantly in heat. But she did like sex. A lot. And intimacy in general. She enjoyed kissing and cuddling and holding hands. She couldn't imagine being in a relationship without those things.

Tasha looked up, her dark eyes a little hopeful. "But the idea of making love..." She lifted her shoulder a bit, smiling sweetly. "That sounds like it could be nice. Like a physical manifestation of that feeling." Then her shoulders slumped. "But making love kinda necessitates that you *be* in love, right?"

Ro didn't believe that sex had to come packaged with love, but she understood the sentiment. She'd had enough bad romantic and sexual encounters to know that, even if it wasn't love per se, sex went down better with at least affection and trust.

And a little foresight, if one could find it, never killed anyone.

So Ro bit her lip, still a little hesitant even as a plan began to form in her head. "I think I might have an idea about that."

Tasha arched her eyebrow. "About what?"

"About knowing someone." For all its troubles, some days, being puck had its advantages.

The other woman's eyes narrowed suspiciously. "What do you mean?"

Ro rolled her shoulders, a bit uncomfortably. "Pucks and pans have some prophetic abilities." She held up her hands cautiously. "I'm not great at it but I could show you, if you want."

Incredulity still sharpened her gaze, but Tasha leaned in with interest. "Show me what?"

Tasha would like this, Ro was sure of it. Or at least she hoped Tasha would. One could never know for certain until they were in it. But Tasha had questions, had doubts, and Ro could give them both answers. Tasha just had to give it a chance. Grinning, Ro cocked her head invitingly. "What it's like to make love."

*   *   *

Tasha stiffened indignantly. This was the weirdest date she'd ever been on. "So when I said that I like to move slowly, you thought the first date would be the best time to try to get me into bed?" Had she not been listening at all?

Ro shook her head. "I'm not trying to get into your bed." She picked up her tea and took a sip. "I'm trying to get into your head."

Uh-huh. Tasha snorted and instinctively took a sip.

But the second the sweet brew touched her tongue, the world changed.

The black and white cafe burst into brilliant color. The backs of varnished wood chairs bloomed into looming, leafy trees that canopied the cafe. Even the scent of the place was different, the aroma of coffee and pastries mixed with more earthy smells like rain, mud, and growth. The soft jazz music that had been playing over speakers stopped, replaced by lilting live music playing that reminded Tasha of whatever flowing song Ro had played before, echoing not just in her eardrums but in her soul.

The voices in the cafe had changed as well. The quiet chatter became a strange harmony of sounds, some higher or lower than human vocal cords were capable of. Some spoke languages Tasha didn't recognize. She looked around. The business execs in suits were all gone and in their place were people with scales and fur and feathers chatting to each other or on phones. The student, nose-deep in a book, suddenly had wings that fluttered to the beat of the music streaming through her headphones. A strange sound made Tasha turn. She gawked at a gargoyle — this small, gray, compact creature that looked so stony they shouldn't have been able to move — in an apron, of all things, as they bussed tables.

"Try not to stare."

Tasha dropped her gaze immediately. She wasn't entirely sure she wanted to see more anyway. "So everyone here is…"

"Magical?" Ro's voice sounded tired and a little sad. "Mostly. There are quite a few staff members who are half-human, like me, and at least one person I know of who is fully human. I don't think he's on shift today though. But, like I said, this is a haven place — a place for magical people to be who they are without worry. We don't have to wear glamours or hide here because the whole place is hidden from everyone but us."

"Is it okay that I'm here?" Tasha didn't want to cause trouble or anything.

Ro nodded. "You were invited."

"And if I wasn't?"

"You wouldn't be here." Ro pointed to runes carved and painted in the cafe's corners. "Haven places have layers and layers of spells — glamours and way-wards and protection charms — so humans don't notice them."

Tasha studied the runes, amazed by the magic. "And now that I know it's here?"

Ro shook her head. "Without an invitation, the human mind can't see past the spell." When Tasha looked at her skeptically, she continued, "Have you ever woken up from a dream and tried to fall back into it? You can try, but it's not really up to you."

That sounded convenient. And a little terrifying. "So why invite me in the first place?"

Ro fidgeted a bit. "Being magical in the human world is a double-edged sword. Some humans look at us and see the stuff of dreams. Others see…"

Nightmares.

Ro gestured to the cafe. "Haven places give us a safe space to see and be seen."

It was a way to test who could be trusted and who couldn't. Given the recent rise of humanity-first rhetoric, Tasha supposed she could understand the need for caution. "And the tea?"

There was a pause before Ro sighed. "Is part of a seeing spell. So you can see the world as it is." Another pause. "So you can see me as I am."

In her head, Tasha ran through all the pictures on Ro's profile. Her hat. Her sparkling eyes. The wild twist of her hair. The blush of her cheeks. And that smile. She thought about every email and message and chat they'd shared. Every fandom they'd gushed over. Every memory — office gossip, past relationship stories, exchanges with friends — they'd shared. She thought about every time she'd imagined what Ro might be like in the moments building up to this date.

"Tasha?"

Swallowing hard, Tasha looked over at Ro, who'd taken off her hat and coat and was shaking out her curls. Two slim, short, blunted horns peeked out from the silken cloud atop her head. Her shoulders and arms were covered in soft-looking wool a shade or two lighter than her hair. Her eyes, which had been dark brown, now seemed more like dusk falling over the city. Endless umber burned and blended with plums and wine, while the promise of sunlight hid beneath the dark.

Magic.

Shyly, Ro smiled, the expression on her face like a resigned *ta-da*. She tousled her bronze hair nervously. "Hi."

Tasha felt her stomach clench, not unpleasantly. Though still a bit weakly, she smiled back. "Hi."

Ro coughed and rubbed her arms, disturbing the tight, short curls, too casually. "Not too weird?"

Tasha took in the woman sitting across from her. Sure, Ro did not look the way she had in her profile pics. But, even with her limited dating history, Tasha knew that was true of most non-magical people too. And, while she didn't look the way Tasha had expected, she somehow looked exactly how she should.

This was Ro.

So, Tasha shook her head. "Not too weird."

Ro gave a small laugh, her shoulders sinking a bit in relief. "You say that now." She cocked an eyebrow and laid her hands palms-up on the table. "Want to see if that's still true after seven years or so?"

Tasha tilted her head curiously. "It won't be real, though, right?" They'd only just met.

"It'll just be in our heads, but it'll let us see what our future could be like, if we were to go down that path."

Did she want to? Even just imaginatively?

They'd just met, but if she did this, Tasha would see what getting to know Ro would be like. She'd literally be able to know, on the first date, whether things could work out or not.

Tasha held the bespelled teacup in her hands. "The magic only lasts an hour?"

Ro nodded.

"After that, your world goes back to the way it was."

She could do this. See what it was like. A part of her — a part she rarely let herself listen to — always wondered if there was a scenario that would feel intimate enough. If she'd ever experience the kind of love she longed for, if it even existed.

If there was ever a chance to take a leap of faith, wasn't this it? Looking around the strange, beautiful, amazing cafe, how could she not at least want to believe?

So, taking a deep breath, Tasha sat up straight. Setting aside the cup, she held out her hands, so clammy and cold she wanted to apologize. But instead, she pressed her palms against Ro's and said, "Show me."

* * *

It was the curse of threes.

Ro watched Tasha worry her bottom lip between her teeth and crinkle the menu in her shaking hands. Ro shook her head, wondering how Tasha could still be so nervous after three months of dating.

She'd been like this on their third date too. Tasha had been terrified that Ro would be expecting the traditional Third Date Kiss. Instead, very aware of her fears, Ro had spent the whole night warming Tasha's cold, clammy hands in hers. It wasn't that Ro hadn't *wanted* to kiss Tasha. But watching the credits roll with Tasha's warm, soft hand in hers had felt more intimate than most of the kisses she'd shared with others.

She'd hoped that would have wordlessly reminded Tasha that they weren't on a timetable. They didn't have to play by anyone's traditions.

Yet, three months later, here they were.

Ro wondered if they'd have an awkward three-year anniversary dinner as well. Now that was a thought. Honestly, she didn't think she could handle it if they were still dealing with this after another three years. Because, underneath the neurotic worry over numbers, she knew the real underlying anxiety.

Apparently, in the dating world, every milestone happened in threes. The kiss on the third date. Sex after three months. Marriage or moving in by the three-year mark. A bunch of rules that apparently everyone was expected to know and adhere to. And that Tasha could not.

Ro had deliberately picked a restaurant they'd been to several times. A familiar space that might not be *their* place, but could be one day. Sighing, Ro pried the menu from Tasha's grip. "You know what you want. You always get the avocado turkey melt, light mayo, with tater tots instead of fries and either a strawberry shake or a Coke. Either way, you've been looking at that menu too hard for too long." She reached out and laid her hand palm up to her. "Talk to me."

Tasha frowned and stared at Ro's hand, unsure. "I know that you said we're okay." She swallowed and clutched her hands together tightly. "That you're okay, but..." She shook her head.

After years of being told the opposite, it would be hard for someone like Tasha to believe.

Ro didn't know how to fix that. Wasn't even sure she could. She was pretty sure this was one of those things Tasha had to change for herself. But Ro hoped she could help. "What are you afraid of?" Because Tasha clearly was.

Tasha scoffed. "What?"

"What are you afraid of?" Ro reached for the easy answer. "That I'll leave if we don't follow some arbitrary timetable sold to us by romance novels and *Cosmo*?"

Tasha let out a small chuckle. "So we're okay?"

Ro smiled. "We're okay."

"And you're not disappointed by waiting?"

You're not disappointed by me? Ro could hear the unasked question hanging over them. How to answer? She didn't want to lie, but the truth felt terribly complicated. She laid her hand on the table again, open and inviting. She waited until Tasha took it, pressed their hands together palm-to-palm, before smiling. "I want to kiss you, Tasha. I want to hold you and caress you and, yes, I want to sleep with you. And I have since we were just avatars on a dating site to each other."

Tasha's face scrunched and she started to slip her hand away.

But Ro held firm, still gentle yet with purpose. She held still and waited while Tasha decided whether to tug her hand away or stay. She was glad when Tasha took a steadying breath, held her hand, and looked into her eyes. Ro smiled. "But, more than that, I want you to want that." That was the truth. Ro felt it, fully, in every word. She let her thumb caress circles over the back of Tasha's hand, feeling her bones held together beneath the soft, resilient skin. "I want to wait for that."

For a moment, Tasha's hand tensed and her face creased with worry. "What if that never happens?" Her voice was so quiet.

Because *that* was what really scared Tasha. Oddly, it didn't scare Ro. Maybe it should. There were no guarantees that it would happen.

But it could. And neither of them could know. Until they did.

Ro swallowed. Okay, yeah, that was a little scary. But that just meant it mattered. And that was good, right?

Ro looked at their entwined hands. Yeah, this was pretty good.

"I'm willing to stick around to find out." She wrapped both their hands with her other one. "Are you?"

Tasha bit her lip, but nodded and smiled. "We're okay."

*   *   *

Sitting on the couch, both lounging across the overstuffed armrests, Tasha could tell Ro's mind was not on the TV show. She turned to sit cross-legged on the broken-in cushion and faced her girlfriend. "What are you thinking?"

Ro shook her head. "Nothing. Just a weird thought."

Tasha arched an eyebrow. "About what?"

Ro rolled her eyes. "You really want to know?"

That felt evasive. It made Tasha wonder if she did. She nodded but held her breath when Ro let out a heavy sigh.

Ro shrugged her shoulders awkwardly before turning to face Tasha too. "I need more from our relationship."

More? Tasha let out her breath slowly. She shouldn't have been surprised. Ro had lasted longer than most — had been more than beyond patient, unlike anyone else Tasha had known. She shouldn't be surprised.

This shouldn't hurt.

Ro held out her hands. "Don't get me wrong. I like being with you and I don't want to change or rush you." She sighed and slumped her shoulders. "But I need something more. I need to know that we're moving forward. That, no matter how nice things are with us right now, there's more for us. I'd like to see if we can come up with some kind of compromise."

"Like what?" Tasha crossed her arms over her chest, having heard this all before. Did Ro want to *just try* sex, sure that Tasha would feel differently about it, while in the moment? Did she want her to push past her reservations and just *fake it till you make it* her way through?

"Do you touch yourself?"

Tasha straightened. "What?"

Ro blushed, but repeated, "Do you touch yourself? And not just, you know, here." She made sweeping gestures over her torso, from breasts to lap. "But everywhere."

"I…" Tasha felt her cheeks flush. "I'm not really comfortable with that."

"With talking about it?" Ro leaned forward. "Or doing it?"

Tasha shrugged. "All of it."

Ro pursed her lips and nodded, like she'd been expecting that answer. "Do you want to stop talking about it?"

Yes. Except. "I don't like talking about it, but I feel like we should."

"We don't have to, if you don't want to."

Tasha knew that. But she could feel all their unsaid words swirl like a cold, dense fog between them. Was that really doing either of them any good? Better to just have the fight, then deal with the consequences. If this was the end of them, well, better to know that now too. Tasha braced herself. "Just say it."

Ro sat quietly for a long moment as if struggling with the same fog Tasha felt. "You told me that you aren't comfortable getting intimate with someone unless you really know them, right?"

Tasha nodded.

"Then don't you want to get to know yourself?" Ro's hands fisted and she dropped her gaze. "I'm afraid to touch you. Because I don't want to cross any of your boundaries. I keep waiting for you to tell me what you're comfortable with, but it just occurred to me that maybe you don't know. And both of us not knowing what feels good to you isn't a great place to start building intimacy, right? I hate the idea of you having to tell me if something I've done feels wrong; I'd rather hear you ask me for what feels right. I mean, wouldn't you like to know what feels good to you?" She peeked up at Tasha. "I know I would."

Tasha opened her mouth, but promptly shut it. She'd never really thought of it like that. For so long, touching herself, like so many other things, had felt like one more expectation, one more obligation she couldn't meet. One more so-called *natural, normal* part of being human that she didn't understand.

Sure, she'd tried it before and felt more confused and frustrated than anything. So she'd stopped.

But maybe instead of thinking of it as trying to figure out what the fuss was, what other people got out of it, maybe she ought to just think of it as trying to understand herself more. Think of it as getting to know herself.

"No pressure." Ro turned her attention back to the screen. "We don't have to do anything right now. Like I said, it was just a random thought."

One that, without any obligation or baggage weighing it down, Tasha thought might be worth exploring. She sat back on the couch and stared at the TV screen. Maybe. Without turning away from the show, she cleared her throat. "I'm not sure how I like to be touched." But, Ro was right, she would like to know. "But, until I do…" She took a deep breath. "Can I, maybe, touch you?"

She felt the cushions shift beneath her as Ro straightened on the couch. "How would you like to?"

Tasha's face burned with embarrassment. This was why she'd always avoided conversations like this. But Ro was right; nothing would ever change unless she did. "I like holding your hand."

Out of the corner of her eye, she saw Ro reach out a hand to her.

Tasha grasped it, feeling the tension between them begin to ease. "This is okay?"

She knew Ro wanted more, needed more. But this was something, a step forward; the question was whether it was enough.

Ro squeezed her hand. "It's great."

* * *

Listening to music and lounging on the couch with Tasha, Ro waited for her roti dough to rest and tried not to think too much about tonight. Dinner with Tasha's mom, who didn't quite like Ro — yet — but who was at least beginning to appreciate that she made Tasha happy. Ro knew that she wasn't most people's idea of a perfect partner for their child — much less Tasha's traditional parents — but, for Tasha, Ro would do her best.

And it wasn't as if she could have made a worse first impression. Being puck, Ro had never *had* to come out. Fluid and free sexuality had been a given in her household. If anything, the idea of trying to explain the *lack* of sex in her relationship with Tasha would probably blow her dad's mind.

But, for Tasha, it'd been different. She'd never told her parents about her sexual orientation. When Ro had asked her why, she'd said it'd never felt like she had to. Why would she, when she'd never dated anyone of any gender long enough to want to introduce them to her parents?

Until Ro. This white, half-puck woman who was about as far as you could get from the nice, Indian boys Tasha said her mother used to set her up with.

Yet, despite the awkward memories of that first meeting, of trying to explain their relationship to Tasha's mom, Ro found herself smiling. She kinda liked being the only one Tasha had deemed important enough to take that step with. It made her feel honored, special.

It made her want to *be* special. Ro's dad firmly believed that the best way to ingratiate yourself to people was by bringing them an offering, and her mother believed that good food always made the best gift. Ro just hoped her roti tasted as good as Tasha's mom's.

Nervously, Ro tapped the rhythm of the song playing through her headphones against the sole of Tasha's foot.

"Hey!" Tasha yanked her foot back. "Massages, not tickles."

Ro smiled sheepishly. "Sorry, you know me and really good refrains; I lose my head."

Tasha rolled her eyes. "Now I've lost my place in my book." She swiped her finger across her tablet. But, even as she grumbled, she straightened her leg so her foot fell into Ro's waiting hands. A not-so-subtle sign.

Well, yes, ma'am.

So, with fifteen minutes left until she had to check on her dough, Ro resumed rubbing the supple flesh, feeling the stress of Tasha's day melt away in her hands. Tasha moaned as she worked a particularly stubborn knot. It shouldn't have been a big deal, but that small sound — accompanied by the tensing then loosening of Tasha's muscles — hit her hard.

It was such a small thing. A comfortable kind of closeness. Almost an insignificant intimacy. With any other person, Ro would have taken it for granted.

But, with Tasha, it felt different. Like a treasure discovered or a truth known.

* * *

Tasha trailed Ro by a few steps as they headed back to the car from Faere Trade.

Ro crushed her hat to her head. "I told you that would be a bad idea."

Tasha sighed. "I just wanted my friends to see your world, so they'd stop being so worried about me."

"Your friend couldn't stop staring at everyone — including me — like we were some kind of exhibit at a zoo or a circus. And her boyfriend kept accusing me of the worst stereotypes."

Richard had not been happy about having to drink the tea to see past the magic. He kept asking about ingredients and FDA ratings.

Ro turned on Tasha. "What did you tell them about me? They practically accused me of abducting you, drugging you. Taking advantage of you. Questioning why someone like me was even with someone like you when 'everyone knows what pucks like.' As if all I am is a pair of horns and an out-of-control sex drive."

Tasha winced. She knew what it was like to have people think they knew everything they needed to know about you just by taking one look. It wasn't something she'd wish on anyone. Much less Ro. And by her friends!

Ro shook her head. "Maude is your best friend and *that's* what she thinks of me. How is it that all they see when they look at me is bad storytelling and fear-based folklore?" Her gaze narrowed on Tasha, her jaw set and her eyes watery. "And if that's all they see, how do I not wonder, when you look at me, what exactly *you* see?"

Tasha didn't know what to say to that. Of course, she didn't think that. They both knew she didn't; they wouldn't be together if she did. But there wasn't a way to defend herself without sounding, well, defensive. As if the problem was Ro not understanding her rather than Tasha's friends not understanding Ro. And that was Tasha's fault. "I'm sorry. I should have listened to you."

She'd talked to Maude and Richard about Ro, tried to prepare them. Or at least she thought she had. Maude was her best friend and Ro was important to her; of course, she'd told Maude everything. How much fun they had together. How sweet and funny and talented Ro was. How even her mom was coming around about their relationship. How patient Ro had been with her. How comfortable — even eager — she made

Tasha feel. How so many things that had in the past seemed obligatory or tedious or even nerve-wracking felt right with Ro.

And she'd thought that Maude understood. She'd said that she did. She'd been excited and happy for Tasha.

But somewhere between suspicions over spell-spiked tea and seeing gargoyles and fairies and pucks for the first time, all that happy excitement had given way to all the supernatural-panic news stories and humanity-first political rhetoric bombarding them from the media.

Ro had told her that would happen, and Tasha had assured her that Maude and Richard were different. That Tasha was different. That she could *make* it different.

Tasha sighed as they approached the car. "I'm so sorry."

Ro walked over to the driver's side door. "I just want to go home."

Alone. She didn't say it. She didn't have to.

Tasha bit her lip. "A musician."

Ro looked up from her keys. "What?"

"You asked what I see when I look at you. I see a musician who can make me laugh or cry or wonder with a song. I see a geek who loves space operas over superheroes because stuffing old mythology into capes and spandex doesn't make tired stories new. I see someone who held my hand while I came out to my mom and who learned to make my mom's roti and naan, and her own aunt's pita and baklava, to bring all of us closer. And I see a woman who's loved me for months now, but never pressured me while I figure out what love means to me." She smiled, her own eyes beginning to tear up. "And I'm so sorry I couldn't make them see that too."

For a long moment, Ro just looked at her. Tasha fought not to squirm, suddenly very curious what Ro saw. She wondered whether Ro thought Tasha was worth the effort.

But then Ro smiled. She opened the car door and unlocked the passenger side. "Let's go home."

* * *

Ro opened her eyes. "Good morning."

Tasha was touching the vale between Ro's breasts, where her wool was naturally thin, more a soft peach fuzz than the full curls that covered most of the rest of her body. The unprotected skin there was sensitive and tingled with each brush of Tasha's lazy fingers.

Ro smiled and stretched, wriggling beneath the slow tease. "What are you thinking for breakfast?"

Tasha paused thoughtfully before pressing her lips to Ro's shoulder. "Pancakes?"

Ro felt Tasha's hands stroke down her belly. "With turkey bacon?"

"Mmmm. And eggs."

Ro's eyes fluttered shut at the sweetly insisting feel of Tasha parting her thighs, making room for herself between Ro's legs. "Scrambled?"

Tasha shook her head then nipped the spot on Ro's inner, upper thigh, just at the wool-line. The spot that she knew drove Ro crazy. "Poached." She licked that sensitive bit of skin. "Just a little runny."

Ro bit back a groan. "Hash browns would go better with that than pancakes." She imagined the thick, flowing yolk soaking the warm potatoes, practically tasting it on her tongue.

Tasha placed a kiss below her belly, just above her mound. "But I'm craving something sweet." She nuzzled the thicker, coarser curls between her legs. "All that melted butter and warm syrup." She made a low hungry sound.

Ro gripped the sheets at her sides. That did sound good.

The tip of Tasha's tongue dipped between the folds of Ro's labia, teasing the ready flesh and making Ro groan.

It had taken a long time to get here, but as Tasha slipped a finger deep inside her, Ro knew it'd been worth it.

Tasha licked and nipped at her, as she thrust within her. Heat bubbled throughout Ro's whole body, spilling in aching sounds from her throat and liquid heat from her core. Pressure built and built inside her, threatening to snap.

And then it did.

Sensation flowed and rushed through her, overwhelming her. Her body shook and shuddered as pleasure stole her breath. The intensity of it, like a psychic burst inside her, was so much she felt lost within it.

Until Tasha's gentle weight settled on Ro's chest, grounding her to the bed. Ro clutched Tasha to her, clinging to her soft steadiness, while her rocked world settled.

With a smug smile on her face, Tasha smacked a kiss to Ro's lips. "Now *that's* a good morning."

Ro laughed and kissed her back. She hugged her tight around the waist, squeezing an excited squeak from that sweet mouth. "Yeah, well, you certainly do know what pucks like."

*   *   *

Tasha blinked, staring at the cafe again. She could still feel everything. Even as the memories, the exact details of it all, began to fade.

She wanted to cling to the memories, wanted to fight to keep them.

But, no matter how hard she tried to focus her mind, she couldn't.

"Why can't I remember it?" It was so frustrating to be able to remember the feelings the experience evoked, but not the experience itself. It was like something that was never really hers had been stolen from her. It shouldn't hurt, but damned if it wasn't tearing her apart.

Ro rubbed the backs of Tasha's hands. "It's easy to create a fantasy." She shrugged wistfully. "Much harder to live it."

Tasha frowned. "Was any of it real?" It'd felt real. Almost more real than the rest of her life. But now... Her mind felt so muddled. "Was that really you? Really me?"

Ro nodded. "My sight lets me see and show potential futures. It shows what, given the two of us together, might happen. It was really you, really me." She tilted her head hopefully, her hair shifting to show more of her horns beneath the curls. "So, if you want, it — or something like it — could be real."

Tasha nodded back. She took a sip of her tea, more to give her hands and lips something to do while her mind tried to puzzle this all together. She set down the cup. "That all happened in less than an hour."

The corners of Ro's lips lifted a bit wryly. "A whole lifetime in less than twenty minutes."

"You know, even after all that, it'll take a lot longer than twenty minutes for me to feel comfortable enough to get intimate with you again, right?" Warm feelings aside, it wasn't as if anything had concretely changed. They were still virtually strangers. In the fantasy, they may have known everything about each other; in reality, they still didn't. She didn't want to say how long it would take because she didn't really know — it just had to feel right — and she didn't want to scare Ro away. But she also didn't want to make promises that she couldn't keep. Tasha forced a laugh, trying to lighten the mood when she felt so weighed down by her insecurities. "And you know what pucks like."

Ro nodded and looked at her, really looked at her. She gripped Tasha's hands in hers tightly. "Yeah, you."

Sonni de Soto is a queer storyteller of color, who believes that the romance and speculative genres too often don't get the credit they deserve. They tell us a lot about humanity. What we desire and fear. Our values and taboos. They allow us to explore sides of ourselves that we can't anywhere else. They allow us, as storytellers, to showcase the soul. de Soto has had the privilege of publishing novels and stories with Cleis Press, SinCyr Publishing, and many others. To find more from her, please visit **instagram.com/sonni_de_soto** and **patreon.com/sonnidesotoallaccess**.

For content notes, see page 244

Gold Medal, Scrap Metal

by Lauren Ring

CAMERAS FLASHED THROUGHOUT THE CHEERING CROWD, lighting up the lunar night as Jinx Montoya's gleaming hovercar barreled down the home stretch. As the finish line loomed ahead, Jinx pushed her thruster to its limit, trading stability for a little more power. This was going to be close. Another racer clung to her side as tightly as a bumper sticker, threatening her hard-earned lead and pushing the limits of safe flying distance.

Jinx set her jaw and tightened her grip on the controls. The other driver should have known better than to play chicken with her. As the star rookie of the Luna Circuit, the media darling and the sponsorship idol, Jinx had too much to lose. Besides, Prilla deserved a champion, not some loser who washed out in the semifinals.

Instead of swerving away and sacrificing her speed, Jinx edged toward the other hovercar, close enough to touch. Close enough to crash. The hovercars flew wingtip to wingtip for one exhilarating moment.

Then Jinx pulled ahead and sped to victory.

The semifinals were over at last. Adrenaline pumped through her veins like lightning as she climbed out of her hovercar, slapping it on its side before the pit crew pulled it away. One more win and it would all be worth it. She would finally be worthy.

143

When she returned to her garage and saw the grim expressions on her crew's faces, the thrill of the race faded. Jinx had won, yes, but barely. The finals next week would be full of faster, better racers. If she lost her edge now, she was doomed.

Jinx stripped off her racing suit and flung aside her helmet. Outside, the lunar paparazzi swarmed like flies, surrounding the garage with a buzz of chatter. Jinx frowned. She loved attention — basked in it, even — but only on her terms. These cameramen were nothing if not predatory.

"Montoya," her coach called. "The press want me to do an interview, unless you're finally willing to talk to them. You gonna survive on your own or do I need to call a babysitter?"

Jinx flipped her off, shrugged on a camera-blocking dazzler hoodie, and headed out. She needed something to help her clinch the lead, and there was one place she could always count on for the rarest spare parts. She just had to go down to Earth for a while.

It was a short flight to the terran surface with the latest in lunar transport tech. Jinx touched down near her best-kept secret: the Castle Junkyard. She had to take a long, winding path from the landing pad to shake off the few cameramen who had managed to follow her, and the heat of the day clung to her, inescapable. Still, it was all worth it when she arrived.

Outside the Castle, heaps of scrap metal and spare parts gleamed like jewels in the sunlight. A neon dragon flickered above it all, breathing pixelated fire that spelled out *DEALS DEALS DEALS*. The crenellated towers of the front office cast cool shadows across Jinx's face. As a child, she had sworn that if she climbed them, she could touch the clouds.

The rusty bell on the door jingled as Jinx walked in, a far cry from the tech she was used to up on the moon. The store itself was full of an eclectic mix of new and old, from real gas engines to a mag drive only a few years out of date. To the side, a huge window looked out over the expanse of the junkyard.

Jinx pulled off her hood and headed to the counter, where an older man fiddled with the settings on his holo display.

"Is the princess here?"

"In the back." He didn't bother to look up from his display. Jinx was the only one who used that nickname.

"Thank you, my liege." Jinx swept into a mocking bow before heading around the counter to the back room.

The scent of motor oil filled the hot afternoon air, and fumes stung Jinx's eyes. She blinked away tears, and when her vision cleared, there was Prilla.

Prilla, the princess of the junk castle, stood next to a motorcycle that looked older than the lunar expansion. Her golden locks were swept back in a bandana as pale pink as a peony, and her plump cheeks were rosy red from exertion. She wore her usual overalls and a heavy flannel shirt, both featuring hand-embroidered petals: her signature.

Prilla often made her own clothes, since most of the plus-size fashion down on Earth wasn't suited to her taste. The best styles could only be found in expensive lunar boutiques. Anything affordable was either limited to straight-sizes or about as attractive as a rusty hubcap, according to Prilla. She wanted to *shine*.

"Hey, princess." Jinx hooked her thumbs into her pockets and leaned against the entryway. "Where'd you find that little showpiece?"

Prilla looked up from her handlebar repairs and huffed.

"Jinx Montoya," she said, "haven't I told you not to bother me when I'm working?"

"Sorry." Jinx stepped forward. She wanted to ask about fixing up her hovercar, but cutting to the chase would mean less time with Prilla. "I thought maybe I could lend a hand."

"The famous Jinx, dirtying her hands?" Prilla giggled. "A minute with you costs more than a hundred of these bikes. Don't waste your time."

"It's not wasting it if I'm spending it with you." Jinx shot Prilla a dazzling grin. Prilla rolled her eyes and bent back over the bike. She was immune to Jinx's charm — they'd known each other for too long. Prilla wasn't some fan Jinx could woo with an autograph and a smile. Prilla was the bubbly lightness of lunar gravity and the roar of engines on the home stretch. Jinx wouldn't dare make a real move without at least one championship title.

"All right, champion, pass me that socket wrench." Prilla stuck out a hand and wiggled her fingers at a nearby table. Jinx obeyed, flushing a little at the nickname. Prilla wasn't reading her mind, though. She was referring back to their schoolyard games of princess and champion, when Jinx had always valiantly fought for Prilla's honor.

"Yes, ma'am." Jinx handed over the wrench. Prilla took it, then paused. "Why did you really come here?"

"I wanted to see you."

"Be honest." Prilla kept staring down at the engine. "You must have more exciting things to do up there on the moon."

"It's not all that great." Jinx shifted uncomfortably. She wanted nothing more than to sweep Prilla away on a grand lunar vacation, but that would mean exposing her to the prying eyes of the media. What kind of champion would Jinx be if she let the paparazzi get hold of her princess? The tabloids were never kind to anyone she associated with. It could get messy, and then both of their reputations would be destroyed.

"I can always tell when you're lying." Prilla put her hands on her hips. "Spill it, Jinx."

"Well, you probably saw the news this morning." Jinx rubbed the back of her neck. "I didn't do so hot in the race."

"Didn't you win?"

"Barely. I need to do better if I'm going to make it through the finals next week."

"And you need me to help you out again." Prilla sighed and set aside her wrench. Then she smiled, making Jinx's heart flutter. "Well, what are you waiting for? Let's go junk hunting."

With the push of a button, the garage door rattled upward, revealing the sun-drenched stacks of steel that lay only steps away. Jinx was breathing in the scents of Earth dirt and desert air when Prilla grabbed her hand and tugged her forward into the junkyard.

It took Jinx a moment to process the fact that they were holding hands. The heat of skin on skin almost overwhelmed her. She stumbled forward, holding tight to Prilla's oil-smeared hand as Prilla weaved deftly through the heaps, stopping here and there to pick through the debris.

Jinx's thoughts drifted into fantasy. She pictured facing a cheering crowd, slinging one arm around Prilla's waist while holding her championship trophy high. The paparazzi and their flashing cameras stayed at a respectful distance — this was Jinx's fantasy, and she got to make the rules — while shouting their praise and adoration.

"How about this?" Prilla held up a dented piece of equipment. Right. Not a winner yet. Jinx shook the daydream from her mind. "You need a new mag drive?"

"New?" Jinx pointed at the dent in the drive.

"I'm doing my best here." Prilla pouted. "Someday, Jinx, I'd like you to visit just to take me out to lunch."

Jinx's cheeks flushed hot as she realized her mistake.

"We could go to lunch," she stammered. "I didn't realize you would want to."

"You really need to come down to Earth, and I mean that both ways." Prilla tossed aside the dented drive and kept walking. Jinx hurried to catch up.

"Princess — Prilla — I'm sorry, I thought you were too busy for me these days. You work so hard."

"I could say the same about you." Prilla picked up part of a coolant rig. She looked it over, then set it back down. "I always assume you're off partying with moon models and drinking free champagne."

"Only when I win."

"Right, right. That's why you're here."

"That's not what I meant." Jinx rubbed her forehead. She was sweating again, and not just from the heat. "It's not all fun and games up there. Half the time I'm just wishing I was down here with you, like old times."

Prilla crossed her arms. There was a softness in her eyes that vanished when she blinked hard. Jinx began to realize how much of Prilla's life she had missed in her long lunar absences.

They kept searching, but the heat of the day was fierce, and it soon overwhelmed Jinx. She sat down on the wing of a junked spaceship, took off her dazzler hoodie, and tied it around her waist, letting the slight breeze play across her toned arms. Prilla hesitated, then joined her. Together, they stared up at the clear blue sky, marked only by jet trails and distant rocket launches.

"Remember when we were kids?" Jinx asked, still looking away from Prilla. "We'd run around with old antennas, swordfighting 'til it got dark. You'd ride on the back of my bike past the hovercar track and tell me someday I'd be out there too."

Prilla sniffled.

"Prilla?" Jinx glanced over to find her wiping away tears. "Did I say something wrong?"

"No, I'm all right." Prilla managed a small smile. "I really thought you were gone, Jinx. It's been so long since we talked like this. Every time you visit, it's just for parts."

"I'm sorry." Jinx wanted to tell her the real reason for her visits, but she couldn't, not yet. She had to be a real champion first. Everything was all tied up together, the finals and Prilla and the moon and the junkyard, but they were almost to the finish line. "I'll be a better friend from now on, I promise. I'll work harder on that than on racing."

"As if," Prilla laughed. "I'd be happy to be your second priority, though."

"All right. It's a deal."

There was a bright flash in the distance. Jinx squinted, trying to find its source among the glints and reflections of the junkyard, but Prilla's gasp drew her attention away.

"Look!" Prilla cried, kneeling at the back of the spaceship wing. "This thruster is still intact. I bet I could jury-rig it to propel your hovercar."

"How long would that take?" Jinx bent over the wing and helped Prilla pry out the thruster.

"Bring her down here tomorrow and I'll have the fix ready for the finals." Prilla hefted the thruster over one shoulder. The bright afternoon sun struck her bandana, making its pink cloth glow golden like a crown. Jinx never wanted to stop looking at her.

They headed back to the garage in comfortable silence. Prilla's tears had dried, and Jinx was busy daydreaming about lapping her competitors and streaking across the finish line. She had fought so hard for so long for this victory, and she was so close she could almost feel the engine thrumming in her ears. If only Prilla could be there, waiting just past the checkered flag...

Back in the garage, Prilla tucked the thruster under her workbench and picked up the socket wrench once more.

"I'll see you tomorrow," she said, tucking a curl behind her ear.

"Tomorrow," Jinx echoed, her eyes fixed on the curl.

That night, Jinx tossed and turned, her thoughts a whirlwind of stress. Sure, Prilla wanted to see her more, but what if she didn't like what she saw? Jinx wasn't as carefree and suave as she wanted to be, but none of the models she danced with ever cared to look past her mystique. They only saw the charming hovercar racer at the top of her game. Prilla knew the young child and the scruffy teen. Soon she would also know the worried wreck.

Jinx awoke the next day at the crack of dreary dawn, ready to supervise the transfer of her hovercar to the Castle. Her anxieties had faded with sleep, and she was optimistic about the upgrades Prilla had planned. Standing there in her apartment, facing the Earth from high above, she felt victorious already.

She of all people should have known better than to jinx herself.

The transport itself was flawless. There wasn't a single scratch on the glossy hull of Jinx's hovercar. The Castle's garage was open and ready. But Prilla wasn't there.

"Tom?" Jinx peered into the front room. "Where's the princess?"

"Should be in the back. She's on the clock." The man at the counter didn't look up from his holo display.

Puzzled, Jinx returned to the garage. With the movers gone, she could now hear the faint sound of crying coming from the connected bathroom.

"Prilla?" Jinx knocked on the door. "What's wrong?"

"Jinx?" Prilla yanked the door open. She had a crumpled tissue in one fist, but she looked more angry than sad.

"What happened?" Jinx demanded, trying to make herself seem bigger, taller, more protective. Prilla didn't respond. "Who do I have to fight?"

Prilla sighed and her shoulders slumped. The anger went out of her eyes, which worried Jinx even more. Jinx held out her arms and, when Prilla nodded, swept her into a tight hug.

"I'm sorry," Prilla whispered into Jinx's ear. Jinx squeezed tighter, trying to stop herself from crying too.

"Don't be sorry, princess. Whatever happened, it won't happen again."

"It was the tabloids."

The pit dropped out of Jinx's stomach like a hovercar with a failing mag drive. She stepped back, clinging to Prilla's hands.

"What did they say?" she asked, as softly as she could.

"It was pictures of us." Prilla's tears flowed freely as she spoke. "In the junkyard. All the headlines were — well, they wanted to know what a star like you was doing with someone like me. They said I was a distraction from racing, and then they started changing your odds. I'm sorry, Jinx, I didn't mean to cause any problems."

"Prilla, you didn't deserve that." Jinx gritted her teeth and pushed aside her fears about taking a sponsorship hit so close to the finals. "I'll fix this, somehow."

"Oh, Jinx." Prilla laughed, but her tears didn't stop. "Always the champion. But why bother? They're right."

"They're wrong." Jinx propped her hands on her hips. "You're *helping* me. You're fixing my hovercar, aren't you? Besides, even if you didn't lift a finger, you'd still be worth more than any lies the paparazzi could spin up, Prilla. Always have been, always will be."

"That's nice of you." Prilla tried to smile.

"I mean it." Jinx stepped up to Prilla, then grabbed a nearby screwdriver and held it out to her. "I'll prove it. Come to the finals with me."

"Really?"

"I know it's been a while since we've really hung out, but it would mean a lot to me if you cheered me on."

Prilla took the screwdriver.

"I'd love to," she said, and this time her smile reached her eyes.

"I'll win for you," Jinx promised. "Then in the victory interview, I'll tell the whole world how wonderful you are."

"Sure you will." Prilla rolled her eyes. Then she set her jaw, grabbed her bandana, and marched over to the thruster. "It looks like we're on a deadline, then."

"You think you can fix her up in time?"

"Are you doubting my skills?" Prilla dragged the thruster over to the hovercar. "I'll have her done early."

"Early enough to go shopping with me?" Jinx asked. She was pushing her luck, but then again, she did that for a living.

"You're buying."

"Of course."

"Then it's a date." Prilla tied up her hair and slid her mechanic's platform under the hovercar before Jinx could respond.

As soon as the airlock sealed on Jinx's ship, she yelled and punched the air. Prilla was coming to see her race, at long last. No more hiding from the paparazzi and sneaking away to the Castle in secret. Jinx was going to take the moon by storm, with her beautiful princess by her side. The tabloids wouldn't know what hit them.

The day before the final race in the Luna Circuit, Prilla called Jinx. Her cornflower-blue eyes were wide and bright on the vid-wall of Jinx's apartment. Jinx checked her reflection in the preview screen — a few swipes at her hair made her handsomely disheveled, not a total mess — before accepting the call.

"Your hovercar is ready," Prilla declared. "The thruster needed some tweaking for cross-compatibility, but everything works."

"That's great." Jinx yawned and pulled her blanket close. "It's *early*, Prilla."

"Well, yeah. Aren't we going to go shopping?"

"How long could that take?"

A long time, it turned out. Prilla bounced in and out of stores, holding up dresses in the mirror and running her hands along racks of blouses, trying to find that one perfect outfit for the finals. Jinx knew she should be out practicing with her new thruster, but somehow it didn't feel as important as it did the day before. She knew how to race. What she hadn't known was how much the smile on Prilla's face could make her heart sing.

At a plus-size boutique on the far side of the moon, Prilla stopped and stared at a lace gown.

"Synthetic spider silk," she murmured. "Tensile strength off the charts."

"Is this a dress or equipment?" Jinx asked.

"What's the difference?" Prilla selected a few sizes from the rack and held them against her chest. "I'm going to try it on."

When Prilla emerged from the dressing room, she was radiant. The dress skimmed her curves and dipped low at the neck, then fell into soft ruffles at the bottom. It looked like spun silver, shiny and chrome, soft and strong. Prilla fiddled with the hem.

"Do you like it?"

"I love it," Jinx blurted. "Princess, it's perfect. That's the one."

"I thought so too," Prilla said, beaming. "I'm so glad they have it in my size. Thanks for waiting for me for so long, Jinx."

Jinx wanted to thank Prilla for waiting for *her*, for sticking around through all those years of distance and missed connections. If she was going to be close with Prilla again, though, maybe she should stop keeping secrets. She cleared her throat.

Prilla's smile crumpled as she stared over Jinx's shoulder. Jinx turned to see a cameraman lurking at the entrance of the store, snapping photos of them. Her newfound confidence died in her chest.

"Jinx," he called out as he swapped the lenses on his camera. "Over here, Jinx! Can I get a closeup?"

"I'm a little busy right now, sorry." Jinx faked a smile. She couldn't have any bad press the day before the finals. "Come see me at the track tomorrow and I'll see what I can do."

Prilla backed away, heading for the dressing room. Splotches of red stained her cheeks and her hands, now in fists, were shaking.

"Who's the girl?" the cameraman asked Jinx. When she didn't answer immediately, his casual smile became a shark-like grin, and he stepped forward. "Come on, I saw her in the papers. She's gotta be something to you. She's the chick from those junkyard photos, right? Did you buy her that dress? Must be a new thing. You didn't seem distracted in the semis."

"We're just friends." Jinx gritted her teeth, fighting her urge to chuck the nearest high heel at the paparazzo's head.

"Does she know that? It looks like she's angling to get her fifteen minutes of fame out of you." The cameraman cast a disdainful look at Prilla.

At that final indignity, Jinx leapt to her feet. She was shorter than the cameraman, but fiercer too, and he retreated as she approached. She grabbed the strap of his camera and yanked him forward, all politeness abandoned. Protecting her reputation was important, sure, but she needed to stop letting her ego hurt Prilla. What kind of champion would she be if she didn't protect what was really important?

"I don't know why you make it your business to insult beautiful women," she said, "but it stops now. If you ever want to show your face at one of my races again, you'd better leave us alone."

"Are you threatening me?" The cameraman squirmed in Jinx's grasp, trying in vain to slip away.

"Apologize to the lady," Jinx demanded, tightening her grip. The cameraman swallowed hard.

"Sorry, miss," he said. Prilla didn't smile, but she did unclench her fists.

"Good enough. Now go." Jinx snapped the lens cap onto his camera and pushed him away, just hard enough to make him stumble. With a nervous glance behind him, the cameraman scurried away.

Jinx slumped against the wall and put her head in her hands. She was not going to look good in the tabloids tomorrow. Hopefully her fans would see that she was just trying to be chivalrous, but Jinx knew the cameraman would find some awful way to spin the situation.

"You didn't have to do that." Prilla's soft voice broke through Jinx's clouded mind like a ray of sunshine. No matter what headline showed up tomorrow, it would be worth it.

"Of course I did." Jinx smiled up at Prilla. "I told you, I'm trying to be a better friend. How was that?"

"That was a good start." Prilla smiled, and Jinx's heart swelled with affection. "Are you sure, though? Right before the finals?"

"I'm sure," said Jinx, and meant it. After all, she was a racer first and foremost. All that really mattered was winning.

The next morning, Jinx woke early, as she did before every race. Her coach met her at the track and her crew went over the final checks of her hovercar, noting the fine workmanship on the new thruster. Her competitors shook her hand and her fans took her picture, clearly not put off by whatever the mall paparazzo had written about her. The whole time, though, all Jinx could think of was how Prilla had looked in that silver gown. She searched the stands, more anxious for her princess to arrive than she was for the race to start.

She was still staring at the stands when Prilla tapped her on the shoulder.

"I wanted to see you before you raced. Here," she whispered, handing Jinx a handkerchief. It bore Prilla's embroidered signature of petals and blossoms. "A token of my honor for my champion."

"Prilla —"

"Don't say anything," Prilla scolded her. "You've got to get going. Just get out there and make me proud."

"Of course." Jinx tucked the handkerchief inside her racing jacket, nestling it just above her heart. She didn't dare let herself think about what it might mean. "I'll see you at the finish line."

As Prilla snuck back out of the pit, Jinx climbed into her hovercar. She activated the mag drive and lifted off. Her car hovered steadily above the track. All system lights were green. With a few deft movements, Jinx glided to the starting line.

The announcer was speaking, but Jinx couldn't hear him over the rush of blood in her ears. Even her first race hadn't felt like this. This time, she wasn't just racing for herself. This race was for more than gold. If she won, she would finally feel worthy enough to confess to Prilla.

At the sound of the starting gun, everything melted away. Jinx peeled off the starting line and headed for the front of the pack. There was no cheering crowd, no waiting princess. There was only the track in front of her.

Something felt off already. Jinx hadn't had time to practice with the new thruster, and it didn't handle the same as her old one. Her hovercar was faster, yes, but wilder too. Jinx gritted her teeth and clung to the wheel. She just needed to stay on course and she could win this.

The racers on either side of Jinx nosed their way forward, jockeying for position. Jinx was picking up speed now. Her hovercar sped down the track as if it had been shot from a cannon. Jinx glanced to either side, set her jaw, and increased the thruster's power.

Another hovercar swung into Jinx's field of view. Its engine steamed as its driver barreled full-throttle down the track. Jinx bit her lip. She needed to conserve her fuel and coolant for later in the race. As much as it stung her ego to be passed, she didn't need to stay in first place the *whole* time.

Lap after lap zipped by in Jinx's rear camera display. Another hovercar passed her halfway through the race. If this race had been last week, she would have challenged it, but with Prilla watching her, she couldn't risk a crash.

The counter of remaining laps dwindled, and Jinx started to relax. The new thruster still had power left to give on the home stretch, and she was getting the hang of steering with it. No one else had passed her, so she only had two hovercars to beat.

Just before the final lap, Jinx poured full power into the thruster. She zipped forward in the span of a heartbeat, catching the two winning racers by surprise.

Too much surprise.

One of the hovercars swerved sharply out of the way. It swung off the magnetized track and its side dropped to the asphalt, sending up sparks as it scraped forward.

With her regular thruster, Jinx would have been able to avoid it with ease. In her panic, she steered as she always had before. Of course, her hovercar didn't respond as it would have before.

Jinx drove for her life as she careened forward, just missing the last racer ahead of her. She could barely stay on the track at this speed. The finish line was so close, but if she made one wrong move, it would all end in flames.

Prilla's smiling face and silver silk dress filled Jinx's mind.

"I'll make you proud," Jinx murmured.

She eased off the thruster.

The hovercar she had dodged earlier sped past her to cross the finish line in first place. Jinx edged out a few of the racers that had overtaken the crashing hovercar, finishing in a respectable second place. The noise of the crowd was deafening. Jinx tried not to look at them as she coasted back to her pit.

She turned off her mag drive and returned to solid ground as the runner-up of the Luna Circuit.

With shaking hands, Jinx unzipped her jacket and pulled out Prilla's handkerchief. She traced the embroidered petals and waited for the paparazzi to swarm her.

Instead, the first person she saw was Prilla herself.

"You did it," Prilla exclaimed, throwing her arms around Jinx's neck. After a startled, frozen moment, Jinx hugged back.

"I got second," she mumbled.

"Better second than dead. I saw the way your hovercar was handling out there."

"Are you proud?" Jinx couldn't meet Prilla's eyes.

"I couldn't be prouder."

"Prilla, can I tell you something? Before the cameras get here?" Jinx folded and unfolded the handkerchief behind Prilla's back, intensely aware of Prilla's arms around her neck.

"Of course."

"I'm in love with you." It came out in a rush, spurred on by the adrenaline shock of the race. "That's why I slowed down. Staying alive to tell you that was more important than winning."

Prilla's gaze was soft yet serious. Jinx fidgeted, feeling her face burn hot. Before Jinx could try to play her confession off as a joke, though, Prilla tilted her head up and spoke.

"Jinx Montoya, I've been in love with you from the first time you called me princess."

"Well." Jinx was sure she was red enough to match Prilla's lipstick. "I'm sorry I can't be your champion."

"You'll always be my champion."

The paparazzi finally arrived just as Jinx grasped Prilla's lace collar and pulled her forward. They closed their eyes to the camera flashes and melted into a long-awaited kiss.

Lauren Ring (she/her) is a perpetually tired Jewish lesbian who writes about possible futures, for better or for worse. Her short fiction can be found in *Pseudopod*, *Recognize Fascism*, and *Glitter + Ashes*. When she isn't writing speculative fiction, she is pursuing her career in UX design or attending to the many needs of her cat, Moomin.

For content notes, see page 244

Half My Heart

by Rafi Kleiman

THE RATTLE OF THE BASS THROUGH THE FLOOR and up into his throat always made Vic feel like a werewolf during the full moon, like he was bursting from his skin, like he was about to become something new. K was pressed warm against his side by the crush of the crowd, screaming, pitched up high to be heard over the noise. The horde was bleeding out ink and endorphins, rolling to the sound of thrash guitar and synth-punk heartbreak. He could feel the vibrations in the soles of his feet, even through his boots, all the way to his skull.

Vic and K rocked with the crowd's messy wet rhythm, struggling to stay on their feet as they strained toward the stage barrier. The dusk-skinned Big on bass, all four arms engaged, hiked one leg up on an amp; sparks shot into the hot air like summer fireworks. A tech rushed to replace it with one of the dozens stacked backstage, leaving the wreckage of the first crumpled on the stage.

The crowd rippled like a storm current. Vic's mouth was papery, his skin sticky with other people's sweat. He could taste it on his lips, salty and sick as he shouted along. Every part of him was shoved up against someone else: his chin nudging into a back, a pointed elbow near his shoulder and knocking up against his jawline, the thrashing plant-like tendrils of a nearby Faygen slapping at his ankles. He shoved back,

157

baring his teeth into a smile, and pushed forward like he was going to get anywhere. He felt tapping on the bare, tattooed bicep of his bio arm, and he turned.

K shot him a sharp, wide grin, pointing up, then tugged on the ponytail of the bearded person on their other side. The person angled towards them, strobe lights highlighting the artificial spikes extending from their cheeks, and K pointed again, jutting their index finger into the air. The incomprehensible mess of sound around Vic pitched down as K was hoisted high, leaving a bubble of space by Vic's ear for the cacophony to fill. Hands poured in to catch them, and the crowd rushed to fill the space where they had been. Vic watched as K was propelled forward, towards the stage, their head tipped back as they let out a wheezy giggle that was completely lost in the noise — though Vic knew it so well he could practically hear it anyway. K's heart hammered double-time in Vic's chest. With the crowd of strangers pressed tight on either side, he felt a strange sort of feedback loop, caught between the wet heat against his bio arm and the electric sharpness of his synth, the difference between nerves he had grown and those that had been coiled in metal. He tasted copper.

Vic lifted his eyes and screamed to the ceiling, letting the crowd toss him this way and that, giddy from his stomach up.

* * *

After, amid the crackle of biodegradable cups and tickets being crushed under heavy boots as the crowd slowly thinned, he found K again. He caught them by the sweat-slick shoulder, their artfully ripped t-shirt hanging halfway down their arm. K slung a damp arm across his neck and tilted their heads together.

"Hey, loser," they said, and Vic reached to ruffle the front of their hair as his other hand dug for gum in the pocket of his ripped jeans. "You have fun?"

"Always do," Vic replied, and ripped the wrapping off the gum stick with his teeth. His tongue felt rough in his mouth, scraped by all the sins he'd bitten out tonight while the mob around him couldn't hear, all the horrid whispers ground under the heels of the people around him. He stuck the gum between his teeth, and turned to K. "Hey," Vic said, twisting in their grip so he could thumb the corner of their wet mouth with his bio hand. "You're bleeding."

"Shit," K said, their studded tongue automatically flicking out to chase his finger. "Must've bit myself. How bad is it, doc?"

"Somehow I think you'll live. We'll see how bad it hurts tomorrow."

"Right! I wanna get that bassist's number," K declared, too loud and too close to Vic's ear. "Musician's fingers times four, hot damn."

"What would you even do with all of those? Just because someone's hot doesn't mean they have to use all of their hands at once. You don't have enough tits for that."

"I have plenty of tits! In this outfit, at least." They laughed, a little wild, still rushing with the adrenaline of the show. "No, uh, I don't know. She'd find something to grab, probably. You crashing at mine?"

"Yeah," Vic said, and felt the relief of home sink into his gut. "Might as well."

"Cool. Just use your own damn toothbrush, this time. It's in the cabinet for a fucking reason." K pushed off, giving him a toothy smile, and Vic almost overbalanced. "I'm going to go flirt with that bassist while they finish packing up."

"The band is backstage, she's gotta be with them."

"I know a guy," K said, sounding entirely unconcerned. "Wait for me here?"

"Yeah," Vic said, pushing his gum up flat against the roof of his mouth with his tongue. "But if you actually get back there I'm going to be shocked."

"You have so little faith in me!" K called over their shoulder, as they slipped off in the direction of the broad-shouldered security by the stage barrier.

Vic found an isolated corner to slump in, playing mindless games on his communicator and shoving his gum around in his mouth. He was going for his third straight combo in a matching game when he heard a voice directly in front of him, slightly accented but easy to understand.

"I like your arm."

Vic looked up to see a Faygen, dressed in scene-ready DIY with rips and spikes, a mohawk-like ridge of spiny leaves crowning their head and twisting lines etched across their green-tinted skin. Vic was sort of impressed; Faygens didn't often go for body mods, considering the plantlike nature of parts of their bodies, but if the tattoo-style carvings were a natural occurrence, they were a very convenient one. In response, Vic bent said arm at the elbow, the slick rose-engraved synth skin flexing with the movement.

"Yeah," Vic said, trying his best to make his voice come out friendly. It often didn't, no matter how badly he wanted it to. "So do I. That's why I picked the design."

The new arrival held out a hand, long-fingered and covered in rings, both metal human-style rings and more traditional ornaments made of natural matter. "I'm Twist. Or, well, that's my common name, anyway. You don't wanna hear the long one. He/him."

"Vic," Vic replied, extending his bio hand to shake. The rings felt interesting against his skin — some cold, some humming with an odd warmth. Like all Faygens, Twist was lacking any discernible fingernails. "He/him too." Twist nodded, and while it was always a little hard for Vic to tell when his conversational partner didn't have pupils, he could swear he felt him give Vic a fairly complimentary up-down glance.

"I saw you earlier, and I, uh," Twist drew his hands back into his pockets, rocking back onto the inch-high heels of his boots. "I seriously had to ask if you're, you know. Available. I saw you with someone before, are you guys —" Twist trailed off with a vague gesture that utilized both his hands and the flexible spines atop his head.

Vic understood well enough. He would've taken pity even if Twist had been human (stars knew he'd had enough trouble with words in his lifetime), but he also knew Faygens had used significantly less verbal communication before first contact, and still didn't do it much among themselves — he wasn't gonna make this guy wait and flail.

"That's K," Vic said, with a nod. Right on cue, though it couldn't possibly be related, he felt a hum of triumph in his chest that could only come from K's heart, beating half-and-half alongside his own. He wondered if it was related to their quest to make it backstage. "They're — we're committed but platonic. And nonexclusive." He smiled, a little sharper than he intended. He couldn't help it — it was just how his face worked. It wouldn't be the first time he had scared someone off without meaning to. Sometimes Vic was amazed he had managed to make any friends at all. "And you?" he asked. "Are *you* available?"

"I have a boyfriend," Twist said, with a grin. "But we're not exclusive either. He'd be first in line to yell at me if I didn't ask for your number."

That was oddly flattering. And Twist was real cute, and clearly had good taste in music, so — Vic held out his communicator, his smile growing. Twist scrambled to pull his own from his vest and shoved them together, clinking their sides together. His hair tendrils were moving in a way Vic wasn't sure he was conscious of, coiling in little twists. Vic wondered if that was where his name came from. The new contacts popped up on both screens for confirmation almost immediately, and they pressed yes at the same time.

"I'll message you?" Vic suggested. "I mean, it's late tonight, but —"

"Yeah, yeah, yeah," Twist agreed, bobbing his head in a continuous little nod. "Uh, we could get — coffee, or food, or something? I don't actually drink coffee. I could drink something else while you drink coffee, though."

Vic bit down on his lip, suppressing a laugh that might be taken the wrong way. He was doing so well thus far — or at least he hoped he was. He didn't want to screw it up now.

"I do drink coffee," he confirmed. "Coffee's good."

"Great," Twist said. He glanced around, offered Vic his hand for an awkward fist bump, and took a few steps back. "My ride is here and she's probably gonna kill me if I take much longer, so."

"Bye," Vic said, feeling flushed and pleased. "Don't get murdered before we can get, you know, drinks. Coffee."

"Yes," Twist said. "Yeah. G'night, Vic."

Vic raised his synth hand in a wave, and watched Twist turn and just about sprint out the venue door. The majority of the crowd had filed out in the post-set crush, leaving only die-hard fans or folks hanging around to wait for someone.

Twist had barely cleared the doorway before K crashed into Vic's back with zero warning; communicator in hand and a smile on their face that told Vic they were just as pleased with themselves.

"So," Vic said, amused. "I can tell you got the number. How did you even get back there? For real."

"I *told* you," K said, waving their communicator in a triumphant celebration before stuffing it back in their pocket. "I know a guy. You don't know the guy." They gave him a mischievous look that spoke volumes. "And you got something too, didn't you? There I was, chatting up that gorgeous bassist — Svayna, by the way, she's cool — when my half of your heart started hammering a fucking drumline on my ribcage. I almost lost my rhythm."

"Well, you love a challenge," Vic said, rolling his eyes. "And if you got her number, I can't imagine it threw you off *too* badly. But. Yeah. A guy came and asked for my number, too."

"You give it to him?" K asked, eyes glinting like they already knew.

"Sure did."

"Is he cute?"

"He is," Vic confirmed. "And no, you can't hit on him yet. I'll let you know."

They shrugged, unbothered. "Fair enough!" they chirped, and hooked an arm through his, beginning to drag him towards the door. "Let's head on home."

Home. Vic liked when K called it that, even if it wasn't quite true.

* * *

One high-speed hover rail ride later, they arrived at the single-bedroom apartment K rented. They both made a beeline for the kitchen, where they ate cold fowl legs with their hands for a post-show refuel, standing up in the hazy light that hovered above K's kitchen table. Sometimes after shows they stopped at one of the numerous little stalls and stands that sold hot, handheld meals from all corners of the galaxy and all manner of cultures. All the encores tonight had kept them too late for even the most dedicated (or adventurous) chefs. After the amount of jumping and bouncing and rocking they'd done to each song, food was a necessity.

After they'd eaten, Vic went to the bathroom to brush his teeth — and did, indeed, use his own damn toothbrush. Shirtless, mouth rinsed and tongue tasting of mint, he stared down the mirror. There were three scars on his chest: two horizontal, from his top surgery, and one vertical scar in the direct center of his chest, from the surgery that had traded half of his heart for half of K's. Vic and K had both chosen to keep their paired scars, but Vic was still deciding whether or not he wanted

162

the other two fully gone. Each application of silvery scar gel faded the color, the shape. If he persisted in putting it on, all of his scars would be barely a whisper, almost nothing left behind.

Vic couldn't be sure, yet, if the the look of them was something that would keep stirring pride, but he had plenty of time to make the choice. The gel didn't stop working, no matter how healed you got.

K barged into the bathroom without knocking, but Vic was too familiar with this to jump. They crowded close to the mirror to check that all their piercings were intact, no beads or barbells lost in the crush.

"How's it looking?" K asked, twisting in the mirror to count the earrings dangling from their cartilage.

Vic knew what they meant right away. "Not bad." Vic turned to see himself from another angle, enough room left in the mirror to see the recent flatness of his torso from the side. " I'm just seeing how the scars are doing."

"I'm still not used to you with no nipples," K said, and stuck their tongue out at their reflection. Vic wasn't sure if they were looking at their tongue piercing or just making faces.

"I didn't have any use for them."

"Could've pierced 'em," K offered. They took a step back, apparently satisfied that their facial hardware was properly positioned.

"Pierce your own," Vic said back.

"Maybe I will," K said. They reached down to grab a generous handful of their own chest appraisingly, even though they were still dressed. "But I'm not super sure how that works with the, uh —" K jiggled their wrist in Vic's direction, the studded cuff strapped to their skin catching the light. "Speaking of," K said and reached to twist the cuff's centerpiece gem, a miracle of shiny circuitry. Their chest shrank in response, retreating into their torso. K assessed themselves in the mirror, and nodded. "I think that'll be more comfortable for tonight. I got what I wanted out of 'em, anyway."

"That bassist's number?" Vic guessed, with a snort.

"Maybe a little bit." K bit down on a grin. "And, I mean, you know, appeasing the fluctuating nature of my comfort with them, but..." Vic nodded. He'd wanted his none of the time, but he could still understand K wanting theirs occasionally. "Anyway," K said, nudging him in his naked ribcage. "I gotta shower before bed. I'm sticky. And not in any of the good ways. Are you joining me, or taking the second shift?"

Vic considered this for a moment. "I'll go after you," he said.

"Sure thing," K said, and reached up to ruffle his hair. "But you *are* showering before you get in the bed, or I'm going to torch it, and my couch isn't big enough for both of us."

Vic, laughing, ducked out of the bathroom before they could mess up his hair any further.

When Vic returned to K's bedroom, clean and still damp, K was already tucked under the covers, wearing glasses and sitting up with a sleek tablet in their lap to read from. He had his own drawer in K's dresser; it took no time at all to pull on a pair of boxers and some socks.

"Is that a new shirt? Why does it say 'carnal knowledge' on it?" Vic asked.

K looked down at the shirt in response, as if to check it was really there. "Disgusted looks from the elderly?" they offered.

"We're alone in your bedroom," Vic said, climbing into the empty side of the bed.

"You never know where the elderly may be lurking," K quipped, quick and easy. With a single touch, their tablet went dark. "And you really can't fucking talk about my clothing choices: you sleep in *socks*. Fucking weirdo." Vic responded to this by kicking out at them with one of his socked feet. They continued, unphased. "Are you staying up, or can I turn the light off? I'm honestly beat — I'll definitely pass out even if we leave it."

"Stars, do you really think I have any juice left in me after tonight?" Vic wiggled under the blankets until he was comfortable, his bare leg pressing hot to one of K's. They automatically hooked a calf over his. Vic's frantic two-toned pulse was slowing already.

"I dunno," K mused, drawing out the syllables. "You *are* pretty juicy."

"Shut up and turn the light off or I'm leaving out the window," Vic replied. K barked a laugh and hummed a simple note at their lights, launching the room into darkness.

It took a little more shifting to get comfortable, but eventually Vic fell asleep, lulled by the sound of K's breath and the half of their heart beating steadily in his ribcage.

* * *

Vic wasn't sure what woke him, but the room was still dark and he tasted bile on his tongue. His chest was constricting with rapid breaths, his stomach twisting in nausea and confusion. All he could do was try to focus on physical sensation, on each detail as they presented themselves to him. The bed was firm and still beneath him, but his body was decidedly not. The blankets had been pulled almost entirely off of him, and his feet were cold — he'd lost his socks, somehow. His mouth was dry from panting. K's hand was gentle in his hair, their body pressed against his side, and as his ears stopped rushing he realized they were talking. It took another long moment to be able to understand what, exactly, they were saying.

"You're okay. Hey, you're all right. Vic, hey. Look at me. Vic. Victor. Victor Gains, my love, half of my heart, I have you, you're here, you aren't anywhere else, you're real and I have you and I won't let anyone hurt you."

Vic sucked in a noisy breath and turned towards them, eyes searching in the dark. He caught on K's face, and could just barely see them start to smile when he did, the glint of their teeth an odd comfort.

"Hey," they said, slightly nonsensically. "There you are. It's okay, I have you." Vic reached out with his bio arm and K was there, chilly fingers twining in his. "You awake?" they asked, and Vic nodded, not sure his voice would carry. "Okay, good," K said. "Let's do heartbeats?"

It took Vic a moment to focus in on the rhythmic thud of the dual heartbeats in his chest, and another before he was able to calm his breathing enough to try and sync his half-heart with K's, noticeably slower and sweeter. Vic's other heartbeat pounded in K's ribcage, but they stayed, breathed with him, squeezed his hand at a regular, slow pace until the disparate parts of the hearts in Vic's chest were beating in time.

Eventually he squeezed K's hand in return, and their smile bloomed again.

* * *

More than a decade earlier, K and their brother Rakhim had moved to the planet that Vic had lived on for his entire life. K had one human mother and one Polychrome mother, and their parenting style was quite unconventional for humans and quite conventional for Polychromes.

165

Modern humans didn't do communal child-raising as often as their ancestors once had, but Polychromes did, and when K and Rakhim's mothers had been offered exciting new positions on a starship, they had sent their fourteen-year-old children to come to maturity in the welcoming arms of their mutual partners and friends in Vic's neighborhood.

K, who had chosen their name in the style of their Polychrome mother, was adopted and looked like neither of their parents. Rakhim, who had chosen his name in the style of his human mother, was a gene-splice baby who looked like them both, with his human mother's prominent nose, and his Polychrome mother's downy feathers on his head and multicolored patterns on his dark human skin. Their new household was a mix of species and cultures — a joyful, friendly clash.

They weren't bitter about their new arrangement. Especially not K, who took to it like a new adventure, comfortable in the knowledge that their mothers would never send them to people they didn't love and trust. They had hologram calls whenever their parents were within range, and gallivanted from place to place without asking permission in a way Vic couldn't fathom happening in a human-only family. All of this combined made them like no one else he had ever met.

Vic only had one mother, and when she had left him for a starship ticket, she had done so without looking back or leaving a forwarding address. She had left him alone with a father who never understood him and barely seemed to know he existed, a man he had already learned to avoid. And he *was* bitter, then and perhaps always. He was so bitter that when he first met K it had driven him crazy trying to understand how they managed not to be. They had both come a long way since then, but Vic still wondered if it would ever be far enough.

*   *   *

When the last post-nightmare tremors had subsided, and an offer to talk about it had been declined, Vic and K lay together in the newly dawning light that had only barely begun to creep past K's curtains. It was silent now, but K was shifting in a way that meant it wouldn't be for long, and Vic wanted it over with.

"What?" he asked. He was ready for something he'd heard before after episodes like this one; K murmuring *Move in with me* in low tones, an invitation too tempting for Vic to truly consider accepting, something they'd fought about before. Some of the worst fights they'd ever had were centered on that question, and on an answer K never understood.

Vic had never really *helped* them understand — the two of them had just gone back and forth until the soles of their words wore down from overuse. But Vic would rather have a temporary oasis than ask for too much and shatter it, leaving him with none at all.

K cleared their throat and turned to press their shoulder to Vic's so they were lying side-by-side, staring at the slowly lightening ceiling.

"I'm going to ask a question I don't think you've ever really answered before," K said, glancing at Vic from the corner of their eye. Vic's heart immediately ticked up. But when K reached for his hand, he let them take it. They had somehow repositioned enough that K was now grasping his synthetic fingers — the buzzy electric feeling he got from it was a nice counterpoint to the tension of the discussion. "But you have to not get mad."

Vic swallowed, waited.

K waited, too, but when he didn't say anything, they tightened their grip on his fingers and continued. "*Why* don't you want to move in with me?" They gave a lopsided shrug with the arm not connected to Vic, like they knew they were retreading old ground, but forged forward nonetheless. "I know we've sort of talked about it before. I've asked. But you never seem to actually answer. I don't think you've ever told me why. I know you don't like living with your dad."

Vic's throat was dry, again. He swallowed once more, trying to clear it.

"I don't like living with my dad," he admitted.

"I know," K repeated. "So why don't you live with me? You like being here. I know you do. You keep half your stuff here. I just don't understand why you insist on keeping the rest there and having to go back for it over and over. You've never told me."

The following silence was long and slow, as Vic considered what words were too much.

"I don't think you'll get it," he said, finally.

"Try me," K responded. There was steel in their voice. "Really. I'm not — I'm not letting you get away with slipping out of the conversation again. You've known me for years, Vic — don't you trust me?"

"Of course I do," Vic said, painfully earnest to his own ears. "You know how much I trust you."

"But you won't tell me *why*. You don't have to live with me, if you don't want to. But you won't tell me why."

Vic closed his eyes because even the weak light in the room was too much, and he didn't want to see K's face as he bared a bit more of his shrinking soul to the person that already knew most of it. He was never sure what part of it would be too unlikable to look at.

"It takes money," he began.

"I'm already paying for it," K interjected.

"No, you have to let me finish. If I'm doing this, you have to let me finish." He waited, and when K did nothing but squeeze his synth hand again, Vic continued. "You live in a one-bedroom apartment. I do odd jobs. I haven't figured out a single solid ambition yet, I pay for body mods and shows and I don't think about anything beyond it. You won't have your own space anymore, if I'm always here. You won't get to bring anyone home. I can't contribute. You'll get —" This one stuck in his throat, almost too much to scrape from his tongue, just another secret like the ones he had screamed last night among the music and the movement. It was silent now, with no crowd to swallow it unheard. Just K, just the room quiet and still, and the knowledge that if he got out of this now, they'd try to pry it from him again, and eventually they would succeed, because he had no real justification for keeping it from them. Vic's eyes stung, shut tight against any hint of sight. "You'll get *tired of me*, K."

The silence, again, this time worse.

"Never," K said when they found their voice, fierce. "*Never*, what are you even talking about? So what if I can't take people home? For one, if someone can't host me, I can and will bang in a bathroom stall —" Vic laughed despite himself, which he knew was exactly what K had intended. "And two," K continued, still ferocious as a burning warp core, sharp as a tiger. "Do you really think that's more important to me than *you are*? I'm not hearing anything about not *wanting* to live with me. I'm just hearing that my favorite person in the galaxy thinks he's a burden."

Vic's chest tightened, the word *burden* hitting like a shot somewhere deep and bloody. He could hear K falter, hear their voice crack, and their next words came out more quietly. "I just… I don't think you know what you mean to me."

"Half my heart," Vic countered. "I'd have to be an idiot to not know what I mean to you."

He cracked open one of his eyes just in time to see K give a weak little smile. "I guess that's fair," they said. "Just — you act like I don't know what wakes you up at night feeling like you've been buried alive. You act like if you ask too much I'll leave. I don't know if the elective heart surgery was enough of a hint, but in case it wasn't, I'm in this for the *long haul,* Vic. What do I have to do to prove it?"

"It's not about you," Vic said, urgently. They needed to know that much, at least. "It's not about anything you've done wrong. It's about me. It's about how I'm —"

"What?" K asked. "You're what, Vic? I've known you our entire adult lives. I've never known anyone better, or anyone I've loved more. We're at least as defective as each other. We've traded tattoos and war stories. You *know* where my cracks are. Why would I mind yours if you don't mind mine?"

Vic's throat felt rough as sandpaper. He truly didn't want to cry, but he wasn't sure his body would cooperate.

"I don't mind," he said, and it came out hoarse.

"I fucking know you don't, asshole," K said, an eye roll in their tone. "Do you think I'd love you this much if I thought you were judging me for it all the time?"

"I guess not," Vic admitted.

"Then can you trust me?"

"I do trust you."

"Vic, can you trust me not to *leave*? Can you trust me to tell you if there's a problem? Can you trust *us* to work on it?"

It felt like too much, but also something like cleaning a cut, or like poking at a bruise that you didn't want to fade. It felt like leaving his scars unhealed.

"Yes," Vic gritted out. It didn't come easy, or right away, because first he had to make sure he meant it. He couldn't say it if he didn't mean it. K's relief sighed out of them in a way that Vic could feel. Their fingers knotted more tightly between them on K's bed.

"Then… you don't have to decide right away, and it doesn't have to be *here* if you want more space, but, as something to work for, as something to trust, as a goal we are well and truly fucking aiming for —" K turned on their side to face him properly, matching his eyes without fear. "Vic. Move in with me?"

Vic pitched forward and pressed his face messily into the crook of K's neck, aware that his cheeks were hot and his breath was fast and his voice was going to crack. He still tried to sound nonchalant when he spoke, just because this had all been too heavy to end on, and he wanted to make K snort.

"Yeah. Okay."

K didn't snort, but they did nudge him a little bit. "You're a jerk," they replied, reaching up to cup his cheek. "Okay, jerk, let's make a home."

Vic's breath left him in a rush, but light remained, filling his ribs like liquid gold in their joined hearts.

Home.

Rafi Kleiman is a queer, Jewish, nonbinary author of speculative sci-fi and fantasy. They know firsthand the value of being able to see yourself reflected in the media you consume, and believe it's vitally important that people of all types, especially those who have been historically underserved, are thoughtfully represented in fiction. They love modern fantasy, bad puns, mythical creatures of all kinds, and live punk shows. They believe thoroughly in the power of hope, community, and friendship, but also believe that necromancy is pretty cool and maybe not that big of a deal. They are occasionally on Twitter **@mothmanlives**.

For content notes, see page 244

Venti Mochaccino, No Whip, Double Shot of Magic

by Aimee Ogden

COFFEE AT CARDINAL CUPS always comes with an off-menu bonus.

One of Jojo's regulars pulls up to the drive-thru with his Wednesday morning office order: three frappes, two lattes, one soy mocha. He always leaves a good tip, and he always pays with a credit card. Credit card users are great for customer service witches like Jojo, who need a full name to do their best work. "Have a good one, D!" she says, handing him the carrier tray, and she knows he will because his coffee comes with a nice cantrip that'll help him send all his emails for the next week with zero typos and exactly the right number of exclamation marks.

The next guy, however, who throws his frappe (he wanted salted caramel, not just caramel-caramel!) at the drive-thru window? He paid in cash, so no credit card receipt to get his details from. The plastic cup has his first name Sharpie'd on it, though, so she sends a little hex after him. Nothing much: an ingrown hair, or maybe a mean hangnail. An hourly-wage sort of satisfaction. The owners don't know why or how Jojo keeps the right customers coming back and sends most of the wrong ones packing, but they sense she's got something to do with it. A little

171

operant conditioning, in her opinion, could really do a person good. And in most of these cases, that person is Jojo.

On Thursday morning Jojo's favorite and most frustrating regular arrives at the counter for her traditional order of a muffin and a cinnamon spice latte. "And can I put a name on that?" Jojo asks, a reluctant smile already pulling at her mouth.

The regular smiles back. It wrinkles her nose and the corner of her eyes, making new constellations out of her freckles. Jojo wants to map out every line of the corresponding star chart. "Hermione Granger," she says. And blushes? Maybe? Jojo studiously avoids looking too closely.

"Hermione Granger it is." She scribbles in black marker as the regular drops a dollar into the tip jar. She always pays in cash, too. No real name means spellwork is silk-slippery, impossible to make stick.

Harold comes in on Friday mornings for Senior Dollar Coffee Day. Jojo pulls up a chair so he can sit close to the counter (the stools are too tippy for him) and show Jojo pictures of his granddaughter at her latest piano recital. She only has a first name — he always pays in dimes, with a quarter for the tip jar — but she does what she can and sometimes when he leaves his hand is gripping his cane a little tighter.

Later that day Mrs. Cynthia "I WANT TO SEE YOUR MANAGER" Nielsen stops by after her yoga class. Jojo has to make her drinks an average of three times before they're "right." Once Cynthia had the gall to tip from the Take a Penny dish; this time she signs a 0.00 with a flourish on the credit card receipt. Jojo is a little disappointed to think she'll never get to hear the story of Cynthia ripping the world's most noxious fart in the middle of the yoga studio next Friday.

The regular is back on Saturday morning, a pile of study books under her arm. When Jojo asks for a name, she says "Eleanor Roosevelt," which goes with the history textbook in the crook of her elbow. When Jojo calls for Ms. Roosevelt's order, it doesn't get as many giggles from the shop as the pop culture references do. But the regular smiles, and that's plenty good enough.

"Enjoy the coffee," Jojo says, through the heat in her cheeks.

"You, too," says Eleanor Roosevelt, then cringes as she realizes.

Jojo opens her mouth to say she's heard the same thing a thousand times. But then — she peeps a name penned onto the top of a notebook page. Susannah R. — she feels a secret, wicked thrill that she's never felt before for a bit of magic so benign. A wish, something small, already on its way to coming true and given the last tipping point into reality: a lost bus pass suddenly found, maybe, or a half-grade better on a final exam. Finally. She grins stupidly, and Eleanor-slash-Susannah offers back a curious smile, and then the pause zips past awkward into mortifying so Jojo retreats back to the espresso machine.

A mom comes in with a pair of toddling twins. They split a raspberry Danish and the mom slams a redeye before crawling on all fours to collect the crumbs. On the credit card receipt, she scribbles "25% sorry math." Jojo sends her off with a doggy bag for the leftover Danish and, though she doesn't know it yet, the best and deepest night's sleep she's had in three years.

The gross guy who keeps asking if she has a boyfriend comes in between four and five, when the shop is mostly empty. He pays in cash; "Josh" isn't much to go on so she hasn't yet conditioned him to associate Cardinal Cups with canker sores. "What are you doing after you get off tonight?" he says, leaning on her display of artisanal truffles. "Because you could be *getting off*."

"She's got plans." It's none other than Susannah R., punctuated by the door chime. Josh says something unpleasant about a threesome but Jojo barely hears him because Susannah R. is standing in the shop for the second time that day and stammering, "I mean, if she wants to."

She does. "I love it when wishes come true," Jojo says. This time, Susannah's nose-wrinkling smile does a little magic of its own on her knees.

This story was originally published in *Daily Science Fiction* (2019).

Aimee Ogden is a former science teacher and software tester; now she writes stories about sad astronauts and angry princesses. Her first novellas, "Sun-Daughters, Sea-Daughters" and "Local Star" debuted in 2021 from Tor.com and Interstellar Flight Press respectively. Her short fiction has appeared in magazines such as *Clarkesworld*, *Analog*, *Fireside*, and *Beneath Ceaseless Skies*. Aimee is a graduate of the Viable Paradise workshop, and she also co-edits *Translunar Travelers Lounge*, a magazine of fun and optimistic speculative fiction. She lives in Madison, Wisconsin, with her spouse, twin children, and a dog named Commander Riker.

For content notes, see page 244

since we're here tonight

by Xu Ran

THEIR FIRST NIGHT ON THE TRAIN IN SPACE, Ren turns to Asa and says, "I think I have an ear infection."

Asa doesn't even look up from the mirror, his lips downturned as he holds one shirt and then another up to his front. "Levi'll have something for that," he says, and so Ren goes to find Levi.

Levi's compartment is the one next to Ren and Asa's, on the opposite end of the train from Song Jian and Elliot's first-class compartment. The three of them had chosen their roommates by drawing straws when they'd first gotten on the train, and Levi had ended up with one to himself. Ren had offered to switch, but Levi and Asa had exchanged a look and told them it was fine. *We've spent more than enough time sleeping in the same room already,* Levi had said, and Asa had nodded and begun complaining at length about all the bruises he'd accrued from climbing into Levi's window on the second floor.

Ostensibly, Levi is only a few steps away, but since it's past ten, the gravity fields outside have been lowered for the night. Ren grimly tightens the drawstrings of their uniform pants and grips the ledge of the sliding compartment door; when they feel the shields release and contract around them as they carefully inch out into the hallway, they swing onto the guardrails that run along the ceiling for this purpose.

"Shut the door after yourself!" Asa hollers. Ren glances back, but the compartment door is already sliding closed automatically.

Ren keeps a careful hold on the guardrails until they get to the next compartment door, and knocks with an elbow. Levi answers after only a bare second, raising his head until he spots Ren half-pressed to the ceiling. His face is shiny like he's just put moisturizer on, like he's already showered and ready for bed. "Oh," he says, and smiles. "Come on in."

Ren lets him take one of their hands and tug them into the compartment, holding on until Ren lowers themselves back to the floor. The door closes.

Levi squints at Ren. "You look pale. What's wrong? Why are you here so late?"

"I have an ear infection," Ren tells him. "I think. Asa said you'd have something for it."

Levi makes a considering noise in his throat and tugs at Ren's elbow, pulling them to sit on the bunk pressed against one of the compartment walls. "Let me go look. Lie down."

So Ren lies all the way down on the soft bunk and tilts their head up so that they can watch Levi walk to the very back of the compartment, where a hydraulic door hisses open to reveal a tiny private bathroom. Levi kneels and rummages in the cupboard squeezed beneath the sink.

"Ah," he says, after a moment. He looks back at Ren. "I think the antibiotics must be with Elliot. Remember, because —"

"I remember," Ren says, and sighs. Elliot and Song Jian's compartment, all the way up front because of Elliot's parents, is a long way away. They aren't looking forward to trying to get all the way there without the gravity shields.

"Sorry," Levi says, frowning in sympathy.

"It's not your fault," Ren says. "Do you have something for the pain, at least? It feels like one side of my head's been blown out."

Levi clucks disapprovingly, frowning deeper, and begins rummaging once more. Ren lets their eyes slip shut to wait. The sheets of the bunk are familiar with the scent of Levi's raspberry-and-peach shampoo. They breathe in, breathe out, and let it calm them.

"Did you eat dinner, Ren?" Levi's voice echoes as if coming from very far away.

"Mm," Ren says vaguely, knowing Levi will understand. The pillow is very soft beneath their head; lying down helps regulate some of the pressure in their infected ear, and now that the pain has abated slightly they can feel exhaustion from the day tugging them gently under.

"Okay, then I think you can take this one … hold on, let me get you a cup of water. I'm going to put a sachet of vitamins in for you too, is that all right?"

"Mm," Ren says again, too comfortable for words.

"Sit up for a second, then."

There's a moment of quiet, and then the mattress dips. Ren opens their eyes with effort and finds Levi's face hovering closely in front of theirs. Levi slides an arm around Ren's shoulders to help them sit up, and then Ren obediently lets Levi slide a pill into their mouth, obediently swallows it with the water, obediently drinks it all. They lick sugar-sweet vitamin residue off their lips when they're done while Levi sets the cup aside. When Levi makes to get in with them, they shove over on the bunk to press against the wall.

The bunk's really only supposed to hold one. Space is a commodity in space, and all of the train's measurements are nearly too exact. Two is a tight fit, but not impossible. Ren finds themselves immediately comforted by Levi's proximity.

"This is nice," Levi sighs, and throws a leg over Ren's hip so that they might fit together better. He pulls the duvet up over them. With the both of them still for more than a few moments, the lights in the compartment click off automatically.

The dark feels almost as impenetrable as space. Ren's positive that if they put a hand in front of their face right now, they would be able to see nothing, nothing at all.

Levi's hand slides into Ren's hair, scratching gently at their scalp, smoothing through tangles. "Your hair's growing out," he murmurs softly, into the curve of Ren's ear.

"I know," Ren says. "I want it to, though. I've wanted it to for a while."

There's a short silence as both of them consider how much harder Ren's life on Earth would be with long hair.

"Well," Levi says bracingly, leg tightening around Ren's waist, "we're all here now. In a few Earth days, we'll be on the new colonies. There's no more point thinking about that sort of stuff."

Ren thinks about space, instead. They say, "I think it would be nice if the compartments all came with windows of their own, like Elliot and Song Jian's compartment."

Levi sighs, keeps petting Ren's hair. "You and Asa both," he says, a little ruefully. "I really don't understand the appeal. There's nothing to even look at out there, doesn't that terrify you?"

"It's like staring into nothing, because space is the absence of things," Ren says. They rearrange their head and open their eyes to stare at the bottom of Levi's bunk, above their heads. "It's calming in that way, I think. Doesn't that make sense?"

"No," Levi says immediately. "I could do the same thing on Earth. Why would I come to space for that?"

Ren frowns. "I don't get it," they confess, and then turn onto their side to look at Levi. "Where on Earth can you look at space?"

Levi sighs, but he leans in, presses the curve of his smile against Ren's forehead before leaning away again. He tucks a piece of Ren's overgrown hair behind their ear and keeps his hand there. "On Earth, I never had the time to look out the windows the way we can here," he says. "So whenever I did, it felt pointless, looking for something I was never going to have."

"But I don't think this is the same," Ren says. "You're in space now. You can look out the windows now."

"I can look out, and still see nothing," Levi says wryly. "When I stare into space and see nothing, it reminds me of that feeling. So that terrifies me, that I've come so far and risked so much and still nothing has changed."

On Earth, Ren never saw Levi outside of school. He was always at school or work or leaving to go to school or work after his dad had left, because his mother had no inclination to take care of five kids by herself. He was always doing things for someone else and never for himself. Ren thinks that getting on this train was the first selfish thing Levi ever allowed himself.

"But if there's nothing when you look outside," Ren says quietly, "then, Levi, all the bad things are nothing, too."

Levi pauses. "I guess — if nothing matters, then nothing bad matters."

"So you do get it."

Levi laughs quietly.

Ren says, "I do still miss Earth, I think. A little."

"Already?" Levi teases, but his voice comes out just this side of wistful.

"I know it's pointless. We'll be on the new colonies soon, like you said."

"Ren," Levi says, then hesitates.

Ren closes their eyes again. Quickly, they add, "Do you think we'll have more to eat than meal flakes when we get there?"

"Elliot and Song Jian will, and they'll share," Levi says, with conviction. He pauses. "Ren — it's going to be good, all of us there together. It's going to be better than what we had."

Ren breathes. They feel the steady rise and fall of their chest prompting the steady rise and fall of Levi's. They miss Earth, but this, at least, they don't have to miss. Even if there's nothing out there, they'll still have this.

"I should get those antibiotics," they say, into Levi's hair. "I love you."

Levi presses a kiss to the side of Ren's head. "You're going to be just fine."

* * *

Ren spends a few minutes in Levi's bathroom throwing up, helps themselves to his mouthwash tablets, and then continues on down the hallway towards the front compartments.

It's late enough now that even the floodlights have shut off. The way is illuminated first by emergency strip lights on either side of the hallway, and then a strange glowing several meters down. When they draw in closer, they realize that it's coming from one of the viewing pavilions. The hydraulic door is shut but there's a crack left for safety purposes, enough to tell Ren there's light inside, there's someone inside.

They peek in before they make the conscious decision to. They say, "Asa?" in mostly a whisper.

Mostly a whisper, but in the emptiness, it carries. The door senses them and slides the rest of the way open. Asa had been pressed up against the glass at the far end of the viewing pavilion, but now he looks around, looks pleased. "Ren!" he exclaims.

"What are you doing here?"

"I was going to Levi's compartment to look for you since you took so long, but I got distracted," Asa says, a little ruefully. "Did you find Levi?"

"Yeah, but he said the antibiotics are all with Elliot, because —"

"Oh, yeah," Asa says, nodding. "You want me to go with you? How badly does it hurt?"

"Not too bad," Ren lies.

Asa frowns at them and moves towards the door. "Come in here and let me take a look."

Ren scrunches up their face. "What can you even see?" they ask, but they slide along the guardrails until they're right outside the viewing pavilion entrance. They reach down for Asa and let him pull them through the gravity shields. Asa catches them and heaves them upright before they can crumple to the ground, and then tugs them in gently. Ren obediently turns their head so that Asa can press a hand against their bad ear.

"The pain's not bad, you said? It hasn't gotten any worse?"

"It's only been a few minutes," Ren says, a little exasperated. "Besides, Levi gave me something for that already."

Asa hums a little, still holding onto them. Ren leans themselves very carefully against Asa's shoulder. Having something to press against like this does help relieve the pressure a little, and they want Asa to keep holding onto them.

"You want to stay awhile and look at the stars with me, or do you just want to get the antibiotics?"

Ren feels too comfortable to move. They say, "Let's look at the stars."

Asa presses the crease of his smile against the top of Ren's head. Then he turns them both around, steering them towards the end of the pavilion where triple sheets of reinforced, pressure-regulating glass are all that's between them and the rest of the universe.

The rest of the universe consists of nothing, nothing at all. Ren peers at the darkness for a moment, Asa's hands steady on their elbows. Looking out like this, like nothing has changed. Like they're still staring at the view from their apartment rooftop, from all the nights they've spent camped up there because they didn't want to sleep at home. The machinery of the train rumbles on beneath their feet. It looks like they're drifting aimlessly in space, not quite moving, but Ren knows that's not true. They know that it only looks like this because space is so vast, because everything else is moving so much faster than they are. They know that they'll be on the new colonies in three Earth days, far too fast for regret.

Asa says, "Can you believe, just a few hours ago, the Earth was our whole world? And now we're here, looking at all of this?"

Ren can believe it. It was in the documents they signed before getting on the train. But now that they're here, the universe spread before them, it feels different. They say, "Asa, what do you think would have happened if Elliot hadn't managed to get us all tickets?"

There's a brief pause. Asa's hand slides into Ren's, as though scared that if he doesn't hold on properly, Ren might drift right off. "I think," he says, his voice very careful, "that we'd have continued being unhappy on Earth."

Ren thinks about being unhappy on Earth. They think about feeling small and overwhelmed and constantly exhausted at the thought that no one wanted them the way they were. They think about all the separate reasons why they're all here now, each other their only familiar things left, why Song Jian had asked Elliot to get them all tickets onto this train, why they'd all agreed to leave an entire planet behind. They say, "You don't think things would've changed eventually?"

Asa asks, uncharacteristically subdued, "Do you?"

Do they? They've all made a decision. It was the right decision. What they don't know is if it's going to continue being the right decision, or what may happen after the dust settles and the urgency of this decision has run its course. But there's no point thinking about those things now, when it's already far too late.

So Ren says instead, "What do you miss most about Earth?"

Asa hums, considering. His hand grips Ren's, steady as ground. Ren knows Asa has never been great at staying still, but he tries hard for Ren. Asa says, "It changes a lot. But right now, looking at all of this — I think it must be the certainty of things. You know, routine. Something to depend upon, something to look forward to, things that you're used to. You get up in the morning, you have a coffee, you try and make do the best you can, you go to sleep, then you do it all again. The things you do every day don't change, really. There are always things that are for certain, down on Earth. You can be sure of things, on Earth."

Ren thinks they might miss that, too. They say, "But you hate doing the same things every day. You hate routine."

Asa laughs. "Ren, I *have* just gotten on a train in space."

Ren shrugs, a little embarrassed. "Well — you said —"

"I do like change," Asa agrees. "I think change can be good, or that most things can be good if you want them to work out badly enough, if you try hard enough. It's only that I liked knowing who I was and the things I had to do, and I no longer have that here — which isn't a bad thing. It's just that it's going to have to be different now, and I have to try again, and that's never easy in the beginning. But trying is the best any of us can do."

Ren thinks Asa is as scared of what they might find on the new colonies as the rest of them. "Is that — are you talking about your father?"

"I knew the things that were expected of me," Asa agrees. "My father wanted a lot of things for me — a college education, a steady career, all the things he cared about. I went along with it all, because I didn't mind. But I suppose that's why Levi asked me to come along. He thinks I should have a choice in my life. He's looking out for me. He thinks the things he wants are the things everyone wants."

"Do you?"

"What?"

"Want to be here," Ren clarifies. "Want the things that Levi wants."

Asa smiles and swings their joined hands between them. "I do want different things from him. Maybe it's because I always had time for myself but Levi's time was only ever for his family. But I also don't think Levi's wrong or selfish for leaving and wanting me to leave with him, even if I know he's thinking it. Everyone is entitled to ask for things that make them happy. You know, towards the end, I only ever saw him outside of class when I was sneaking into his room to sleep with him?"

"I know."

"So Levi wants things to be better, so much that it makes me wonder if things could be better for me, too. Levi makes me want more than what I had. And if Levi wanted me to come along with him, then of course I was going to come. I've never thought to ask myself what I wanted before, but now I guess I'll need to try."

Ren thinks about looking at nothing and feeling like nothing, right here on this train. Maybe for now there is nothing, but things change. Space is vast, after all. Change is scary, but that doesn't mean it can't be good. Things are usually what you make of them. That's why they're here.

Ren raises a hand absently, to press around their bad ear. Asa shifts to look at him. "Is the pain getting worse?" he asks again, concerned.

"It'll pass."

Asa looks at them. He smiles. "Yes," he agrees, "it will."

* * *

Ren spends five minutes convincing Asa they'll be fine going by themselves before leaving to continue down the hallway to the first-class compartments. The night appears to have grown darker while they were talking to Asa, although they know logically that's not possible. Space is also the absence of light.

A curtain dividing the VIPs from the rest of the train lights up and asks their purpose for coming since they don't have the right identification chip to get in. They tell it Elliot's name, and they assume Elliot must be alerted somehow because they're guided down the hallway with rapidly flickering lights, and plopped down in front of a wide-eyed, sleep-rumpled Elliot holding open his door.

"Elliot," Ren says. The gravity shields in Elliot's suite of rooms kick in too suddenly for them to balance, and they find themselves sprawling to the floor.

Elliot hooks his arms beneath Ren's armpits and drags them upright. "Shhh, Song Jian's already asleep," he says, voice hushed. "What are you doing here so late?"

Elliot's pajamas are very soft. Ren fists his dangling sleeves in their hands for something to hold onto, the nausea suddenly making them breathless. "I have an ear infection," they say, swaying a little. Their ear is ringing. Where there had been nothing before, it is now full of white sound.

Elliot tugs them in to press into his side. "Steady, Ren," he says softly, sounding worried, and then, "Guess we'll have to wake Song Jian up after all. Come sit down."

Instead of a bunk bed pushed against a wall to make way for a narrow walkway between the compartment door and a cramped, utilitarian bathroom, Elliot helps Ren down a foyer with a mirror along the length of one wall, into a living room with a dining table, couch, a large black screen, and a wall of glass windows like in the viewing pavilion with a bar counter running the length before it. There's a sliding door at the back of the room, which presumably opens up into the master bedroom and ensuite. It's not that luxurious for Earth, but it's luxurious in space, where everything is in sharp demand.

Elliot maneuvers them both onto the couch, where Ren sinks gratefully into the cushions and lets Elliot gently push them to lie down and stick a pillow beneath their head. Ren's eyes have slid half-closed by the time Elliot's arranged a throw blanket over them, but they're shaken awake what feels like bare seconds later by Song Jian's warm hand on their shoulder.

"Ren," Song Jian says, voice still scratchy with sleep. He hates being woken in the night with how difficult he finds getting to sleep, but Ren can tell he's making an effort to keep his tone soft. Elliot is standing beside him, hovering anxiously. "I've got the antibiotics, can you sit up for me?"

The antibiotics are Song Jian's own, pilfered from the hospital. Ren lets him pull them upright and feed them medicine and then water to wash it down.

Song Jian sits down on the couch beside them when they're done with a heavy sigh of exhaustion and pats at Ren's hair awkwardly. "You want painkillers, too? Something for the nausea? Elliot said —"

"Levi already gave me something for the pain, it's getting better," Ren lies. They worry a little at their bottom lip, looking at Song Jian. The dark circles beneath his eyes are huge; his pajamas hang too loosely off his frame. He's been starting to look better now after they'd gotten him away from the hospital a few days ago to prepare for the journey and Elliot's said that he'd been sleeping fine in his guest bedroom, but at the same time, the train lacks the proper facilities to take care of him in the way that he needs during and after an episode. They've all been worried, even though his most recent medication's been working well so far with few side effects. "Sorry for waking you."

"Nonsense," Song Jian says dismissively, but sags on the couch. "Although — Elliot, you may need to carry me back to bed."

Elliot just nods. "Ren, since you're already here, do you just want to sleep with us?"

"Sure," Ren says without thinking about it. They've stayed over at Elliot's place so many times before on Earth. Just because they're on a train in space now doesn't mean that such simple things need to change. "But I don't want to sleep on the couch alone."

"Brat," Song Jian says half-heartedly. He reaches out for Elliot. "Come on, then."

Elliot reaches out, too. Together, the three of them stagger into the master bedroom, supporting each other. Elliot and Song Jian don't have a bunk bed like the rest of them; instead, there's a fluffy, size-adjustable mattress. Elliot carefully lowers first Song Jian — who groans and rolls onto his side — and then Ren onto the bed before going to fiddle with the settings on the panel. The bed slowly expands enough to fit all three of them comfortably.

Ren lies down, too. They press their bad ear into a pillow that smells like Song Jian and feel immediately better.

"Goodnight, Ren," Elliot murmurs sleepily, settling in. "Wake us if you need anything. Song Jian, if you're sick in the night —"

"Yeah, yeah," Song Jian mutters, sounding already half asleep.

Ren closes their eyes and tries to follow suit, but their mind is restless. They open their eyes again to find that they've adjusted to the darkness, and stare up at the ceiling. Instead of the plain white of the compartments at the back of the train, there is an intricate series of carvings that run all along the ceiling of the room. Still not exactly the height of luxury back on Earth, but here in space, where everything, *everything* is valuable —

Objectively, Ren thinks, Elliot had the most to leave behind on Earth. Maybe he didn't really have a family, or people he loved outside of the four of them, but he had a life. A job. A future. Money, a means of survival, more secure than everyone else. If the rest of them had nothing, then Elliot had enough to give everyone a little something. Asa said if they hadn't gotten tickets, they'd have continued being unhappy on Earth, but Ren doesn't know that that's true. They don't know that Elliot was unhappy on Earth.

Song Jian's soft, rumbling snores have filled the room. Elliot whispers, "Ren, you're thinking so hard I can't sleep."

Ren turns over. They look up the perfect slope of Elliot's nose to his serious eyebrows, his dark eyes, and say, very quietly, "Elliot, why did you get us tickets here?"

Elliot looks back at them. "What?" he asks, in a tone of voice that means he's understood the question but not what Ren wants him to say.

Ren says, "Were you unhappy on Earth?"

"Ren," Elliot says.

"Do you miss it?"

Elliot sighs.

"It's okay if you think I won't like the answer," Ren says, as earnestly as they can. "I just want to know what you're thinking."

"It's not that," Elliot begins, and then pauses, like he's wondering himself. After a moment, he says carefully, "None of us had reasons to stay. Or, reason enough to stop us, anyway. It's not that there isn't anything to miss, it's like — no matter how bad it might get on the new colonies, it wouldn't be worse than what we were already living with. And in some ways, we already knew it was going to be better. We were going to be together."

"No," Ren says. "That's not true. Maybe for the rest of us, yes, but you had reasons to stay. You had so much more than this, on Earth."

Elliot says quietly, "The things I had aren't important. You guys are. And if you weren't happy and wanted to leave, then I was going to be the one leading the way."

Just over a year ago, they snuck Song Jian out of his hospital room for his birthday. They found an empty recreation room, where they could sit and be together. Asa, draped over Levi's lap, reached up to the ceiling and said, "I wish we could be up there, and not down here."

They were found by hospital security and chased away before anything could come of that conversation. But barely three weeks after that, Elliot got them all tickets onto this train in space. And now, in just a short few Earth days —

Song Jian rolls over with a soft wince; Ren knows his muscles get stiff easily. He stopped snoring a while ago, although Ren was still thinking too loudly to notice. He says, "You did lead the way, Elliot. Without you, none of this would've been possible."

There's a brief silence, like maybe Elliot was thinking too loud as well to notice Song Jian's been awake and listening in. Ren doesn't know if it counts as eavesdropping when this is technically Song Jian's bed too, and they like that Song Jian listened even when Ren didn't ask him to.

Elliot says, "That's unexpectedly sweet of you, Song Jian," in that strange, dry way they have with each other that Ren knows means affection.

"I meant it literally, actually," Song Jian says, also sounding strange and dry. Elliot laughs.

"But, still," Ren says. "Were you two happy, on Earth?"

"No," Song Jian says immediately and absolutely, but that was to be expected. What is it like, to know things in such black and white? Ren supposes Song Jian would know surest, out of all of them. He spent his whole childhood in and out of hospitals, and then after he turned fifteen, stopped coming out of them. They said it was for his own good, but Ren visited dutifully with books and flowers every weekend, watched Song Jian become paler and thinner and not the least bit better, so they don't know. They don't know.

"Do you think you're going to be happier, where we're going?" Ren asks.

Song Jian says, "That's not really what it's about, Ren."

"Happiness isn't a place," Elliot says. "If you're unhappy and go somewhere else looking for it, that's still not guaranteed. It's not a sock you lost in the laundry, or a coin the vending machine ate, or anything else like that, anything you can lose and find again. It's more a thing you make. For yourself, for someone else. You have to try for it. And I thought, if it's easier for everyone to try out here, without all those things on Earth you all wanted to get away from, then I thought we should do that. We should try, at least."

Ren remembers what Asa said. They say, "That's the best any of us can do, to try."

"Yes," Song Jian agrees. He's quiet for a moment, then he adds, "People don't listen when I say these things, so I don't really say them anymore. But, Ren, they told me if I insisted on leaving, I was putting myself in twice the danger. I don't think that leaving was the wisest decision, and I don't think I'd advise anyone else to do the same. But for me, I thought I was going to die twice as fast if I stayed in that hospital."

"*Song Jian,*" Elliot says, horrified, half-rising from the bed to look around Ren.

"It's true," Song Jian says steadily. "There are some decisions you have to make yourself, for yourself. I don't know if I miss Earth, but I do know this is a decision I made for myself."

Song Jian turned twenty-one two weeks ago. He was able to sign his own discharge papers then. Ren still isn't sure his parents know, even now, that he's on a train in space. They're not sure Song Jian bothered to tell them, or if he was too scared. But Song Jian's right, that no one has ever listened to the things he wanted before. There's only so far to run on Earth, but space is limitless. That's the point.

"We're on a train in space," Elliot says, determined. "You're going to get better. The new medication's been working fine for months. The hospital wasn't doing anything else for you, anyway."

But that's not the point, Ren thinks. The point is that Song Jian was able to make his own choice. That's already something more than what they used to have.

Song Jian yawns so wide his jaw cracks. He says, "Anyway. I don't know about you, Elliot, but I've never once found again a coin the vending machine ate."

Elliot laughs, surprised. "Ah, Song Jian," he sighs, but nothing else.

The silence settles. Ren blinks up at the dark ceiling, then closes their eyes against it. Song Jian's snuffling breathing has started up again; on their other side, Elliot crowds in on them, warm and giving.

A spark of green lights up the space behind Ren's eyelids. When they drag them open, they see that a hologram is being projected from the bedside table on Elliot's side, an image of Asa's narrow face and Levi's sharp one, from their identification papers. A scroll of text appears just above it, and a flat, robotic voice reads it out for them: *ASA TENOR and LEVI COSTEL here for ELLIOT RHODES.*

Song Jian makes an aggravated noise. "Why?" Elliot groans, swatting at the hologram. His hand only passses right through.

"We could just ignore them," Song Jian suggests.

"I can get the door," Ren offers, but all of them end up going anyway.

*   *   *

The suite doors open to Asa and Levi tumbling in, one after the other. Elliot yawns as he leads the way into the room, squinting disapprovingly down at the tangle of limbs on the floor. "Why is everyone here? It's sleep time. This is not where all of you sleep."

"We were looking for Ren," Levi says, frowning, at the same time Asa exclaims, "Levi came to the viewing pavilion, and I told him Ren had been there but left an hour ago, and they weren't in either of our compartments, so we got worried."

"I'm here," Ren says helpfully, peering out from where they're holding Song Jian's elbow to help keep him upright.

"Well, obviously," Levi says. "But we didn't know that. We thought something bad happened, maybe." He glances around the room and whistles a little. "So this is how the one percent live, huh."

Elliot raises his eyes to the ceiling for a moment. "Song Jian, go back to bed. Everyone else — go sit on the couch, I guess. I'll make hot chocolate if everyone's staying."

"I don't think I'll be able to fall asleep again tonight," Song Jian says, and staggers over to collapse on the couch. Levi and Asa immediately look guilty, starting towards him, but Song Jian waves them off.

"Can I help make the chocolate?" Ren asks eagerly, drifting over to where Elliot's standing at the long bar counter along the edge of the living room.

"Could you get the mugs out? They're in the bottom cabinet."

So Ren stands next to Elliot while he puts the stove on and warms milk and breaks in chunks of real chocolate to melt, and Ren gets to help add in spoonfuls of sugar and stir it all together. Elliot ladles it out into the waiting mugs, and Ren puts theirs beneath their nose immediately to breathe it in. When they bring it all over to the couch, there's just enough space for everyone to cram together, shoulders pressing against knees pressing against ankles.

"How's the ear infection, Ren?" Asa asks, both hands cupped against the warmth of his mug.

"Better," Ren says, drawing their legs up on the couch, and finds themselves surprised that it's become true. They aren't sure if that's due to the painkillers or the antibiotics or something else entirely. "I think it'll be gone by tomorrow."

"You need to finish the course of antibiotics anyway," Song Jian mumbles. "To make sure."

Elliot says, "The couch spins around to face the windows. Does anyone want to watch the stars?"

Levi shudders and shrinks back into the cushions. "Why do you all like looking outside so much?"

"What's wrong with space?" Elliot asks, sounding genuinely curious.

Levi darts a look at Ren. "Well, it's — it reminds us of everything we've left behind, doesn't it, and we don't know what might happen from here on. If this was the right decision. Isn't that scary?"

"We all agreed —" Song Jian begins, mouth set argumentatively.

Ren interrupts, "That's why we're here in the first place. Isn't it?"

Ren had very few things on Earth that they thought of as worthy of missing, of regretting leaving behind. Like Elliot, their family never really bothered with them. Like Song Jian, they've always liked the idea of going where they wanted and doing things for themselves. Like Asa, they've spent a lot of time being wary of asking for more, wary of things changing, because even if things weren't good, they were at least good enough. Like Levi, they've stared constantly out the window thinking *what if*.

They've spent a very long time content with feeling invisible in their home and wanting to be invisible at school. They've spent a very long time just existing, and being unhappy. Their family had never really had anything, so they had even less for Ren. But Ren thinks about being allowed to miss things, even when those things were objectively terrible — when they had to hide constantly at school, when they always took the long way home, when they were never allowed to be only themselves in front of anyone else. But just because something hadn't been good doesn't mean that you can't miss it anyway. And just because you miss the way things used to be doesn't mean that you can't look forward to the way things could someday be. So, in the end:

"Levi, it isn't all for nothing. We're all trying. We're all here. You told me earlier that there was no more point in thinking about the things left behind. But I also think... we're allowed to miss them."

Levi swallows. "Yes," he says.

Ren hums. They wind a finger beneath the hem of their sleep pants and tug at them. They're not as soft as the ones that Elliot and Song Jian have, these ones mass-produced and uniform-issued when they'd been assigned compartments on the train. But they're still better than what they used to have. They miss a lot of things on Earth, but that doesn't mean things won't get better here if they just allow themselves to try.

"I think it's okay to miss things and have regrets and wish to turn back time, even if none of that's possible," Ren says. "I just think you have to let yourself look forward too, because change can be good if you try. I can't say if this is the right decision, but it's one we made for ourselves. Aren't things already better, with the five of us?"

"Ah, Ren," Asa sighs. Elliot's smiling.

"You have to make happiness for yourself, if you want it, but the nice thing about that is you can make it anywhere you like," Ren says. "And, you know, space is vast."

"For what it's worth," Song Jian says, after a moment, "I'm very glad I'm on this train with all of you."

Ren says, "Me too." And because it's something they mean, "It's easier to try with the people you want to try with."

Levi's tipped over so that his head is in Ren's lap, legs stretched over Asa's. Asa has begun to massage Levi's calves without being asked, even though he's pulling a face as he does it. The blackness outside no longer feels so all-consuming when Ren's surrounded so completely on all sides with warmth. Song Jian drops his head between Elliot's shoulder blades, and appears to instantly fall asleep there despite his earlier protests.

"Is this a party now?" Elliot asks, sounding amused.

"Well," says Ren, smiling, "since we're here tonight."

Xu Ran grew up moving between multiple countries and therefore has a lot of feelings about the idea of home. She enjoys drinking black coffee instead of water, eating cake instead of actual meals, and spends most of her free time putting things into online shopping carts before taking them out again.

For content notes, see page 244

I'll Have You Know

by Charlie Jane Anders

WHAT DO YOU GET YOURSELF on your hundredth birthday? New shoes? Cake? A season pass to the 0p3rA for their V#rd! retrospective? To hell with all that. El puts on a nice shirt, scrolls on down to the Endocrinthology Center, and tells Dr. Webbo, "I wanna do it. Today is the day."

Dr. Webbo refocuses her view from enhanced scan to actual, which means she's staring right at El. "Are you sure?" she asks. "It's a big step, especially at your age."

"Yeah. I'm sure. I've had a hundred years to think about it, right? I want to start hormones and nano-therapy. I wanna transition from male to female."

El only squirms a little, on the medical bench inside Dr. Webbo's private office, which looks just like a secluded meadow full of wildflowers.

Dr. Webbo asks El more questions, but meanwhile the doctor's already using her left index finger to click "yes" on a bunch of boxes. El produces a hologram of her therapist, Dr. Russell, winking and giving a big thumbs-up, but luckily, the process of gender transition has gotten easier and less gatekeeper-y since the last time El looked into it.

El always pictured the first gender-confirmation treatment being a kind of glittery mist blown into her face from a cupped palm, like fairy dust. And yeah, that's one of the options, but there's also a kind of body paint (starts blue, turns pink, very on-the-nose) and a lozenge you can put under your tongue. But El wants to make a wish and snort fairy-dust, so that's what she goes with. Head rush!

"You should start noticing the effects pretty much immediately," Dr. Webbo says. "Your body will look and feel different, and you might have some mood swings. Good news is, you're healthy enough that you could live another twenty-five years, or even thirty, to enjoy your new gender." She gazes at the enhanced scan view. "But… why don't you tell me about your dreams?"

El's head is still swimming from the sparkly flakes, and she has a hard time remembering any of her dreams. "Boring. Weird," she says. "A lot of shoe salesmen trying to get me to wear birdcages on my feet. I wake up feeling amazing, though."

El is too busy doing a happy dance inside her mind to pay full attention to all Dr. Webbo's questions. She should have done this decades ago. *Today is the first day of my life as a woman,* El says to herself. *I finally found myself, and it only took a lifetime.*

"Hmmm…" Dr. Webbo furrows her high forehead, causing her locs to shift around. "Says here that you're only on the most basic sleep package. Your dreams are keeping you young, but they're not teaching you anything."

"What if I don't want my dreams to teach me?" El says. "I still learn the old-fashioned way: by making a series of increasingly disastrous choices."

Dr. Webbo doesn't even laugh at El's joke, which, let's be honest, was only half a joke. El did try to re-skill as an interior-decor coder at age eighty-three, right when all of the decor-scripting languages were becoming obsolete. And then there's the matter of El's roommate, whom we'll get to soon enough. Changing gender is probably the first smart move El has made since her late forties.

"This is a quality of life issue." Dr. Webbo uses her Serious Doctor voice. "However much time you have left, you need to have the best experience possible. I'm going to mark on your file that you declined any dream-enhancements, but I'm going to send you some literature."

"Okay." El suddenly feels self-conscious about being argumentative, because she should be trying to turn over a new leaf. She's starting her second century on this planet, she just finally took the plunge and flipped her gender. Today of all days, she ought to be gracious. "I'll totally think about it. I'll talk to my roommate even."

Dr. Webbo knows all about El's roommate, so she just shakes her head. "I would avoid discussing this with Goaty, if I were you."

*   *   *

El still doesn't feel any different when she leaves the Endocrinthology Center — but the world looks quite transformed. Her gender marker changed in every datasink while she was finishing up her birthday check-up with Dr. Webbo, so everywhere she looks, the shops are advertising these wraps that morph from sundress to corset dress at sunset. Cartoon characters and knights in armor call her "Ms." or "Ladyperson" as they pass on the scroll, and even the trees appear fluffier. Of course, every window and streetlight offers El various hundredth-birthday deals, which she's dreaded (one reason she gave herself something else to celebrate today.)

The newsbubbs are full of occurrences which would be terrifying on their own, but which collectively form a gaudy tapestry. The artificial reef we built off the Gulf Coast has been singing again, mostly Stevie Wonder and Aretha Franklin. The Martian robot commune is threatening to shoot down any humans who approach. Five million people are threatening to go on an emotional-labor strike. The Patent Office is once again recognizing Inaction Patents (for new and innovative methods of refraining from doing something) and has already received thousands of applications.

By the time El gets home, her back aches and her knees are doing her a mischief, and all her euphoria at finally making the big change is fully wearing off. All she wants to do is sit down, maybe watch some stories. But of course, her roommate greets her at the front door, bouncing and demanding to hear every single detail.

Goaty is seven feet tall and teal-colored, except for a purple beard, and today they're wearing a long crimson necktie and some Bermuda shorts on their woolly goat body. Plus very serious square-framed glasses.

"Not much to tell," El tells Goaty. "Just a routine checkup. Oh, and I changed my gender at last. Feels good so far."

"You don't look a day over ninety." Goaty claps their hoofs.

Goaty's ingratiating tone makes El suspicious, so she squints at them. "You've lost another two percent of your value."

"That's the trouble with a floating exchange rate," Goaty says in a fake-cheerful tone. "Sometimes it just don't float the way you want."

When El decided to put all of her retirement savings into a new cryptocurrency, she never expected to end up actually sharing her apartment with the evolved form of Goatcash. For the first few years, Goatcash was fine, accruing value faster than a flesh-and-blood goat could chew through a trash pile. But something happened — El still isn't quite sure what — and now Goatcash is a sentient being, who lives with her. And sometimes devours all of her junk food, usually while taking terrifying dips in valuation.

"Today of all days, I don't want to have to worry about you," El says. And then she can't help mentioning the exact thing that Dr. Webbo told her not to mention to Goaty: "My doctor thinks I should get my dreams enhanced."

"Whoa. I've never dreamed, unless you count my birth, when I experienced delusions of currency." Goaty strokes their glorious lavender plume of beard with their left hoof. "But don't you kind of want to make the most of your dreams? I've been watching you sleep, and I have to say you're pretty uninspiring."

"You've been… watching me sleep." El can feel her microbiome go feral.

"What?" Goaty turns shrugging into a dance. "You always watch me sleep."

"That's only because you sleep all the time." El snorts. "You should get a job. Whatever kind of jobs they give to failed cryptocurrencies."

"I'm a success on my own terms!"

It's just barely night-time, but El feels exhausted. Big day. She crawls into bed and feels the gel slowly ooze over her, getting in her pores. While she sleeps, the gel will rejuvenate her cells, like always, and stimulate her neural pathways. She only looks up a few times to see if Goaty is there.

Sometime in the middle of the night, the "literature" that Dr. Webbo promised arrives. Instead of the usual dream-nonsense, El's ninth-grade volleyball coach, Mr. Rayford, is standing next to her first real boss, Jayjay Manter, and they're both talking to El about the benefits of enhanced dreaming.

"Just think. You could learn a language, or even become a juggler." Mr. Rayford juggles three volleyballs.

"I dunno," El says to these authority figures, whom her conscious mind barely remembers. "I worry there's a thin line between sleep-learning and indoctrination."

"All learning is indoctrination," says Jayjay, with the smirk that El remembers from all those awful staff meetings. "Information is never truly content-neutral, right? The point is, you don't want to be left behind."

El keeps arguing with them until she wakes up, feeling crampy. Goaty is making a big show of not looking at her.

*   *   *

El can still remember being in her mid-fifties and desperately wanting to transition from male to female. It was right after her divorce from Bessie, which had felt like the end of her life, even though the marriage had only lasted seven years. Back then, one thought stopped El in her tracks: *what if I'm just too old?* The idea of starting over at age fifty-four, or fifty-five, just seemed insurmountable, and El pictured everybody looking at her and going, *Who do you think you're kidding?* But after El decided not to take the plunge, she kept meeting people her own age and even older, who'd transitioned "late," and seemed serenely happy in their own skins.

For decades, El kept finding reasons to hold off, like, *Why not wait until after the Robertsons' picnic?* Or, *Maybe once I've made myself indispensable at this new job.* And then there was always another occasion where El probably ought to make an appearance as a distinguished older gentleman, rather than... whoever she was going to be after transitioning. And that was part of the problem, really: El had a hard time visualizing the person she was going to be, and how people were going to react to her, and she was really good at convincing herself that it was fine either way.

Until one morning, El woke up and realized that: A) She was ninety-nine years old, and B) She no longer gave a shit. And it was not too late at all, because it was *never* too late, and whatever El did, she would still be the same person, in most of the ways that matter. And trying to be "taken seriously" is a foolish game.

"Here's what I don't get, though." Goaty is doing some painfully incompetent goat-yoga. "You're happy to alter your body, and to some extent your mind, by flooding yourself with female hormones and nanotech. But you don't want to enhance your dreams? You could learn to code in Whut, or understand the new disunified ultrasymmetry physics."

"Could I finally understand why I put all of my money into a cryptocurrency that keeps trying to eat my drapes?" El grumbles, lowering herself into a duct-taped recliner.

She keeps noticing weird sensations, as if she can actually feel her fat redistributing to her chest and hips, and her skin softening. She almost cried at an ad for shower-grout caulk.

"Hey!" Goaty stops in the middle of violent planking. "I never promised to keep gaining value. Or to be a perfect roommate. All I promised is, I would solve the Byzantine General Problem. Have you been attacked by a Byzantine general even once, since you invested in me? No, you have not. Success!"

Later, El reaches all the way into the back of her closet for the dress she bought twenty years ago and never wore, and she feels a moment of panic as she slips it on. Like this dress could burst into flames as soon as she clasps the clasp. Her skin is so sensitive, all of a sudden. "What's the point of dying without ever once getting to be real?" El says out loud. She wiggles her thumb and a mirror appears, revealing a round-faced woman with her white hair in a bob, who could be one of the old ladies on that comedy show El used to watch. She looks cute, but unremarkable. Which… is perfect.

This is the person El was trying so hard to visualize, back in her fifties.

She hasn't really been aware of her own body for a decade or two, other than as a flawed vessel that could break down at any moment. What if her body could be a source of joy once more?

*　*　*

El goes out and scrolls to the tea-dome, where some friends around her age are getting wasted on Lapsang Souchong and shortbread. Everybody congratulates El on the birthday and transitioning and just generally still being a work in progress.

Turns out Yen and Harriet and a few others have been doing the "enhanced dreaming" thing. "I woke up having memorized all of Samuel Coleridge," says Harriet with a laugh. "You don't want to be left behind."

"I can do my own taxes now, thanks to the enhanced dreaming," adds Aaron. "You don't want to be left behind."

"Why do you all keep repeating that phrase?" El says.

"Which phrase?" Yen asks.

El repeats it: "'You don't want to be left behind.'"

"I never said that," Harriet protests.

But then fifteen minutes later, they're talking about something else, and Harriet randomly says, "But then again, you don't want to be left behind." And then immediately denies having said it.

That evening El has a hot date with a 117-year-old non-binary person named Ray, who insists on getting a pitcher of margaritas, because what's one more artificial liver replacement? They eat nothing but chips and guacamole. Ray is extremely cute, with pink streaks in their hair and a velvet jacket. But they mention that they're also doing the "enhanced dreaming" thing — and they also randomly keep saying, "You don't want to be left behind."

El ends the date early, even though she was having a pretty good time.

* * *

The weird sales pitch is back in El's dreams. This time, it's Dr. Lathorp, the marriage counselor who kind of took Bessie's side. "I'm glad you're working through your gender issues at last," Dr. Lathorp says, with maximum condescension. "But listen, you need to sign up for the enhanced dreams. Everyone over ninety is doing them."

"Is it only older people, then?" El feels even more suspicious than before.

"Younger folks don't need it." Dr. Lathorp sounds exactly the same as when she called El a supporting character in her own marriage.

"Yeah, I think I'm gonna pass," El says.

"I'm trying to help you." Dr. Lathorp is scribbling with a pen that has no ink. "You don't want Dr. Webbo to report that your faculties are impaired, or you could get put on Supported Living. You might not be allowed to leave your house without supervision, for instance."

"If you were going to threaten me, you shouldn't have chosen the form of someone who was so bad at their job." A chill is going all the way through El's bones and she suddenly doesn't feel super confident of breathing.

When El looks again, Dr. Lathorp has turned into the state legislator that El interned for in college, Mitch something-or-other. Mitch is holding out a piece of paper and saying, "Come on, sign this, will ya? I have places to be."

El ignores Mitch in favor of studying her surroundings. They're in Mitch's old office: glass case of softball trophies, shelf of unread books, beautiful desk supporting a crappy computer. El starts pulling books off the shelf, because she's remembered two things: dream geography is bullshit, and El studied interior-decor coding for five years.

There, at the back of the bookshelf, El finds a ragged hole in the fake wood. She pushes her hand through, and then her whole body, until she's in a dank secret passageway. Somewhere behind her, Mitch something-or-other keeps explaining the many benefits of dream enhancement in a stentorian tone. El keeps going down the passageway as it gets deeper and narrower, until she finds a bunch of roots dangling from the dirt over her head.

El can't help giggling at the literalism, as she pulls on the roots and gets herself root access. As she suspected, there's been some corruption here: a malicious codeset that embeds instructions like, DON'T VOTE, NEVER CHALLENGE AUTHORITY, STAY AT HOME, YOU DON'T WANT TO BE LEFT BEHIND. She wishes she had a way to make screenshots of all this, and then her dream helpfully provides an old-school digital camera, like from her youth.

"I'm leaving now," El tells Mitch, who's followed her down into the tunnel. "People are going to find out about your scam. If you know what's best for you, you'll clear the hell out of my dreams."

"But —" Mitch something-or-other sputters. "You're making a terrible mistake."

"Terrible mistakes are kind of my thing," El says. "But you know what? I'm a success on my own terms." She doesn't even realize for a moment that she just quoted Goaty. She hopes they never find out, because they'd be insufferable.

She pushes her way back into Mitch's office, and keeps shoving through doors, until she finally pushes out of the gel's dreamscape.

Back in the real world, El sits up, with the last of the gel evaporating off her skin. Goaty is lotus-positioning at the foot of her bed, staring at her.

"Whatever you just did, you should do it way more often," Goaty says. "You've never slept this entertainingly before."

El just rolls her eyes, and searches her image folder for the screenshots she took of the secret code at the heart of the enhanced-dreaming program. "You know what?" she says to Goaty. "I think I'm turning into the kind of old lady who makes trouble."

Goaty is too busy trying to eat her only dignified pair of pants to answer.

A version of this story was first published in *MIT Technology Review* (2019).

Charlie Jane Anders is the author of *Victories Greater Than Death*, the first book in a new young-adult trilogy, along with the forthcoming short story collection *Even Greater Mistakes*. Her other books include *The City in the Middle of the Night* and *All the Birds in the Sky*. Her fiction and journalism have appeared in the *New York Times*, the *Washington Post*, Slate, *McSweeney's*, *Mother Jones*, the *Boston Review*, Tor. com, *Tin House*, *Conjunctions*, *Wired Magazine*, and other places. Her TED Talk, "Go Ahead, Dream About the Future," got 700,000 views in its first week. With Annalee Newitz, she co-hosts the podcast Our Opinions Are Correct.

For content notes, see page 244

The Cafe Under the Hill

by Ziggy Schutz

THERE IS A CAFE WHERE THE SUN IS WARM but never too bright, the pastries are always fresh, and everything knows not to use their real name.

The barista is always beautiful, the cashier always stunning, although their proportions shouldn't quite work, something always a little too long or a little too sly. Their smiles seem genuine, though, as they serve coffee to "Stardust," "Sister," and "Customer 87." Their eyes are dark and reflect the light, and they never seem to age, even though they have both worked there for years.

They do accept money there — any currency will do. They also love making deals — a month of coffee for a bit of hair, a custom birthday cake for one hundred smiles. They even give some things away, although everyone who goes there knows better than to accept anything for free.

All sorts of people frequent this cafe, folk Fair and Foul, storybook creatures sharing sugar with nightmares, and always, always humans, who can only find this place if shown by a friend or truly lost.

Humans are the barista's favourites.

Christopher walks into The Cafe Under the Hill at 9:35 on a Thursday morning, his time. He holds the door for a shadow, grins at a couple on their first date, and walks up to the counter. He moves with a grace and a confidence that is almost Fae-like, even as his kind smile betrays his humanity. His tight, short curls are a shock of blond against his warm brown skin, sitting like a crown against his temples.

It is his first time here.

"What can I get for you?" asks the cashier. She is here every day, and greets most guests with their usuals already rung up. Her goat-pupil eyes seem to spin as they take in their newest customer.

"I'd like... A slice of carrot cake, please. And an iced latte."

"Want any flavouring in that?"

Christopher takes his time answering that one, bushy brows scrunched up like caterpillars as he considers the question. "Is luck an option?" he asks finally.

The cashier nods. "Of course!"

A laugh explodes from the boy, who is probably a human twenty, twenty-one. His excitement is that of a child, regardless of his age. So many humans are delighted by anything even slightly out of the ordinary.

"I'll get that, then! Anything that helps with a happy ending. With soy? Or any non-dairy option. For here?"

She types in what might be his order and what might be gibberish, or something else entirely in a language the Fair Folk have neglected to share. "That will be seven. And three pennies, if you have them. Older than ten years."

He takes a moment to count out exact coin. This cafe does not take card and does not give change.

She takes it, popping a penny into her mouth and the rest of it into a drawer.

"Oh! What's the name for the order?"

"Christopher," says Christopher.

The barista, midway through his latte, freezes. Their curls frizz with the tension, all standing on end. They turn to meet eyes with the cashier.

Most people choose names that are obviously not theirs. That are nobody's at all.

"An interesting name," the cashier gets out, shaking off her surprise.

"Thanks!" says Christopher. "It's mine."

The other patrons have started to shift, uncomfortable. It's been so long since this happened. None of them have ever been around to see it.

"Christopher," calls out the one making the drinks. A bell tolls, although no one has moved to ring it.

Do not give the baristas at The Cafe Under the Hill your True Name. Everyone knows that.

Everyone, that is, but Christopher.

"Thanks!" he says again, and takes his order to a table. He eats, seemingly oblivious to how everyone around him is pretending not to stare.

Once he's finished, he busses his plate and glass, and heads for the door with a wave.

"Christopher," says the cashier, and even though it is no one else's name, every human and every creature flinches.

All but Christopher.

"Have a good one," he says, and with a twinkle of his fingers he is out the door.

He has left. He shouldn't be able to, but he did so anyway.

"We're closed," says the barista. No one moves.

The cashier raises her voice. The lights flicker. "We are closed for the day!"

Everyone scurries out, the spell-that-was-no-spell broken. With a wave of the barista's hand, the door locks.

The two Fae, who helped place the floorboards for this shop so long ago, who are indistinguishable from the roots of this place, stare at each other for a moment immeasurable.

"But it was his name," says one to the other. They know each other's True Names, a marriage of trust and power as well as love. But even they do not speak them here, the traps they have set not clever enough to spare its creators if they slip up. They said them once, out loud to each other, far away from here, and then had to make do with compliments and endearments. That is how it is, for most Fae. Calling a lover by their name is as foolish as it is dangerous. Instead, they try to pack as much affection as they can into words that don't really belong to them at all.

"Darling," says the cashier to the barista.

It is not even the names that they crave. It is the intimacy, the trust.

"Sweetheart," replies Darling. "What happened?"

It is the promise of forever.

"I don't understand," says Sweetheart. "It was his True Name."

Darling reaches out, sending their power down past the floorboards, into the ground where their traps still glow, even after all this time. They are fine, as hungry and as patient as ever. It is not a problem with the traps.

Sweetheart reaches up, makes sure every roof tile is still overlapping just so, checking for leaks and for secrets. Nothing is hiding, everything is hidden.

There is nothing else they can do, with the information they have. The next day, the store is reopened. Only those who were there the day before know something has happened, and they don't dare speak of it. For all that this cafe is a comfort and a port in a storm to some of them, they know that it is a place to visit and move on from, and none of them want to draw the wrong kind of attention lest the doors and windows cloud over and become a cage.

Christopher doesn't come back the next day, or the day after. But a week or a month later, he walks in with a friend. She has big eyes and clever hands and a haircut that says pixie but a height that says dryad, and she is none of these things at all — only human.

"This is Abigail," he says, and that is true.

"It's a pleasure to meet you," Abigail says. "I've heard a lot about this place, I'm excited to finally be able to check it out." This is also true.

No trap springs. Abigail tips well, gets whipped cream on her nose when she sips at her hot chocolate, and laughs when Christopher points it out. They leave together, uncontested.

Sweetheart pulls at her hair until the colour strips right out of it, leaving bits of blonde all over the floor. Darling sweeps it up with the cafe's worn broom, humming something comforting for only Sweetheart to hear.

Fae are not cruel, because cruel is a human word. It's not that they long to see Christopher and Abigail suffer. It's that there are rules, rules that even they have to follow, and these two have come into their space and broken them, and they do not know how or why.

To understand, you have to look at the rules themselves, and ask yourself one very important question.

What makes a name True?

For most, it is in the gifting, the parent or maker looking at a being and giving them something without asking for anything in return.

There is power in that, when it is done honestly. And most do not question this, even as they earn nicknames and accolades and move further and further away from that moment of naming.

But for some, they look at that name and tear at it, pulling it apart like they are looking for the seams. For some, the name itself betrays something about a nature they do not wish to have. Something given freely, but not without cost, the name a summary and a symbol of everything in their life that was misunderstood at their beginning.

Christopher was given a name that meant princess, and found himself longing to be a prince instead. So he reached deep into himself and delved for a name that felt right, a name that fit, like a shirt finally sitting on shoulders that had always felt too thin, or a chest that had always taken up a little too much space.

Names have power, and so do words. To take an old name and declare it dead is to kill a past that was never really yours. It wasn't something anyone did on purpose, but Christopher has always been the curious sort. When he first stumbled into the outer circles of the Fair Folk's business, he wondered what that would mean for him, freshly named as if freshly born, bearing a name that is less a gift and more a reward for surviving. Survival he wears in the bruises on his knuckles and pressed into his ribs. He is curious and he is brave, brave to the point of foolishness, like any proper prince from once upon a time.

So, he takes a chance, and introduces himself as Christopher.

Things freely given leave paths connecting us all. Whether out of kindness or out of tricks, they leave openings, openings that can be exploited. To know someone's True Name is to know someone's true beginnings, after all. As if you were there at the moment of their naming, and so there to dictate their future too. But if that name has died, if that story has changed genres at the request of its hero... well. How does knowing someone's new and truest name give you power over them, when it took such strength and power to claim it? When the whole point of it is to be Known?

Christopher went into the woods and dug a hole and cast an old name into it, returned it to the earth even as he forged himself a new path. Abigail climbed the tallest of mountains and tossed her old name to the winds, let it be torn apart around her even as she donned her new mantle.

The renaming is not new. No, humans have been doing that as long as they've existed, no matter what the history books say. The Fae have always delighted in it, come to consider those humans who claimed their own gender or decided to do away with the concept of it entirely to be closer to Fair than the rest. No, the renaming is not new. What is new is the deliberate way Christopher wears his journey, Abigail her triumph. What's new is the openness.

Humans have been finding new ways to break the old rules since the first one stumbled into a ring, slipped their way through the dirt, and found themselves under the hill. That, more than anything else, is what makes them human. The curiosity, the drive to change.

Darling and Sweetheart have never seen it laid so bare before them, this phenomenon of humanness. The anger comes from an itch, an itch to understand without the knowledge of how to ask.

Perhaps they would have learned on their own, in time. But that is not what happens. What happens is that Christopher and Abigail walk in a few days later, a new friend with a new name beside them.

"Hello," says Christopher, who orders for all three. "Instead of paying today, I thought we could trade."

Darling leans over the counter, close enough that Christopher can see the years in their pupils, like the rings of a tree. "What would you like to offer as trade?"

"I can tell you how we did it," says Christopher, because his kindness is a human's kindness, and his curiosity is the kind that breaks things but also takes the time to learn how to put them back together again.

They sit down around cups of coffee with luck mixed in, and Christopher and Abigail and Javier take turns talking about burials and Sweetheart and Darling hold hands as they listen, and when the humans leave and the shop is empty Darling turns to Sweetheart with a light in their eyes that brings to mind the revel they met at, how those bright eyes shone across a crowd and Sweetheart knew she would spend her whole existence following those particular stars, if Darling let her.

The shop closes for a day. That is all they need.

There is a cafe where the sun is always warm but never too bright, where the ice cubes don't melt and the tea is never bitter. There is a hole underneath its floorboards, where certain things are buried.

The owners wear nametags and love to call each other endearments, names like darling and sweetheart, but more than anything they love to call each other by their names, Arbutus and Orion, always said like it's the first time they've ever gotten to address each other out loud.

It's said if you go there you will fall in love just by being near them, because some emotions are just too big for anyone to keep inside their own skin.

Abigail and Javier still visit often, and they are never asked to pay — although they often do anyway, with stories more often than any coin. And of course, Christopher has become a fixture of the place. Arbutus always greets him by name when he walks through the door, and Orion thanks him by it, too, when they hand him his order.

He says their names like they're old friends, and Orion thinks they understand why the Fair Folk have always been so fascinated by humans, as if stealing them away like that will help to figure them out.

"To think," Arbutus says with a smile. "All they had to do was ask."

Humans and Fae share a certain cleverness. The only difference is that Fae hint at it while humans delight in showing it. Arbutus cannot begrudge them this. After all, so many of them do so with a smile.

Orion nods, and kisses their lover, and says her name like a promise of forever (which it is).

If you find The Cafe Under the Hill, let yourself walk in and approach the counter. The new cashier will greet you with a wave, will recommend anything as long as it's got carrot or luck in it, and he won't eat the pennies, but if you want, you can tip him with a story.

As long as it has a happy ending. He's rather fond of those.

This story was first published in *Vulture Bones* (2018).

Ziggy Schutz (she/her/he/him) is a queer and disabled author writing out of the Pacific Northwest. She finds herself drawn to fantastical stories and hopeful endings, and is always searching for the moments between, where he can catch his breath. She can be found on Twitter **@ziggytschutz**.

For content notes, see page 244

(don't you) love a singer

by TS Porter

REALITY BUCKED AND TWISTED. The *Sweet Crescendo*'s deck dropped out from beneath Kait's feet and then rose up to smack her tumbling into a wall, which fell away from her arms as she fell toward it. Another twist, and she was thrown back into a heap on the heaving deck. The entire left side of her body ached from the bad landing. There were screams, and the crashes of cargo crates splitting as space and time conspired to tear the ship apart.

This was how it happened. This was how it ended, just another interstellar freighter lost in subspace with all hands. The lead chanter was down — dead or just injured, Kait couldn't tell. There was blood, the scent of it in the air and the red splash of it in an uneven arc across a twisting wall. Or was that the floor?

Kait briefly caught sight of Maya, her mouth open in a panicked scream. She reached for her but space twisted again, violently, and Maya was gone. Kait couldn't see Danicai anywhere.

Another gravitational wave, and the entire ship squealed under the pressure. The terrible sound arrived in Kait's ears uneven, shifted red and blue. One of the pilots' safety harnesses failed, and they were thrown out of the high bird's nest to fall in uneven fits and jerks toward the bucking deck.

This was how they died. This was why Kait's renny had tried her entire youth to steer her away from spaceships and singers. The lead chanter was down, and their second wasn't taking up the job. Kait could not stand, could not stomp to keep time, but she managed to brace herself in the crack between two cargo crates. She breathed deep, filling her lungs from the bottom of her boots up to the back of her throat, and slammed her right fist against the twisting floor. The ringing sound carried out through the ship. Two, three, four, and she opened her mouth.

"Weigh heigh, and up she rises!" Kait belted out, with all the force she could project. It was one of the oldest of shanties, from back when the ships it was sung on were wooden and sailed across oceans of water.

"*Weigh heigh, and up she rises,*" a few other voices answered. A few more stomping feet or pounding hands joined her in keeping the beat. They were all off-rhythm, with spacetime twisting around them.

"Weigh heigh, and up she rises!"

"*Early in the morning!*" More voices, gathering, strengthening.

Kait could do this. She might be a new hand, one of the most junior singers aboard with only six months under her belt, but the way her renny told the story she'd been born singing. Renny sang around the house, and Kait couldn't remember a time when she didn't have a tune on her tongue, when she wasn't adding her own verses to the classic songs.

She'd always loved to watch the ships come in. Sailing crews had seemed larger than life to her. Whenever they could, Kait and Maya would go down to the shipyards and watch the singers disembark from their spaceships, exulting in full-throated song. They were barrel-chested, their voices bigger and stronger than other people's, their friendships tighter. They laughed and sang and held each other close, and it made Kait's chest hurt with want to watch them.

"Don't you go and love a singer," Renny would warn her when e caught her at it — her beautiful renny with er often-broken heart. E didn't follow er own advice. The lovers e brought home, now and then, were singers more often than not. Some of them could be persuaded to teach Kait new shanties, new harmonies. They taught her breathing exercises to expand her lung capacity, and how to sing at volume without harming her voice, and she'd practiced endlessly.

It wasn't the singers Kait loved — she'd figured out early that she was ace, and never wanted anything to do with romance — it was the singing. She'd been born full of song, and she wasn't letting the *Sweet Crescendo* go. Not without a fight.

"Drunken Sailor" were the typical words to this shanty, but those irreverent lyrics wouldn't be right. Kait couldn't gently poke fun at anyone, not when she didn't know who on the crew was injured, or even if Maya and Danicai were alive or dead.

Maya had been her best friend since their school days. They understood each other like no one else ever had, and could have entire conversations in duet, much to the annoyance and confusion of their classmates. When Kait had proposed that they hire on to a freighter company, she did it in song, and Maya had taken her hand and harmonized with an argument she'd been composing to convince Kait of the very same thing. They'd never considered going without each other.

She'd been so scared when Danicai had joined her in orbit around Maya, loving her in ways Kait didn't. She'd trusted Maya not to leave her, but she'd been afraid that Danicai would try to steal all of Maya's love and attention from her. Instead Danicai had taken them as the unit they were and twined both voice and life around them to gently and sweetly strengthen Maya and Kait's endless duet into a tercet. Kait had gained another friend as dear to her as the breath in her lungs.

Kait couldn't tease them without knowing they were safe. Any words would do for the shanty she was leading, so long as they could be made to fit the measure. What she needed most was hope, and she couldn't be the only one.

"Sing loud so the Captain hears you!" Kait sang.

"Sing loud so the Captain hears you."

"The Captain and the pilot hear you!" Looking up, Kait could see Captain Smith and the last remaining pilot frantically working on the ship's controls. Trying to bring the *Sweet Crescendo* back into balance.

"Early in the morning."

And then, restart. "Weigh heigh, and up she rises!"

It was a tedious, monotonous song, by design and intention. What mattered was the beat. Subspace was treacherous and twisty. If you could build a ship that punched through into subspace, if you could find the right place to punch back out, you could travel light-years in a matter of hours — but that was only *if* your ship wasn't torn to shreds by the warped spacetime.

For all the years of study humanity had put into it, nobody had yet discovered a technological solution that worked better than a crew of singers. Put them in a line from stem to stern, all singing a shanty together, with a captain and a pair of pilots listening above them. If they could keep the whole ship in time, keep any part of it from redshifting or blueshifting away, then they just might make it safe out the other side of the subspace jump.

There was no resource more valuable to an interstellar freighter than singers, and a good lead chanter. Massive lung capacity, a clear voice, and an unshakable sense of rhythm were their stock in trade. Even when reality twisted, even when up and down no longer had meaning — when present and past were too close or far from each other — a singer had to follow the lead chanter.

And if the lead chanter went down, somebody had to sing in their place. If Kait was the first one to gather the presence of mind to lead, she'd *do* it.

"Never let the redshift take us," Kait sang, up to the Captain holding the whole crew's life in their hands, echoed by more and more singers as the verses continued. They knew as well as she did that their lives were on the line. There were no lifeboats and no escape pods that could save them, not in subspace. A ship's crew lived and died together. If a ship went down mid-jump, it went down with all hands.

Kait's life had been full of love and music before she'd joined the crew of the *Sweet Crescendo*, but it was nothing compared to how much she found aboard. The kind of people who could keep singing through the disorienting confusion of a jump were the ones who never stopped singing anyway. There was always someone humming, someone tapping out a beat, someone starting a song. Kait fit right in for the first time in her life.

Jan, who'd been a ship's singer for decades, elected themself the unofficial parent of the entire crew. They went out of their way to make sure the junior singers knew their way around the ship, and were comfortable in their bunks, and had everything they needed. Everyone on the crew was eager to share their favorite sights and sensations in new ports, their best remedies for a sore throat, and tips to manage the motion sickness of subspace. A thousand tiny kindnesses, and they added up to a family. They were there for each other, always. Even those who didn't get along well weren't cruel. A crew had to be able to work together seamlessly, had to trust and depend on each other, to sing their ship through subspace. Kait could not bear to lose a single person.

"And neither let the blueshift claim us!"

"Early in the morning!"

This trip was a milk run, easy money, or it should have been. Ah, but subspace was an unpredictable beast. Its moods ran treacherous, and a smooth trip one way could be death on the return. A sinkhole, unnoticed, could rip a hole out of a ship. Twisters could pull it to bits. Kait didn't know which they'd run into here, or if it was another hazard altogether. All she could do was sing, keep time, and call out lines.

"Our good ship will hold together." It was a prayer, a plea, as much magic as Kait could let herself believe in when the voices of the crew rose up to echo hers. She couldn't see anyone, from her shelter. None of the friends she lived and sang with, every day. She couldn't tell their individual voices apart in the resounding chorus. All she could do was hope.

"Our voices hold the ship together!"

"Early in the morning."

"Weigh heigh, and up she rises."

The song could go on forever, for as long as the lead chanter could come up with verses. They didn't have to make sense. Any phrase that fit worked. Above her, the Captain and pilot were still frantically fighting their controls. They hadn't given up. Kait kept the time, and called out the verses they needed to bring the ship back into line.

She sang about going home — her renny was watching the skies for Kait's ship to come back, like e'd watched for er loves who did not always return. E had sobbed in Kait's arms the day she'd hired on as a singer. "How much more must I suffer for having loved a singer?" e cried. "The ships are taking my baby too." And Kait left anyway, because her heart beat in time with a sailor's shanty from the day she was born.

She sang for Maya, the best friend whose soul fit together with hers like puzzle pieces. They'd sung together up the gangplank onto the *Sweet*

Crescendo their first day as sailors, and every day since. She sang for Danicai, who made Maya so happy and could make anywhere feel like home. Kait didn't know what she'd do without either of them crowding into her bunk to watch ridiculous vids together when she was down, or cuddling her when she was homesick, or walking arm in arm with her as they explored the markets of strange worlds — taking care of her as she took care of them. Kait still couldn't see either of them. She couldn't see *anyone*. All she could do was sing, and hear the unified voices of the crew joining her.

They were more in time, now, even if the ship was still warping wildly in spacetime. The danger was not over, but the singing at least gave them a chance.

Kait sang about the ship. She and Maya had chosen the *Sweet Crescendo* because the pay was good, and she belonged to the Silver Star line, which had the best safety record out of all the freighter companies. They brought more singers home safe than any other line. It had been a calculated decision, but the ship had become so much more than just another freighter to Kait. The *Sweet Crescendo* was more than just the materials that made her up, more than just the cargo she could carry. She was the kindness of the old hands, looking after the new singers. She was the warmth of a Captain who smiled often and knew the names of all the crew. She was the way the crew's voices resounded through her belly. She was the spirit of all of it together, and the heart of the vessel that held true and did not betray them even as subspace tried to rip her apart.

Time was unreliable in subspace. There was no way to tell how long the jump was taking, besides the number of verses sung or the slow decrease of the water in Kait's canteen, sipped during responses as she prepared the next call. Her right hand grew numb, pounding time on the deck, and her left hurt too much to take over. It seemed to her that this was a far longer jump than any she'd been on before.

Kait sang, on and on, about anything that kept the verses flowing, and gradually the heaving of the deck settled back to the regular shimmy and roll of traversing subspace. Kait climbed out of her cramped nook to stand and stamp as she sang.

Maya was on her knees nearby. She had a terrible scrape across her cheek, blood dried on her pale skin, but she was alive. She was alive, and she was singing, and her face opened in a brilliant smile when she looked up and saw Kait holding a hand out to her.

"Hand in hand and sing together," Kait called, and Maya sang it with the whole crew as Kait pulled her to her feet. Their fingers laced together, and they didn't let go.

Danicai crawled out from between two crates and stumbled awkwardly toward them on stiff legs, relief clear. Danicai clung to Maya's hand on one side, and reached for Bran with the other. Bran held another, and another, and another — all those who could still stand, helping each other to their feet. To Kait's other side, Jan very gently took her left hand, old singer smiling through a split lip as they sang. There were more beyond them, so Kait stood in the middle of an unbroken line of singers from stem to stern. The ship's doctors were bustling, now that they could move through the ship, and Kait couldn't tell who they were tending to. It was enough, for now, to see that most of the singers were on their feet.

They finished, one last chorus of "up she rises." Then, because the monotony of a single shanty could become unbearable, and they'd been singing this one so long — and because it no longer suited Kait's mood and *she* was the one leading now — she switched to a new song without losing a single stomped beat.

"Oh, we'll be all right, if our friends are by our sides!"

"Oh, we'll be all right, if our friends are by our sides!" The joy of the response reverberated through the ship, as the singers all took up "Roll The Old Chariot Along." Another very old shanty, familiar to everyone. This one had the space for harmonies, and they combined beautifully throughout the ship. Kait didn't usually sing the melody, but it didn't feel wrong to be leading, just this once, through the repeated lines of the verse, and then bold through the chorus.

"Oh, we'll be all right, just as long as we can sing!" Kait squeezed Maya's hand. They lived and died by their voices, together; and today they lived.

Maya's deep brown eyes were shiny with a hint of tears. She tugged Kait closer, and Kait leaned down so Maya could press her scraped forehead against Kait's bruised one, so they sang against each other's mouths. "We'll be all right, when our pretty Kaity sings," Maya sang, just to Kait, the chorus of voices blocking anyone else from hearing. Kait briefly rubbed noses with her before she faced away to lead in the chorus again, and Maya turned to Danicai for comfort.

The unmistakable vibration of the *Sweet Crescendo*'s subspace engines ran through the deck, rumbling up through Kait's boots. The wave of relief nearly took her feet from under her. The Captain had found a place to punch back out. The trip was almost done.

"Well, a little time ashore wouldn't do us any harm!" Kait sang, keeping on time through those last few crucial seconds. The rest of the singers echoed her in an exultant shout. The rumble of the engines rose to a roar, and the singers' voices rose to outmatch it through the final chorus.

"We'll roll the old chariot along,
And we'll all hang on behind!"

The fabric of the universe strained, twisted, and then *snapped* into place like a stretched rubber band suddenly released. The twist and roll of subspace was gone, replaced by the static stillness of mundane space.

If Kait was a real lead chanter, she'd have repeated the last line at half time to bring the song to an official close — but it sounded like every singer in the ship was cheering, and her legs finally did give out on her. Kait grabbed Maya as she went down, and they crashed to the deck together in a bruised tangle of limbs. There was no music in Kait's mouth now, only sobs.

Danicai was only a second behind Maya, dropping to the floor to hold Kait along with her, and they held Danicai back just as tight. They hardly noticed Captain Smith's voice projected through the ship, unnecessarily giving permission for the singers to stand down and telling them how soon they'd be in port.

"We almost died," Danicai whispered, voice shaking. "I can't believe it, we almost *died*."

"You sang us through," Maya cried against Kait's neck, voice thick with tears. "As soon as I heard your voice, I knew we were going to be OK."

Someone — *someone else thank all the stars and galaxies* — started a celebratory song. Kait didn't recognize it, but the lyrics were about storms ending. It didn't have the call and response of a shanty, and nothing depended on whether Kait joined in or not. It was just a song for the joy of singing.

"Up now," Jan urged, holding a hand out to Kait's group. Maya took it.

Bran was there too, helping Kait and Danicai to their feet. "Looks like our greenhorns are real sailors now. You've weathered your first gale!"

"And you led the singing through it, too." Jan held Kait back by both shoulders, smiling proudly at her. "You'll be the stuff of legend, girlie."

More and more singers were gathering around. The celebratory song grew, even as the injured were being triaged for medical care. Captain Smith and the pilot were rappelling down to the deck, to check on the crew and their fallen pilot.

Kait had followed this crew's voices from port to port, singing their way through subspace together — and in the deadliest danger, they'd all followed hers.

"Don't you love a singer," Kait's renny had warned her, again and again.

Maya and Danicai were bracketing her, holding her close, and people were calling their congratulations to her group of greenhorns, or reaching out to touch Kait in thanks for leading them. All of these, her friends. All of these, people she'd trusted with her life and who'd trusted her with theirs. *Her* people, every last soul aboard the *Sweet Crescendo*.

It wasn't a single singer Kait loved; it was an entire ship full of them.

Kait didn't know the song they were singing, but the chorus was simple. She kissed Maya's cheek, and Danicai's, and she smiled as she lifted her head and let her voice rise to join the harmony.

TS Porter is a strange fae beast collecting sticks for nefarious purposes. Their short stories have appeared in *Vulture Bones* magazine and the *Enough Space for Everyone Else* anthology, as well as in various other small-press anthologies. Their novel and novellas can be found and purchased on Smashwords. TS's physical location and momentum vary, but home is always online. They can be found at **ts-porter.tumblr.com** or on twitter as **@TSPorterAuthor**.

For content notes, see page 244

The After Party

by Ben Francisco

THE LAND OF THE DEAD IS A PARTY that never stops, and you can stay as long as you want. You've been dancing for weeks now and you have no intention of stopping anytime soon.

It's the best party you've ever been to. The DJ is an alchemist, always sensing exactly the right song for the right moment: the tune that will crescendo the crowd's energy as it rises, like a thrilling roller coaster, then slow it down when the energy needs to ease back, like a gentle rocking chair.

The sky is your ceiling and the ground is your dance floor. No matter how far you travel, the party's still there, across dense forests and cobblestone plazas and valleys dotted with shamrocks and dandelions. But your favorite spot is here, where the shore meets a forest of redwoods and you can dance in the sand or the waves or the trees, as you please.

People are wearing body paint and glitter and capes and wings — not costume wings, but *real* wings that flap and glide and furl and unfurl to the beat of the bass. People are dressed and undressed and in between, and every body is shining with its beauty: lean bodies, fat bodies, hairy bodies, smooth bodies, male bodies, female bodies, bodies that transcend male and female, bodies that have been shaped by their wearers into a fully realized dream of themselves.

Your memories of that other place are fuzzy, that place where gravity held everything down and rules tied everyone up. You vaguely remember that some bodies were treated as better than others, that you used to look down at your own body and feel shame that certain parts were too big and others too small. That seems so quaint now, the idea that a body and its parts should only come in certain sizes, as if you were an appliance whose pieces had to come in exact specifications in order to be assembled properly.

The beat slows down, and you take a break from dancing and wander to the lounge by the beach. The chairs and sofas and pillows are so comfortable they hug your skin like an entire wardrobe of satin. The tables are covered with fruits that are sweet and juicy and cool, and hot teas that smell of lavender and cinnamon.

You grab a pomegranate and sink into a plush couch, savoring the elated aching of your muscles from the delight of the dance. You hold up the fruit in your hand and feel the urge to talk to it, like in that monologue with the skull from that famous play everyone always quotes in the other place. You have the urge to declare, "Alas, poor Pomegranate, I knew you well!" But that would be a lie; you barely knew Pomegranate at all. Your whole life in the other place, you avoided pomegranates on principle, because the work-to-fruit ratio was far too high for any sensible person to waste time on them. It's only since you got here that you've begun to understand the genius of the pomegranate, the way the labor it requires is intrinsic to its succulence.

As you tease out the seeds from the husk, someone approaches you, his face familiar. "I've been looking everywhere, and I've got to say, this was the last place I thought to look," he says, pouring himself an orange spice tea with honey and lemon. The scent of honey and lemon helps you remember. He always took his tea with honey and lemon. That was his hangover helper, along with two ibuprofen.

A series of memories come back to you, like rewatching scenes from a movie you saw long ago. Going to an ATM to get cash for him, knowing what he would use it for but not knowing what else to do. Sitting through a professional meeting with him in a conference room as he madly constructed a mind-map of post-it notes, knowing he was high but not knowing if your other coworkers could even tell the difference. Him leaving to "party and play" the night before checking into the clinic, because it just makes so much *sense*, he said, to have a proper fond farewell, while you waited up all night for him, knowing exactly what he was doing and not knowing what sense even meant anymore. A vicious cycle of knowing too many things and not knowing so many more.

He stands over you, stirring the honey into his tea. "Do you remember me?" he says, and you nod slowly. "It's easier to remember when we're near each other. Near other people we knew — before." He pauses, slowly sipping his tea. "I've been looking for you, because… I never actually got to do the steps down there. I mean, I went through the motions, but I never *really* did them. So I guess that's what I'm doing here. Working the steps I spent a whole life avoiding. Steps two and three are a lot easier here." He chuckles and waves his teaspoon around at the food, the lights, the dance floor that stretches to the horizon. "I mean it's pretty hard to deny a power greater than ourselves with all this around us."

You laugh because it's true. It's funny how people would debate those things, arguing that everything was small, not seeing that even the smallest things contained infinity.

"So number nine is a doozy," he says. "Feels like I've been working on it for eternity already, and I'm still on the top part of the list. Because that's where you are, right near the top of the list. Of the people I cared about. Of the people I hurt. I want you to know… I know how much I hurt you. How I put you in so many impossible situations. And I want to thank you for trying to help me even when you had no idea how to. Even when *I* had no idea how to help myself."

He puts down his tea, and locks his eyes on you. You didn't realize that tears could happen here; up until now it's only been smiles and dancing. But as you look at him, you realize that tears are part of the splendor too. "I'm sorry," he says.

For a moment, you feel the tug of your former self, the urge to judge and recriminate, to remind him he's apologized a thousand times before, that his actions have consequences that he can't undo with two too-easy words. But you're larger than that now. Now you have the wisdom to know so many differences. And you know that this time *is* different, that he means the words he says. Your eyes dance with his eyes, following their lead into the territory of tears.

"I forgive you," you say, and he drops onto the couch and hugs you, a hug with his full self, the way he used to hug before those tiny crystals of dark magic took away your friend, your brother.

"I wish I could give you something," he says. "Something to thank you."

The song transitions, to an upbeat remix of a ballad about the healing of beautiful broken hearts. You jump up. "You *can* do something! You can dance with me!"

He laughs as you drag him to the dance floor. "Is this the afterlife or the upside-down?" he says. "*I* was always the one trying to drag *you* out to the parties."

The crowd parts to make space for the two of you, and you need it, you need all that space to leap and dance and twirl each other around. Suddenly you're not dancing on the floor anymore, you're dancing on air, gliding over the crowd in a flight of ecstatic joy.

Still soaring, you pull him close and whisper, "I always understood, you know. How you wanted to get somewhere… higher. You just took a wrong turn trying to get up here."

He hugs you tight, embracing you in the air. "That's a kind way to put it. And you've always been kind."

You and your friend dance for hours, and the DJ seems to be playing just for you, playing songs from all the times you shared together. Even the songs you got sick of because they were on a loop at all the clubs for an entire year — even those songs seem perfect now. You dance a dance that's much more than nostalgia, it's the making of a new album that has the greatest hits of the past and a whole new set of rhythms that were only just invented.

Then he says, "I've got to go. I have a lot of rounds to do." He hugs you goodbye.

You keep dancing by yourself, and the music is even better now than it was before — how does it keep getting better when it was so absolutely perfect from the start? Such questions are unanswerable; your only answer is to dance out all the joy that's surging through your body.

You're taking another break, crouching on the shore, letting the tide wash over your feet and the bassline wash over your ears. It's nighttime now, though the passage of time is hard to gauge here. You haven't seen a clock or a watch or a tiny screen measuring the passing of seconds since you got here. You don't miss the clocks or the screens or the schedules, not at all; they were what kept you away from this for so long.

That's when the two of them find you. For the first time since you've been here, your volume of delight comes down from 11. You hope this won't take long, that they won't try to keep you from the dance floor.

"We want to share something with you," she says, "if you'll come with us for just a minute."

"Things are different now," he says.

"I'm not leaving the party," you say, unmoving from the sand.

They look at each other, nodding, as if they expected this.

"Then we'll do it here," she says.

"The music is nice," he agrees.

Your father turns to his left, and an oven rises out of the wet sand. Your mother turns to her right, and suddenly she's in front of a wood-top island that's traveled from the kitchen to the ocean's edge. In a flurry, your parents are chopping and whisking and sautéing. The music shifts to a soft jazz beat as the scents of garlic and butter and cilantro fill the air. Your parents smile as they work, dividing the labor effortlessly, which is jarring, because they could never be in the same room together, especially a kitchen, for more than five minutes before the shouting started. And your father never knew how to cook anything other than eggs over easy.

"I've learned to cook here!" your father says. "For a while, I was having trouble finding my way, figuring out what I was supposed to do. Then I found the feasting courts — have you been down that way?"

"No," you say, confused about where the feasting courts could be. It's all one endless dance party from horizon to horizon.

"When I found the feasting courts," your father goes on, "I realized *this* is what I've been missing. I spent my whole life trying to fix things, but I never learned to *make* things. To cook things up!"

Your mother lets out a harrumph. "Five decades of marriage and I've got to wait for the afterlife for this man to finally learn to cook."

Your father laughs. This isn't like they used to fight, the take-no-prisoners mutually assured destruction. This is different, the playful sparring of two people deeply in love.

You find it all quite disorienting.

"So we wanted to find you," your father says, "and offer you this feast!"

"We wanted to give *you* something for a change," your mother says. "Even when you were a little kid, sometimes you took care of us more than we took care of you."

A kitchen table appears on the wet beach, the waves lapping against its wooden legs. *Your* kitchen table, the one from the house you grew up in. Your parents set the table with the feast that they've created — mofongo, pasteles, collard greens, crème brûlée — every single one of your favorite dishes. Your father lights candles and your mother pulls up a chair for you, inviting you to sit.

Part of you still wants to go back to the dance floor, the jazz two-step calling to your feet. But the scent of the meal made just for you is seductive, and you appreciate that your parents have made such an effort. You wonder if that's part of the magic here — that it's easier for people to find the power inside themselves to make the effort.

You sit with your parents and eat. The food tastes like home. Not the home you had, but the home you *almost* had, the home that could have been perfect if things had been just a little bit different.

As you eat, your parents tell you about their wanderings. You had no idea there was so much more to this place, that this world kept going beyond the party. But then you only just got here, and the party's demanded all your attention, like a lover that's been waiting all night for you to come home.

Your mother cracks open the top of her crème brûlée as you finish the meal. "We've been here a while," she says. "And we think we're almost ready to go up to the second floor."

"There's a second floor?" you ask.

"Oh yeah," your mother says, gesturing toward the forest. At its edge, an old wooden staircase ascends into the heights of the redwoods. You've seen it before but always assumed it led to a treetop pavilion, a special section of the dance floor with a spectacular view of the ocean. You've been meaning to check it out, but haven't had the chance. "We needed to see you first. To share this meal with you. To offer you a little nourishment. To thank you for all the ways you nourished us."

"I spent so much time trying to get you to be something you weren't," your father says. "When the whole time you were this kid who was perfect just exactly as you were."

"Thank you," you say, and you can tell it's what they need to hear. The music shifts from jazz to salsa, and the three of you smile at one another. You all stand up and dance around the kitchen table as the tide comes in, your feet splashing in unison with each other and with the congas.

Your mother takes your hand. Your hips and her hips move as one. It's familiar and comforting to dance with your mother, just like you used to when you were little.

Then the beat shifts to a rhythm you never expected. Your mother twirls you around and passes you to your father. He extends his right hand, much to the surprise of your left hand. He places his other arm around your shoulder, shocking your shoulder blades. He's positioning himself to follow, inviting you to lead.

This is even more disorienting than the feast, but the compass of your body manages to find its bearings. You take your father's extended hand, and place your other hand on his back. You guide him through the dance in the shallow waters. Splash-splash left. Splash-splash right. His body follows yours as easily as his smile. You feel, for the first time in your existence, living or dead, that your father is seeing you. A tiny team of tears finds its way from your eyes back into the ocean.

The song ends. Your parents kiss you goodbye and say they've done all they came to do, that they'll see you on the second floor when you're ready.

For a moment you wonder about these people who keep finding you, how all of them seem to have a mission, a list of things they need to get done. Should you have a list too? You used to have so many lists, in so many places. Post-it notes, memo pads, email reminders, taskmaster apps. In life, you made list after list, lists of all the lists you had to make, so many lists you nearly drowned in them.

No. No lists for you here. Your only mission is to dance.

The music goes on. The sky is clear, and the stars, the planets, the constellations are all swirling to the beat, the most spectacular light show you've ever seen. Even the Milky Way is dancing, that river of lights undulating to the soaring orchestral rhythms. You dance for hours with those celestial bodies.

Then you see him. Smiling, shimmying his shoulders as he dances towards you. He's still so sexy. It irritates you that he's still so sexy.

"Hey, tiger," he says, dancing in a circle around you. He knows you love it when he calls you tiger, like Mary Jane and Peter Parker. "I've been looking for you. Never guessed that you'd be here. I thought for sure you'd be in the library. Have you been to the library? It's just like this, but with books, every book there ever was, whole cityscapes of books. You'd totally love it."

You half-smile, but you're determined to resist being manipulated. Redemption may have been possible for the others, but not for him. What he gave you was a scar, not a wound, and scars last, even longer than the bodies they lived on.

You come to a standstill on the dance floor. "You lied to me," you say.

He stands still too, just a foot away from you. "I lied *so* much," he says. "And my lies enchanted you, every one of them."

You spent the last decade of your life preparing for this moment. You have whole monologues prepared, treatises on all his wrongs, interrogations of all his untruths. But it does you no good that you ran your lines so many times; you still aren't ready to perform off-book, not for this, not for him. Of all the lines you rehearsed, all you can remember is one, one single question that you never got the answer to: "All those times when you said you couldn't kiss me because I had severe halitosis, was that a lie too?"

"Total lie," he says, grinning. "Except one time. The first time, your breath really was terrible. That was what gave me the idea. All the other times, I just didn't feel like kissing you, and that was the easiest way to get out of it."

You knew it. You always knew that was a lie too. So much smaller than all his other lies, but the one that might have hurt the most, like a hatchet as small as a paper clip.

The music gets ominous, and all the joy scatters away from the dance floor like cockroaches running when you turn on the kitchen light.

"I lied so much it was like scratching an itch," he says. "I did it without thinking. But here's the funny thing: now I never lie. Here, I only say true things."

This conversation is nothing like the others. He's not even trying to apologize, this person who hurt you worst of all — who made you lose your faith, not just in him, but in yourself. In everything.

You wish he would leave. You wish the happy music would come back.

He looks up at the Milky Way, still dancing above, oblivious to your misery. "The truth is we should have broken up three years earlier. I was terrified of you seeing... how broken I was. My soul did somersaults so you wouldn't see how much I was hurting. I made up all those lies to... please you — and to manipulate you. I turned away from you when you kept reaching out. And I never even told you why. It wasn't because I didn't have enough love for you. It was because I didn't have enough capacity. I wish I'd been strong enough to love you right. I owe you that much truth, at least."

He's dancing around an apology. Even here, he still can't say the simple words *I'm sorry*. Part of you wants to be large, to forgive him anyway, like you did your friend and your parents. But you're not that big yet.

"Okay," you say, and that's the most you can offer. The music shifts to a pop remix you've always loved. "I'm going back to dancing now."

You can see in his eyes that he's disappointed you haven't given him your forgiveness. You're stopping him from getting through his list. Part of you feels some satisfaction in that, though you know you shouldn't, not here, not in this place where delight makes old grudges nothing but needless weight.

"I was going to go upstairs soon," he says, "you know, check out the famous second floor. But maybe I can dance near you for a bit?"

"I guess that's fine," you say, which you guess it is. Before all your affection ran into the shadows, before you found out all the ways he lied, you used to love dancing with him.

You dance, not *with* each other, but *by* each other. You never touch, but your eyes meet a few times each song. He looks at you with adoration, with desire. You can't remember the last time he looked at you like that — not since long before you separated. You can't deny how nice it feels.

A while passes, and then he gets close to you again. He clutches your shoulders and looks you up and down, like you're a skyscraper and he has to crane his neck to take in all of you. "Is this really all you've seen?" he says. "Just this party?"

"Well, yeah," you say. "It's the best party ever."

He erupts in laughter. You don't quite understand the joke, but you sense there's nothing mean-hearted in his laugh. It's a laughter

of irony — or appreciation, maybe — and you get the feeling he's laughing at himself and the world as much as he's laughing at you. "That is so rich," he says, wiping laugh-tears from his eyes. "That is so perfect. You spent your whole life taking care of everyone but yourself, going through all those lists of things that had to get done. You never slowed down enough to enjoy the party. So here you are.

"I'm going upstairs soon," he says. "You were my last one. But before I go I'd like to ask you for two more things, even though I've got no right to do that. Can I give you one last kiss? The kiss I should have given you a long time ago? And can I tell you one more true thing?"

There were so many nights when you lay awake desperate for a kiss goodnight, craving the touch of the person right there on the other side of the bed. It comforts you that at least one of your regrets is mutual.

"Yes," you say, "you may kiss me. But only if it's wet and passionate and sends shivers through my soul."

He looks into your eyes like you're a goddess and you just answered his prayers. He comes in close and kisses you and your mouth is full of fireworks and his hands are touching you in all the places you love to be touched and just at that moment the DJ transitions to a new song, and it's *your* song, the song that you and he loved long before the sexless nights, when the two of you were at your best, two heroes at the beginning of a romantic adventure, except this time the adventure doesn't disappoint, it keeps going and going just like this kiss, which is the quest and the map and the magic elixir all at once.

He kisses you like he never wants to stop, but eventually the music shifts to a different song and you pull away, because your tongue is tired and your legs are ready to dance again. He steps back and watches you dance, still catching his breath. "That was amazing," he says. "I was so dumb not to do that every single second you were in my reach."

You nod as you bop to the beat, because it's true, that was dumb of him.

"So here's the last thing," he goes on. "The other true thing I have to tell you. You deserve that kiss. And so much more. You deserve all the joy in the world, because you are wondrous and lovable and sexy and sacred."

You're having trouble hearing what he's saying, because you sense that there's wisdom in it, and that feels deeply unfair — the last thing this person should be allowed to do is offer you wisdom. An amazing kiss is one thing, but wisdom is where you have to hold the line.

He reaches out to run his fingers through your hair. "I'm sorry I stopped you from seeing your own beauty. I hope that here you get all the joy and desire and love that you deserve."

You stop bopping, shocked that he actually said the words.

He's about to turn away, but you grab him by the arm to bring him back, because you just realized something important. "Wait," you say. "It wasn't just you." You pause. You want your words to be true, too. In life, you used to be so diplomatic that you'd make yourself small in the name of preserving foreign relations. Death is demanding more directness of you. With the world and with yourself. "I stopped saying yes to dancing. You always used to ask me to go out dancing with you, and sometimes I'd go, but then at some point I stopped completely. I always had... something else. Work. Friends who needed help. Things that... seemed more important."

He leans back, thumbs in his pockets. "You always had your lists. And they kept multiplying. A hydra you could never defeat."

You laugh. That was how you saw yourself then, a hero fighting an undefeatable monster. "Now I don't have any lists."

"And I don't have any lies," he says.

You're starting to understand the ecology of the magic here. This place strips you down. Of lists, of lies, of whatever was holding you back.

"Which came first?" you ask him. "Was it you saying no to kissing or me saying no to dancing?"

Tears here should no longer surprise you, but from him they do. He almost never used to cry, even as you broke each other's hearts. But he's crying now, crying openly as he never did in life. "I don't remember," he says.

"I can't remember either," you say. It's perplexing yet clarifying, the way you suddenly feel less certain of your own story. And then you say: "I wish I'd gone out dancing with you more. I wish I'd said *yes* more — yes to so many of your invitations. I didn't have the capacity either. I'm sorry I wasn't... ready. For you." You look at everything around you, the dance floor, the luminous bodies, the swirling constellations. "I wasn't ready... for this. For joy."

"I know," he says. "Joy takes work too." He hugs you one more time. "Hopefully I'll see you upstairs later. But you really should check out the library first, you'll love it."

It's true that you always loved libraries. The books, the quiet, the potential for productivity. "I think I need to stay here a while longer," you say, smiling. "I've got a lot of important dancing to do."

He nods and smiles back at you as he dances away, toward that old wooden staircase at the edge of the woods, the one that leads to a second floor that's somehow higher than the sky.

You wonder what it's like up there, if the music's even better, if such a thing is possible.

Maybe you should check out the second floor too.

But first you'll dance for one more song. It's a good one that just started.

Ben Francisco is a gay genderqueer Puerto Rican writer. Their stories have been published in *Fireside Fiction, Lady Churchill's Rosebud Wristlet, PodCastle, Realms of Fantasy, Shimmer Magazine, Best Gay Stories*, and From *Macho to Mariposa: New Gay Latino Fiction*. Their stories range from magic realism to space opera and have been known to feature oversexed ghosts, depressed precognitive psychics, and pantheistic vampire aliens who reproduce like moss. Ben is a graduate of the Clarion South and Taos Toolbox writing workshops. Outside of writing fiction, they have two decades of experience in the nonprofit and philanthropic sectors working for gender justice, immigrant rights, LGBTQ rights, and racial justice. You can find them on Twitter **@BenFranciscoM**.

For content notes, see page 244

The Mountain Will Move
If You Ask

by Jaxton Kimble

ROMY YATES IS THE ONLY REASON I'VE SURVIVED this expedition so far, and now I've gotten her killed.

Okay, stop spinning out, Ianto. Specific language. Concrete facts. Romy isn't dead. Yet. And I have other things I can actually accomplish, so eyes front.

I check the farabine tank seals for the third time, even though the rover's diagnostic came back clean the first two. There's no evidence of breach or damage. This is good news. Except now I've run out of excuses to avoid the med tent on the mountain side of camp.

Romy insisted camping against the mountain made us more secure. One less quarter to watch. The jagged crags and peaks and dark overhangs of granite are a range of menace to me, but I'm hardly qualified to make safety judgments after today.

Maybe one more excuse: the glow at our campsite's exposed edge. I turn away from the mountain face and check on Siddhi on watch. Her hair's tied back in a raven ponytail, shining with moonlight. She leans against a rock crag with a wiry tree winding around it. It's grown since yesterday; the rock, not the tree. Siddhi's field jacket is torn in several places, but she's intact after the attack, same as all of us except Romy.

The sepia of Siddhi's complexion turns to rings of pale lavender at her wrists and knuckles. That's her tell, and the fact that it's glowing means she's using her bent. Intensifying ambient light for her eyes so night reads clear as day is the first trick she learned. I won't be sneaking up on her. I make sure to give a broad wave at a polite distance anyway.

Siddhi raps her knuckle on the rock growth. Her admiration slips through the psychic wisp that connects us all. "Right again," she signs. "This keeps up, we'll have a wall inside two days."

This world's topography is elastic. Shifts here aren't tectonic, they're fluid. Sometimes it's slow like the growths around the camp or a valley on the trail that wasn't there the day before. Sometimes it's explosive. I feel the tide of those changes as well as I can smell primrose on the wind, though I don't like calling what I do a bent. Hell, local flora manage my gimmick without trying: the tree trunk corkscrewed around Siddhi's crag? It was bone straight this morning. It twisted itself to avoid uprooting.

I start to speak aloud, then catch myself. One more careless, hurtful slip. No, Ianto. Stop. Focus. Now: sign. "Any news?" I need to change the subject before I spin out again.

"All clear out there." Siddhi jabs a thumb at the surrounding scrubland. "Was about to ask Burhan for an update. Come with."

I don't want to, but I didn't want to come out here in the first place. It wasn't a question when Romy picked me for her team. It's not a question now. At least, it's not a question I'd ask out loud.

Lavender light flares at Siddhi's knuckles and wrists. A glowing ball pops into existence above us and lights the path. We head for the mountain face and leave the newly-grown crags behind us, their presence a geological underbite pulsing at the base of my skull. Then it's buried by a pulse of pain through the wisp as Siddhi trips and smacks her knee on the ground.

"You okay?" I sign.

"Fine." She's already on her feet again. "Didn't notice the ridge."

Dammit. "Because it wasn't there." The ground was level until a step before we reached this spot. Then the ridge kicked itself up and caught Siddhi's foot. That kind of mild pitch and flow to the ground feeds right into my proprioception — I don't have to pay attention to account for it. "I'm so sorry."

"No worries."

"I have one job," I sign. "Keep all your feet on a safe path." I don't have to pay attention for myself. I have to pay attention for *them*. Siddhi's pain is already fading, but Romy's screaming agony this afternoon, her shoulder torn open, I can't forget that. Shouldn't forget it.

Fucking focus, Ianto. Foot to path — *mind* to path — every step accounted for until we come up on the med tent.

Romy's relief washes over us both at the same time. I let go of self-recrimination as Romy pushes through the flap and into the gas lantern's glow. I'm used to being the waxy, sweaty, pale one — it's unnerving on Romy. Okay, her black skin is never pale, but the smooth shine of her complexion's gone waxy. The shortness of breath, the glass to her gaze, none of these are Romy.

"Slow down!" Burhan calls, stalking out of the tent herself, frowning. Her worry is as bright in our minds as the red streaks of her tell in her midnight hair and beard. Catching sight of Siddhi, she repeats it in sign. "I told her to slow down. She's still hurt."

Siddhi frowns. "How is she hurt? You healed her on the road." Burhan's bent is flesh.

Burhan shakes her head. "I closed the wound," she signs with broad, terra-cotta fingers. "But the haedama fangs don't just bite — they poison."

"You can't purge it?" Siddhi asks.

"Dorofei could extract it or transmute it," Burhan signs. Dorofei is Romy's second. They took the other half of the crew on a longer, more stable trail to another possible farabine tap. Twice the chances. Sure, twice the chances of me mapping our people into danger.

"Ianto." Romy pulls herself tall and traps me in her wide, deep-set stare.

"I... yes. Sorry." I stop leaking my whine through the wisp.

She waves it off. "You were checking the tanks. Copacetic?"

"Tanks secure, levels stable."

"Then we don't need Dorofei running after more," Romy signs. "Send them a message to meet us —"

Romy's turn is sudden. Siddhi rushes to break her fall when she collapses.

"Dammit," Burhan hisses. I feel his gender shift in the wisp as he focuses. He runs his fingers through his hair, red streaks starting to glow, then blows into his hands. Romy wakes with a groan at his touch.

"The poison?" Siddhi signs.

Burhan cracks his neck. "I sloughed the infected flesh and forced it to grow replacements, but I've been trying to explain: the toxin's still there."

Romy cocks her head to the right, eyes flashing with a red glow. Romy's bent is the wisp, and when we're close enough, it lets her channel our bents through it. She takes a beat to get her bearings, then signs, "I see what you did. Stick close, I'll maintain it myself."

"For how long?" Burhan's last shift was ephemeral. I feel her slide back to *her* as strongly as I feel her worry.

Romy signs to me instead of answering Burhan. "We need a path to Dorofei."

"What about you?" How can I look somewhere else when that's how we got here? I killed Romy watching everything but what I needed to, and getting into trouble I couldn't solve myself.

"Ianto, I need you in the now." Romy pushes past my surging guilt. "Dorofei."

Immediate problem, Ianto. I close my eyes and open my senses. The others say my tell looks like indigo tears spread down my cheeks. They don't see the topography in it that I do. They also don't see the four of us flaring bright on my mental map. I pull back and expand my view until I make out the glowing pinpricks of Dorofei and their team. Stable paths call to me while variable paths wriggle their turns and dips in spacetime patterns I pull apart like tangled string.

I open my eyes. "They're on the opposite side of the mountain. The fastest route that won't fall out from under us while we're on it runs north. With the rover, should be about a day and a half."

"You're sure?" Burhan asks.

"He's sure." Romy pushes herself to her feet. "We pack and get on the road, and we've solved two problems in as many days: poison managed and farabine en route for delivery."

"No," Siddhi demands. The wisp conveys how few shits she gives that it's technically countermanding a superior. "You rest in the rover's sleep alcove. We'll pack."

* * *

On my way back from gathering the resource collectors from the perimeter, I swing by the lab tent. The flap's closed. Burhan and Siddhi have put up a soft wall in the wisp, the psychic equivalent of a sock on a doorknob. It seems like exactly the wrong moment for sex, but I have enough trouble with the tasks at hand to get distracted by consenting adults. I snag a crate of supplies off the stack Burhan and Siddhi gathered before they started doing none-of-my-business. Burhan could have boosted her muscles to carry them all in one go, but one crate's all my natural flab can manage.

Without Siddhi to pump the lights, patches of shadow cover and weave through delicate grass and striped night flowers. I walk without worry. The ground can't surprise me, and this time there's no one I can put at risk. Romy opens the rover's back hatch.

"You're supposed to be resting," I say. I'm slightly out of breath, so it's harder to speak aloud, but my hands are full and Siddhi's otherwise engaged, so I work with what I've got.

Romy raises one thick eyebrow. She had will enough to scale the walls protecting every axis of privilege against the threat of her existence. She left those gatekeepers scattered in her wake to claim this commission. I don't know why she picked an albatross like me, but I know it wasn't because she needed a nanny.

"Sorry." I hand over the crate and swing the RCs onto the tailgate. "We're packing up the lab tent, then it's just the med tent to go. Best to be on our way; I'm getting the tingle of a roil coming."

Tension slices through the wisp like a paper cut. Romy puts a finger to her lips before I ask. She slips from the tailgate to the ground and folds up the hatch. I follow her nod out to the wavering night. Romy punches the rover's exterior light array on. A pair of reptilian heads, their long snake necks growing from a single antelopian body, twist up at the light and motion. Several other pairs join them.

Fuck.

"Haedama!" I flood panic through the wisp. Romy brandishes her sword and doesn't flinch. Exactly like last time.

Two sets of fanged jaws strike before I register the motion, but Romy yanks me clear. "Down!" Her voice is steady but firm. Its scaly necks twisted up in each other trying to reach me, the creature tumbles off balance. So do I.

When Romy took the bite for me this afternoon, I told myself I was too distracted collecting the farabine to notice. What the hell's my excuse now?

"Are you all right?" Romy's distraction puts her between me and the jaws again.

"Look out!" My yell is barely in time. One set of jaws clanks hard on her sword, and she twists the blade to trap its teeth like a stuck gear. The other head's still free, mouth unhinged and fangs glistening.

The world turns white. I'm frozen in the memory of last time, of unadulterated pain tearing through the wisp until we were all screaming in unison as Romy fell. I had one job: call out the hazards on the path. But Romy fell.

Assurance eddies through the wisp as Burhan jabs broad fingers between the haedama's razor teeth before they close, crimson glowing in her hair. The teeth scrape across her skin like it's stone. She grunts low and grabs the first head when Romy wrests her blade free.

Romy's gratitude washes through all our minds. Her next slash takes off both snake heads.

I jump at a touch on my shoulder, but it's Siddhi. That's why the world turned white — she amped up the light.

Burhan, hands now free of poisonous fangs, signs, "We were just —" She freezes under Romy's glare.

Not an hour ago, low-grade static in my head was all it took to distract me from using the right language. Romy just eluded death for the second time today, and she still has the focus to magnetize her sword to the quick-draw plate at her thigh so she can sign. "Excuse your libidos later. Fight's not done."

Siddhi rolls her eyes, ignoring the dressing-down. As the other haedama stalk closer, she waves for my attention and signs, "Get behind me."

I start to argue, but then the tingle from earlier intensifies. Siddhi's the only one looking at me, so I sign and yell at the same time: "Roil!"

The haedama cower and back off.

"Don't say those things understand you." Burhan's signs barely register through the gurgle and twist and not-actually-a-smell of copper underneath the haedama.

"The world's about to drop out from under them, and they can feel it," I sign.

"Where's our safe line?" Siddhi asks.

I point.

"Stand back. This is mine."

No one asks if Siddhi's sure. She takes three steps back and raises her hands, arms stiff, palms out. She's not signing now, she's working. These gestures aren't any more necessary to access her bent than me closing my eyes to check the ground below us. It just helps to have a focal point. The lavender rings covering her lithe joints brighten. There's a waver like the air over desert stone. Siddhi pushes her hands against nothing and the ripple encircles the haedama as their not-quite-gazelle lower halves bound for safety. Smoke pops on their scales as soon as they cross into the shimmer. With loud yelps, they leap back inside the ring. I guess this means Siddhi's not limited to the visible spectrum.

The ground around us rumbles. We brace against the roil. The ground turns to chaos, swirls and surges and melts. Rock screeches and splinters. Sod rockets up beneath us. I don't know if it's the speed or the terror robbing my breath, can't separate the howl of wind from the tumult of the others.

The explosive churn of earth climaxes into a new hill with a sharp cliff. We whiplash to a stop as fast as we started. Forewarning be damned, it catches me off balance. I lose my footing and fall back on my ass. Pain screams up my spine as I roll head over heels and end up facedown with a mouthful of sod.

"Nice work, Ianto." Romy's on her feet. They're all on their feet but me. I spit out grass and mud, but the metallic flavor lingers.

"You okay?" Burhan offers me her hand. She nudges through the wisp to check on me there, as well. I wave off the hand and resist her probe in my mind. Other than sweat dripping from her red-streaked beard and the tip of her knife-sharp nose, Burhan's fine, and I don't have it in me to be the weak link once again. I close my eyes, topography tickling my cheeks, and verify what the haedama's distant shrieks have already told me.

"Crevasse on the other side drops a good fifty feet." I wave to the new cliff edge. "The haedama aren't going to be a problem."

"What about you?" Burhan asks again.

"I'm fine."

"Are you — ?"

"I'm sure." It comes out sharper than I mean it to be, but it stops the questions. I push myself up, biting down a hiss of pain at the movement. "Let's go."

"That might be a problem." Burhan points down the steep slope, where rocks bubble up through the grass.

"Last gasps of the roil," I assure her.

"More than a gasp." Siddhi's palm shines a spotlight down to the base of the slope. A moss-covered boulder has the rover hoisted off its wheels on the left side. I'm ready to point out the rover's wriggled off more precarious perches before when I catch the tangerine whiff of its biofuel.

Burhan bounds her way down first to confirm: "Farabine's intact, but a rock spar's lanced the fuel line."

"And Dorofei has all the bents to fix it and synthesize fuel on their team," Siddhi signs.

"That makes it three problems instead of two we solve when we get there." Romy's soothing confidence washes over our concerns.

"How do we manage that without the rover?" I ask.

"Last time you looked for pathways that could fit the rover. Now we just need one that's wide enough for a set of shoulders. More chances. Give it a go."

Options slither across the back of my eyelids, shape and reshape themselves as I roll forward from now to when our feet would hit them. I open my eyes to dismiss the tangle. "More paths, yes, but nothing gets us there in less than a week on foot."

"I don't think the toxin's going to give us that long," Burhan signs.

"We've got a stopgap," Romy signs.

Burhan shakes her head. "The effort's going to slow you down, or me if I'm spelling you, and it'll wear us both down sooner rather than later."

Siddhi signs, "And you both have to sleep."

"Won't be a week if we go straight there." Romy pins me with her eyes. They flare dark almost-purple blue as she channels me. I frown and close my eyes to focus. There. A cave system that isn't formed yet: arrow-straight between us and Dorofei. And under the crushing weight of the mountain.

I shake loose the chaotic fractals. "It'll be another week before it opens, Romy. We don't have time to wait."

"Which is why we aren't waiting for it."

"I don't —"

"You're going to open it. Now."

"You can do that?" Burhan raises an eyebrow. She and Siddhi both leak surprise over the wisp.

"No. I can't. I sense the shifts, pattern-match fast enough that it *looks* like I'm making the ground do things."

"That's exactly what you can do." Romy signs.

Cold radiates along my spine, which makes the throbbing worse. "I'd know if I —"

"You grok that stalagmite?" Romy points to a fairy ring of iridescent mushrooms.

"What stalagmite?" Burhan asks. The ground beneath the mushrooms is flat, but I can't miss the building tension.

"Ianto?"

Runnels of topography drip past my lashes, itch the back of my throat. The ground is flat now, but when I roll the map forward, there it comes, loam-covered rock stabbing upward.

"It'll grow in… an hour, maybe?" I sign.

Romy nods. "Or…" Her eyes flare. The mushrooms skitter and split as the shaft of earth rises. Now. Early.

The others fade to the background as I cross to the shimmering fungal caps, moved by instinct to a new array on the spike. This shouldn't be here, but sure enough, it jibes with my internal map. I reach out, but as my fingers brush the mossy surface, it sinks back toward flat earth.

"No." I catch it. Not with my hands. With my will. The map around me closes in until it's this singular piece crackling along my cheekbones, but I hold the ground, force it to keep its shape.

"Romy!" Burhan's voice breaks my concentration. The stalagmite finishes falling, the mushrooms once again a flat ring. I turn to Burhan and Siddhi easing Romy to the ground. Romy's eyes wash red and her breathing suddenly steadies.

"And that's why you have to do it," Romy signs. "The ground on this world's already elastic. Unlike flesh or light, if you move it with will, it's got no problem snapping back when you let go. Poison's not quite the same, but it's got no problem laying waste to the same pieces of me every time I take a break from fortifying myself."

Busy fighting off the encroaching smog of blame and regret and helplessness, I forget myself crossing to Romy. I don't favor my stride right, hissing as pain jolts from the bottom of my spine.

Siddhi's sculpted eyebrows dive for the bridge of her nose. "Liar," she signs. "You *are* hurt."

"I'm fine."

Siddhi swipes the back of her hand under her chin, calling me a liar again.

"Siddhi and I can check the farabine tank and put together field packs from the rover," Romy signs. She amends at Siddhi's frown. "Fine. I will rest, Siddhi will prep. Let Burhan take care of you."

* * *

I spit out the last of the sod and clear my throat until I find my voice. "I'm an idiot."

"You're not an idiot," Burhan says, surveying the med tent. The supply bin's contents got jostled around, and we needed to right the exam bench, but otherwise the tent fared far better than the rover.

"I'm the only one who knew what the ground was going to do, and I'm the only one who fell. What else is that?"

"Balance, which has nothing to do with your bent."

"Bent." I snort. "I'm... dented at best. Closer to the warp in a wet tabletop. *You* lot are bent. Hell, Siddhi expanded into infrared back there like it was nothing."

"Siddhi's a show-off." Burhan's smile does a horrible job of selling the critique.

"Like you don't find it attractive."

"I find plenty attractive." Burhan winks. Siddhi's not the only show-off.

"If Romy had channeled me and left me behind to find the farabine tap —"

"She'd have had a weaker sense channeling from a distance. Besides, you're both alive because she was standing watch, which she couldn't do if she was busy concentrating on the ground. If you're done with the worst *would you rather* game ever, turn around and let me get a better feel for the problem." Burhan slides a hand down my back. "Vertebrae intact, no torn muscles. Ah. Yeah, that's a broken tailbone. Hang on." Warmth spreads from where she grazes me. I taste aluminum. There's a sharp moment of increased pain I hiss through, then relief as Burhan's bent notches everything back into place.

There's another sensation, this time through the wisp. Burhan's gender shifts again, and I'm acutely aware of the cup of his hand at the crest of my ass. The warmth rising in my cheeks has nothing to do with his bent and everything to do with him.

"So, now we've dealt with the proximate trouble, I think you need a release to help you re-focus, yeah?" Burhan circles in front again. His bright eyes trap me.

"You don't have to," I mutter.

He raises an eyebrow. "I don't have to do much of anything. I want to."

"Still, you —"

Burhan pulls his gloves on, the tight black leather ones that tell me he's settled and here and ready. That same sense comes through the wisp, but our link is adjacent to the mapping part of my mind. My map-brain slips and surges and reshapes itself so often, it's exhausting to find my way through it. The gloves are a concrete symbol that anchors the world.

I nod, suppressing a shiver as Burhan puts up a privacy wall in the wisp.

Without context, Burhan's gaze sliding up and down my body, the crooked twist of his full lips, would read as sinister. I suppose it reads as sinister with context, but context says this is sinister I want.

"Shirt off." Burhan stands an arm's length away. He could take it off himself if that's all he wanted.

I cross my hands at my waist and pull the shirt up and over in a rush. He snags it before I free my wrists. I tug. He twists the fabric taut and I stay bound in it. He's gained half a foot and bulked out while my shirt blocked my view.

Burhan takes his time circling behind me. He has the same forced lack of urgency when he pulls the shirt free of my hands. I keep them raised, let him trail his fingers down my forearms. He cups my elbows, then inverts his grip at my flabby biceps and swings my arms behind me. A brief pressure on my hands demands I keep them together.

My breath shudders at the warmth on the back of my neck, the tease of whiskers. If they want, the others can press through the mental border we've built in the wisp. Fear twists into the knot building below my stomach.

"Always with the worry." Burhan parses the wisp better than me. If he were distracted, I might be able to hide something from him, but not here, bound up in his will.

"Romy's so close," I quiver. Burhan's better than me, but the wisp *belongs* to Romy.

"Shh." Burhan slides a gloved hand over my mouth. He follows through his tease with the rough scratch of his beard as he kisses my neck. Trying to hold back my moan turns it into a whimper as his free hand brushes my nipple. He licks the edge of my ear. "Now that's what I want to hear."

My own hands hold their place, a breath away from his thick thighs, as his hand slides down my stomach. I whimper-groan again.

"No?" He's playing with me. My knees buckle. He grabs me around my waist as I recover, and his defined torso presses into my back.

He loosens the hand over my mouth enough for my *yes, Sir* to be clear.

"Pants," he says. My hands, freed by the command, fumble to tap the release. I shove to pop my erection out from the waistband. Burhan wraps a glove around it and I don't bother to drop my pants any further. Leather means his bent works on the gloves, makes them as frictionless as any lube. He muffles me again, because we can cordon off the wisp, but we can't keep Romy from hearing when I let loose.

He starts slow, but I'm already worked up enough that it doesn't take much time for the rhythm to rise. Whether it's wisp or bent or mundane instinct, he feels the tension spread along me before I do.

"Not until I say."

I mumble and nod under his hand. I breathe, short and rapid, holding off as he edges me, as the world stops sliding and shifting around me and becomes a single, building, ever more focused point. I don't know how loud I am, whether Burhan's hand tightens over my mouth to muffle me or stimulate me and holy fucking god I don't *care*. He pinches my nose closed, licks his way up my neck, and breathes his permission in my ear.

My fingers dig into thin air and the ground reaches up to meet them. Rock tears through the floor of the tent. Granite pylons twist and curve with the arch of my spine, then splay outward and melt with my release. My mind races along the path under the mountain. I could wrench it open in the burning center of this moment — but it's already gone. One final, desperate gasp, and I collapse.

I'm on the ground again rather than inside it, catching my breath collapsed back against Burhan's soft but firm body.

"That was new," he chuckles, a tremor on my spine. I blush.

"What about you?" I play my fingers along his forearm.

His voice is soft now that we're past the need for firm. "No, I'm good."

Of course he is. He enjoys it. The wisp confirms that much. Doesn't stop me wishing this weren't yet another case of getting better than I can give.

* * *

I said before that my tell isn't tears to me. This time, though: yeah. Tears. And sweat.

I catch myself before my knees slam into the ground. I don't need another medical intervention, thanks.

"Try again," Romy signs.

"I. Can't. Do. This." I have to wrestle my exhausted brain to recall each sign, but at least no one hears the choked-back sobs I couldn't hide if I spoke aloud. I've been at this for an hour, and all I've managed is pushing the rock face enough to eke in a handful of steps if we walked nearly on top of each other. When I try to tunnel further, the entry snaps shut behind the bubble of my attention.

Siddhi stoops into view. "You have to."

"Relax and find your focus." Burhan circles behind me, but when his bare hands rub my shoulders, they just tighten the knots.

Romy pushes off the rock she's been resting against. "You can —"

"I can't!" My raw voice joins my signs unbidden, cheeks and neck hot. You don't yell at Romy, but I need them all to *stop*.

"Tell me." Romy isn't angry, but she's not letting me slide. Her eyes pulse red from another internal sweep to clear ongoing damage from the toxin. The interval between sweeps is shrinking.

It can't be worse knowing than not, can it? So ask and lose one more distraction, Ianto. "Why did you pick me? I understand Siddhi and Burhan, but I'm no more useful than the sensors on the rover. I'm not bent enough to —"

"Bent is bent," Romy signs. I ignore her pain slipping through the wisp. "It's who we are as much as what we do. I spent the better part of three decades fighting everyone from my family to old school military brass to stop them misgendering and deadnaming me. Believe me when I say I know what it is not to be seen, Ianto. To feel you're not enough." She lets it show in a pinched smile and a deep breath, the fight we can't win with swords or magic, the poison that threatens without a single bite. "And believe me when I say: I see you. You're the one who can do this. Cut the path. I promise to lead us through."

"It's a mountain." The crush of granite in my mind makes the sign feel heavy.

"And it will move if you ask." Romy's smile is patient. "I'm not saying it's easy, but for you, it's not impossible. It's all right to feel overwhelmed. Remember, you don't have to reshape the world. Stay small. Concrete. Make enough space for us to fit through together."

"We'd be sealed off. In the dark with just the air we —"

"I can shore up our lungs." Burhan's touch converts my barest gasp into a supercharge.

"I'll bring the light." Siddhi raises her arm, fingers flattened against her thumb. She opens her fingers, and the sign fills with an actual bright white glow.

241

Romy's eyes shift from crimson to indigo long enough for her to find the right spot in the rock face.

I close my eyes. I don't need the breadth of it all. Just one, searing focal point, like the one Burhan helped me find in the tent.

The rock recedes ahead, along the natural cave path that will be here next week. I let Romy take my hand and lead me forward. *Not the world*, I tell myself. I can't see where we're going, but Romy can. She shares her insight, I make the space.

We make our way under the mountain, and Romy is going to live. We're all going to live, because together we'll bend the world we need.

Jaxton Kimble is a bubble of anxiety who wafted from Michigan to Florida shortly after having his wisdom teeth removed. He's still weirded out by the lack of basements. Luckily, his husband is the one in charge of decorating – thus their steampunk wedding. He has far too many 80's-era cartoon/action figure franchises stored in his brain. His work has appeared previously (as Jason) or is forthcoming (as Jaxton) in *Cast of Wonders*, *Diabolical Plots*, and *Escape Pod*. You can find more about him at jaxtonkimble.com, or by following **@jkasonetc** on Twitter.

Content Notes

The Ghosts of Liberty Street (page 2): mention of transphobia, perceived mortal peril, description of hypothetical bomb shelter use/death

Custom Options Available (page 18): sex, references to past indentured service, earthquake, mortal peril, implied offscreen mass casualties

The Invisible Bisexual (page 28): sex, brief casual transphobia/ queerphobia

Frequently Asked Questions About the Portals at Frank's Late-Night Starlite Drive-In (page 39): references to animal harm, references to death, references to alcohol, bullying, allegorical queerphobia and queer erasure

The Perseverance of Angela's Past Life (page 52): queerphobia, internalized fatphobia, alcohol

Sea Glass at Dawn (page 66): injury

unchartered territories (page 79): queerphobia, mention of parental abuse

Midnight Confetti (page 87): childbirth, smoking, alcohol, mention of motorcycle crash

black is a flower (page 96): parental death, animal harm, major character death with reincarnation

Sphexa, Start Dinosaur (page 101): brief reference to past racist/ transphobic bullying

The Frequency of Compassion (page 105): transphobia, injury, mortal peril, parental death, nonconsensual telepathy

What Pucks Love (page 121): sex, allegorical racism, parental death

Gold Medal, Scrap Metal (page 143): car crash, harassment, implied fatphobia

Half My Heart (page 157): PTSD episode, reference to parental neglect

Venti Mochaccino, No Whip, Double Shot of Magic (page 171): sexual harassment

since we're here tonight (page 174): chronic illness, reference to long-term hospitalization, reference to parental neglect, vomit

I'll Have You Know (page 191): alcohol, mind control

The Cafe Under the Hill (page 200): brief reference to physical abuse

(don't you) love a singer (page 207): injuries, mortal peril/references to death

The After Party (page 216): death, references to past drug addiction/emotional abuse/child neglect

The Mountain Will Move If You Ask (page 228): sex, injuries, mortal peril, animal harm, internalized negative body image

Our Community

Thank you to our Kickstarter backers for making this anthology possible!

Let's keep bringing brighter and better futures to life, in stories and in the real world!
— **Michael Haynes**

Keep going, everyone. There's a future waiting for all of us, and it's as beautiful as we can imagine it to be. From an agender queer who never would have even known to dream my current wonderful life as a teen, there's so much to keep hoping and fighting for.
— **Jamie Perrault**

Thank you for all the people (myself included) you've inspired to be who they are!
— **Léon Othenin-Girard**

Being unapologetically queer is revolutionary. Never forget that.
— **D. Ann**

He waka eke noa!
— JLand

May this book bring you hope.

I am delighted that these stories are available and have been published. Things have come a long way from when the queer representation you could find in the big bookstores and libraries was riddled with hostile stereotypes. I think the speculative fiction of the future will continue to find ways to get necessary queer stories into the hands of readers. There's so much more out there to explore. Onward, to the future!
— **Silver Adept**

Everything is a queer thing!
— **<3 Murray**

Those who write new futures breathe life into all of us. Love to the creators.
— **RK Popkin**

Thank you to every Queer storyteller who shares their universes with us.
— **H. E. Casson**

Kamimakuna, "Praise the Sun!"

We are everywhere. You are not alone.
— **Ray Lardie**

"In our hands is placed a power greater than their hoarded gold / Greater than the might of armies magnified a thousand-fold / We can bring to birth a new world from the ashes of the old / For the union makes us strong." — Ralph Chaplin, "Solidarity Forever"
— **JC Cat**

For the Indian queer kids out there, it does get better. <3
— **V.R.**

Sometimes people expect a lot from us when all we want to do is just be. If your highest goal is just existing, you're doing great, be you, enjoy it.

— **Alannah O**

The futures we write about where being queer is so normal that people don't think twice? Someday, those futures will be here. Until then, keep writing, keep hoping, and keep dreaming. It WILL get better.

— **Alessandor Earnest, the Imp of Editing**

When you transition, try to mold your ideas about your transition around hope for the future and not fear. Unforeseen things will happen, but it's better to move forward with a positive frame of mind if you can.

— **Lily Morgan**

Stars often don't see the light they emit. Two things are easier to give than receive: love, and hope. May we share them widely, and set ourselves the goal of accepting them.

— **Emile H.**

It's okay to NOT KNOW. Figuring out who you are and how you feel is hard. People who are questioning are all welcome.

— **Amanda DeLand**

This is for my childhood self, who didn't know queer was an option; my current self, who is so delighted for representation; my future self, who certainly has more to discover; and for my child, who will one day be old enough to read this book too.

— **Pyrrh**

"We need, in every community, a group of angelic troublemakers." — Bayard Rustin. I am incredibly proud and so full of love for my enby descendent, half of the team behind this anthology and an angelic troublemaker from the day they were born. May you all unfurl your wings with joy, and make good trouble every day of your lives! Love,

— **Jed's Mom**

Understand one another for the better.
    — N.K.Q. Thomasson

Your stories are worth telling.
    — Lydia Rogue

The future is ours: everything is going to be okay.
    — Morgan Pasquier

Tomorrow belongs to the people who show up. I'll see you there.
    — Spider B. Perry

I don't know who's reading this or when they're reading it, but I know it will eventually land in the hands of someone who needs to hear this, so here goes. The most important thing to take from these stories, and other works of queer speculative fiction, is that, no matter how outlandish or fantastical the technology gets, no matter how impossible it feels, there is one part that is absolutely, irrevocably true, and that is the depiction of a future for our community. Queerness is a beautiful and complex narrative, one that stretches on forever in both directions. Just as we have a past, we have a future, and I believe it is a bright one. So read these stories, and enjoy a look to the future — laser guns and spaceships optional.
    — Susan Mesler-Evans

You have made it to this point in your life. This beautiful, messy, imperfect, wonderful, amazing point. So keep going. Keep going. Keep going. Keep going.
    — Rory

Hell or high water, we will absolutely create the world of our dreams.
    — Candace Hudert

A B Sigler · A Barrett · A. Gray Lamb · A. Plumb · A.C. Wise · A.J. Sass · Aaron B. · Abuelita Héctor · Ace Malarky · Acorna Starfall · adanska · Adelai · Adria Bailton · Aerylaance · AJ Hartson · AJ Knight · Alana Melnick Haddox · Aleksandra Hill on behalf of khōréō magazine · Alexius Serefeas · Alice Tsoi · Alicia Gibbons · Alicia Williams · Alison Lam · Alison Sky Richards · Allie Kleber · Ameenah, Choco Dreamsicle · Amy Smift · anatsuno · Anaxphone · AncestralLizard · Andan · Andi C. Buchanan · Andi Kent · Andie Larson · Andrea Horbinski · Andrew Hatchell · Andrew Hays · Andy H. · Andy Purkiss · andytuba · Angela Li · Ann Cofell · Anna Cook · Anna G · Anna Tiferet Sikorska · Annie Haggard · Ari Tillett · Arianna Emery · Ash B. · Ashe Azrak · AURELIA LEO · Aurelie Le Borgne · Austin Valeske · Austine Decker · Awn Elming · Ays · B "Pineapple" Annsa · B.H. · Bartimaeus · Beatrice Waterhouse · Belle · Ben Nash · Ben Weiss · Bernadette Bauer · Bess Turner · Beth Morris Tanner · Blue · Bo B Boy · Bookwyrmkim · Brandy G. · Brian Leone Tracy · Brigid Keely · Britt Taylor · Britta Lundin · Brittany S · Brooke Williams · Brooks Moses · Brynn · C. C. S. Ryan · C.Lee · Cait Greer · Calliope · Cameron E · Cara Murray · Carrie M · Caru & Angela · Casey Casas · Cass Morris · Cassandra Evans · Cat Chapman · Catherine Lundoff · Catherine Sharp · Cathy Green · Cecilia Tan · Ceillie Simkiss · Céline Malgen · Charles Payseur · Chelle Parker · Chelsea Johnston · Cheryl Morgan · Chimedum Ohaegbu · Chris G · Chris McCartney · Chris Salcedo · Christine Hanolsy · Christopher 'Vulpine' Kalley · Christopher David Lawton · CJ Fox · CJ Gibson · CJ Ward · Clara Ward · Clayton N · Clémentine Blachère · Cliff Winnig · Cole Lopez · Colin Kerford · Colombe and Simcha Gralla · Cristov Russell · CrossroadsDog · Crummy · Crystal M. Huff · CS Smith · D Franklin · D.F. Pendrys · D.J. Sylvis · Dan Arndt · Dan Hallock · Dana Ross · Darling · DaveBearMN · David Edmonds · David Grinspoon · David Matthewman · Dawn Vogel · Debbie Phillips · Dee Morgan · Dee Shull · Demetrius Bagley · Devin Spencer · disco · Djibril Ayad · DK Jones · Dr Jobo · Duncan M · E Clark · E. C. Ambrose · E. Catherine Tobler · E.J. Kelly · Eleanor Pender · Elena Jimenez · Eli Western · Eliana Dimopoulos · Eliza Blair · Elizabeth Sargent · Elizabeth Sweeny · Ellie Campbell · Ellie Yee · EMH · Emily Aviva Kapor-Mater · Emily Mooshian · Emily Williams · Emma · Emma Lindhagen · Enfys Book · Ephraim Mallery · Eric A Jackson · Eric Jordan · Eric Starker · Érik Drolet · Erin Black · Erin Cashier · Erin Subramanian · Erin Yarborough · EstanceDH · Ether Nepenthes · Eva · Evan Finnian · Evelyn (they, them) · F. C. Moulton · Fabienne Schwizer · Falterfire · Felix Simonson · Fiona Hopkins · Fool's Moon Entertainment, Inc. · Frederick Aeightch · Fredrick L. Doss · Geneva Langeland · Geneviève Paquin-Saikali · Geoffrey Lehr · Georgina Primrose · Gillian Fenwick · Ginger Kautz · Glen Brixey · Glyn Morgan · Gogs Herriott

Grace P · Gretchen Z · Guin Kelly · GV Pearce · H Lynnea Johnson · H. Baxter · H. Emiko Ogasawara · Haipollai · Hale Fannar Ethan · Han · Han Kane · Hanna J · Harley Victor · Harrison & Aiden Webb-McFarland · Haz Bain · Heather ♥ · Heather Rose Jones · Hethenea · HockeyBabbler · Holly J · Illimani Ferreira · Imogen Malpas · Iphy · Isabel Sepúlveda · Isana Skeete · Iz M-R · Izzy Wasserstein · J.A. Fitzpatrick · J-Brickey · Jackie Daggers · Jacob Mattison · Jade & Sara · Jade Robeck · Jade Shields · Jae Steinbacher · Jaelen Hartwin · Jahnavi V. · Jaime Ratcliffe · Jake Lawler · Jam · James Lucas · James Stanphill · James Starke · Jamie Bliss · Jamie Perez · Jaq Greenspon · Jasmine Stairs · Jason A. Bartles · Jason Peterson · Jasper Love · Javier Quintero · Jay Edelson · Jean-Paul L. Garnier / Space Cowboy Books · Jed Hartman · jen h. · Jenni Hughes · Jennifer Barnes · Jennifer Berk · Jennifer Rhorer · Jenny and Owen Blacker · Jess Belmont · Jess Draws · Jesse the K · Jessica (JP) Petriello · Jessica Eleri Jones · Jessica Guggenheim · Jessica Lopez · Jessika Lopez, la reina feminista · Jett Jones · Jill Rose · Jinx · JJLeggo · Jo G · Jo Miles · jodez4 · Joe Decker · Joel A. S. Butler · Joelle Parrott · John H. Bookwalter Jr. · John Kusters · John M. Gamble · Jon Duckworth · Jonathan Gilbert · Jordan McEntaffer · Joseph Soonsin Lee · Josh Messinger · Joshua Buergel · Josie Quinn · JT · Julia McDermott & Rob Batchellor · Julia Mono Rose · Julia Rios · Julian Stuart · Juliana · Julie Andrews · Julie L Spradley · Justin Myers · jvw · K. C. Alexander · Kal Clintberg · Karen Healey · Kat Kourbeti · Kat Wenger · Katalina Watt · Kate M. Eidam · Kate Malloy · Katherine Delzell · Katherine Gladhart-Hayes · Katie Fouks · Katie Redderson-Lear · Katri Leikola · Kay James · Kayden Persephone Black · keerawa · Keith Chaffee · Kel-l Miklas · Kellen DeRuy · Kelly Hoolihan · Kelly Kleiser · Kendra · Keshet Roman · Kevin Grove · Kevin J. "Womzilla" Maroney · Kevin North · Kimberly M. Lowe · Kit Leveret · Kit Stubbs, Ph.D. · Kristin Rollins · Kynerae · L Bright · Lacey Stewart · Lady Insomnia · Lara Eckener · Lauowolf · Laura Tabea Mattern · Laura47 · Lauren M · LaurenZannah · Lawjick · Leah Leslie · Leah Rachel von Essen · Leane · Leon W Fairley · Leora Spitzer · Leucosia · Ley Mabe · Lilly of the Void · Lily · Lily Frenette · LionessElise · Lisa Eckstein · Literati Press Comics & Novels · Llinos Cathryn Thomas · Lou Weaver (he/him) · Lucy Fox · Lucy~Nyah~Chan · Lyn Shaffer · M. J. Pettit · M. S. Vacchio · M. Scott Boone · M.K. Fisher · Maggie Block · Maggie Hermanson · Mahj · Malda Marlys · Mallow Leo Flapjack; Mallowsap Proudburrow · Maresah · Margaret Bumby · Margaret Moser · Margot Atwell · Marguerite Kenner and Alasdair Stuart · Marie Blanchet · Marie Oak · Mark W. · Marlowe · Mars Robmann · Marsh J. Lynx · Martha S. · Martin Stein & Scott Saxon · Mary Beth Case · Matt and Camille Knepper · Max Turner · Megan Green · Megan Miller · Mel Weed · Melissa Shumake · MerrillBea · Michael Andersen

Michael Kahan · Michael Kwan · Michael M. Jones · Michael Steingas Barber · Michèle Breton · Michele Howe (neverwhere) · Michele Wellck · Michelle Sorge · Mike Falter · Mike Selinker · Minerva Cerridwen · Mira Mechtley · Miriam Roberts · Molly Campbell · Molly M. Berg · Monica Barner · Monique Cuillerier · Moon · Morgan Pualani · Morgan Stone · Nakarem · Narrelle M Harris · 'Nathan Burgoine · Ness & Phoenix · Netthauser · Nick Coveney · Nicole A. · Nicole Bruun · Nicolette Molina-Madril · Nivair H. Gabriel · Olivia Montoya · Oriene Shiel · Paige Kimble · Pandeism Anthology Project · Paris Lavender · Paula F-C · Pauline Westerbarkey · PBK · Penny Hart · penwing · Peregrine · Peter M Howard · Phoebe Barton · Phoebe Harris · Piper · Piper Jones · Preeti Ramaraj · R J Theodore · R Zemlicka · R&C OkhDougall · Rachael · Rachel (@biriyaks_keeper) · Rachel Alexander · Rachel Brittain · Rachel Coleman · Rachel Dilkus · Rae Helmreich · Raine Wynd · Rakie Bennett · raksha · Random Yarning · rathiri · Ray · Ray Rodriguez · RCF · Rebecca Burton · Rebecca Holt · Rebecca Slitt · Reetz McGee · Regis M. Donovan · Reiley Elizabeth Daniels · Ren Hutchings · Rena Rocford · Renaissance Press · Rhonda Z · Rhyolight · Richard Gropp · Richard Leis · Riot Fae Dice · Risa Wolf · RJ Pedie · Rob Funk · Rob Lake · Robert Tienken · Robyn Moore · Rocket Bae · Rocky Halleron · Rory Hatchel · Rory Sims · Rosa María Quiñones · Rosco · Rose Hill · Rosier Cade · Ruth F. Simon · Ruth Sachter · Ryan Wyatt · S. "Jet" Pak · S. Chen · S. Naomi Scott · S. Wittenberg · Sabrina Nobile · sabrinix · Sae · Sam Atchison · Sammie Patton · Sara Harville · Sarah Bea · Sarah Goslee · Sarah Hester · Sarah Merrill · Sarah Scott · Sarah-Rhiannon · Sasha Sienna · Satsuma · SDZ · Sean Dyer · Selwyn's Sanity · Shana Hausman · Shannon M. · Sheila Dee · Shelly Cerullo · Shenwei Chang · SI CLARKE · Simo Muinonen · Sonia · Squishy · Stef Maruch · Stephen Ballentine · Steve Kuerbitz · Steven Anderson · Stewart C Baker · Sumana Harihareswara · Susan "JJGYET" Richfield · Susan Hamm · Susan Tarrier · Suzanne Musin · Sydney P · Sylvia Greer · T · Tad K · Tali · Tamar G. · Tania · Tansy Rayner Roberts · Taryn Husband · Tasha Turner · tekla hawkins · Tess M · That Awesome Tyra · The Battey Family · The Blerd Newsletter · The House of Roses · Thea Flurry · Theo Galadriel · This Wicked Day · Thom Watson · Thomas J. Spargo · Thomas Zurkan · Tibs · Tiffany & Benjamin Moore · Tiffany Morris · Tiffany Stockham · Tim Sauke · Tina Gilman · TK & EK & Kat · Tobi Hill-Meyer · Tony & Mark · Toretha · Tristan Thyme · Tyler Hinman · Vae · Valerie N. · Vicky Soper · Viktoria · Vivian Wiener · W Assaf · Wayan Mjöll Ingudóttir Williams · Weronika Mamuna · Wesley Teal · Wilbert Bishop · Wren Alyssa · Zachary "Pup GIR" Ledbetter · Zara Kazmi Barsotti · Zoe Brook · Zoe Kaplan · Zuki · and 318 supporters who chose not to be named

Isabela Oliveira has been a professional editor for years, from technical documents to pop culture content. While attending college, she kept busy as the poetry editor and later the editor-in-chief of her university's literary journal, the *Salmon Creek Journal*. Isabela started speaking on panels at fan conventions in 2016 and has been at it ever since. These days, she's working as an editor by day, and an occasional podcast co-host, a crafter and maker, and an aspiring voice actress in her free time.

Jed Sabin is a jack-of-all-trades with professional experience as an editor, writer, scientist, project coordinator, and logistics manager. At age 17 (before Kickstarter existed!) they successfully crowdfunded and produced a geeky pin-up calendar that was featured on Neil Gaiman's blog. They were editor-in-chief of their college student newspaper, and they worked as an editor on the popular Kickstarter-funded *Maze of Games* puzzle novel. Their writing has been published by *Daily Science Fiction* and *Wired Magazine*.

* * *

Our heartfelt thanks to the village of talented creatives who contributed to this project; to Christy Maggio and Katje Sabin for valuable advice in the early planning stages; to Charles Payseur, dave ring, the Mermaids Monthly crew, and everyone else who enthusiastically promoted and supported the funding campaign on social media; to Bogi Takács for eir giant list of queer specfic anthologies, which was a treasure trove of inspiration and education for us; to Gretchen Treu and Hayley T. for their generous time and expertise; to our librarian friends for their feedback; to our cultural consultants for the essential work they do; to all the incredible authors who submitted stories to this project; to all our campaign backers, including those who chose not to have their names listed in the book; and most of all to RB and V, for bringing us water and making things possible.